T0117006

# Death's Crooked Shadow

GORDON N. MCINTOSH

iUniverse, Inc.
Bloomington

Death's Crooked Shadow

Copyright © 2011 Gordon N. McIntosh

iUniverse books may be ordered through booksellers or by contacting:

iUniverse
1663 Liberty Drive
Bloomington, IN 47403
www.iuniverse.com
1-800-Authors (1-800-288-4677)

ISBN: 978-1-4620-4851-9 (sc)
ISBN: 978-1-4620-4853-3 (hc)
ISBN: 978-1-4620-4852-6 (e)

Printed in the United States of America

iUniverse rev. date: 9/29/2011

For Cathie and Will.

*Every murder turns on a bright hot light, and a lot of people… have to walk out of the shadows.*

Albert Maltz
Author and screenwriter

# Prologue

The man's car was parked in the alley behind the alderman's house, in the shadows, away from the yellow glow of the sodium streetlight. By the time he had lugged the suitcase up the basement stairs, wheeled it across the tidy patch of lawn and past the garage to the alley gate, he had sweat through his shirt and summer suit. He hefted the case into the Buick's trunk and quickly shut the lid before the inside light gave him away. He guessed the case weighed over fifty pounds, maybe ten of it audio- and videotapes, the rest being cash. Most of the bills would be hundreds; the alderman considered smaller denominations insulting. The money couldn't help the politician now. The long career of Chicago's most powerful alderman was coming to a spectacular end.

The only signs of life in the alley were the random flash of a firefly and the reflected gleam of a cat's eyes before it darted into a passageway. The sultry air was heavy with the smell of fresh tar from a neighboring roof. Was it a portent of the hellfire awaiting the alderman and those around him?

He didn't turn his headlights on until leaving the alley and heading toward downtown Chicago, where he was to deliver the suitcase. After punching in a private number on his car phone, he waited, expecting to be told the location of the covert meeting—and the end to his responsibilities.

"Hello," an unfamiliar voice answered on the sixth ring.

Something was wrong. No one else was supposed to be involved in the handoff. "Who's this?"

"Who's dis?" the stranger countered.

"This isn't your phone. Who are you?"

"Officer Donovan, 12th District. You know the guy with this phone?"

"Yeah. Where is he?"

"*Who* is he?" Donovan asked.

"You first. What's the matter?"

"We found this phone on a homicide vic."

The man hung up, pulled to the curb, and breathed deeply. His pulse rate was galloping; he felt like he was falling. The last man he could trust, the only one who could protect him, had been eliminated, meaning he too had been exposed. There was little time. They may already have discovered his wire-transfer sleight of hand, directing their money to a different account. It wouldn't take long to learn he'd carried away the alderman's videos and cash. Carelessness, an informer, or a suspicious bank officer—the reason didn't matter; he would be their next target. He didn't intend to wait.

Two blocks from his house the man heard the sirens and saw the fire trucks rumbling by. From the corner, he could see that the whole east wing of his home was ablaze. Firemen were hauling out hoses, shooting streams through broken windows, and soaking down the roofs of adjacent homes. A crowd was gathered behind the police cars, and a TV van was pulling up on the periphery. There was no telling who else might be in the crowd, and the man couldn't risk finding out. They were closing off every point of their vulnerability.

His office in the McCollum Building downtown would be next, but it would be more difficult for them to access. He had time to remove his computer hard drive and sanitize the place. Then Bernard D. Sutherland planned to disappear.

# CHAPTER 1

**C**hicago's June had been its fickle self, balmy teases interspersed with chilling reminders of the long, gray winter. As if newly arriving from other climes, Mother Nature had chosen Independence Day to prove she hadn't lost her fire, punishing the city with record temperatures. Day after day the sun bore down, its intensity stifling the slightest breeze. Area governments issued ozone alerts, opened temporary cooling shelters, and asked citizens to look out for the homeless and elderly. Those who had been eager for summer had second thoughts as they listened to triple-digit forecasts.

Doug Sutherland loosened his tie and unbuttoned his collar. Sweat trickled down his back, a drop from his temple plopping onto the front page of his newspaper. He stood, opened a gap in the venetian blinds, and squinted into the white glare. Eastward, through the canyon of office buildings, he caught a glimpse of the lake a half mile away. Dozens of sailboats drifted on their moorings, aimless in the calm. His sloop was one of them, and if there was any wind offshore he intended to find it that afternoon. Worst case, it would be cooler on the water than in this boiler of an office. What was wrong with the building's goddamn air conditioning?

As if in answer, his secretary stepped into his office, fanning herself with a handful of envelopes. "I called the manager again," Eileen said. She was a pretty, single mom in her mid-thirties. Her long hair was dirty blond, and due to an addiction to chocolates, her figure was slightly on the chunky side. "A compressor went out. They don't know when it will be fixed."

"Welcome to summer." He watched as Eileen wiped her forehead with the back of her free hand. "If it's not working in an hour, you can go home."

"That's just as bad. I'll go to a movie. It's always cold at theaters." She looked at the envelopes she had been fanning with and said, "Oh, here's your mail. Sorry for the sweat."

Sutherland flipped through the mail and stopped at a familiar envelope.

The statement had arrived as always, marking the end of June and another fiscal year. His name and address showed through the envelope window, and in the upper-left corner were the names of the deceased founders of one of Chicago's venerable law firms. Sutherland tossed the envelope on the pile on his desk. He didn't have to open it. The report would contain the same information as always. The amounts varied each year, but the long-term trend was positive. The holdings of the trust had doubled since it was formed. As if he cared.

For years, as regular as the summer solstice, the statement found its way to him. Despite the exigencies of college, law school, marriage, a daughter, divorce, and a few career changes, he'd only dipped into it once, and that was when he was desperate. He'd felt sullied afterward, corrupted, as if by touching the money he shared in his father's guilt. He'd reimbursed the trust as soon as he could and swore never to draw on it again. One day he would donate it to a good cause. In the meantime, he tried to forget it along with the other traces of his father.

Doug Sutherland glanced at that morning's newspapers resting on his desk. He had made the front page of both Chicago dailies. After months of quiet coverage in the back sections, he and the McCollum Building were big news again. Hardly the type of publicity anyone would have chosen.

The *Sun Times* featured a two-column-wide photo covering the demonstrators marching in front of the old building. In the *Chicago Tribune*, Bill Jamison's column described the futile last-ditch efforts of the preservationists to obtain a court order stopping the McCollum's demolition. Six months earlier Sutherland had finally won approval to tear it down and redevelop the site. In another few weeks, it would be history, its terra-cotta façade and signature fenestration consigned to photos and memories.

An hour later, after a conference call with his attorney and a discussion with a potential lender, Sutherland clicked onto Yahoo's weather page. The temperature had risen to ninety-five. It felt close to that in his office. His shirt was sticking to his back, and the ice cubes in his Coke hadn't lasted two minutes. With the air conditioning out of order, it was no use. Sutherland told his secretary, accountant, and staff of five others to go home.

The sky was white hot as Sutherland stepped out of the building. He put on his sunglasses and draped his suit jacket over his shoulder. He was meeting a few friends at the yacht club in twenty minutes and taking the tender to his boat. No racing today, just a relaxed sail beyond the swelter of the city.

As he walked he thought about the newspaper articles and the critics of what Sutherland was doing with the McCollum Building. It had been owned by his father, Bernard, and along with a number of other properties, it had been placed in a trust with the young Sutherland as beneficiary. The building was old, vacant, and dilapidated, but it was one of the last remaining buildings influenced by the Luis Sullivan school of architecture. And despite its age and poor condition, its location made it desirable. It commanded one of the few undeveloped corners in Chicago's Loop, and if it hadn't been tied up in the trust, it would have been acquired years before. As the trust's beneficiary Sutherland was entitled to everything in it, but he had insisted on purchasing the building at a market price. It was a risky financial stretch, but it was better than benefiting from his father's tainted legacy.

Sutherland's iPhone rang as he was walking east along Madison to the Grant Park garage. He recognized his foreman's number.

"Doug?"

"Yeah, Jack. What's up?"

"I'm at the site. You gotta get over here."

"What's the problem?"

"Not on the phone. You gotta see this. We had to stop work."

"It won't wait? You can't handle it?" He could almost feel his hands on the helm, an onshore breeze cooling his face and filling the sails.

"Not me. This is your call."

"All right. Fifteen minutes. This better be good."

# Chapter 2

The skull lay encased in a shattered section of Greek column. The jaw hung askew, exposing a half-dozen blackened fillings. In the shadows below the skull, Sutherland could make out the concave cast of the neck and shoulder in the hardened plaster, the muscle and sinew long since shriveled away. But the skull's most eye-catching feature was the missing upper-front tooth, conferring the appearance of a cartoon hillbilly.

"Jesus," Sutherland said, jumping up from his crouch, stumbling over some of the bricks littering the site.

He removed his hard hat, wiped his forehead with his sleeve, and took in the scene before him. The McCollum waited in the summer glare, a crumbling shell resigned to the wrecking ball swaying overhead. Under the bleached sky, building and shadows looked surreal, a charcoal fantasy by Salvador Dalí.

Stripped of its terra-cotta façade, the building revealed cross sections of offices, each floor a slice of stained walls stacked twelve high to the caved-in roof. Blackened shafts cut vertically through the floors and yellow-brown stairways zigzagged from level to level, stitching the fractured floors together.

Sutherland recalled standing with his father here, in the building's lobby, remembered the promise that someday this "grand old lady" would be his. Since that time the city had erupted into a skyline of glass and steel, elegant giants towering over the old McCollum. Viewing the destruction before him, Sutherland felt confused and uncertain. Was it really economics that forced the demolition, or was he merely destroying another memory of his father?

A shower of masonry and stone cascaded to the foot of the ruin, forcing him to cram on his hard hat and retreat a few steps. While he waited for the dust to settle, a wave of stale air pricked his nostrils—musty drafts descending stairways and shafts, dying exhalations of the condemned structure. Ghosts, he thought.

Sutherland's two-way radio crackled and he unsnapped it from his belt. Yelling over the diesel crane still clattering twenty yards away, he said, "Jack? Was that you?"

From the construction trailer at the edge of the site, his demolition foreman's voice squawked over the radio. "Yeah. You find it yet?"

"Right in front of me."

"Should we forget it? Means nothing but trouble. Some poor slob stuck in the column," Jack said, "from a hundred years ago. We'll lose days, more maybe, if we call the police."

Sutherland thought about Jack's comment. A hundred years? The man buried here when the McCollum was built? No. It didn't take an expert to know the difference between the original construction and this more modern addition. But the foreman was right about delays: they meant thousands in cost overruns, temptation enough to dump the column's contents into one of the waiting trucks and forget about it.

"What you think, Mr. S? It's history. Who cares?" Jack said.

Sutherland's inner voice echoed the foreman's words: *Let it lie.* He already had enough to think about, financial issues to deal with. After a long pause, Sutherland said, "Hold on a minute. I'll take another look."

"You're the boss." Even over the static, Sutherland sensed the foreman's disapproval.

Sutherland surveyed the pile of rubble once more, noting how the remnants of the ten-foot column lay across the field of crumbled brick. It was cast plaster and broken, a five-foot section leaning against a rubble mound, smaller pieces scattered nearby, the construction not original—a renovation during his father's era. Reinforcing wire mesh still connected parts of the plaster like ligaments in a severed limb.

He scrambled over loose debris to the column and squatted, studying the shadows between the pieces, trying to ignore the skull's hollow stare. Pulling his flashlight from his rear pocket, Sutherland went down on one knee, probing with the beam of light the section of column lying cracked open above the skull. Inside he could see the fossil-like imprint of a human hand—the right palm, thrust into the plaster, making a perfect mold. Another, smaller fragment of the column lay a foot away. In it were molded an impression of the nose, eyes, and forehead. Below the nose, where the mouth would have been, the form of the man's other fist pressed against the mouth. And in the grip of what had been that fist, there remained a section of PVC pipe extending from where the mouth must have been, through the plaster to the top of the column.

Sutherland had to hold back a violent urge to retch. The significance of the scene was undeniable. The victim had been buried in the plaster alive, sucking last breaths through the tube.

While Sutherland picked his way out of the building's shade, shielding his eyes from the sunlight, he envisioned the condemned man—one hand squeezing the tube, the other straining upward into the muck, lungs heaving, laboring for precious air. Swallowing back bile, Sutherland reached for the radio.

"Jack," he said into the two-way, "call the police."

# Chapter 3

Two hours later in the air-conditioned trailer jammed against the construction barriers, Sutherland said good-bye to Jack, his foreman, leaving him to deal with the police and their paperwork. Sutherland couldn't help them with the dead body's identity but was able to place the time of death as sometime in the two-year interim between his freshman year in college and when he returned from his wanderings in the Caribbean and Mexico. He knew the building well, having followed his father from floor to floor on many visits there, and he had first seen that column—now the unidentified man's coffin—when he'd returned after his father's death.

The crime scene technicians intended to close down the job while they removed the skeleton and searched for evidence, efforts that could take at least another day. Sutherland waved an *adiós* to the Latino detective handling the investigation and opened the outside door to a rush of hot air. From the top of the stairs, he surveyed the busy scene around the McCollum's corner site.

Three police cars had squeezed against the construction barrier surrounding the lot. Behind the squad cars, parked in the shadow of the McCollum, was a white van, the top a jumble of microwave dishes and antennae, its decal declaring the presence of Channel 2 News. Circling in front of the main gate a handful of protesters, veterans of the attempt to designate the McCollum a landmark, brandished placards bearing slogans from their lost battle.

SAVE THE McCOLLUM

*Don't they ever give up?* he thought. While he watched, a white Mercedes limousine eased to the curb, shimmering in the heat like a mirage. Sutherland squinted for a better look and, when the car came to a stop, read the license plate: JULES. The tinted rear window slid down and Jules, the man himself, hailed from inside. "Doug. Over here."

Jules Langer. No avoiding him now that he'd been spotted. Sutherland descended the trailer's stairs and picked his way through the traffic toward the limo. When he arrived at the car, Jules Langer was peering through the open window at the police cars and television vans. A white-haired chauffeur in a dark suit sat behind the wheel. The smell of new leather hit Sutherland on a wave of cool air as he drew near the window.

"Doug. What's going on? They clamping down on amateurs?" Langer was the president of Langer Development, a heated competitor. He was forty-one with striking blue eyes, salt-and-pepper hair, and a cultivated tan. The only flaw in his handsome features was a slightly receded chin, a suggestion of timidity that he more than compensated for by his unflagging ego and penchant for expensive clothes. "And you. You been in a wrestling match?"

Sutherland glanced down. His shoes were ash colored, his navy suit pants were streaked with dust, and perspiration stained his blue shirt like an indigo rash. He stooped to see his reflection in the driver's window. His face was sweaty and smudged, one wide streak obscuring the half-moon scar on his cheekbone.

"It's a dirty business, Jules. Remember when you used to do it?"

Langer chuckled, but the laugh didn't conceal the resentment. Sutherland was the new kid on the block, this being his first downtown office project. Langer had built a half-dozen high-rises in the preceding ten years. Yet Sutherland had won the intense competition for Broadwell Communications' Midwestern headquarters—the anchor tenant that would enable development of the McCollum site. Langer had needed Broadwell for America Tower, his plan for a seventy-story building on an empty lot that lay fallow two blocks away.

"There an accident?" Langer was looking across the street at the news team setting up a camera. "Somebody hurt?"

The image of the skull and breathing tube was still turning in Sutherland's mind. "We found a body."

"Who?"

"Just bones. The police thought from when it was built, but I told them it's more recent. It's definitely murder."

Langer blew out a long whistle. "Maybe the building's cursed. All the problems you had getting approval. Doubt your new tenant will take this too well. Good thing you've got a lease executed, right?" He smiled knowingly.

Sutherland could imagine wheels turning behind Langer's blue eyes. The lease wasn't finalized, and with all his contacts, Jules Langer would know it. There were some minor unresolved issues, even though they'd been working on it for months. "Don't get your hopes up, Jules," Sutherland said. "This happened a while ago, while I was in Mexico. Nobody's going to care."

Langer massaged his jaw with a manicured hand as he stared across the street. "About the time your father went to prison?" He never missed an opportunity to needle, didn't even bother to disguise it. Sutherland learned long ago not to let him get under his skin.

"The skeleton's in a column. Your dad's company might have done the construction." Miles Langer, Jules's father, had run the construction company that had evolved into Langer Development after the old man died.

Langer's eyes widened and he swallowed hard. "The body was in a column? During that time you were gone?"

"Yep. It was one of two that stood in the lobby. Probably fabricated somewhere else, shipped to the building for installation. Some sick fuck buried the poor bastard in plaster. Alive."

Langer had a distant look in his eyes, unfocused, his nose wrinkled up, as if straining to remember something. He shook his head slowly, as if denying whatever he was thinking. "Couldn't be," he said.

"Couldn't be what?"

Langer blinked, as if rescued from where his thoughts had been. "Nothing," he said, a waved hand dismissing his comment. "There was just the skeleton? Nothing else? ID maybe?"

"Police may find something. Anyway, I gotta go. My whole schedule screwed up. Gonna cost me a couple days."

"Lucky this didn't turn up a couple months ago. A few Broadwell board members were against your project because there was already too much hair on it. The preservationists, your father's history, being a felon and all. Then you barely squeaked by council approval."

"Who was lobbying the council, Jules? Who planted that in the Broadwell directors' minds, Jules?" Sutherland asked, knowing full well Langer had close contacts with Broadwell high-ups.

"I came this close." Langer held up his hand, a half inch between his index finger and thumb. "You got in under the wire. A thing like this …"

"What's this got to do with it?"

"A dead man. In the building your father owned. Now you. If it was murder, who killed him? Tell me that. No one wants to be associated with that much bad publicity. Broadwell's got problems enough."

Langer had a point. Sutherland had barely edged out Langer's project. Although he had letters of intent on Broadwell's lease and his construction financing, neither was finalized. Anything could happen. Judging from the look on Langer's face, the scheming had already begun. Yet behind those calculating eyes there seemed to be anxiety as well. Langer knew or suspected something else. What?

Langer straightened his perfectly tied half Windsor knot and said, "Broadwell may be wishing they'd signed with me." He flashed a plastic smile, flicked a salute, said something to the driver, and the limousine pushed into traffic to the blare of car horns.

# CHAPTER 4

A few hours later, Sutherland was back in his sweltering office, having nothing better to do. After he'd found the body and knew he'd be tied up with the police, he'd notified his crew to take his sailboat out themselves. No sense ruining everyone's afternoon. His shirt completely unbuttoned and shirttails out, he was finishing a review of some construction documents when the office phone rang. With the whole staff gone because of the failed air conditioning, he picked it up himself.

"Hello?"

"Is dis Sutherland?" The caller's voice was forced and raspy, adding to the static on the line.

"Who's calling?"

"Dis Junior? Sutherland's kid?"

When was the last time someone called him Junior? Twenty years?

"What's this about?"

"You the guy doing the McCollum Building, right? Wrecking it down?"

"Yeah, so?"

"It's on the TV. The police and all? Found a dead guy?"

"Yeah, I know. I was there. Who is this?"

"Remember Danny Delaney?"

How could he forget a name like that? One of Chicago's most colorful characters. He was still a legend long after he'd disappeared.

"What about him?"

"That was him."

Is this guy for real? The infamous Alderman Delaney? If he was really the body in the McCollum Building, it would solve a fifteen-year-old mystery.

"Why are you telling me? It's a police matter."

"Gonna be lotta questions. Like who done it. People pointin' fingers."

"And what?"

"Maybe your old man done it. Was his building."

"You saying he did?"

"He'd be a suspect."

"He's dead. What can they do to him?"

The question seemed to stop the caller. Only silence.

"If it was Delaney, the police will figure it out," Sutherland said. "So what do you want?"

"I got Danny's notebook. Everything what happened. Names and shit. Payoffs."

"You trying to blackmail me? Forget it."

"Fuck no. Thought you'd want to buy it."

"Sorry. Sell it to Geraldo or a TV channel." He glanced at the front page of the *Tribune*. Seeing his old schoolmate's byline, he said, "Or try Bill Jamison at the *Tribune*. He's always hungry for a story."

"I gotta get something for it. It's worth somethin'."

"Why come to me?"

"Your old man always treated me good. Not like a lot of 'em. You'll see." He hung up.

*I'll see?* he thought. As far as Sutherland was concerned, he'd already seen too much. What else did he have to worry about?

# Chapter 5

Later that day, in Langer Development's offices, Jules Langer studied the mirrored alcove enshrining a shimmering representation of America Tower, the developer's concept for his new seventy-story office building. The model rested, as it had for the last two years, on a marble pedestal, a sleek rocket on its launching pad.

Jules Langer contemplated the building's glass and stainless-steel details and shook his head. A rocket to nowhere, unless his fortunes changed, and today he saw a way to make that happen. The discovery of that body at the McCollum could be his opportunity to wrest the Broadwell Communications deal from Sutherland. The worrisome aspect of the unearthing was the real possibility that his father's company really had installed the column where the body was found, as Sutherland had suggested. Some of the company's records went back that far, but not in sufficient detail to check individual projects. Langer hoped no one else had information pointing his way.

Telling himself to think positively, he punched in a telephone number and waited, listening to the ring tone.

"Posner here," a man answered in a nasal New York accent.

"Maury, Jules Langer."

"Don't bother, Jules. The answer's still no."

"Be nice to me, Maury. You may be begging to finance me yet."

"You lost Broadwell. Just deal with it."

"It's not over 'til it's over. America Tower's gonna out-Trump Trump." Standing in front of his desk, Langer glanced at his reflection in the mirror, juxtaposed with America Tower's model. How many times to how many people had he said those words? It didn't matter, he still believed them.

"Call when you've got an anchor tenant, Jules. I can't finance empty buildings." Then the dial tone once again droned, and Langer replaced his receiver for a few seconds, long enough to ready himself. It was time to capitalize on the day's discovery. Glancing at his image in the mirror, he said, "Smile, baby, smile," picked up the phone, and dialed the first of the New York phone numbers he had called many times before. His supporters on Broadwell Communications' board would want to know about the latest piece of the McCollum drama. A dead body. How would their shareholders react to that kind of publicity?

# CHAPTER 6

The smell of stale beer and smoke hung in the bar like a toxic smog. So much for Chicago's smoking ban. Suspended from the shadows, dusty lamps dropped light cones on a grimy floor and a half-dozen sticky-topped tables. It wasn't the Ritz, but Bill Jamison needed a story. The comprehensive corruption story he'd been working on promised to be a blockbuster, but he didn't have all the pieces nailed down. He still lacked irrefutable proof connecting shady deals and a circle of financiers, real estate magnates, and government officials he was investigating. In the meantime he had to rely on whatever dirt he could dig up to keep his byline in the public's eye.

He took another step into the saloon and scanned the room for a likely face. Three men sat hunched over the front-to-back bar, two drunks argued with the bartender, a derelict slept at a rear table. No one showed interest except a scruffy man in the near corner. Jamison walked to his table.

"You the guy that called?" Jamison asked, appraising the stranger's unshaven face, protruding stomach, and once-white tee shirt.

"You da reporter?" the man growled.

"In the flesh."

"Gimme a beer, then we talk."

Jamison stiffened. He hadn't eaten dinner and had driven across half the city to this dump. Now he's supposed to take orders from this lowlife? "I look like a waiter?"

"You'll do."

The man watched Jamison through tiny, dark eyes. His swarthy skin appeared clammy, reminding Jamison of how warm he was himself. He could use a beer. "What d'you want?"

"Old Style. Two." He raised two stubby fingers holding a well-chewed cigar.

Walking to the bar, Jamison grinned. He knew the type. Italian—West Side. He'd gone to school with greaseballs like him.

A car commercial blared from the TV perched above the row of dusty bottles behind the bar. Then the picture changed to the image of George Spanos, a US congressman from Chicago and the front-runner to win the election for the governorship of Illinois in November. He was standing in front of a senior citizens' center, his collar open, his shirtsleeves rolled up, looking like a man of determination and action. With his strong chin and chiseled features, he could have been the model for the sculptured statues from his parents' homeland. Wiping perspiration off his forehead, perhaps demonstrating how hard he was working, he was denouncing his Republican opponent, calling him a flip-flopper, when the bartender muted the audio. "Can't stand that prick," he said to one of the comatose men at the bar. "He was a sleazy state senator, one of them lying sons 'a bitches in Washington, now he wants to come back and fuck us some more." Then he noticed Jamison standing there and said, "Whataya have, Mac?"

"Three Old Styles. Make sure they're cold, if you don't mind." *Goddamn dump isn't even air-conditioned,* he thought.

While Jamison waited for the beers he contemplated two gallon-sized jars, one containing pickled eggs, the other, knockwurst floating in a murky fluid. He was hungry, but not that hungry.

"So what you got for me?" Jamison asked, placing three beers on the table.

The man grabbed a bottle and chugged. Jamison noticed his right ear poking through his hair. It was disfigured, a cauliflower. An ex-boxer or wrestler. Very *ex*, from the look of him.

"Watch the news. Already saw it on the six o'clock." The man wiped his mouth with the back of his hand.

Jamison turned to see a news announcer filling the TV screen, a pretty woman with short, blond hair. He imagined how he would appear on TV and frowned. He knew with his narrow face and red hair and beard he looked like a leprechaun. The television scene changed to a black reporter standing in front of the McCollum Building.

"This's it," Jamison's companion said.

The bartender turned the volume back on as the blond reporter was saying, "A body was uncovered today during the destruction of a Chicago landmark. A local historian is suggesting we may be witnessing the outcome of a century-old murder …"

Jamison glanced sideways at his tablemate, who chortled around his cigar. The TV reporter continued, telling the viewers how in 1905 Percy McCollum's brother disappeared after a family dispute and how foul play was suspected. Jamison didn't care. A century-old crime was not his road to fame and fortune. Fresh muck, the more sensational and slimier the better, was how he'd make his name – like the rats' nest of financial and political chicanery he'd been investigating for the last several months.

The man across from Jamison snorted as the reporter was wrapping up. "In a way, this victim's fate was like the McCollum's, for although the demonstrators behind me fought for its life, they lost the battle." The camera panned the broken walls of the building and then the line of sign carriers playing to the camera. "Back to you, Mary Beth."

Jamison watched until the picture faded into the studio. Talk about a line of pap and bullshit. *Where do they get these guys?* he thought. *All face and no brains. And this meeting is a waste of time.* He turned to face the man snickering across the table. "You have a name?"

"Scooch," the man grunted.

"Scooch? That it?"

"That's all you get." He jammed the cigar into his mouth.

"Right. Spelled like it sounds, I'll bet." Jamison took out his notebook from his jacket.

"What's that?" Scooch asked, pointing.

"Notes. In case you say something I can use, such as why you called?"

The man leaned forward and asked, "What's it worth?"

Scooch's breath forced Jamison back in his chair. He swallowed hard. "That beer's all it's worth so far. Know what investigative reporting is, Mr. Scooch? Current stuff, living people, scandals, bribery, corruption—that's my bag. So if it's hundred-year-old bodies you got—*arrivederci*, Scooch."

Scooch leaned closer toward the reporter and whispered, "Wasn't no hundred years. More like fifteen, he disappeared. A big alderman."

An alderman? Fifteen years ago. Jamison would have been in college then, but he vaguely remembered something about a councilman going missing. But would he pay for a story like that? Not if he could help it. "Who cares about a dead alderman? They all should be shot."

Scooch looked disappointed and wary. "Sutherland said you'd be interested."

"Doug Sutherland?" How would Sutherland know this slob? And why give him Jamison's name? They hadn't seen each other for at least a year.

"Dat's him," Scooch said. "Said you were okay—that I'd be unanimous."

"Anonymous. And you'll be real anonymous if you don't tell me what this is about. How d'you know Sutherland?"

"His father was okay to me. So I called to tip his kid about Danny being in the building and all."

Bingo! Danny Delaney was his name. Alderman in the First Ward who practically ran the city council. "How'd you know about Danny?"

Scooch finished the one beer, set the empty down, and let out a loud belch. "How much's it worth?"

"For what? You know who killed him? Or is this nothing but gas?" Jamison smiled at his own joke.

"I got Danny's notebook."

"What's in it?"

"Numbers, names … shit."

"Let's see."

"It ain't here. Anyway, a thousand bucks first."

"I look like an ATM? Besides, I have to see what you have." But Jamison didn't want to lose this one. A murdered alderman's notebook, a guy as powerful as the mayor?

"You ain't the only reporter." Scooch grinned, his eyes sinking deeper into his fleshy face.

"By the time you get someone else, this story's gonna be dead as Danny. You think the police won't find out who the body is?"

Scooch glared at Jamison and hoisted the second bottle, draining it.

Jamison looked at his Timex. "Look, if we hurry I can make the late edition. If I miss it, your information's worth shit. Now it's worth five hundred."

A few seconds passed before Scooch said, "Eight hundred."

"Only if it's good. I'll get a teaser in the late edition now, then we'll talk about that notebook."

"Gimme another beer first," Scooch said, scratching his belly.

Jamison hurried to the bar, dredging his memory for more of Danny Delaney's controversial history—decorated vet, lawyer, party ward boss, powerful alderman of dubious ethics. He was never indicted, but there were plenty of rumors before he disappeared.

While Jamison waited for the beers, he called the paper on his cell phone and enlisted a news assistant for some hurried research. Then, with three more beers, two yellowish eggs, and a plum-colored knockwurst in a bar napkin, he scurried back to Scooch's table for some dinner and serious conversation.

# CHAPTER 7

When Sutherland stepped from the harbor tender onto *Circe* that evening, he found two members of his regular crew napping in the sailboat's cockpit. They had already taken *Circe* for an afternoon sail, returned, and then busied themselves on cleaning and minor repair tasks until the heat got the better of them. Once on board, it took five minutes to start the engine and cast off the mooring line. By six thirty they were motoring past the harbor lighthouse through the gap in the breakwater.

They found a light wind a mile offshore, just enough to fill the main and genoa and push them along at five knots on a calm lake. Sutherland let his first mate take the helm while he made margaritas and poured taco chips into a bowl along with the guacamole his bowman had brought. He felt at home on his boat—the easy movement, the murmur as the water rushed by the hull. Forgetting the events of the afternoon would take more than an evening sail, however.

He had plenty to worry about. The engineering firm he'd hired was a month behind, the architects' designs far exceeded Broadwell's budget, his financing wasn't locked in place, and the lease wasn't finalized. A man dead in a building was small stuff. It would cost him a day or twos' delay, only a drop in a large bucket. So why couldn't he forget it?

The month Danny Delaney disappeared, Sutherland had been on an archeological dig in Mexico near the border with Guatemala. A year and a half earlier, he'd been a student at Cornell when the news of his father's indictment reached him. Upsetting as it was, he had confidence that it would be proven a mistake, that his father would be exonerated before the weekend. Then came the reports of his confession and the hyped-up headlines about the corruption that had almost brought down the mayor. Angry, resentful, and propelled by the profound sense of betrayal he'd felt, Sutherland sold off his furniture and personal effects to his fraternity brothers and took off to the Caribbean with only his backpack, passport, and two hundred dollars.

His father, a presumptive pillar of honesty and moral rectitude, had been exposed as a corrupt fraud and hypocrite. How could he face that pretender again? Or continue benefiting from his illicit earnings, money he'd earned colluding with amoral politicians and power brokers, dealing in kickbacks and payoffs?

Simple answer: he couldn't, and so he didn't return from Mexico until learning of his father's death. Within two days of his return an FBI agent interviewed him and made him fully aware that after Bernard Sutherland's release from prison, he had picked up where he'd left off with Danny Delaney and cronies. As a result, despite their many overtures, Doug Sutherland had meticulously avoided doing business with any of them. Jules Langer's father, Miles, had died of cancer some time after Delaney went missing, but the rest of the circle was still around. Let them worry about Delaney's legacy. That is, if it was really the alderman they'd uncovered in the McCollum.

At eight o'clock, they came about and set sail on a broad reach back to Monroe Harbor. A long swell had been building from the north, the result of a squall line crossing northern Wisconsin. If it only would come their way, it would bring a welcome respite from the last few days' heat. By the time they reached the harbor breakwater, an onshore breeze had freshened, and they slid past the lighthouse at nine knots under a spinnaker. When Sutherland checked the barometer, he saw the pressure had fallen enough to encourage wishful thinking. Maybe tomorrow would be cooler.

# CHAPTER 8

Jules Langer sat at his desk in a high-backed, leather armchair that he occupied like a throne when visitors entered his office. He pulled the *Chicago Tribune* closer and skimmed the short article again.

### BODY DISCOVERED IN McCOLLUM BUILDING
#### Sources Believe Missing Alderman Found
#### by Bill Jamison

A body was uncovered yesterday in the ruins of the McCollum Building in Chicago's Loop. Police disclosed that the body was found during the building's demolition, in a section remodeled in the nineties. Though the authorities haven't yet confirmed it, reliable sources believe the body to be the notorious politician and power broker, Anthony "Danny" Delaney. He was the long-time alderman of the Chicago's First Ward when he disappeared under suspicious circumstances fifteen years ago. The police have ruled this death a murder and should confirm the victim's identity within days.

In a related matter, the whereabouts of alderman Delaney's notebook has also been ascertained, a discovery that may shed light on the alderman's alleged activities and even on his death.

Langer picked up his Montblanc fountain pen and underlined *notebook* in bold, blue strokes. Late the previous afternoon, after he'd finished his New York calls, he received a phone call from a crude-sounding man who wanted to sell a notebook supposedly belonging to the dead man discovered in the McCollum. At first Langer thought it was a prank, Sutherland or someone working for him having him on. But when the caller mentioned Danny Delaney, his alarms went off, evoking conflicting thoughts of opportunity and danger. Langer agreed to buy it, sight unseen. When he asked how much and where they could meet, the man said he'd call back. Langer felt a pang of anxiety; he couldn't let someone else get their hands on that book.

Langer read the byline again and shouted to his secretary, who was at her desk filing her nails just outside his door. "Linda, call the *Tribune* and get me Bill Jamison on the phone. He's a reporter."

"The newspaper?" A stunning, dark-haired woman in her late twenties appeared at the door. She was the latest of a string of assistants he had hired since his divorce, each tenure lasting until the romance or his tolerance for incompetence waned.

"What other *Tribune* is there? And if he's not in, leave a message to call here and get his cell number if you can."

"Can I tell him what it's about?"

"This morning's article. Say I have information for him."

The contents of that book could be dynamite, whether as a threat to Langer himself or an opportunity to resolve a long-endured problem. Either way, he wanted it and knew he wouldn't be alone in that regard.

Langer had never directly dealt with Danny—Langer's father had always insulated him from the man. The alderman had been an impossible man to fathom, a question of which of several descriptions or definitions one chose. He was certainly an astute politico who looked after his constituents. He was also an opportunist who used his well-connected law firm and city council position to line his own pockets. The pivotal question and the one frequently asked was if and where his activities had crossed the line from technically legal yet ethically questionable, to outright illegal and criminal. From the little Langer was privy to, one thing was clear: if there was a notebook, it would attract a lot of attention. Though Langer himself was sheltered from any illegal activities that might have taken place back then, this story could open a can of worms about current arrangements.

# Chapter 9

US Congressional Representative George Spanos was halfway through his *New York Times* crossword puzzle when his wife, Lizzy, interrupted from the other side of their breakfast nook table. "Did you see this *Tribune* article, hon? The one about the body?"

Their two children, a sixteen-year-old boy and a girl of seventeen, had been picked up for their tennis matches, leaving congressman and wife to finish their abbreviated morning ritual in peace. Normally when he returned to Chicago from what he considered the drudgery of his Washington responsibilities, Spanos had more time to relax. That all changed after he was tapped to run for governor. In another half hour, he would be carried off in a limo on a whirlwind tour of appearances, from senior centers to ghetto churches. Being the front-runner didn't matter. Polls could be deceptive and there were months to go before the election.

Spanos, his pen poised, searched his memory for a five-letter word for dog genus. Canis? "What body?" he asked.

"Uncovered in a building downtown. Chicago. They think it might be that alderman."

Fourteen down. Pulitzer Prize economist … He looked up, suddenly interested. "Alderman? Who?"

She consulted the *Tribune* article and said, "Danny Delaney, but they're not sure yet. Isn't that a case you worked on? When you were with the prosecutor's office?"

What a memory she had. Probably why she was such a competent librarian and schoolteacher. Back then they had recently moved to Chicago from Philly, and it was his first year on the job. She had delivered their son that summer, and he'd been working twelve to sixteen hours every day while she struggled with two infants at home. He remembered it as the worst year of his life, the content of which he had tried unsuccessfully to forget. How could he when there were those who constantly reminded him and held it over him? The irony was that he was a sitting US congressman and potentially the next governor of Illinois, a situation that was the direct consequence of his unforgivable actions of that nightmarish year.

"That was when John Durham was murdered, right?" she asked. "The lead FBI guy? I remember the case fell apart after that because I got to see you again."

"Because the evidence was destroyed and we had no case. Let me see the article." He reached for the paper. After reading it, he took a deep breath and let it out slowly. Delaney. That's what started it all.

# Chapter 10

After he'd left the last of the phone messages to the Broadwell Communications directors, Langer felt optimistic again. Swiveling around in his chair, he scanned the photographs covering the wall behind his desk. His mood sank immediately when he glimpsed the empty spot, now a darker rectangle against the sun-bleached paint. His former wife's portrait had hung there, and the void was a painful reminder of his divorce, its cost, and the maddening publicity surrounding it. She had made his life miserable for two years, alleging that their marriage was never consummated, that he was impotent, that he had an unnatural relationship with his sister. Even after he agreed to her demands, she continued feeding the gossip columnists, stopping only after his lawyers went to court to silence her. After five years he still vacillated between covering the offending reminder and leaving it as deterrent against thoughts of another marriage. It kept his romantic ventures superficial and short-lived.

The rest of the wall was a showcase of racing sailboats, their brilliant spinnakers ballooned and pulling, so real one could hear wind and surf, the winches grinding, sails pulsing, the helmsmen's shouts—so real Langer felt his usual race-day queasiness just looking at the heaving hulls and whitecaps. His eyes locked on his favorite, a shot of two yachts, crews aligned on the windward rail, crashing toward a finish line bow to bow. One boat was his, *Julia*, named for his sister. The other was *Circe*, Doug Sutherland's racing sloop. Langer had won that race, the only time he had ever beaten his rival.

He had named the boat for his twin, hoping it would bring luck. It hadn't worked. Not for the boat and not for Julia. His glance fixed on a photo of Julia in her wedding gown. The groom wasn't in the picture, but the thought of Reginald Tunney, his brother-in-law, made him reach for his roll of antacids. He chewed on three of them while he gathered his resolve. Danny Delaney's notebook could be his opportunity. Its contents could be a threat to Tunney, a bargaining chip for whoever held it. Last evening's call from the man offering to sell Delaney's notebook was an omen. He had agreed to meet, and the man promised to call back. If it went as planned and he acquired the notebook, Langer might finally have the leverage to free his sister from his sadistic brother-in-law.

# Chapter 11

The man called Scooch chose the meeting place again, a Polish cafeteria near a CTA train stop. It was late morning when Bill Jamison walked in and found Scooch sitting under an overhead fan at one of the few occupied tables. The air smelled of pierogi, borscht, and sour seasonings Jamison couldn't identify.

Crumpled napkins and cloudy glasses and plates smeared with congealing drippings cluttered the table. Jamison sat opposite Scooch, who grunted a hello through a mouthful of apple pie.

"You see the paper?" Jamison asked.

"Mmm hmm."

"Now we get down to the details." He placed his cell phone next to his notepad on a clear section of the table directly in front of him. The phone was on and set to take photos. He intended to get a shot of Scooch and anything else he could.

"How about payin' up first." Scooch belched and held out a gummy palm.

Jamison pulled a white envelope from his sport coat, separated half the bills it contained, and handed them to Scooch. "Twenties. Half now, half after I see what you got." Scooch grabbed the bills, counted them and stuffed them in his pants pocket. Then he searched among the heaped plates to reclaim a half-smoked cigar and jammed it into his mouth. He didn't attempt to light it, and given how soggy it looked, Jamison doubted the disgusting thing would burn.

"So far your information holds up," said Jamison. "Police didn't believe it at first."

"You tell them about me?"

"I don't even know your real name."

Scooch removed his unlit cigar, leaned forward, and whispered, "Fascucci. Angelo Fascucci … so they call me Scooch … get it?"

"Ingenious." Jamison edged back from Scooch's breath. "Okay, Angelo …" He wrote the name in his notebook as he spoke, "How'd you know about the good alderman?"

"He married a cousin of mine. Gave me things to do."

"Things?"

"Around the office, errands, you know."

"You involved in him disappearing?"

"Without him I got no job, nothin'." Scooch leaned heavy arms on the table.

"How'd you get the book?"

Scooch replaced the cigar between his teeth then looked to each side and confided, "Night he disappeared, Danny had all kind of visitors, like normal. Nothing for me, so I sacked out in his basement office. I woke up and gotta piss like a racehorse. So I go to the crapper in the basement, which was near the cubbyhole where he had his safe, and on the floor is this notebook. Dropped it while getting stuff from the safe or somethin', I figure, so I grab it and head upstairs to give it to him.

"Half up the stairs I stop. I listen, see, and I hear guys talkin'. What I hear, they got Danny in some factory or something. Guy says Danny's a stoolie. Gonna bury him in the McCollum after they torch his house, destroy what records he hid."

"You recognize the guys?"

"You kiddin'? I just want outta there, 'cause they're talkin' about torching the place. I snuck back down the stairs and went out the alley door with the book."

"You bring it here? Let me see."

"Rest of the money first."

Jamison handed Scooch the envelope. His own money for Christ's sake—didn't waste his time asking the damned newspaper.

After stuffing the cash into his pocket, Scooch retrieved a black leather five-by-eight-inch notebook from inside his work shirt. The edges between the covers were grimy and yellowed.

Jamison reached for it.

"Uh uh." Scooch set it down in a small space he made among the dishes. "It stays there."

Jamison opened the cover to the first page and scanned it. He saw columns of clear handwritten numbers, dates, initials, dollar amounts, and abbreviations. He was reminded of the tables of logarithms that confounded him in college. "What's this mean?"

"Nothing to me. Didn't know he had the thing."

Jamison turned the page to more of the same. He scanned down rows and noticed that in addition to dates, initials, and dollar figures, there sometimes were Loop addresses and a column headed "Tape No." There were cryptic notations in some rows, initials that looked like abbreviations for bank names with their account numbers or wire transfer codes. He felt his heartbeat race as some of the abbreviated names registered possibilities. With a little research, he might be able to match the dates with people and buildings. These could be payoffs or kickbacks. He stopped and made entries into his own notebook, turned a few pages in Danny's and transcribed more. Scooch looked on warily, chewing on the unlit cigar.

"Why don't you let me take this, get a copy of it?" Jamison asked, trying to hide his excitement. The flunky obviously didn't know what he had.

"I look stupid?" Scooch said.

Jamison stifled an urge to answer and leafed past a half-dozen pages, comparing the dollar amounts. They ranged from a few thousand to tens of thousands. Then, one larger number stuck out at the bottom of the last page of entries. He pointed to it and said, "Whose initials are these?"

Scooch leaned forward and squinted at the page. "Fuck if I know."

Jamison wanted to copy this, but he could see that Scooch was getting impatient. So he reached for his cell phone and said, "Just a sec, I've got a text message," and while pretending to read his screen, he snapped off two shots: one of the open page and one of his wary table companion. Before Scooch could object, Jamison replaced the phone and turned his attention back to the book.

The second-to-last dollar figure was five million, next to the words "wire transfer" with a fifteen-year-old date, the initials BS, and a series of numbers, maybe an account and a routing code. None of the other amounts exceeded five digits.

"Look at that. Five million," Jamison said. "We're talking major bucks here. And what's this on another line, the MWPF? Isn't that a pension fund?"

Scooch stiffened, then came alive as he snatched the book from Jamison's hands and pulled it up to his face. He wrinkled his nose and squinted, his lips moving as he read. Then he began pulling on his bad ear, perhaps his way of recalling something. "That night," he said finally, "Mr. Sutherland and Danny were talking secret-like when Mr. Gorman was out of the room. Mr. Sutherland said the others were in for a big surprise when they found out he didn't send the money to the usual bank. A wire or something like that. Nobody ever cared what I heard. Didn't understand, anyway."

*Because you're dumb as a post*, Jamison thought. "Benjamin Gorman? Head of the pension fund?"

"That's him. Mr. Gorman."

Jamison reached for the book. "There's more there. Let me see."

Scooch pressed it to his chest, protecting it from Jamison's reach. "That's all you see," he said. "I gotta think."

"How much you want for it?"

"I gotta think." He closed the notebook and stuffed it inside his shirt.

"I just need a copy. Just a copy," Jamison said, on the edge of his chair. "We can go right now. There's a place down the street with a machine."

Scooch scratched the stubble on his chin. "Five grand for a copy. But the money first."

*Impossible*, Jamison thought, but quickly said, "Where can I call you?"

"I'll call *you*."

"But don't sell the original, okay? Not even show it. What if you're robbed?"

Scooch nodded. "I'll send it someplace safe."

Jamison stood up then asked a question that had been nagging him. "Why'd you wait so long? What you been doing all these years?"

Scooch's eyes darted away. He pulled at his gnarled right ear and then shrugged. "Didn't mean nothin' to me," he said. "Threw the thing in a trunk and forgot it until I heard about the body in the McCollum. So I called Mr. Sutherland's kid."

"Why him?"

"I used to deliver shit to his old man. Treated me good. Didn't want his kid blindsided about Danny and thought he might buy the book."

"All those years? Where were you? Doing time?"

Scooch shrugged. "Small-time shit. Never killed nobody or nothin'."

A few minutes later Jamison breathed in the afternoon air, grateful to be free of Scooch's aura. He hurried to a spot across the street and watched the restaurant door. A moment later Scooch appeared and headed toward Division and the underground train station. Jamison followed, planning to keep him in sight until he reached whatever sty he called home.

# Chapter 12

The promised cold front had stalled over Minnesota, leaving Chicago to swelter another day. Fortunately the air conditioning problem in Sutherland's building wasn't as serious as thought, and it was repaired by the start of business. When he arrived, his office felt like a meat locker, as if the management was making up for the failure.

He spent Tuesday morning focused on the latest designs and cost estimates for Broadwell's regional headquarters, the building that would replace what remained of the McCollum. *Architects!* he thought. If he agreed to everything they suggested, he'd be 20 percent over the pro forma.

At twelve thirty, a baritone voice jolted Sutherland out of his concentration.

"Mind if I bother you a second?" Dan Dixon, a balding black man with horn-rimmed glasses, stood at Sutherland's door. Dixon was Broadwell Communications' project manager for their new Chicago headquarters. He crossed the Tabriz carpet and plopped into a chair facing Sutherland's desk. "You look worried. You okay?"

"The budget is all," said Sutherland, trying a smile. He liked Dan. They made a good team.

"I thought maybe it was about the body."

"No big deal. It'll delay us a couple days, but I can make it up."

"Cops know anything yet? Other than it was the alderman?"

"If they do, they haven't told me."

"I hope it dies down soon. This kind of thing …"

Sutherland put his pencil down and studied Dan's face. The tight lips, the clenched jaw suggested a problem. "There something wrong, Dan?"

Dan shrugged, his hands palms up. "I spent yesterday at New York headquarters working on the user's wish list. While I was there, the news about the body came up. The corporate counsel was a little concerned. A couple board members have been asking questions."

Sutherland let out a breath. "Jeez. Ask me, he should worry about getting the damn lease finished. What's he worried about?"

"You know, bad publicity. If it got out of hand."

"Nothing we can do. Whatever happened, happened. Besides, it has nothing to do with your company."

"I know. I'm just passing along his concerns. With the shareholder's lawsuit and rumors about the SEC looking at us, the company has to be very careful about everything, including who it does business with. You should have heard the internal debates about your problems with the preservationists. A few directors wanted to drop you then."

"Jesus. I didn't kill the alderman. What are they thinking?" Sutherland clenched his fists, felt his face heat up.

"Take it easy," Dan said, holding his hands up, leaning back in his chair. "It's probably nothing. Just wanted you to know." He stood up hurriedly. "Look, I've got to go. I'll keep you posted."

"Yeah. Thanks." Sutherland turned and looked out the window. The view was dominated by Chase Tower, its soaring lines rising out of sight. At thirty floors, Sutherland's building wouldn't reach Chase's hip, but it was to be one of the few downtown office developments in years and Sutherland's triumph. But without Broadwell, he couldn't build. He'd never get financing.

He swiveled in his chair and admired the renderings of his new building that hung on the opposite wall. Stainless steel and green glass. Nothing fancy, but elegant nonetheless. If all went well, in another eighteen months, Broadwell would be moving in, and Sutherland would already be on to his next projects. And why wouldn't all go well?

Ten minutes after Dixon left, Sutherland retrieved his phone messages from his secretary's desk. "Some reporters called," Eileen said. "They want your comments on the body at the McCollum."

"If they call again, tell them to ask the police."

"And a man from the FBI just called." She ripped off the top sheet of her notepad and handed it to him. "Wanted to know when he could come by tomorrow. I guess it's about the body."

"Everything's about that body. I've got meetings with the architects most of the day. If he wants to see me, it'll have to be first thing."

He crumpled and threw the reporters' messages in the wastebasket. Another was from Kelly, his ex-girlfriend. No hurry there, though he wondered why she'd be calling. The final call was from Bill Jamison. Odd that his name sprung up again after so long.

Sutherland dialed the number on the note, and Bill answered.

"Long time," Sutherland said. "What's up?"

"I called to thank you for giving Scooch my name. You read my article this morning?"

"Who's Scooch?"

"The guy that called you. You told him to contact me. That's what today's article's about. Danny."

Sutherland tried to recall what he'd said to the anonymous caller. "It's not like I know a lot of reporters. What'd he tell you?"

"A lot. But it's what he's selling. Why didn't you want it?"

"An old notebook? What for?"

"I think your father's in it."

"How so?"

"His initials, anyway. And according to this Scooch guy, he was with Danny the night he disappeared."

"Even if they're his initials, it's old news. Nothing they can do to him now."

"It raises some big questions."

Like why'd a supposed pillar of virtue go to jail for bribery? "Why waste your time on old news, Bill? There's plenty corruption today."

"But this is murder. And I'll bet there's some juicy bits you didn't know. You ready?"

Sutherland sighed, weary of allegations he was past caring about.

The reporter went on. "According to the public records, Danny owned a small interest in the McCollum. Your father bought him out for a hundred thousand a month before Danny disappeared."

Why hadn't Sutherland known that? Then again, why should he? Doug Sutherland's company had bought an undivided, 100 percent interest in the McCollum from the trust his father had created. He had no need to delve into its history; that was the title company's responsibility. As long as the deed was free of claims and everything legal, he wouldn't have concerned himself about its chain of title.

"And that's not all," Jamison continued. "If the book and Scooch are right, it looks like a certain BS had something to do with sending millions of dollars to a numbered account somewhere. Benjamin Gorman's pension fund is mentioned too, so possibly the money was taken from there."

"Somebody's initials and your choice of words, *possibly*, aren't very convincing. You making this up?"

"Listen. Someone named BS embezzles five mil, your father buys out Danny, Danny disappears, and so does your father, supposedly committing suicide. Think there's a story there?"

What could you say to a question like that? "Slow down, buddy. Where does your suggestion of embezzling come from? You're jumping to conclusions. You don't even know if the notebook's real. You have it? Has it been authenticated? Have the police confirmed it's him?"

"It's him. And this guy's sure it's Danny's book," Jamison said. "He

31

wants too much money for it, but I sneaked a picture of a couple pages. I've already dug up some good background and have more research in the works on these names, initials, abbreviations, and shit. On the surface, it's not easy to decipher, but who knows? Abbreviations that could stand for *commissioner*, *lieutenant*, and *alderman*."

"If you don't know for sure, how can you print it?"

"I'm simply reporting on Danny's notebook's contents, along with the background. After I meet with Benjamin Gorman, I'll know what I have. Like this stuff about money in and out of what may be Panama and Cayman banks. Secret accounts? Has to mean something, you think?"

Only that his father's trust fund once had an account in Panama, but that tidbit was too juicy to feed to a hungry reporter.

# Chapter 13

First-time visitors to Sutherland's apartment always thought he'd just moved in. He'd lived there since his divorce and liked it simple, unadorned, just as it was. In the words of Mies, less is more. That evening in his apartment, Sutherland paced his large living room, an old habit that helped him concentrate. His route took him around an island of couch, chairs, and coffee table, past the stereo, flat-screen TV, and two abstract oils to the north window, where he continued east, head down and focused.

First the caller says it was Danny Delaney's body in the McCollum and suggests that his father might be a suspect in Danny's death. Next, Jamison says the caller remembers a discussion between Danny and Bernard Sutherland about millions of dollars, maybe stolen. If the caller was right about Danny's body, did that add credence to the rest of it? Sutherland had been in Mexico and wasn't aware of the chronology of events. Who died first: Danny, as Jamison implied, or his father? Was a large amount taken from Gorman's pension fund? And the most crucial question: could his father have been involved in Danny Delaney's death?

The Internet would have the answers to the initial questions, but whether his father was capable of murder was something else. As he clicked onto the *Chicago Tribune*'s web page, he couldn't dismiss the image of the body and its missing tooth, a gap into a darker history. Maybe he shouldn't go there.

After two hours of pointing and clicking, Sutherland leaned back in his den chair and reflected on what he'd learned. He'd accessed dozens of newspaper articles dating from the time of his father's conviction. Most of what he'd read told him nothing new. Bernard Sutherland had confessed to trying to bribe the mayor. He'd served a short prison term and had disappeared from his yacht on Lake Michigan a few months later. It was ruled a drowning; whether it was an accident or suicide couldn't be determined.

Nothing in the news of the time reported a multimillion-dollar theft, pension money or otherwise. One article mentioned that Sutherland's father had once been on the board of directors of the state's pension fund, so there was definitely a connection. But Benjamin Gorman, the head of the pension fund, was quoted at the time that they were achieving record returns. If there was stolen money of that magnitude, Benjamin Gorman would have known. So what was Jamison or this Scooch character talking about?

Gorman had been in Sutherland's father's house on several occasions when he was a boy. As recently as five years ago, the pension boss had tried to finance one of Doug Sutherland's projects, but he declined. He wanted nothing to do with his father's acquaintances.

He felt as if dead men were dragging him into places he didn't want to go. His father implicated in Danny's death? After embezzling millions of dollars? Sutherland's adult life had been plagued with the belief that his father had been guilty of bribery, but these other crimes weren't as easy to repress. Especially in light of Broadwell Communications' aversion to controversy.

Wouldn't it be easy to clarify? Jamison planned to talk to Gorman. According to Sutherland's web research, the former pension fund head was still living in the city's northwest side. He had been forced out of his position as president under the shadow of irregularities a few years ago. Since when had irregularities been a problem in Chicago?

# Chapter 14

**WEDNESDAY, JULY 11**

Sutherland stepped into the restaurant and waited for his eyes to adjust to the dim light. The air was heavy with the aroma of garlic, onion, corn tortillas, and grilled beef, and he was struck by the recollection of a dark-haired woman at the stove. For a moment he was in his high chair, his Mexican mother stirring the contents of a large *olla*. It must have been the year before she left, before there was only him and his father. With the memory in mind, he decided he might sample some of Casa Rosa's celebrated cooking while he attended to the real reason he was here.

He consulted the maitre d' and walked toward the rear of the room, weaving through the passageways between tables, looking for the one man he expected to know. But after surveying the sea of diners, Sutherland reached the kitchen having recognized no one.

He stood with his back to the kitchen doors, his gaze sweeping the room again. At the point of giving up, he saw something move to his right, a hand raised in greeting. He turned, and from the candlelight of the nearest table, a ghostly face stared back at him.

"Jesus," Sutherland whispered, shuddering. This was Benjamin Gorman, the man who once controlled billions of union pension money. If he hadn't moved, he could have been mistaken for a corpse.

Sutherland took the chair opposite Gorman at the table. Neither man offered to shake hands.

"A long time, Benjamin."

"Been a while, Junior." His voice was a thin, forced chord.

Junior. Again. A label from the years before, when he'd followed his father around. Sutherland took off his suit jacket and hung it on the chair back. "You have to sit by the kitchen? It's almost a hundred out."

"There's worse things than being hot." Moisture glistened on Gorman's spotted scalp. His overlarge shirt was wet through, his collar open, the greasy tie pulled down. He drank from a glass of ice water and replaced it in its puddle by his right hand. He seemed in no hurry. "Now you're older, you look like your old man—except darker, like your wetback mother."

"So they say." His father had been handsome, but what could Sutherland say about Gorman? "You don't look so good."

"Cancer. Radiation, chemo," Gorman said. He turned his hands palms up, indicating the hopelessness of it.

A waiter arrived and Sutherland ordered a Dos Equis. He didn't feel hungry anymore.

"What drags you to my level, Junior?" Gorman grinned, revealing a perfect row of teeth, comically large in the shrunken face.

"It's Doug, not Junior."

Gorman nodded. "Want to forget the old man, eh? Then why'd you want to meet?"

"I need something."

Gorman arched his left eyebrow. "You? A favor?"

"Nothing that will cost you," Sutherland said. "Anyway, I read you retired."

"Sure you read it." Gorman spit the words. "The fuckers. 'Pension Boss Ends Notorious Career,' the papers said. Libel's what it was."

"Save it. We both know better."

"Bastards never proved a thing. Fuckers." Gorman pulled a large handkerchief from his back pocket and wiped his brow. "So what d'you want?"

Where did he start? So much he didn't know, so much he never cared or dared to ask. Like what really happened during the years Sutherland was away at college, then Mexico? What went on in city hall's back rooms? Sutherland had fifteen years of suppressed questions, but they all concerned the same issue. He cleared his throat and said, "For starters, what exactly was my father into? Guilty of?"

Gorman gawked in disbelief. "All this time … you're just asking?"

"That's right. Just asking."

"He confessed, didn't he? Went to jail for it."

"For bribery. But what else?"

"I look like his confessor?" Gorman waved a bony hand dismissively. "Jesus Christ! What other fucked-up questions you got?"

Not a good start. If Gorman knew more, he wasn't going to make it easy. "What about the money he took?"

"Who told you that?"

"Then it's true?"

Gorman paused and pursed his lips before answering. "It's history. Forget about it."

"Hard to overlook millions of dollars, even in a fund as big as yours. You never reported it."

Gorman's laugh trailed into a hacking cough. When he finally stopped, he said, "You think the money came from the Mid West Pension Fund?"

"Wasn't it?"

Gorman scoffed. "You really don't know? Jesus. Your old man didn't tell you nothin', did he?"

"So whose was it? And where is it?"

"If he didn't tell you, where you getting this shit?"

"A reporter." From his shirt pocket, Sutherland pulled out Bill Jamison's *Tribune* article and flattened it on the table. "Didn't you read this?"

Gorman tilted his head, like a puzzled bird.

"Danny Delaney. They found his body in the McCollum. You didn't hear?"

Gorman slowly nodded. "I don't follow news no more. So that's what this is about. Next you'll be asking who killed him."

"You were a suspect, right?"

"Because some asshole saw me coming out of Danny's the night he disappeared. Police couldn't prove nothing, but a few people still figured me for it." His laugh again faded into a wheeze, and he coughed into his handkerchief.

"So who did?"

"Lots of people wanted him dead. Anyway, what do you care?"

A few days ago, Sutherland didn't know, didn't care. Not about Danny, not about his murderer, not about missing money. Now these questions were worming themselves into his life, jeopardizing his livelihood. Gorman could probably tell him everything he needed to know. Sutherland had to restrain himself from reaching across the table and shaking it out of him. He'd probably kill the pathetic old prick in the process. "Okay then. The money—why wasn't the theft reported?"

"The money's why you're here, ain't it?" He smiled knowingly. Then he shrugged. "There's no harm in me saying. Right after your old man served time, we sold one of the buildings from Danny's ward to some friends, a group of casino owners that were skimming and needed to launder some cash. We priced the property way below market and they paid the difference in cash, which we could use to pay off some of our silent partners, guys who didn't like the limelight. Your old man had been disbarred but still did our finance stuff. Out of the blue, he substituted different wire transfer instructions and sent it someplace."

"That's it? Nobody did anything? None of your cronies?"

"He died, remember? Soon after."

"Millions, and you don't know where it went?"

"It wasn't mine. It was for the fuckin' politicians, police, judges, and the other assholes we had to keep happy."

"Who's the 'we' you keep talking about? Besides Danny?"

"If you don't know, ask the guy that told you about the money."

Sutherland pointed to the newspaper article. "All he knows is what he saw in Danny's notebook."

Gorman's head jerked as if he'd been doused with cold water. He squinted at the article before asking, "A notebook?"

"Some guy had it. What's in it?"

Gorman licked his cracked lips and sipped some water. His trembling hand spilled a few drops as he replaced the glass in its wet spot. Then he chuckled, then grimaced, as if it pained him. "If it's true, it'll keep some guys awake at night."

"That why Danny was killed? He was blackmailing someone?"

"He was going state's evidence. Feds, everybody." The old man seemed agitated; his hands shook and his lower lip began to twitch. "After he disappeared, the cops didn't have nothing, so the investigation died. Never heard another peep. You got the thing?"

"Not me. But some guy thinks he's gonna be rich."

"Dead's more like it. And me with him once they find out I don't have it." Gorman forced his mouth into a deathly grin. "I was at Danny's place that night, after your old man left, before the others came. Before they torched his place they searched everything and discovered he had planted secret cameras and must've been taping his meetings. I took some files—hardly worth anything, it turned out—but I let everyone believe they were important. When they asked, I just smiled and told them not to worry, all his shit was in a safe place, including the tapes."

He glanced right and left, as if making sure no one was watching. Satisfied, he fumbled with the button on his shirtsleeve. After an effort, he exposed his left forearm and rested it on the table next to the candle. Pointing to an eight-digit number tattooed on his paper-thin skin, he said, "My security. I hinted it was the number of a box with Danny's stuff. But now …" He started to laugh then grimaced again. For an instant the sweat on his face, tinged by the crimson candle, looked like blood. Gorman strained to grin. "Now leave me alone, Junior."

He reached into his shirt pocket, extracted an unfiltered cigarette, and lit it from the candle bowl. When he leaned back from the flame, his eyes were closed in pained ecstasy, his gaunt face shrouded in smoke.

Across the street and two doors down from Casa Rosa, in the entrance foyer of a closed store, two men waited. The first was thin with long, greasy hair. He wore a pair of jeans and a Willie Nelson tee shirt, drenched with sweat. He fidgeted, scratched, shifted from foot to foot while his head bobbed in rhythm to some inaudible beat. The other man, wearing chinos and a polo shirt, stood like a statue and was just as solid. His skin was pale, his sharp nose crooked, his short hair blond.

The blond man monitored the diners leaving the restaurant, some waiting for the valet to bring their cars, others walking right or left down the sidewalk. It was almost dark, but he wouldn't have trouble spotting their mark as he passed through the door to the street. They would follow the target down the alley he took to his back door. Afterward, the blond man would deal with the lowlife junkie at his side, giving him the promised bag of heroin. From the edge of his sight, he saw the junkie kneading with his thumb the knife handle in his right hand.

# Chapter 15

In the purple haze before dawn, Vicente Romero scuffed through the shadows of Michigan Avenue's rear alley on his way to work. Overhead, fire escapes hung like blackened skeletons, while murky recesses and darkness waited ahead. Vicente whistled nervously, crisscrossing the narrow alley, avoiding doorways and skirting garbage dumpsters, their sweet stench hanging in the air. *Aliento del Diablo.* Breath of the devil, he thought.

Approaching his building he heard the scrabbling of small feet over the rough stones. *Rats by the dumpster,* he thought, feeling a shiver. His pace quickened as he neared the freight doorway, but after another step he froze, as if slammed in the chest by what he saw.

He had almost stumbled over it: the motionless body of a young man spread-eagled on his back. Even in the dull light, Vicente knew the man was dead. The eyes lifeless glass, the mouth a silent hole. One fearless rat sat by a ragged wound in the man's neck, its eyes staring hatefully, its cruel mouth chewing.

"*Lárgate.* Fuck outta here," Vicente shouted, stomping the ground by the dead man's sneaker, recoiling a step as the rat snarled before slinking into the shadows behind the dumpster.

The dead man lay on a flattened cardboard box, arms spread at his sides, palms up. A wine bottle cap, matches, and a plastic bag with white powder lay by his right side. A heavy rubber band still encircled the man's upper arm. A hypodermic dangled from the scars on his forearm. Seeing the cooker and kit, Vicente crooned, "Can't get no higher, amigo."

Vicente wasted no time. He stooped over the dead man and searched his pockets. He found a wallet, opened it, withdrew the half-dozen twenty-dollar bills, and thrust them into his own pocket. Before he threw the wallet away, he noticed the driver's license and something strange: the name on it was Benjamin Gorman, and the photograph looked nothing like the dead man.

*　　*　　*

Special Agent Mark Branson was sitting in Sutherland and Associates' small waiting area when Sutherland arrived the next morning. As soon as Sutherland entered, the agent closed his cell phone, stood up, flipped open a wallet, and flashed his FBI identification.

He was in his late forties, five-eleven, and blue-eyed with blond, almost white, well-trimmed hair. His navy-blue suit barely disguised a well-built torso.

"Your secretary, Eileen? Said to come by first thing. I hope I'm not too early."

Sutherland glanced at his watch. Eight thirty. "It's okay. Come on in." He led the way past a conference room, several empty cubicles, an office where his accountant was peering into his computer screen, a coffee station, a copy room, and his secretary's desk, which guarded his corner office.

"Morning, Doug." Eileen handed him a note and, seeing the agent, whispered, "Kelly asked me if you got her message yesterday. I told her no. If this keeps up I'll never go to heaven."

"You're an angel nonetheless."

This new note was another from Kelly. "Lunch today?" was all it said.

"Tell her I'm tied up," he said, and he waved Agent Branson into the office. "Have a seat. Coffee?"

"Just had some, thanks."

Branson sat in the armchair in front of the desk. Sutherland took his chair on the other side. He pushed a stack of bills and engineering reports out of the way and said, "So this is about the body? It definitely was Danny Delaney?"

"Yes, sir." He unzipped the cover of a black leather portfolio and turned a few pages of the notebook inside. "Dental records proved it."

"I talked to the police the day he was found. Why's the FBI involved?" If Gorman had been right, probably something to do with Danny being a government witness.

"It's complicated." The agent plucked a pen from his shirt pocket. "You found him, right?"

"Actually a crane worker did. He told my foreman, and he called me."

"So you saw the, ahh, skull."

"Right."

"And what did you think?"

"That somebody was dead. Buried in the building."

"Did you know who it was?"

"How would I know that?"

"Precisely. How would you?" Branson turned a few pages in his book,

41

found what he sought, and said, "How long have you owned the McCollum Building, Mr. Sutherland?"

"I bought it a year ago."

"Yet, according to our information, it was already yours. Aren't you the beneficiary of the trust that owned it? Your father's trust?"

"That's right."

"May I ask why? Why use your own money if it was already yours?"

"Personal reasons. To use your term, it's complicated." Why bring up not wanting to benefit from his father's shady deals? "Is it relevant?"

Agent Branson sighed. "Possibly. Your father owned it when Mr. Delaney was buried there. Did you know that they'd been partners, that the alderman owned a piece of the building?"

"Not until yesterday."

"And that your father bought him out shortly before they both disappeared?"

"This was all new to me."

"So your father didn't tell you any of this. You were old enough. What, about twenty, then?"

"About that."

"So how could that be? Didn't you talk?"

"Not then. Not about any of this."

"Did he keep notes? Leave you any files, his diary?"

"Some I tossed, other stuff I didn't bother looking at."

Branson shook his head, apparently frustrated. "So there's nothing you can tell me? I don't have to tell you, this doesn't look good for your father."

Sutherland wanted to smile, but the truth was too painful. "A little late, don't you think?"

Branson's face reddened, his jaw clenched. "Think it's amusing? You could be affected as well."

"I wasn't even in the country. And yes, I can prove it. I've kept my old passports."

"This reporter from the *Tribune* is writing about a notebook. Did you see or pick up anything like that when you saw the skull?"

"No."

"The reporter claims this notebook is Delaney's. What do you know about that?"

"Just what Jamison wrote." Sutherland made a point by checking the time on his iPhone. "Are we nearly through? I'm sorry I'm not much of a help, but this is all ancient history that didn't involve me."

"But it does, Mr. Sutherland. What do you know about money, millions of dollars, gone missing at that time?"

Sutherland hadn't read this morning's paper. Had Bill Jamison mentioned the money in his column? "Hype to sell papers, for all I know. Why wouldn't it have been discovered long ago?" Let him ask Gorman about it. He'd probably spit in this guy's face. "This whole thing is a waste of your and my time."

"Really?" Branson's eyebrows rose, as if the thought surprised him. "You think so? I'll tell you right now, you may believe you're insulated from all this, but if stolen or dirty money was used to buy all or part of the McCollum, you're going to be ass-deep in this." Branson turned to point to the renderings of Broadwell's headquarters building hanging behind him. "That means so will your project."

*     *     *

In Chicago's Taylor Street neighborhood, a woman in cutoffs and a halter carried a trash bag from her back door to the alley. When she approached the garbage bin she stopped short. She held her nose and cursed herself for not bagging the chicken skin and guts from the night before. The heat had cooked the mess into a putrid stew. Clouds of flies circled and buzzed around the bin. God, she hated flies. And that stench. She'd have to be quick tossing the garbage.

She retreated several steps, took a deep breath, and strode toward the bin. She opened it and in mid-toss, froze, staring at a human face. Alive, she thought, flinching backward and dropping her trash bag. She looked on wide-eyed as the man's eyes shimmered blue-black, dancing with light and chaos like a kaleidoscope, as if he were hallucinating. His mouth lay open, roiling with mute activity. She gawked silently until she realized that the life and struggle on the man's face were the frenzied hunger of crawling flies.

Minutes later the police responded to reports of screams in the alley. They found the woman squatting, her eyes closed, fingers clenched so tightly on her cheeks that they bled. Her life seemed suspended on one anguished note she moaned over and over and over. She hated flies.

# CHAPTER 16

A half hour after Agent Branson left, Sutherland was in a taxi on the way to his architect's office in the west Loop. His cell phone rang, and his secretary announced that Kelly Matthews insisted on speaking to him.

"Tell her you couldn't reach me," he said.

"I heard that, Doug," Kelly answered in an icy tone. "Thank you, Eileen, you can hang up now." Sutherland heard a click as his secretary disconnected.

Kelly Matthews was an attorney for the City, a member of Chicago's Landmarks Commission, and a former flame. Sutherland hadn't talked to her for months, not since the landmark group launched their no-holds-barred campaign to stop the McCollum's demolition. The intensity of the preservationist attack had surprised everyone. In addition to the customary approach—the defense of the old building on its aesthetics and value to the city—they had tried a new tactic: a personal attack on Sutherland and his father's blemished reputation. It was dirty, and in the end it didn't work. The city council had approved his development plans, but not before the trust Sutherland and Kelly had shared had crumbled into as many pieces as the McCollum itself. Not the first time in his life he'd been betrayed by someone he thought he knew.

"Just kidding," he said.

"Then why you don't pick up my calls? Or return them?"

"Why wouldn't I want to talk to you? I even looked for you among the protesters at the McCollum the other day. What were your people trying to prove?"

"They're not my people. That's why I need to talk to you."

"It's your nickel."

"In person. You free tomorrow? Lunch?"

"Kinda hassled now. Another time, Kelly."

But as he started to hang up, hearing her voice ascend in octaves and decibels, he pulled the phone back to his ear. " ... Your stubbornness," she was shouting. "I'm just trying to help."

"Kelly, your kind of help will break me."

"That's not fair. Listen. Someone in the landmark group supplied the dirt about the planning commissioner fixing your zoning."

"Old news, Kelly."

"There's more. You've got to see it—for your own good. Stuff on your father. And Danny Delaney."

Sutherland sucked in a breath. Everywhere he turned, Danny and good old Dad. "Okay. Where?"

"Our lunch place? Noon? It's been a while."

"For a reason," he said and then hung up. He didn't relish facing those hot, emerald eyes. They'd scalded the last time, but that wasn't his principal fear. Truth was, he wasn't sure how he would react, whether he could handle it, whether he could stop himself. He needed more time. But if she had something new about the McCollum, he might as well hear it from her first.

# Chapter 17

The next morning, drenching rain and a north wind broke the city's fever. By dawn the cold front lathered into a gale, sweeping rain in sheets and driving huge whitecaps along the lakefront. Sutherland awoke early and, from his dining room, followed the line of breakers as they crashed against the concrete abutments along the shore, throwing up white walls of spume. While he finished his second coffee, he turned on CNN and skimmed the *Chicago Tribune.* Halfway through Bill Jamison's column he almost choked on a hot mouthful. He had to read it a second time to believe it.

After Jamison's article recounted the events of the last few days—the discovery of Danny Delaney in the McCollum Building and the reappearance of a notebook documenting questionable transactions and illegal money—Jamison ventured into the world of speculation.

> The notebook contains an index of videotapes as well as details of dates and payments made to the movers and shakers of Chicago and Springfield. Included among the prominent men referenced are a sitting federal judge, a high police official, an alderman, a state senator, and a candidate for a high state office in the upcoming election.
>
> Bernard Sutherland, father of the current owner of the McCollum, was partners with Mr. Delaney in owning the very building where the alderman was discovered. Mr. Sutherland disappeared from his boat on Lake Michigan, an apparent suicide, soon after Alderman Delaney disappeared. It is only a matter of time before we connect these dots.

"Jesus H. Christ," Sutherland said, bolting out of his chair. "He's trying to ruin me." Sutherland imagined Broadwell Communications' corporate counsel reading this and fretting over how it could put a stain on the company's image. As if their once-pristine reputation wasn't already being scrutinized because of rumors of creative accounting.

When Sutherland reached Jamison's office number he ended up with his voice mail. "Bill, this is Doug Sutherland. Call me." To think that he was a fraternity brother and had almost been a friend at one time.

*     *     *

Scooch spent an active morning. He left his transient hotel at eight o'clock and, after a three-egg breakfast at a nearby diner, caught the CTA train to Diversey. With Danny's notebook in a plastic bag under his arm, he plodded through the downpour to a copy service and FedEx office near Halsted Street.

Trudging back to the El station, he passed a greasy spoon with a lunch counter and a handful of deserted tables. The inviting glow through the steamed-over windows beckoned him, and he entered. In the middle of his second chocolate doughnut, he noticed the "OPEN ALL NITE" sign and decided this was a perfect place to meet one of his future benefactors tonight. He pulled out some change and went to the pay phone to make his call. Tonight he'd make an easy five grand, the first of many payments.

*     *     *

"There's a police detective here to see you," Eileen said, poking her head into Sutherland's office. "Are you here?"

What now? He'd already told them all he could about finding the alderman's body. "Police, FBI, why not? Next it'll be the CIA," he said. "Send him in."

A minute later a tall, lanky black man in a Chicago Police uniform walked in. His wind jacket was wet, and the plastic cover to his hat was covered with droplets. "Mr. Sutherland? I'm Officer Hendricks."

"Have a seat. This about the alderman again?"

"Alderman? Err ... no," the man said as he sat across from Sutherland. "Nothing about any alderman. Just a few questions about you meeting with a Benjamin Gorman. You had dinner with him at Casa Rosa's, is that right? Wednesday?"

"Yeah. Why do you want to know?"

"What time did you leave the restaurant?"

"It was getting dark. Why?"

"You left alone? He stayed there?"

47

"He was smoking a cigarette, the idiot. Probably what's killing him. What's this about?"

"You notice anybody when you left, maybe in the lobby, or outside?"

"Look. I had one beer with him, we talked, I left. So? What's the problem?"

"He was killed. Sometime after he left. According to his housekeeper, you were the last appointment he had."

"You think that I …?" This was rich. Delaney in his building, now Gorman after they meet. What's next?

"We're not saying that," the officer said. "We were hoping you might have seen someone. Waiting. A junkie was found with his ID and the knife that killed Gorman. You see anyone, someone that didn't fit, maybe?"

Sutherland remembered Gorman's agitation upon hearing the news of Delaney's notebook. His fear that his make-believe protection had evaporated, that the others, whoever they were, would know he hadn't taken Delaney's records. So was it a junkie, or the "others," who'd killed him? Sutherland didn't know, but he guessed the latter.

"No, but I wasn't really looking," he responded.

The officer stood, evidently satisfied that he'd done his job, perfunctory though it seemed. "If you think of anything, please call us," he said before leaving a card on the desk and walking out.

After replaying the conversation in his mind, Sutherland couldn't think anything new the officer might have learned from the exercise. This was what his taxes paid for. Sutherland, on the other hand, had become aware of how prescient Gorman had been. The cigarette he'd lit before Sutherland left would have been his last.

# Chapter 18

George Spanos sat in his office in the Longworth Building across Independence Avenue from the Capitol Building in Washington DC. He had flown back to the Capitol for a vote on immigration the night before, after another day of campaigning on Chicago's south side. He had a copy of the latest *Chicago Tribune* on his desk. "Jesus," he said to himself as he removed his reading glasses. How could that be? Danny had a notebook? An index of videos. "What the fuck," he said out loud.

Mat Guzmán, one of his interns, stuck his head in the office and said, "Something wrong, sir?"

Spanos tossed the newspaper on the desk in disgust. "You're fuckin' right there's something wrong. Some reporter's trying to smear me. Didn't you read the damn paper? You're supposed to read the thing and tell me what I need to know. That so hard?"

"I'm sorry, sir, but he didn't mention any names. He just said a high state office. Could be any candidate, so why would anyone think it was you?"

Guzmán had a point. Problem was, if it *was* Delaney's notebook, and if it contained names, it could easily have been Spanos that the reporter meant. That could be explained away with an innocent explanation. But if the true context were to come out, George Spanos's political career would go down in flames. Possibly worse. "I don't care, he said. Get me the number of the *Trib*'s general manager or editor. They've already endorsed me, for Christ's sake. How can they let a rogue reporter smear me?"

"Yes, sir," Guzmán said, and he retreated from the office.

Spanos waited for him to leave before picking up his phone and dialing a familiar private number. In a moment, he heard the irritating, reedy voice.

"Good morning, Governor."

"Not if that fuckin' notebook has legs. What do you know?"

"The notebook's probably authentic. How else would that reporter get that stuff? We're working on it, don't worry."

"We can't afford this. The election's months away."

"We could lose more than you, Georgie. More than just an election. So keep kissing those babies, eating those hot dogs, and pumping those black hands. We'll take care of it."

Spanos heard the phone disconnect and replaced his own receiver with a bang. As if he believed it was that simple. It wasn't the notebook they needed to worry about. Its contents would be considered hearsay and couldn't seriously hurt anyone given the statute of limitations. But despite his anxiety and the pressure he was under at the time, Spanos clearly remembered the secret meetings he'd attended at the alderman's home. Were their discussions being taped? If so, and if those tapes still existed and were publicized, it would be disastrous. The smooth road he'd sped along for the last fifteen years would run off a cliff.

# CHAPTER 19

The rain continued. It took Sutherland ten minutes to flag an empty taxi for the short trip from his office to meet Kelly Matthews. On the way, the cab passed what remained of the McCollum Building. The long arm of the wrecking crane leaned like an abandoned fishing pole, its lead sinker dangling without a hook. The police hadn't finished their examination of the site, and the rain would only delay their inspection more.

Is this what it had come to: a stillborn dream? Originally he had wanted to renovate the McCollum, restore its faded beauty, polish the old gem to what it had been when he'd first seen it as a boy, when his father doted over it. But it had been neglected too long, the costs were too high, and the old design didn't function for the demands of the new century. Tenants wouldn't pay the high rent it would take to invest that kind of money. He had shown them the numbers—Kelly, the landmark people, the preservationists. Tearing the dilapidated building down, building a modern high-rise was the only way he could make it work, the only way he could avoid losing the building and the site altogether. But they wouldn't see the reality. Their idealism transcended dollars. So they fought him. And they played dirty, alleging deals had been made and that Doug was no more than the greedy son of a convicted felon.

But he fought back; he secured Broadwell Communications as an anchor tenant, and with the unexpected help of the commissioner of planning, he won. In the process, he had destroyed the object of his father's pride and been betrayed by Kelly, the one woman he'd ever been truly close to. And now, because of Broadwell's concerns and these ghosts of the past, the dream was in jeopardy. It might have been better if his father had given it to charity instead of to him. Maybe it was some kind of punishment.

In the restaurant, as Sutherland shook out his umbrella, he glimpsed Kelly's chestnut hair in a nearby booth. *Here goes.*

"Doug," she said with a wry grin. "What a surprise, only fifteen minutes late."

"Couldn't get a cab." He sat across from her, placing his umbrella at his feet.

"You didn't want to come."

"Hey, I'm here." He picked up the menu.

Kelly had a narrow nose, high cheekbones, and a full, curvy mouth that was currently verging on a smile. With her large eyes, she always looked engaged, captivated with the people and things around her. She wore creamy linen slacks and jacket with a melon-green silk scarf at her neck.

"I ordered your usual for you," she said, "well-done ground bovine flesh with fried onions and hot peppers."

"And you're having chicken salad."

"I'll eat the burger if you don't …"

"No, I'm starved."

She sipped her iced tea, adjusted her scarf, and pursed her lips slightly— her about-to-broach-something-awkward look. After another drink of tea, she said, "I read that *Tribune* article this morning. What's your take?"

"You enjoy it? Substantiates the crap your people have been throwing."

"Not fair, Doug. I know when I've lost."

"Some of your nutty group doesn't—picketing in the heat the other day."

He saw her lips tighten, her eyes harden. Now he was in for it. You didn't win arguments with Kelly—you hoped for a draw. She called it tenacity, he called it stubbornness, but then the same could be said of him. He shifted his glance to the patrons off to the side. Then he studied the water glasses, the bread basket, the silverware, the salt and pepper shakers, and finally his watch.

"How did we end up this way?" she asked. "I was doing what I believed in."

"Kelly, we've been through this. A renovation wouldn't work. Your people tried to put me out of business." He looked into her eyes, those wet, green eyes doing it to him again. "Look, let's call a truce. What's this about the dirt?"

She smiled gamely and agreed. "Truce." The waitress arrived with their food, asked if there was anything else, and scurried off.

"Okay, the dirt," Kelly said, reaching for a french fry on Sutherland's plate. "One of the landmark staff was a fanatic on preservation. Up to him, you wouldn't tear down an outhouse if it was older than a year."

"Was? Past tense?" Sutherland spooned some jalapenos onto his hamburger and bit into it.

"He quit a couple months ago. When they got around to cleaning out his files they found this." She produced a manila folder from the seat beside her and handed it to him. It was labeled "Sutherland."

He opened it to find a paper-clipped sheaf of photocopied news articles, letters, and handwritten notes. The top sheet had a blurry photograph of

Doug's father next to the news lead: Sutherland Sentenced Two Years. He swallowed. The unchewed mouthful went down in a painful lump.

"Read through it, you'll find letters," Kelly said.

He scanned a three-month-old letter to the *Tribune*, attached to fifteen-year-old clippings, and felt the old anger return. "The smear campaign. How could you let them do this?"

Her mouth tightened into an angry line. "You really think—"

"The guy worked for you, didn't he?"

"For the Landmarks Commission, but I didn't know he was—"

"You could have stopped it. What did my father have to do with this?"

"Doug, I didn't know."

"You could've … oh never mind." He flipped through the pages, stopping here and there, browsing through old articles about his father, other letters to newspapers. "How long have you had this?"

"A month. You had your zoning … thought I'd let it die. But when this Danny Delaney thing came up, I had to tell you—your father's knowing Danny and all. It's big news. The papers might print more of this stuff."

"Doesn't matter now." He picked up a letter. "Damn. Look at this. That crap about the commissioner."

"You have to admit it looked fishy. Your own lawyer, now the commissioner, endorsing your demolition. She's normally tough on development."

"She was never *my* lawyer. She handled my dad's estate—years earlier, when *her* father was commissioner. I'd like to believe she did it because it was the right thing, not because our fathers were once friends."

He looked back at the folder again and grimaced at another headline:

SUTHERLAND LOST IN LAKE MICHIGAN
SUICIDE SUSPECTED

"Your guy did a lot of research," he said.

"That's another thing, it wasn't him. One of his co-workers told me he got it in the mail. Anonymously. Someone using the organization."

"*Your* organization. And it almost worked." Sutherland scanned the room, looking for the waitress. "Thanks for bringing me this. I'll buy lunch."

"You hardly touched yours."

"Not hungry."

Kelly bit her lower lip. *Here comes another awkward subject,* Sutherland thought.

"How's things on the home front?" she asked.

Sutherland's home front meant his daughter, who lived with his ex-wife. After their divorce, Margo had moved to California and had lived with a wealthy millionaire. The arrangement only lasted a year, and she had recently returned to the Chicago suburbs and her roots. Over the course of Sutherland's relationship with Kelly, she and his daughter had become fairly close, often seeing one another when Doug was tied up at work.

"Jenny's fine. Why?"

"She called. Still wondering when we're getting back together. You gonna talk to her about it? It's not fair her asking me."

"I did tell her. She was in a regatta with me two weeks ago. She's just too young to understand. That why she called?"

"Not just that." Kelly folded her napkin and leaned forward, her eyes on his. "At her age she needs role models. She sees her mom, and you, and gets confused. You seem successful, but you never seem satisfied. Margo doesn't do much at all except play around and shop. A dilettante, Jenny calls her."

"Margo's not a dilettante at one thing—spending money. She used to have ambition and higher standards. I hope Jenny doesn't follow after her. One princess is enough."

"Your standards are a little tough for a thirteen-year-old."

"Why?"

"You're too hard on everyone, especially yourself. I think it's the victim's syndrome."

"What's that?" he asked, catching the waitress's eye, scribbling in the air for the check.

"Just my own observation. First it's your mother abandoning, then your father disappointing you, then Margo, and now I suppose it's me. No wonder you're so wary about trusting anyone. Everyone will ultimately screw you over."

"That's bullshit, Kelly," he scoffed, feeling himself tense up, his defenses rising. "Can we change the subject?"

"Sorry I hit a nerve. Anyway, is Margo as shallow as Jenny suggests?"

"She say that?"

"No, it's my inference. She doesn't badmouth her mother."

"Good. It's just that after Margo stopped working she changed. She called me the other day wanting money. I had to remind her that I gave her everything she wanted—a debt-free house, alimony, and child support."

The waitress came with the check and Sutherland handed her a credit card.

"Another victim of divorce lawyers," Kelly said.

"Worth every penny, though things looked better for me then. Now with all that's happening, my future is a little more tenuous. What else did Jenny say?"

"Just wondered why couples like you and Margo, or you and me, can't keep it together."

"You have any answers?"

"I haven't had any more success than her mother," Kelly said with a sigh. "You're a tough customer. Anyway, she's coming downtown over the weekend. Do the father thing and spend some time with her."

"The father thing," he repeated, glancing again at the "Sutherland" folder.

"Any good memories?" she asked, indicating the folder. "He must have left you with something."

Sutherland, considering the question, saw his father's face in the sun as they sailed, his loping gait when they played softball, the half-glasses he wore in the hours spent reading together by the fire. Despite being a single parent, his father had always been there, always pointing the way. The newspaper clippings sensationalizing his father's crime, his punishment, and his suicide spoke of a different man, and Doug couldn't make the connection. The latest revelations didn't help. Could he be a murderer as well?

"Did he leave me anything?" he said. When he'd returned from Mexico months after his father's death, Doug found he'd inherited a modest six-figure trust. "Sure, the McCollum and a few other properties, all of which were heavily mortgaged. Two financed boats and some personal stuff, not to mention all the lies, duplicity, and a zillion questions. It gets worse. He may be implicated in Danny Delaney's death, something that could derail the McCollum project altogether."

"Sorry I asked," Kelly said.

He didn't hear her comment. His mind was still on what his father left him. The elder Sutherland's house had been burglarized and set afire before the son's return. The office wing of the house was totally destroyed, but the rest was untouched. During the months of probate, most of the contents had been given away or auctioned. The only remaining records dated back years before and had been in the garage. Doug had carted them to a storage warehouse without so much as a second glance. Looking back, given his feelings at the time, he was surprised he hadn't burned them as well. He wondered whether there had been material relating to this Danny mess in that fire. Was the burglary the result of someone looking for the alleged money or tapes? In any case, the only other remaining material from that time had been removed from his father's office in the McCollum. Sutherland remembered where they were.

The waitress returned, and Sutherland signed the receipt. He stood and said, "You said Jenny's coming downtown?"

"Sunday afternoon."

"I'll call her. I want her to find something for me."

He picked up his umbrella and Kelly's folder, placed a brotherly peck on her cheek, and walked out the door before the effects of her familiar perfume made him say something stupid.

*     *     *

From the lobby window, Kelly saw Sutherland stride away, his umbrella bent against the downpour sweeping across the plaza. *What a perfect metaphor,* she thought.

# CHAPTER 20

Seven rain-drenched blocks from Millennium Park, Jules Langer sat at his conference table, a fifteen-foot-long polished slab of granite. The morning overcast seemed to seep into the room through the floor-to-ceiling windows, but he tried not to let the gloom affect him. *Maintain a positive attitude*, was his mantra. *Find the silver lining.* Even Bill Jamison's latest article in the *Tribune* that was spread before him wasn't going to bring him down. He finished off his coffee and read the two-column piece for a second time. Most of it featured Danny Delaney's public career drawn from old newspaper accounts, but the last sentences captured Langer's attention:

> Though the mystery of the alderman's whereabouts has been finally solved, we are left with new questions, the most important being, who murdered him and why? Could his recently surfaced notebook help with those answers? After all, wouldn't a record of transactions, details of the backroom deals of which he had been accused, offer some clues? Shortly, with the notebook available for inspection, we will learn the truth. The first of its surprises will be revealed in a future edition.

Langer wouldn't have to wait; he would know what the damn thing contained after this evening's meeting. Scooch should be calling soon to tell him the time and place.

The darkness outside made the windows act like murky mirrors reflecting Langer and the bright lights of the conference room. Gazing at his reflected image, he straightened his tie, smoothed his hair, and nodded his approval. Then he caught himself, wondering what difference appearances made to the visitor he expected shortly. Eugene Sandler was all business, and anything outside his focus was unimportant and probably invisible. When he'd called the night before to schedule his visit, it hadn't mattered that Langer had a golf date. It would have been rained out, but Langer would have canceled it anyway, wanting to know what the big man knew about Danny's death and the notebook. If he was going to beat everyone else to it, he wanted a head start.

In the eighties when it all began, Jules Langer, Reggie Tunney, and Gene Sandler were together at Raskoff Real Estate, a small firm of brokers, property managers, and investment bankers. The partnership continued for a year after old man Raskoff died of old age, but not long after Danny Delaney disappeared, they closed the company's doors and went their separate ways. Reginald Tunney formed his own management agency, and Langer took over his recently deceased father's business, Langer Development. Sandler left Raskoff Real Estate with his connections and several insights: First, that all apartment and office building owners needed insurance and janitorial services. Second, that those same owners' fates relied on a hospitable local government for permits, licenses, taxes, zoning, and police protection. Soon, buying property insurance from Sandler also ensured a receptive government.

With the explosion of new construction, Sandler's influence grew, along with the stakes. He used pension fund contacts like Benjamin Gorman to finance new projects. And for every new development, he extracted ownership interests for the aldermen, congressmen, and bureaucrats in return for zoning and favors. A few select politicians were major shareholders in his profitable insurance company, receiving their payoffs through dividends. His system made him one of the most powerful men in Chicago.

Powerful, and ruthless in maintaining his dominance. He had ruined more than one man who'd defied him, and Langer could count two large real estate companies that went under after refusing Sandler's "help." Langer wondered how far his ruthlessness could go. Now that it was certain that Danny had been murdered, that the rumor that he'd fled to a friendly tax haven was unfounded, the question was more germane. Were Sandler and his cronies, including Langer's own father, responsible for killing Delaney? Langer didn't want to believe it. Denial was more convenient, and it wasn't too fanciful to attribute Danny's murder to his other connections. No telling how close he was to legal and illegal gambling, and there were plenty of rumors of how he'd stepped on some Outfit toes. The mob was still alive and kicking in Chicago.

Langer's thoughts were interrupted when Eugene Sandler pushed open the door and looked around the room. His body nearly filled the opening, and as the door swung against the wall, a wave of saccharine cologne wafted in. He was in his fifties, five foot ten, and wore a navy-blue, double-breasted suit over his nearly four hundred pounds.

Sandler's face reminded Langer of melting ice cream—strawberry ice cream. It was bright pink, melting down from light-blond hair and spilling over the white shirt collar like a liquefying scoop over the cone. When Sandler was provoked, bright blotches surfaced like strawberries. Langer wondered if they would appear today.

"Morning." Sandler's voice sounded like he had a broken reed in his throat. One expected a deep bass or at least the tenor of a Pavarotti from a man of his size, but Sandler squeaked like a badly played oboe, a sound that produced shivers and surprise the first time someone heard it. It still took Langer a moment to reconcile the man and the edgy sounds he produced.

Sandler sat down at the head of the conference table, opened a gold case taken from his breast pocket, and lit a filtered cigarette with a gold Dunhill lighter, all the time appraising Langer through the tinted glasses he wore for light sensitivity. Smoking wasn't allowed in his offices, but Langer wasn't going to make an issue out of it. He slid his empty coffee mug in front of Sandler for an ashtray.

"Where's Neils?" Langer referred to the Scandinavian-born driver *cum* bodyguard who usually accompanied the fat man.

"He's in the car. We free to talk?" Sandler was sweating, despite the room's air conditioning. "Cameras, recorders off?"

"You're being paranoid," Langer said.

"Your father taught you that trick—listening in on the other side's private discussions during negotiations. Turn it off. And dim the lights while you're at it."

Langer sighed. "Don't take it personally. Just a habit." He rose, walked to end of the table, opened a wall panel, and turned off a digital recorder. With another dial, he turned down the overhead lights.

"Better," Sandler said, spewing smoke. "If we'd'a been more careful in Danny's place, we wouldn't be in the fix we're in. You believe that son of a bitch? Videos?"

"I was only there a couple times."

"Your father was there plenty." Sandler leaned forward on his heavy forearms. "What do you know about this notebook in the news?"

Langer was glad he hadn't had to bring up the subject first. "All I know is from the paper."

"Someone's claiming he's got it. I got a message, but the guy didn't leave a number. My bet's he called you too."

"Why? My father was Danny's buddy, not me."

Sandler looked at his cigarette, holding it in front of him between fleshy thumb and forefinger, contemplating the smoke rising in a thin thread. "The guy didn't single me out. If he knew my name, he has yours. He'll sell to whoever pays. So what did he say? He mention videos?"

As always, as if intimidated by Sandler's sheer weight, Langer wilted. "No. But like you said, he wants money."

"And you agreed?"

"Sure, but I don't know what's next. He's supposed to call."

"We gotta get a hold of the damn thing. Find the tapes if they still exist and silence the fucker before the feds find him. He's got the book, he's gotta know more."

Langer felt the burn rising from his stomach and reached into his pocket for his antacid tablets. Talking about getting the book was one thing, but the guy that had it? He chewed down two tablets and asked, "You suppose he knows what happened to Danny? That reporter wrote he was tortured."

Sandler examined the large diamond on his pinky ring then polished it on his jacket lapel. "Nothing too painful for that prick. He was about to give the feds everything."

"Really?" Langer couldn't remember if his father had mentioned Delaney and feds or not. "But nothing happened. If the feds didn't do anything then, what's the problem now?"

"A couple things." Sandler's face was darkening, the topic seeming to annoy him. "This time we don't have an insider in our pocket. If there's anything to this notebook or it leads to Danny's videotapes, it could break wide open. We'd be up to our asses in feds. Even if we got off, Spanos wouldn't have a chance in the election. Our investment would be down the tubes."

Sandler had said all of that as if Langer already knew what he meant, but he didn't. Sure, he knew about payoffs to inspectors, aldermen, and some police high-ups that his father had had a hand in, but a federal agent on the take and Spanos's involvement, a candidate for governor as part of this, were something new. Then there was that suggestion about *silencing* the guy who had the notebook. Finally he said, "They couldn't have anything on me. I didn't have—"

"Smarten up, Jules. You're with us today, aren't you?"

Whatever ugly kind of business Sandler and Langer's father were involved in back then was sucking Jules Langer into the same muck. It was apparently much uglier than the petty graft, kickbacks, and payoffs he was aware of. In the face of Sandler's worries, Langer's purpose in acquiring the notebook was innocent. He'd merely wanted it for leverage against his brother-in-law, Reginald Tunney. Straightening himself in his chair, pulling his shoulders back, he told himself he wouldn't allow Sandler to drag him down to his level. But he had to be careful. "So what do you want from me?"

"When you hear from this joker, agree to what he asks. Meantime, your father's papers, his records, notes, whatever he kept hidden away—like what he secretly taped in meetings—you still have them?"

"Some."

"Burn it all. Back to your baby pictures if you have to. If we don't find the son of a bitch and that notebook leads anywhere, there could be a shit storm of subpoenas and warrants coming at us."

"That bad?"

"Assume the worst. So we have to deal with this …" Sandler sucked on his cigarette, held it in a moment, and exhaled. "And …" he ignored the coffee mug and ground the glowing tip into the polished granite tabletop, blackening the pearly stone and strewing shreds of tobacco and ash over the lustrous surface, "… snuff it out."

He stood up with a grunt and a heave, sending the chair wheeling backward against the wall. "You hear from him, call me." Then he pulled his suit coat down over his huge girth and strode out, leaving Langer alone in a cologne-flavored haze.

Langer chewed another antacid tablet, pulled out his handkerchief, and rubbed away the dark smudge on the granite. "Don't count on it, you fat fuck," he said to himself, but his macho words couldn't hide his own unease.

# Chapter 21

**D**etective Stanley Vislowski sat at his metal desk in his area headquarters reviewing the papers spread before him—two deaths, two files. He read the reports from the officers at the scenes, statements from neighbors and passersby, and reports from the crime lab and medical examiner. He studied photographs of the scenes and the bodies. It seemed clear-cut, but something bothered him.

"What do you think?" he asked his partner, Detective Manny López, sitting at the adjacent desk reading the sports page.

"Slam dunk, amigo," López said, not even looking up from his newspaper. "Case closed."

They identified Benjamin Gorman's body by his ID and wallet, found near a dead John Doe discovered miles away. The dead junkie's pocket had contained a knife with blood encrusted in its crevices. It appeared straightforward: a drug addict kills Gorman for money, buys heroin from an unreliable source, and accidentally overdoses himself. He wasn't the first junkie to die from juiced smack.

Vislowski imagined what his lieutenant's directions would be: the department's overloaded, this one hangs together, close it and work on your backlog. Vislowski and his partner, Manny López, like the rest of the force, were always stretched, and maybe closing it was what he *should* do. But there were too many connections to jump to simple conclusions.

Vislowski reread Gorman's history with all the media allegations and indictments for kickbacks, fraud, and misappropriation of union funds. The accusations had come to nothing, but a specter of corruption followed Gorman, amplified by his association with Danny Delaney, whose body just happened to have been found several days ago.

Then there was Gorman's housekeeper's statement about his activities the day and evening of his murder. Gorman had two phone calls that day, one from a reporter named Bill Jamison and one from a Mr. Sutherland. Gorman had agreed to meet Mr. Sutherland at a restaurant that night. The officer who had interviewed that Sutherland hadn't made the connection in his report, but odds were that he was the same Sutherland who owned the building where

Danny Delaney was found. It would just take a phone call to find out, and Vislowski didn't want to be accused of missing something that obvious if there was more to this case than it being a random killing. He didn't need another black mark on his record.

"I don't know, Manny. Might be more here," Vislowski said, shuffling through the paperwork.

"Come on, man. We're due for an easy one," López said, dropping his newspaper into the wastebasket. "Let's get out of here. Buy you a beer?"

"You go ahead. I'll catch up," Vislowski said, thinking Bill Jamison might be able to clear this up. Jamison had written those articles about the dead alderman, and he was always scrounging for a story; they'd exchange information. At the same time Vislowski would ask about Veronica, Bill's sister. It had been a while since their little trouble, and maybe she was able to let bygones be bygones.

Still another worrisome piece of evidence bothered him, though. It was one thing to buy into a coincidence between Delaney and Gorman. Maybe John Doe Junkie killed him and bought some bad shit. But what about the tattoo? Vislowski scanned the statement from Gorman's doctor again. There it was: besides explaining about the terminal cancer, the doctor described a tattoo Gorman had on his left forearm, a number of some kind.

Vislowski sorted through the photographs once more, stopping at the enlarged print of Gorman's left arm. No tattoo. But a four-inch patch of flesh had been sliced off like the test cut on a Thanksgiving turkey.

# Chapter 22

Shadowing behind in the rain, Bill Jamison saw Scooch turn into a small diner a block from the El train stop. *This must be the place; it's nearly eight o'clock. Scooch, that fat slob, will probably put away a couple blue plate specials while he waits for his buyer.*

As Jamison edged by the diner, he glanced through the fogged windows. He guessed twelve stools and four tables, and there were three customers besides Scooch—no place to observe inconspicuously. He would have to wait in the rain, as he had an hour ago near Scooch's fleabag hotel. Scanning the area across the street, Jamison saw several closed storefronts with recessed entrances. He could observe everything from there.

Jamison closed and shook his umbrella in the small entryway. He could see the diner clearly, but judging from the darkening sky, he would have to be vigilant to pick out the man meeting Scooch. He gripped his digital camera, hoping it was fast enough for this light.

$$* \qquad * \qquad *$$

Jules Langer opened the door into the warm pungency of grease and onion. Standing at the entrance, he shook his umbrella and slowly surveyed the room. He inspected the lunch counter, assessing the ragged patrons perched on stools and the dull-witted grin of the cook with an unlit cigarette dangling from his lips. In the rear of the diner, he noticed a heavy man in a work shirt reading a newspaper. Langer walked toward him.

Scooch looked up from the paper and beckoned with a furtive jerk of his head. Langer sat down at the littered table.

"Have we met?" Langer asked.

"Yeah. But you look different." Scooch picked up and mouthed a cigar.

*What did this pig look like fifteen years and fifty pounds ago?* Langer wondered. His imagination failed until he noticed the cauliflower ear. It was Danny's errand boy. Langer only saw him once or twice back then. Maybe Scooch was mistaking Langer for his father. No sense enlightening him.

"You do too," Langer said.

"Yeah. Outta shape."

Now it made sense. If the notebook wasn't buried in the McCollum with Danny, his lackey might have it.

"You have it with you?" Langer asked.

Scooch's eyes darted left and right. "Just some pages. Copies. Pay, and you'll get the real one."

"How can I be sure? You called some other people, too."

"Why not? After I talk to that reporter guy, I figure the notebook's worth somethin', so I call Danny's old pals. The names in the book or what I remember."

"How do I know you're selling me the original? There's no copies?"

"'Cause I'm through fuckin' with it. I make a few calls and look what happens." Scooch handed over the folded newspaper. Under an oily smear, the right-hand column bore the headline:

## UNION PENSION CHIEF FOUND MURDERED
### Benjamin Gorman's Death Linked to Dead Addict

Langer skimmed the short piece and said, "The article says it was a junkie. You saying it wasn't?"

Scooch cleared his throat and spit a brown gob into a napkin. Langer averted his eyes back to the newspaper.

"I'm saying I'm not takin' no more chances. The newspaper guy warned me. Soon's I get rid of the thing I'm leaving town."

"Who else you talk to?"

"Never mind. Not gonna happen to me like Danny or Gorman," Scooch said, his little eyes narrowing, his nostrils flaring. Langer could sense the man's fear. "The book's safe. Where's your money?"

"Show me the sample."

Scooch retrieved a package he had been sitting on. He unwrapped the plastic and handed Langer a folded sheath of papers.

Langer examined the five copied pages, bound by a paper clip. It had the columns of dates, initials, dollar amounts, and shorthand notes in chronological order. The dates went back almost sixteen years. It seemed to him that it was an index for computer files or tape recordings. "How many more pages are there?"

"Thirty or so." Scooch held out his sweaty palm. "The money."

Langer reached into his suit pocket and withdrew an envelope, holding in front of him. "There's five thousand here. Now let's go get the book."

"Gimme your address. It'll be sent."

"Bullshit."

"I ain't taking chances. Somebody's keeping it for me."

"That's smart, but why should I trust you?"

"'Cause you ain't got a choice."

"Hell I don't," Langer said, opening the envelope. He riffed through the pack of hundred-dollar bills, gathered half of them, and put them in his inside suit pocket. "There," he said, holding out the package. "That's a down payment. The rest when it's in my hands."

"What the fuck?" Scooch looked offended, but he took the envelope. His lips moved around the wet cigar, counting, as he fingered the bills. "How do I get the other?"

"You tell me. You got my number," Langer said.

"I'll call you tomorrow." Scooch coughed again, but before he could spit, Langer looked away, through the window and out into the stormy night. Across the rain-drenched street a solitary figure stood in a recessed entrance to a closed store. If he was waiting for the rain to stop, it would be a long night.

Langer stood, and with a last glance into the other man's devious eyes, he picked up his umbrella and walked out.

*     *     *

From across the street Jamison saw Scooch's visitor push out of the diner and managed two quick shots with his digital camera. He hadn't been watching alone. Moments before, a man with a black umbrella ambled along the sidewalk on his left and entered the empty doorway thirty feet away. He couldn't have entered the store itself because it was a closed dry cleaning shop.

Jamison crept forward in his entryway, peering to his left for a sign of the other man. A dark form lurked there, just as Jamison had for the past half hour. He retreated backward into the shadows to think. He wanted to follow the man who'd left the diner, to get his license number or another photo. Now what?

He didn't ponder long.

From out of the downpour, wearing a baseball cap and a long, black raincoat and carrying an umbrella, the other man materialized like a wraith. Jamison inhaled sharply, instinctively raising his furled umbrella in defense. The dark figure tilted his umbrella back, revealing shadowy features perverted by the glare of passing headlights. His chin was tucked inside the coat collar, the eyes shaded in their sockets, the skin ghostly white. He said nothing, merely stood there blocking the entrance, tall and looming. Jamison could only gasp.

Without another thought, Jamison lunged forward, elbowed past the menacing form, and bolted into the rain, carrying his furled umbrella with him. He never looked back.

# Chapter 23

**SATURDAY, JULY 14**

Between the Lincoln Park Zoo and Lake Michigan, bordering a narrow lagoon, a running trail continues its meandering route through Lincoln Park, skirting harbors, tennis courts, a nine-hole golf course, and beaches all the way to Hollywood Drive to the north.

Doug Sutherland leaned forward against a maple tree, stretching one calf, then the other. Around him a quiet mist hugged the grass, and yesterday's rains mottled the running path in puddles. An orange sun peeked through the clouds over the lake. Sutherland breathed in, savoring the sweet scent of wet grass and earth.

He had left a message to meet Bill Jamison here, knowing that Bill sometimes ran on Saturday mornings and it might be the only chance he had to dissuade him from sensationalizing Danny's death or, at a minimum, mentioning Sutherland's father. If there was continued unsubstantiated speculation about money and murder connected to the Sutherland name, he could lose the Broadwell deal, which would bankrupt him.

*Where is that jagoff? Was he afraid to show up and face me?*

"Doug," a male voice shouted. *Finally.* Sutherland turned to see Jamison and a red-haired woman jogging toward him in running shorts and tank tops. They slowed and stopped, but not before Sutherland appraised the woman's smooth running form.

"Sis, Doug Sutherland. Doug, my sister, Ronnie."

"Glad to meet you," Sutherland said, returning her measuring gaze. She shared her brother's hair and eye color, but the similarities ended there. The brother was fair-skinned and freckled with a copper beard and careful, emerald eyes, as if he were guarding something. The sister's darker skin lacked the freckles, and her eyes were direct and uncompromising.

"I thought you'd stiffed me," Sutherland said.

"Heck no. You can help me. I've got some questions."

"Not as many as I do. You up for Montrose Harbor?" Sutherland asked, figuring an hour should be enough time to hammer some sense into Jamison.

"Just so you don't make it a race," he replied. "He's always had to beat me, sis."

"You game?" Sutherland asked, looking at Ronnie. "Eight miles?"

"Sure. Let me stretch first," Ronnie said as she bent over and planted her palms on the grass.

Sutherland saw it and marveled—not a hint of effort or break in the knee. He stooped to touch his own toes, barely brushing them on the second try.

Ronnie finished her stretch. "Okay, I'm ready."

They began running silently side by side, muscles loosening, hearts quickening. The only sounds were breathing and footfalls. For the first hundred yards they ran parallel to a rowing crew, the shell skimming along the lagoon, the oars hardly making a splash.

"You were Bill's fraternity brother?" Ronnie asked, settling into a relaxed pace.

"Bill was working on his first novel."

"Still am. Same one, matter of fact," Jamison said, laughing at himself.

"You're a good writer," Ronnie said.

"She's only two years older but still acts like my mother."

"You need someone to push you. You read his recent byline?" she asked, glancing up at Sutherland.

"The alderman was discovered in my building." Sutherland would work into this slowly.

"Ohhh," she crooned. "The one the preservationists fought over. I was rooting for you. They were playing dirty."

"I thought I was all alone for a while."

"Ronnie used to be with the state's attorney's office," Jamison said. "She sees injustice everywhere."

They ran easily at a seven-and-a-half-minute-mile pace, slow enough to talk without strain. As they passed Belmont Harbor, Sutherland said, "What did you want to ask?"

"Tell me about Benjamin Gorman and his fund."

"I'll bet you know as much as I do."

"Doubt it. I wanted to meet with him, but you beat me to it. You might have been the last to see him alive."

"The murderer was. A junkie, according to what the police told me. A cop stopped by yesterday."

"They aren't so sure who did it. But what did Gorman tell you?"

"Not much. He hadn't even heard about finding Danny, and if he knew who killed him, he wasn't saying. About the money, he swore there was none stolen from his fund, meaning your article is fantasy." There was no way Sutherland was going to give Gorman's account of the real source of the money. "This isn't your novel, Bill."

"You think I'm making this up? What did he say about the notebook?"

"Another surprise. He thought all of Danny's stuff was burned and it worried him that it wasn't. Other than that it was a short meeting. An ornery bastard, and really sick. Surprised he didn't die at the table."

"I'd hoped to get more out of him, but he didn't return my calls. Why'd you meet him anyway?"

This far into the run Sutherland felt the endorphins kicking in, fueling the anger for what Jamison had written. "To check on this bullshit you wrote. And Gorman's denial of money stolen from his funds, by my father or anyone, proves it's wrong. He had no reason to lie. If he hadn't been murdered he'd be dead in a month."

"Entries in the notebook," Bill Jamison said. "Your father's initials and millions, another entry with the pension fund's initials. I'm just connecting the dots."

"Dots?" Sutherland shouted, grabbing Jamison's arm, stopping him abruptly on the trail and spinning him so they faced one another. They were breathing hard, sweat channeling down their faces and necks. Jamison took a step back, his eyes wide, mouth open. "There's nothing to connect," Sutherland continued, closing the gap between them so they were nose to nose. "Gorman said so, and anyway, how can you leap from common initials to my father's stealing from a pension fund? It's wild speculation. Keep it up and you'll ruin me."

Ronnie had stopped twenty strides farther on and was walking back to them. "What's up?" she said.

"What do you mean?" Jamison said, still shrinking back from Sutherland's anger. "Ruin?"

"You print rumors about my father and money, digging up age-old bullshit, trying to implicate him … you're worse than the tabloids." He had to control himself or he was about to start swinging.

Ronnie stepped between the two of them and held up her hands protectively. "Easy. What did I miss?"

"I'm only printing what I've seen and what the police are telling me," Bill Jamison said.

Sutherland took a few deep breaths. "Now you're talking to the cops about me? What's your headline tomorrow? 'Doug Sutherland implicated in Gorman murder?' 'Like father, like son?' Anything for a headline?"

"You're trying to gag me?"

"You have no proof for any of this," Sutherland growled, seething.

Ronnie stood between them, arms spread, one pointing at each of them like a referee separating two boxers' clinch. "Calm down, you guys. I don't know what's up, but I'm here to run. How about burning off some of your testosterone and discussing it like adults?"

Sutherland huffed a yes and Jamison nodded. They started off on the trail again, abreast, with Ronnie between the men. Finally, Jamison broke the ice. "Let's face it, there's plenty that needs explaining. I saw your father's initials, an entry about a large hunk of money, Danny owning a piece of the McCollum, him buried in your father's building, then your father himself disappearing, presumably committing suicide. Forget about you meeting Gorman. This is news and I'm writing it. If not me, someone else. You started it by sending Scooch to talk to me."

"And you're squeezing out every ounce of juice and adding your own."

"Don't have to squeeze. It's oozing out."

Ronnie interrupted with a mediating tone. "Doug, the detective that told Bill about you meeting Gorman is an old friend. I'm sure it won't go further."

"If it gets in the paper, it could be the last straw. There's already enough conjecture to derail my deal with Broadwell."

It took a few strides for the point to sink in. Bill Jamison was the first to react. "So that's the real issue," he said. "Broadwell's getting nervous. They've been in a bunker ever since the SEC suspected something. Their stock's tanked and the board's in turmoil."

"Meaning the entire McCollum project is at risk," Sutherland said.

"Okay, I understand," Jamison said. "But this thing's got its own life. Got people real nervous. My editor already got a couple calls from Washington, friends of George Spanos, no less, suggesting the paper let it die. Spanos was on the phone himself to my editor, even though I never even mentioned his name. There's more than just smoke here. That's the other reason I wanted to see you. I need insight on what corruption is going on in real estate."

"So you come to me? Thanks."

"I'm not suggesting …" Jamison said. "But have you seen much of it? Kickbacks, bribes?"

"It goes on, but not me. Never."

"Was one of the players Eugene Sandler? His name's in the notebook next to a lot of entries."

"Not was, is," Sutherland replied. "If you need any zoning or variances or whatever in the downtown area, the alderman directs you to Sandler. You agree to buy his property insurance, use his janitorial company, give him a piece, and you get your whatever."

"You had to do that?" he said.

"It costs me to refuse, but I tell them to cram it," Sutherland said. They were running along a muddy path, the nine-hole golf course on their left, the lake on their right, still choppy and roiling from yesterday's storm. Ahead in Montrose Harbor, sailboats bobbed and pulled on their buoys while seagulls cavorted and screeched overhead.

As they turned east on the Montrose peninsula, Jamison said, "I met a guy who works for Sandler. He has access to documents dating back years that could document Sandler's corruption and maybe link today's activities back to Danny. It'll mean indictments."

"Are you planning to bring the state's attorney into it?" Sutherland asked.

"Why should he bother?" Ronnie said. "They're impotent. I was with the state for a few years, so I know. I couldn't take the system. Too many bad guys getting away."

"Ronnie's connections could help, though," her brother said. "And so can you. I'll make you a deal. I'll be more careful about what could affect you if you help decipher what I got from that notebook so far. Addresses of properties, dates, players, dollars."

"Do you have the notebook?"

"I have photos of a few pages," Jamison said. "This Scooch character is trying to sell it, if he already hasn't. Five grand. Interested?"

"How do I get a hold of him?" Buy it and burn it would be the plan, but why tell Jamison that?

"You can't. He's supposed to call. Meanwhile, can you come to my place tomorrow morning and look at the notes? Any time after eight."

They reached the turning point on the peninsula. From there looking south, downtown Chicago rose from the mist like a dream city—the long tongue of Navy Pier with its Ferris wheel on the east, the tapered Hancock Building rising over the Gold Coast, the ragged skyline of office towers in the Loop, and Sears Tower itself, tall, distant, and imperious, like Everest. Sutherland always liked that view. Except now it wasn't called the Sears Tower anymore, as if changing it to the Willis Tower wiped out its pedigree and role in Chicago's history.

Heading south again, they gradually increased their speed, conversation became labored and monosyllabic, scenery rushed by in a dream-like blur. And with the speed Sutherland felt the pain sharpen and the juices course, pushing him to the finish. With less than a mile remaining, he exhaled one word: "Kick?"

"Nothing left," Jamison croaked. "You go."

Sutherland accelerated smoothly, lengthening his strides and speeding his turnover as the finishing mile marker neared. He wouldn't go all out, just enough under the pain threshold to release that addictive euphoria.

With a hundred yards to go, he heard footfalls overtaking him. *Bill was sandbagging*, Sutherland thought. But it was Ronnie, not Bill, who flashed by, stunning him in a blur of red hair and churning limbs. Sutherland nerved himself forward, straining, ignoring his knotting stomach, sucking in air and pain. He gained inch by inch, but her surprise-won edge proved too great. It took everything he had to finish in a tie.

"You sneaked past me," he gasped.

"You just underestimated me."

"I won't do that again."

Bill Jamison loped the final ten yards to join them. "Who won?"

"Me," they both puffed at once, laughing.

"So who, really?" Bill said.

Ronnie said, "Tell you what. Hundred bucks says I beat you in a half mile. Right now. You on?"

"No thanks," Sutherland said. "Another day."

"Smart man," Bill said. "Going against my sister is a sucker's bet."

*　　*　　*

After recovering their wind and dousing themselves at the water fountain, Sutherland confirmed he would be at Jamison's house in the morning and jogged away toward his apartment.

Ronnie's gaze followed him as he disappeared. "He told this Scooch guy to call you?" Her brother nodded, and she added, "And you think Gorman's murder is related?"

"Vislowski thinks so, too, but can't prove it. Why?"

"Could be nothing—call it intuition or maternal anxiety, but Doug's not telling you everything. Be careful about what he got you into."

"I was already in pretty deep with my research on Gene Sandler. Gorman and Delaney were tied up with him, so it's a natural connection. You're always pushing me to get a story. You're telling me to back off?"

"Murder's not your beat, that's all," she said. "Two guys dead. Doug better be careful too."

"That's not maternal anxiety speaking," he said, smiling.

"Gotta admit, he's not bad looking. Sexy scar—adds a little zest. That why you joined his fraternity?"

"Afraid not, sis. Not my type."

"Hmm. Maybe he's mine."

"You two?" He scoffed.

"What?"

"Trust me. It'd never work."

# Chapter 24

Later that morning, Bill Jamison sat in his cluttered office cubicle overlooking the Pioneer Plaza and the Chicago River. Old news articles, photographs, phone messages, notepads, and loose paper lay scattered and heaped over desktop, filing cabinets, and floor. At times like this, in the confusion of a story's development, Jamison wondered whether it would ever come together and crystallize.

His telephone rang—the call Jamison expected.

"I found the files, Billy boy—in storage." It was Sandy Craig, a Chicago newspaper reporter long retired and living in Arizona. Searching through the archives of Danny's era, Jamison had learned that Craig had written several articles about the alderman's legislative triumphs, political coups, and alleged misdeeds. It wasn't what was in the articles that interested Jamison so much as what things Craig knew but couldn't print.

"You look through them yet?" Jamison asked.

"A little … would've been a good story."

"Still can be."

"Because they found Danny? A book's what to do with it. I'd write it if I weren't burned out."

*Boozed out's what he means*, thought Jamison. "Can you send what you have?"

"That depends, Billy," Craig replied cagily. "I spent a lot of time on this. Can't just hand it over."

"Look, if it's credit you want …"

"Not just credit, Billy. Retirement's not as cheap as it's made out to be."

"I'll take care of you. But there's the time thing here, Sandy. Tell me what you have." *And by cocktail hour you'll forget we even talked*, Jamison thought.

"Want it in writing. Shared byline and book proceeds. Not that I don't trust you …"

"Okay. I'll get an agreement out today. Meantime, I've got to have the highlights—you know deadlines."

There was a silence followed by an exhaled hush. Jamison visualized from years ago Craig's ingrained movements: the cigarette, the lighter, the smoke pluming from nostrils and mouth, the cigarette dangling and twitching as Craig spoke.

"What do you know about Raskoff Real Estate?" Craig began.

"As in Phillip Raskoff? Big outfit fifteen or so years ago. Lots of in with the City."

"Right. Got first crack at city projects, special tax treatment, subsidized loans, zoning variances—you name it. While Raskoff ran things, it never got too dirty. But later, when he left things to others, the real corruption started."

"Who was involved?"

"Eugene Sandler and company."

"Sandler's still at it," Jamison said. He stared into his word processor, tapping as he listened. He was on the right trail. "Who else?"

"Reginald Tunney and Jules Langer were there too. They all left Raskoff about the time Danny disappeared."

"I read about Langer all the time. Runs Langer Development now. Never hear about Tunney. They all dirty?"

"Sandler, yes. He and Jules's father, Miles Langer, who started Langer Development. But I never found anything on Tunney, and Jules was new, just starting out."

"Tell me about Danny."

"Next to the mayor, Danny Delaney was the most powerful politician in town. Especially if it had anything to do with downtown. You wanted anything—approvals for zoning, condemnations, et cetera—you needed Danny. Back then it was easier to conceal ownership in trusts, so Danny and others took their payoffs in interests in apartment and office buildings. Meanwhile, a guy named Gorman got kickbacks for cheap financing through the Mid West Pension Fund."

Jamison stopped keying. "Benjamin Gorman's just been killed."

Craig coughed. "Sounds like Danny's body's discovery has worried some folks."

Jamison shuddered, recalling last night's rendezvous at the diner and the shadowy form in the storefront. "You know why Danny was killed?"

"'Til now I didn't know he was. Probably because the feds had him over a barrel. He was turning."

Jamison wiped the sweat from his forehead. This was getting better every minute. "Informer? There's nothing in the papers."

"I got it from a source in the FBI, but not for publication. They got him on tape and he agreed to cooperate. I could've had the whole story from the beginning, but he disappeared."

"Who were the feds after?"

"Other aldermen, party officials, state senators, cops, real estate developers … a long list. They wanted the mayor, but Sutherland confessed and blew their case."

"Bernard Sutherland?"

"He went to jail for it, but I heard he was a scapegoat."

"Why wasn't Danny's state's evidence thing in the news?" Jamison asked.

"When Danny disappeared, the feds thought he skipped or was killed. The head FBI guy was murdered at the same time, and there were some internal problems with lost evidence. They were left naked with their dick in their hands. Embarrassing, so they hushed it. Couple of us chased the story, but even when I confronted them with what Danny told me, they clammed up."

"Danny told you about this?"

"He told me lots of things that never made the paper. He thought he was untouchable. It was a game. He'd make sure I didn't have a wire and he'd play 'what-if' with me."

"Ever see his notebook?"

"Didn't know he kept one. Why?"

"It turned up. A record of transactions, maybe payoffs, an index to videos he taped. There were some big bucks mentioned with Bernard Sutherland. Millions."

There was silence, then static, then more silence on the line.

"You still there, Sandy?"

"Yeah," Craig said slowly, as if dredging his alcohol-stewed memory. "I was just reading a note about Danny mentioning money diverted from a property sale or something. I looked into it but never found anything. Just enough to make me wonder about Sutherland's suicide, though."

"Why?"

"You're supposed to be a reporter; do your own homework. Send an agreement and I'll see what else I can remember." He hung up.

*Up his drunken ass*, fumed Jamison. *Hasn't had a sober day in forty years. Tells me to do my homework.*

Jamison finished his notes from the phone call, scrolling through the text one more time then adding to his list of items to investigate:

Names and initials: Richardson, Adams, Guerrero, Benning, McMillin, Spanos, etc. Who were/are they?
Ownership/sales of buildings
Partnership tax returns
Background on Raskoff, Tunney, Sandler, Langer

Sutherland: Suicide?
FBI agent death

Scooch had said he'd called Doug Sutherland because of his father. The conviction business would have occurred when Doug and Jamison were in college, about the time Doug dropped out. Jamison recalled the fraternity house rumors after Sutherland disappeared for parts unknown—talk of his father going to jail. But nothing of a disappearance or suicide.

Jamison flipped through the notes scribbled from Danny's notebook, understanding still eluding him. He needed the rest of the notebook. He needed Scooch.

# Chapter 25

The manager of the Biscayne Hotel twisted a lock of gray hair around her forefinger in nervous ritual. It was almost noon and the occupant of room 228 had not appeared—hadn't lumbered down the stairs and out the foyer to his breakfast, his routine since arriving two months ago. She would see him enter the diner diagonally across Belmont, and after half an hour, return with the newspapers. But not this morning.

The manager didn't especially like the man. Like most of the Biscayne's clientele, he wasn't her kind, but Mr. Fascucci ranked near the bottom of the lot. Despite her distaste for the man, she nervously pulled and coiled her dry locks. Had she made a mistake? Had she been careless the night before?

She only wanted to be helpful. The man had arrived out of all that rain a few minutes after Mr. Fascucci returned. Could she tell him what room his friend Scooch was in? Mr. Fascucci staked him in a poker game, the man said. He won big and was here to pay him off and have a quiet toast of celebration. Showing her his appreciation and as evidence of his winnings, he gave her a fifty-dollar bill.

After she told him how to find room 228, he asked what Mr. Fascucci called her, so he could tell him about her courtesy. He also asked whether Scooch left things with her, like in a safe, in case his friend wanted to leave the money there tonight. She had told him no. He'd ascended the stairs and must have left by the back door because she never saw him again.

It was almost twelve o'clock, way past Mr. Fascucci's time. Maybe they'd celebrated too much. There was some noise, she remembered, and the television was fairly loud for a period. If they were drinking that would explain it—Mr. Fascucci was hung over and needed to sleep in.

The visitor was nice enough, very polite, clean, and neat, not at all like Mr. Fascucci, with his sloppy clothes, filthy cigars, and gnarled ear. Come to think of it, he didn't look like he needed to borrow money; he'd worn a nice raincoat, and his umbrella had an expensive-looking handle. But what was the harm?

Still she pulled and fretted with her lifeless hair. At twelve she decided to see if he was all right. She couldn't call—Biscayne rooms didn't have phones—so she climbed the worn marble staircase to the second floor and shuffled down the threadbare carpet to the end room, where she rapped four times. After counting to ten, she knocked more loudly. Again no response. She took out her passkey.

At first she thought the occupant had fled in a rush. The drawers were open and the dresser top was swept clean of everything. But opening the door farther, she saw Mr. Fascucci's belongings strewn all around the twelve-by-twelve room and his suitcase lying open and empty on the floor. The mattress was half off the frame and the bed clothing heaped in the corner with other clothes. The man himself was not in sight.

The manager's eyes were drawn to the closed door to her right—Mr. Fascucci had insisted on a room with a bathroom, saying he was through sharing showers and commodes with other men. Was he in there or not? She wanted to leave, but she had to be certain. That was her job, after all.

The bathroom door wasn't locked. She opened it slowly and noticed a towel stuffed in the exhaust fan. Curious, what was the point of that? Before she saw more, before she opened the door farther, the stench of defecation and stale urine overwhelmed her. She retreated and caught her breath. She could call the police, but what would she tell them? She had a stinking bathroom?

She held her breath and pushed open the door; it hit the bathtub with a hollow clunk. Peering in, she froze, stupefied. There was Mr. Fascucci's bloated form, bound and half naked in a faded blue robe, immersed in the bathtub's brownish water. His mouth was stretched wide, stuffed with a white sock. Over his head and taped around his neck was a clear plastic bag, and through it, his deranged eyes stared directly at the manager, as if shocked by her intrusion and outraged by the absence of his cauliflower ear.

Her scream was heard by every roomer, rat, and cockroach in the hotel.

# CHAPTER 26

Jamison's townhouse overlooked Oz Park, a thirteen-acre island of grass, tennis courts, softball diamonds, and playgrounds at the center of Lincoln Park's residential neighborhood. Every tennis court was being used, and a handful of dogs were chasing balls and cavorting among themselves on the softball outfield. It was a perfect Sunday morning, all sunshine and blue sky. Sutherland settled into a white leather couch and stretched out his tanned legs, the color of his weathered deck shoes. "How long will this take? I've got a race today."

"Fifteen minutes is all we need." Bill Jamison placed his briefcase on the coffee table and sat in an upholstered armchair. He opened his case, retrieved several sheets of paper, and handed them to Sutherland. "I'd like to know more about these apartment and office buildings, not just who built them. Financing, ownership … so forth—anything that might link them or smells a little off."

Sutherland skimmed the typed property names and addresses, all in Chicago and its suburbs. "No problem. What I don't remember or have in my files I can find easy enough. That all?"

"What do you know about these people?" Jamison passed Sutherland another typewritten sheet.

"I know a few," Sutherland said, reading. "You know Sandler and Gorman already. Tunney would be Reggie—Reginald, as he prefers. These others? Richardson, Spanos, Guerrero, Benning, Adams, and McMillin? There is a state senator named Richardson. Patrick, I think. An alderman Guerrero. A judge McMillin, but without a first name, who knows? Got to be lots with the name Spanos, not necessarily our congressman. You see them in Danny's book?"

"That's just what I got a glimpse of. Guesses until we connect them with other sources I'm working on. The notebook had last names or initials, some titles, but if I'm right, those people have secret interests in the properties on the other list. Probably hidden in trusts or other partnerships, but I have a source who can get tax returns that cut through that. They're interesting because I don't think the all the ownership interests were paid for, or they were given as a discount for favors, a sophisticated variation on cash under the table."

"All that from that from a peek at a notebook?"

"That and from a reporter who knew Danny and an accountant who works for Sandler. And this will freak you out: in the archives, he saw a cover letter to a partnership agreement signed by Bernard Sutherland, your father. Apparently he was the lawyer who drafted the agreements. He ever tell you?"

"Drafting agreements isn't illegal. We already knew he did legal work in real estate before he lost his license."

"And went to jail. That's when you left school, right?"

"Caribbean and Mexico for two years." His way to distance himself from his father's ignominious fall and blatant hypocrisy.

Jamison was sorting through his notes, when he stopped. "One more thing. Along with your father's initials …"

"BS could be Bruce Smith, Brian Savoy, Bugsy Soprano …"

"Okay. Next to somebody's initials and the five mil is written 'First Nat.' Did he bank there?"

"Sorry. Harris Bank. And you could never hide a deposit of that size. Did you check?"

A phone rang somewhere in the rear of the house. "Gotta get that." Jamison walked out of the room, scuffing his sandals along the hardwood floor.

Sutherland studied the properties on the sheets while he listened to Jamison's voice rise and fall in the rear of the apartment. The list contained more than twenty developments, all in the Chicago area, all completed in the last eighteen years. But before he could conclude anything more, he heard a yell. "Sonovabitch."

Jamison stomped back into the room, shaking his head and muttering.

"What's the matter?" Sutherland asked.

"That was Stan Vislowski—Detective Vislowski, my sister's old boyfriend. He told me Scooch was murdered yesterday. Police found my name in his room and they want to see me. Of all the fuckin' luck." He plunked himself down onto the couch and buried his head in his hands. "Can kiss that notebook good-bye."

"The guy's dead and you're griping about the notebook?" Sutherland said. "You're lucky. What if he'd given it to you?"

Jamison looked up, suddenly animated, his eyes wide. "That's right. He was going to send it to someone for safekeeping. If he did, we can trace it." He crammed the loose papers into his briefcase and snapped the clasps. "I've got to see Vislowski. Take those papers with you and we'll meet Tuesday or Wednesday on what you've got. Okay?"

Jamison started for the door and then turned back, his eyes gleaming, excited now. "Wait a minute. If he was murdered Friday night, I may be able to identify his murderer. I took a shadowy photo of the man who met Scooch in the diner and another guy was standing right in front of me." With that revelation Jamison existed his house in a whirlwind, leaving Sutherland to see himself out.

*     *     *

Sutherland had an hour before he needed to be on his boat, and Jamison's inference that his father had been involved in the shady partnerships prompted a trip to his rented storage space. When he'd returned from Mexico he had carted his father's undamaged records from the garage and his sailing gear from his yacht club lockers and dock box to U-Storage, a warehouse near the Kennedy Expressway. After his divorce and his move from his suburban home to a high-rise in the city, he had hauled contents of the basement to the same space. It was his father's records, those not damaged in the fire, that interested Sutherland now. These archives might contain tax records establishing whether his father had any partnership interests with Gene Sandler and his cronies.

Sutherland unlocked the padlock on the chain-link door of the cage and stepped in. Two heavy sail bags from his father's sloop were on a shelf to the left next to a cardboard wardrobe containing old clothes. The shelves on the right held golf clubs he never used, skis and poles, an old tennis racket, a rolled-up inflatable dinghy, foul-weather gear, oars, life jackets, and box of shoes and boots he couldn't remember owning. Cardboard boxes containing who-knew-what were stacked at the far end of the fenced-in cage, along with a two-drawer filing cabinet holding his father's records.

When he'd cleared out his father's garage, he had barely looked at the files' contents. There were estate and income tax liabilities to consider, so he'd piled everything into the two drawers and hauled the cabinet off.

In fifteen minutes he'd ruffled through his father's latest five years of tax returns. In all, there were K-1s from at least ten real estate partnerships in those years, but it would take more research to tell if they were connected to Sandler, Gorman, or Tunney. There were also receipts and checkbooks for the last two years of his life. Sutherland stuffed the returns and bank statements into a bag for later study, locked the cage, and left the warehouse, thinking that if the whole building burned down, it would save him the trouble of trashing the rest of the crap he'd left there.

Nothing he'd seen in the files hinted of a large sum of stolen money—understandable, since the alleged transaction supposedly took place later. Most of his father's more current papers had been burned in the fire in his home. Any others would be those left in his McCollum office, all of which were delivered to Sutherland after he returned to learn of his father's death. He hoped that his daughter, Jenny, could find them in the attic of the house that used to be his before the divorce.

A few minutes later, Sutherland turned his Jaguar south on Lake Shore Drive. It was a postcard-picture day. The landmark Drake Hotel loomed ahead, the lake stretched to the horizon on his left, and North and Oak Street beaches were packed with sun worshipers sprawled on the sand, playing volleyball, or tossing footballs or Frisbees. Out on the lake dozens of white sails dotted the sparkling water. In several hours Sutherland would be racing out there.

As he turned into the Chicago Yacht Club parking lot, his mind still lingered on his meeting with Jamison and news of Scooch's murder. Why didn't he buy the notebook when he had a chance? He could have burned it and all its skeletons, allowing Scooch to trudge through life unharmed. And Gorman? By meeting him, had Sutherland put him in harm's way?

No. There were other plots and actors at play. Gorman had made plenty of enemies in his lifetime, and Scooch was destined for trouble from the beginning. Even more ghosts were likely to be exposed by that notebook—or by Jamison, if he kept digging.

# Chapter 27

Nobody won Sunday's race. Minutes after *Circe's* crew executed a spinnaker jibe—four boat lengths ahead of the second-place yacht—the wind died. The calm stalled the rear of the fleet first, increasing *Circe's* lead, but gradually it overtook them all. The race was called after hours of coaxing inches from slack sails.

After a few beers with his crew, commiserating over the win that got away, Sutherland returned to his condominium. He dropped his car with the garage attendant, who asked him whether he had won the race. It baffled Sutherland how these men knew so much about his activities.

As soon as he opened the apartment door he knew he had a visitor; a sweet bouquet redolent of orange blossoms thickened the air. Two steps more and a blond dervish rushed at him.

"Daddy," Jenny gushed, jumping up, planting a kiss on his cheek.

He gave her a warm hug, all ninety pounds of her. "You're red as a beet."

"We went to Oak Street beach."

"Aren't you a little young for that place?"

"I'm thirteen."

"That's what I mean." He tried not to imagine her in her bikini among the oglers on the beach. "What's that smell?"

"Bath oil. I changed."

Blond, with Scandinavian features, Jenny could have been her mother's younger sister except for Sutherland's dimple nestled in her sun-reddened cheeks and the little twist of the mouth, which on her looked impish when she grinned. She wore a navy-blue-and-white-striped shirt, white shorts, and sandals. On the floor by the kitchen table sat her red, white, and blue beach bag, the size of an airplane carry-on.

"You staying tonight?"

"Chelsea's mom's picking me up in fifteen minutes. I've been waiting for you, like, forever, with nothing in the refrigerator. You can tell Kelly hasn't been around."

"Don't get your hopes up."

"Is she going on the Mac with you? It's next weekend isn't it?"

"It is, but she's not going."

"Oh," she said, disappointed. "I was going to ask to come, too."

"When you're a little older, Jenny. The races you've been on only lasted a few hours. The Mac is round-the-clock days, catching short shifts of sleep on sail bags on a boat crowded with a double crew. Besides, your mother wouldn't let you."

"She already said no. She wasn't happy about me coming here today either. I think it was because of what the newspapers were saying."

He felt heat rise in his face. Trust Margo to find a way to stick a finger in his eye.

"Is that why you asked me to look for this?" Jenny said, taking a bulging accordion-type legal folder out of her beach bag. "I had to be sneaky, so she wouldn't know. It was in the attic with some yearbooks. I checked inside, just to make sure."

Taking the folder from her, he set it on the kitchen table, untied the string fastener, and started pulling out the contents onto the table.

"All Grandpa's?" she asked.

"Yeah. Taken from his office." Sutherland shuffled through a handful of papers, including a number of bills and pieces of junk mail and a paper-clipped sheaf of monthly reports from his property managers. Why had he kept it? Probably because he didn't want to think about anything concerning his father at the time. "They gathered up everything from his desk and gave it to me after I returned. I think we can toss most of it."

After giving a few unopened utility bills a swift glance, he pitched them into the wastebasket. When he came to a clipping from the *Chicago Tribune*, he paused to scan it. The article's headline read, "State Prosecutor Missing Three Days, Car Found in St. Louis Airport." It was dated a few days before his father died, and Sutherland assumed the missing man, Daryl Anderson, had been a friend. His father had been a prosecutor once as well, though it been a long time since Sutherland had given any thought to his father's earlier career. Every good thing his father had done had been negated by his guilty plea.

While he was reading, Jenny dug out the remaining contents of the folder. "What's this?" She held up a large brass key embossed with an *M* in fancy script on both sides.

"All the McCollum keys were like that once. They were replaced by card keys or modern locks and latches ages ago. That was probably the last one."

"So the initial stands for *McCollum*?"

"Yep."

"Why'd he keep it?"

"Nostalgia maybe. I remember when he had it changed. The door and lock the key fit were destroyed during the flood when I was in high school."

"There was a flood?"

"In 1992, before you were born. Workers on the river punched a hole in the old coal tunnel under the Loop. The Chicago River poured in, flooding the basements of the McCollum Building and dozens of others, forcing them to be evacuated and costing millions in damage." The sixty miles of tunnel under the Loop were once used to deliver coal to the office buildings, but the practice had been discontinued for decades. In his youth, he and his father would descend forty feet under the street by the McCollum's elevator shaft and explore the abandoned tunnel. It was impossible to forget the utter darkness and the quiet, but the most intense memory was the terror he always felt and his abject need to cling to his father while they sloshed down the eerie tube.

Sutherland's recollections were interrupted by his daughter. "Can I have it? It would look neat if it was shined up. Like on a necklace."

"It's not good for anything else. There's a guy in Winnetka who can clean it up for you. He polished a nautical clock on *Circe* for me. I've got his name in the den. Come on."

"Awesome," Jenny said, stuffing the key into her pocket.

Sutherland returned everything to the envelope and led his daughter down the corridor to the den. "I think I kept his card." He opened the top desk drawer and fingered through a rolodex, an anachronism considering that these days everything was on PDAs.

Jenny browsed the den's shelves, crammed with books and racing trophies, one wall covered with sailing photos. She stopped in front of a picture of a woman with dark hair in braids interlaced with bright ribbons. "Mom never talks about your mom and dad. She tried to hide the newspaper articles about Granddad, you, and the building. That why the interest in his files?"

"Smart girl."

She wandered to another photograph. "That's his boat, isn't it?"

He turned to see her pointing at a classic sloop with a low freeboard and long overhangs fore and aft. He could never look at it without some memory flashing into his mind—now he saw his father and he varnishing the sailboat's brightwork on a spring afternoon. "That's it."

"Looks like an antique," she said, studying the photo. "If you didn't like him, how come you keep it?"

"Your mother tell you that?"

"I guess she must have."

And no wonder. For years Sutherland had worn his bitterness openly, never mentioning the good years he'd spent with his father. "Here it is," he said, handing Jenny a business card.

Just then, the intercom buzzer by the den's door let out a loud, piercing screech. Jenny jumped, dropping the photo on the carpet. Then a deafening, static-distorted voice squawked, "*Mr. Sutherland. Your daughter's ride is here.*"

"*Eeeee*uuuu," Jenny whined, holding her ears. "Gross me out."

"It's your friend," Sutherland said, also wincing from the ear-assaulting noise. "I asked them to fix that speaker."

"Gotta go." Jenny retrieved the photo from the floor, gave it to her dad, and planted a peck on his cheek. "Why don't you give Kelly a call?"

# Chapter 28

After a nap induced by an afternoon of sun, heat, and beer out on the lake, Sutherland spread out the partnership tax returns and agreements he'd retrieved from the warehouse that morning and started reading from the earliest date. He compared the buildings with those Langer had seen in the notebook then tried to match initials and names with players from that era, many of whom were still in business today. After two hours he came to the lamentable conclusion that, as Jamison speculated, his father had indeed associated with Tunney, Langer, Delaney, Gorman, and Sandler, not to mention a handful of prominent former and current city and state officials that he'd identified so far.

On the surface the elder Sutherland's participation didn't appear illegal. These were real estate limited partnerships for the development and ownership of commercial office and apartment buildings. What wasn't evident in these documents were the criminal activities Jamison was suggesting—that some partnership interests were given or discounted as payoffs to others, be they politicians, inspectors, judges, or whomever was needed. What was obvious from the documents was that at one time his father, as attorney, had originated the partnership documents and served as administrator for some of them. The accounting and tax returns were handled by Sandler or his accountant.

So instead of proving Jamison's articles wrong, his original intent, Sutherland's research was digging a deeper hole. Rather than scorning his father for attempted bribery, it looked like he might have to add serial corruption to the list. What's more, he, or members of that cabal, might be guilty of murder. *Give up while you're ahead*, Sutherland said to himself.

He knew he couldn't. Setting aside the pile of forms, he turned his attention to the envelope Jenny had brought. With his home office destroyed, this constituted the only remnants of what his father had been working on between the time he was released from prison and his suicide. Whatever his father had had on his computer had been removed. That left little to go on.

He spilled the contents on the desk and sorted through them. Besides what he'd already seen, there was a checkbook showing a balance of a little over $2,000, an outdated dictating unit, a box of blank tapes, a calculator, several pencils and pens, a ruler, a small stapler, and five blank legal pads. He read through some business letters with no apparent relevance, an unfinished tax return from his time in prison, more unopened junk mail and bills, and several credit card receipts.

Coming across the clipping from the *Tribune* again, he read it more carefully. Daryl Anderson, the missing assistant state's attorney, had been working with the FBI on an undisclosed case. After the discovery of his car in the St. Louis airport, police and FBI spokesmen had not ruled out foul play. Since it had been cut out of the paper the day before his father died, Anderson's disappearance must have occurred a few days earlier. First this state's attorney, then Delaney, then his father. How would you connect those dots?

Frustrated and tired, Sutherland stared at his father's bills and old mail, undecided whether to sort through it or toss it all out. Finally he opted to call it a night. Fifteen-year-old bills could wait.

# CHAPTER 29

## MONDAY, JULY 16

On Monday morning, Sutherland arrived at his office to find FBI agent Mark Branson waiting. Eileen had escorted him to the conference room and served him coffee and the morning papers to keep him busy. She met Sutherland in the lobby. "He's been here for half an hour. I think he was glad you weren't here yet, because he started asking questions. Your appointments for the last week, phone messages, spending habits, like that."

"And you told him?"

"Nothing personal. Anyway, I cut him off when he started asking about your father. What do I know, anyway? Before my time."

"Thanks. Anything else? Messages?"

"Frank Mann and the lawyers need to talk about the lease." Frank was his real estate broker, who had helped land the Broadwell deal. Probably calling to tell him that they were still waiting to hear from Broadwell's attorneys, who'd seemed to be dragging their feet since the SEC had been looking into their company's books. "Also two reporters. And a detective from the Chicago police wants to talk you. Vislowski?" she said.

"When's he coming?"

"Said he'd call back."

"I'm expecting Dan Dixon, so show him into my office when he arrives." He and Dan, Broadwell's project manager for the McCollum, had some design changes to review before meeting with the architects.

Sutherland filled his coffee cup from the office pot and walked into the conference room, where he found Agent Branson at the table reading the *Tribune*. The agent looked up, took off his half-glasses, and assessed Sutherland with half-closed eyes. It was as if he was trying to read something in Sutherland's face. "Morning. How are you?"

"Busy. What can I do for you this time?" Sutherland pulled out a chair from the table and sat across from the agent with his back to the windows.

"Seen this morning's article? Your buddy's?"

"What rumors is he printing today?"

"That Danny Delaney's associates killed him because he was talking to the government."

Sutherland wondered where Jamison got that piece of information. He hadn't mentioned it Saturday or Sunday. Gorman had told Sutherland in the restaurant the night he was killed, but Sutherland hadn't passed it on. Jamison never got a chance to talk to Gorman to learn for himself. Was it widely known, or was Jamison good at digging?

"*Was* he going to testify?" Sutherland asked.

"The article says Danny was going to implicate a lot of important people in town. Some are still around."

"You didn't answer the question. I know Jamison has a vivid imagination."

"Not in this case. He also names your father."

"Again?" Sutherland grabbed the *Tribune* and pulled it across the table. He scanned the article, anxiously anticipating the two words he didn't want to see, *McCollum* and *Sutherland*. But most of the column dealt with known facts about Danny's past, the allegations that surrounded him, and Jamison's spin on what happened—Danny flips, his cronies learn about it, Danny gets whacked. Jamison avoided potential libel suits by posing questions rather than making direct allegations. Was Danny involved in kickback schemes that included deceased associates Benjamin Gorman and Miles Langer, activities that continued to this day with the surviving players? The final paragraph mentioned Scooch's murder, ostensibly killed for the notebook, and maintained that the notebook was still at large. He promised to divulge the names of the living players who had perpetuated Danny's ring of influence and corruption.

It could have been worse. The references to his father weren't new, though Sutherland wished he'd stop hammering at it. "He knows how to sell papers, doesn't he?" He tossed the paper back to Branson. "But you didn't come to show me that article. I'm expecting a client."

"You went to see Benjamin Gorman the night he was killed. Why?"

"Because of Jamison's accusations that my father stole money from Gorman's fund. I wanted to see if it was true."

"What did he tell you?"

"He categorically denied it."

"That's it?"

"A man of few words. And very sick."

"And now very dead. You were the last man to see him."

Sutherland chuckled. "A line right out of the movies. So now I say, his murderer was …"

"You could have had an argument about the money."

"Assuming there was any money."

Branson was silent for a moment, serious, staring down at the table, apparently mulling some decision. He puffed his cheeks, blew out a breath, and said, "Okay, Mr. Sutherland. I'll tell you. First, Delaney was turning state's evidence. Second, the stolen money—stretching the point that taking illegal money is considered stealing—was diverted from a building sale involving money skimmed from gambling casinos. A short time before your father died, he arranged it so the proceeds of that sale were wired to an account other than the one regularly used by Delaney and the rest. It was dirty money, so nobody could admit to owning or missing it. We think he also walked out with Delaney's files, videotapes, and some cash. No one to our knowledge found the money or videos."

"I hope you don't expect me to know anything about that," Sutherland said. "And if Danny turned state's evidence, why no indictments, no trials? It couldn't have been a very good case."

Branson seemed momentarily stopped by the comment. He glared at Sutherland for a full five seconds, his jaw clenched. Finally, tight-lipped and rigid, he said, "It would have been a very good case, Mr. Sutherland. Very good. A lot of important people were going down. I know, I was there."

"If it was so good, what happened?"

"I'll tell you because your father was so much a part of it. The head FBI investigator was murdered the night Delaney disappeared. The same night Danny's taped testimony and affidavits were destroyed when the case's war room was cleaned out and burned. A dead agent and an aborted case. This is personal with me, Mr. Sutherland. Very personal."

"Murdered? I read he disappeared. His car was found in St. Louis's airport."

Branson seemed surprised or confused by the comment. "You've got it mixed up. The man that disappeared was Daryl Anderson, an attorney on the team. The murder victim was John Durham, my boss and the lead FBI agent handling the case. He was shot the night Delaney disappeared, the day before your father died. They never found the shooter, and we don't think it was a random crime. They killed him and had the evidence destroyed to avoid prosecution."

Start with an FBI agent's murder, add a missing fed attorney, toss in a murdered alderman and Sutherland's father's suicide and you have a deadly stew. It gets spicier when Gorman and Scooch turn up dead. Sutherland took a deep breath, thinking the conference room was getting stuffy. He needed fresh air, but he also wanted answers.

"What happened to the guy that went missing?"

"Anderson? He was found."

"And?"

"He was found."

"Have your secrets. But didn't it occur to you that whoever killed Danny took the money and the tapes?"

"We ruled that out. We detained an international banking specialist who was hired by an anonymous party—we believe the killer or killers—to trace the same money trail we were, with the same futile result. On top of that, these recent murders indicate that someone's desperate to get their hands on the notebook and the videos."

"Why now? Didn't they know about the tapes before Jamison started writing about the notebook's contents?"

"My guess is that if they knew about them, they thought we already had the tapes but they weren't that incriminating, especially with the loss of the rest of the case evidence. In a matter of days we closed down what was left of the team, a bunch of clerks and junior lawyers, including me and George Spanos, in subordinate roles."

"So why would they think they were more incriminating now?"

"Your friend Jamison has disclosed some of what's in the book. A few transactions and dates associated with videos. The names or initials may not be specific enough alone, but if there is a tape of that transaction, whoever was involved would know how incriminating it was. If my guess is right, it'd be enough to put them away, and since no legal action was taken years ago, they realize that the government never had them."

"So how does this involve me?" Sutherland asked.

"I told you. We believe your father carried off the tapes that night."

"Bad pun, but if that's the case, it's a dead end."

"Has anyone ever questioned you about what your father left?"

Sutherland had to think a moment before answering. "The only conversations I ever had about my father were right after I returned from Mexico, when I learned about his suicide and they gave me his personal belongings. Fifteen years ago. Might also been some guy from the FBI, but I can't remember more than that."

"I was already reassigned. That was Agent Parisi doing a cursory follow-up. I've seen his notes. No one else?"

"Nothing that made me think twice about it. Most of those who knew my father and what happened tiptoed around the whole thing. Anyway, why would I know? I wasn't around."

"Point is, the existence of that notebook suggests that the tapes and files may still exist. We're going to follow this, which means you might be hearing more. If you do, the best thing is to get us involved."

"I've got nothing. Old tax returns which you've probably seen already."

"Years ago. But somewhere out there there's money stolen from some very unscrupulous people. And maybe tapes that could put them all in jail. They don't know what you have or don't have." Branson shrugged and smiled. "And here's what we're all thinking: why wouldn't he tell his only son?"

"Who is the 'they' you talk about?"

"I can't say, except your reporter friend is on the right track."

"You're after indictments? Justice for an FBI agent's murder? Can't be the money. Peanuts to the US."

"I've said enough," Branson said.

Sutherland turned and stared out the window at the gray and purple sky, thinking. Suddenly he couldn't hold back a laugh. "What a circle jerk. You guys think my father had it, the other guys think you got it, now you think I know where it is. It's an Abbot and Costello sketch." He stood up abruptly, his patience at an end. "You'll have to excuse me; a client's waiting, and a Chicago cop is coming to see me. He probably wants to know who's on first."

Branson stood up and took a step between Sutherland and the door. His jaw muscles tensed, his eyes stern. "Think you can laugh this off? A buried alderman followed by two related murders, three if you count the junkie, and a lot of dirty money. One name keeps popping up. Sutherland owns the building with the dead alderman, Sutherland diverts the dirty money, another Sutherland—you this time—talks to the guy that finds a notebook and turns up dead then meets Gorman, who turns up dead. I couldn't give two shits about those others, but one of ours is dead. A good agent and a friend. And from the beginning the name Sutherland is at the heart of it all. It's not funny and it's not going away."

"You through?"

"No. If you or your buddy Jamison finds that notebook or anything else, turn it over. If you don't work with us, you're making a big mistake. There are murderers out there, Mr. Sutherland, that aren't as easygoing as I am."

Sutherland sidestepped the agent and led him out of the conference room. As he passed Eileen's desk he said, "Do me a favor? Show Agent Branson out." He didn't say good-bye.

*     *     *

Dan Dixon of Broadwell was waiting in Sutherland's office, leaning over a large set of engineering drawings spread on the corner table. "Morning," he said, looking up. "Meeting over?"

"Yeah, sorry to keep you."

"Was it really an agent? FBI?" He must have heard Sutherland's comment to Eileen.

"Yeah. More of the same. Questions about Danny Delaney."

"It's all over the papers. Including a couple more dead guys. I wish the whole thing would die. It's really complicating things up in headquarters. Not just the corporate counsel's office. A few directors are making noise. All because of those *Tribune* articles."

More likely because of Jules Langer's phone calls to a couple directors. "Are they talking about America Tower?"

"One director called me last night wanting to know its status. Said he got a call from Jules Langer, trying to get back in the picture. He's not the only one. Langer's got a few other champions in management, and this publicity is giving them an opening."

"From what I read, they all should be worrying about more important things. Falling stock prices, rumors about creative accounting, bad investments—and didn't your treasurer just leave under a cloud?"

"Yeah, things are tense in New York. Glad I'm in Chicago."

"Would it help if I called, or went to New York? This Delaney crap is ancient history; it shouldn't be affecting what was, and still is, a well-reasoned and best solution."

"I know, but things are sensitive there. Now especially. I'm not in the loop, but I don't think going there will help. Let's hope some war takes over the headlines."

"There's going to be a war all right. I'm going to find Langer and rip him a new blowhole. His old man was as dirty as anyone. He wouldn't be in business if his father hadn't earned a fortune as one of Danny's cronies."

# CHAPTER 30

Evening sunshine streamed into Jamison's living room, and shouts from Oz Park floated across the street through the screen door. As soon as Sutherland entered and closed the door behind him, Jamison pointed to a photo on his coffee table and said, "Does this man look like a murderer?"

Sutherland walked across the hardwood floor and eased into an upholstered chair. Staring up at him from the photograph was the beaming face of Jules Langer as he stood beside a model of America Tower. "Langer? You got to be kidding."

"I saw him with Scooch at the diner the night he was killed. It was too dark and far away to get a decent picture, but I recognized him. He's the son of Miles Langer, one of the men mixed up with Danny Delaney. He was there to buy the notebook, I'm sure of it."

"Maybe he'd want the notebook, but murder? No way." Sutherland pulled down his tie and unbuttoned his shirt collar, thinking that if Langer was after the notebook, he must have a good idea what was in it.

"Wish I could identify the other guy there that night," Jamison said. "Came out of the rain, scared the shit out of me. He could have followed and murdered Scooch."

"Who murdered him?" came a shout from a feminine voice.

Sutherland turned around to see Ronnie Jamison opening the screen door. As she entered, she continued, "You find out who did it?" Her skin was damp and her red hair pulled back in a ponytail. She wore shorts and a blue, damp tank top, and when she plopped down next to her brother on the sofa, it was as if she'd just finished a marathon and wasn't happy with her time.

"Just speculating," Jamison said, watching her kick off her sandals. "Tough day in the market?"

"You could say that," she said. "Had to cover a bunch of shorts."

"You a trader?" Sutherland asked. "I thought you were an attorney."

"*Was* an attorney. Gave it up a couple years ago."

"You trade full time?"

"My big sister is an action junkie, Doug," Bill Jamison said. "She'll bet on anything and everything, not just stocks and bonds. But enough chitchat, I'm meeting someone in a half hour. Let's get to what you found, Doug."

Sutherland retrieved a list of twenty-five properties from his briefcase. "You didn't need me for this. It's all in the county records. The present owners are Langer's company's affiliates, a Raskoff family trust, Reginald Tunney's company, and a half-dozen trusts and limited partnerships that could include anybody. The rest of these were sold years ago but were once owned by the same names or held in trust, making it tough to identify who's behind them. Some of these projects had been in financial trouble, but none went back to the lender or were restructured, which in itself is amazing. Everyone was having trouble during that time."

"Not if the lender was part of the scheme, like Gorman and his pension fund," Jamison ventured.

"Every player had their part," Sutherland said. "But notice that none of my father's properties are on this list. Nothing here implicates him."

"Except his initials in the book, the fact that he was Delaney's partner in the McCollum and that he prepared the partnership documents. I've another source verifying that there was money taken."

"But five million? How can you hide that kind of theft? It's hearsay, unproven."

"Okay, I hear you." Jamison held up his hands in surrender. "Let's change the subject to these so-called investors." He handed Sutherland a manila folder. "What if I get these for every partner involved?"

Sutherland opened it, scanned the top sheet, and said, "It's a tax return for a limited partnership."

"Right. The general partner sends it to the IRS and a K-1 to each partner. If it cuts through all the trusts and convoluted structures, I'll have the name of every partner. These forms come from Gene Sandler's accountant's files. My guy can get them for every project, going back to Delaney's era. Should've had them already, but the man's jumpy."

"You should be too. These guys aren't looking for that kind of publicity. In any event, limited partnerships aren't criminal."

"Even if they were," Ronnie interjected, "the state's attorney wouldn't give them a second look. Too many years and too many big names."

"Speaking of big names. Take a closer look at that 1099 summary. A certain George Spanos was a limited partner. A Spanos is also listed in the page I photographed from Delaney's notebook. And get this. I learned that he was with the state's attorney's office back then. Talk about a story."

"Careful, Bill. You're talking about our future governor. If you're wrong …"

"I know. I've got to dig a little deeper before publishing."

"Could any of this lead to Delaney's murderer?" Sutherland asked.

"I worked with Vislowski when I was with the state," Ronnie said. "He can't find his ass with both hands. But Billy? He could win a Pulitzer."

"Ronnie, I told you …" Jamison said.

"Have some confidence," she said. "No one else has this information." She pointed to the partnership papers. "And you know where the notebook is."

"Where?" Sutherland asked.

"I'll get to that," Jamison said. "I told Vislowski what I knew about Scooch and he returned the favor. We've had a quid pro quo for a few years now." He looked at his sister. "He asked about you."

Ronnie scowled at him.

"So where is it?" Sutherland asked.

"Police believe the killer took it," Jamison said. "But Scooch told me he was sending it somewhere safe. I'm betting the killer doesn't know that. Scooch died of a heart attack while being tortured. The killer may not have learned anything before he died. Police found a Federal Express receipt and tracked it to an aunt in Niagara Falls. When they talked to her on the phone, she claimed Scooch sent her some gloves."

"Gloves?" Sutherland and Ronnie said together.

"That's what she claimed. I'm going to see her myself."

"You tell the police you saw Langer with Scooch?" Sutherland asked.

"I only just realized it was Langer I saw. But Vislowski told me a few other things. The killer may have left something in Scooch's room: an expensive umbrella. The room was torn apart from searching for the notebook, and the cops found this silver-handled umbrella under a pile of clothes. They figure the killer gave up looking in the mess."

"Fingerprints?" Sutherland asked.

"Don't know yet. But I usually come out ahead in these exchanges because he's still got a thing for my sister."

"He better get over it," Ronnie snapped.

"When I tell him about seeing Langer I'll find out about prints," Jamison said before asking Sutherland, "Has Vislowski talked to you yet?"

"Not him. But I gave a statement at the McCollum site the day we found Delaney, another uniform saw me about my meeting Gorman, and that was topped off by a visit from the FBI. An Agent Branson."

"He visited me too," Jamison said. "Pissed him off that I won't give up my sources. But get this: Vislowski thinks Scooch's murderer also killed Delaney.

They both had their knuckles crushed, and the killer took souvenirs. Danny's front tooth was yanked out."

"Dentist from hell," Ronnie said, grimacing.

"That's not all," Jamison said. "Scooch's ear was missing, and the tattoo Gorman had on his arm had been sliced off."

Sutherland cringed, imagining Gorman's shriveled forearm in the restaurant's candlelight.

Jamison looked at his watch and stood. "I've got to change and go. Why don't you two get something to eat?"

"Somehow, I'm not hungry," Sutherland said.

Jamison laughed and disappeared down the corridor.

"But I could use a drink."

"There's a good bar across the park," Ronnie said.

"You're on."

"I'll even buy. A few drinks might free those secrets you're hiding behind that innocent grin." She smiled, but Sutherland felt the resolve in her eyes. "I'll be right back."

Five minutes later Sutherland heard her footsteps and turned from the window, where he had been straining to see down the street. She reappeared wearing the same shorts but had put on a man's shirt with rolled-up sleeves and the shirttails tied around her midriff. Her ponytail was combed out, and the bright lipstick matched her flaming hair.

"What's the matter?" she asked.

"Did Bill change into black? Leather?"

"Why?" She moved next to him by the window.

"He left through the side door. Someone followed him down the street."

"You sure? Where?"

"The guy was there," Sutherland said, pointing to a bench across the street, in the park. "Sitting by that couple with the dog. As soon as Bill appeared in front, the guy followed."

"You positive?" she asked, her forehead furrowed.

"He kept parallel in the park until Bill caught a cab. You know where Bill went?"

"Meeting his source, Robert Hurley, the accountant with the tax history." She bit her lip, narrowing her eyes. "I better call him."

She reached him on his cell in the taxi and told him he might be being followed. From what Sutherland inferred from Ronnie's half of the short conversation, Jamison told her not to worry. "Just be careful, Billy," she said, ending the call.

"He was dressed in leather, like one of those macho gay guys. What's the deal?"

"Playing a part. You do what you have to do. You probably learned that from your father, but it was up to me to teach Billy."

"Why you?"

"Our folks died when we were young. We were raised by our aunt and uncle, who were older and didn't really like kids. Billy never had a real father to show him how to be a man. I had to be father and mother."

And she still was, from what Sutherland could see.

# Chapter 31

Chicago's Commercial Real Estate Association luncheon was held in the grand ballroom in the Palmer House, one of the oldest hotels in the Loop. Sutherland arrived just before noon, nursing a throbbing head and a stomach growling like a pen of rabid dogs. Margaritas and enchiladas—he loved spicy food, but with too much tequila it was deadly.

Last night he and Ronnie left Jamison's apartment and walked to a restaurant with an outdoor patio. During an alfresco dinner washed down by margaritas, Sutherland temporarily forgot all about Danny, the McCollum Building, and Broadwell Communications while developing an affinity for red hair and emerald eyes, though hers were a lighter green than Kelly's, an observation he quickly put aside as extraneous history. For reasons he couldn't pinpoint, most of the conversation uncharacteristically centered on him and his experiences. She seemed interested in what it was like to be brought up by a single father and why his mother had left them when he was an infant. But she quickly moved on to the time he spent wandering through Mexico and crewing on a charter sailboat in the Caribbean during the period his father was in prison. She wanted to know about the game of squash, his sailing races, and what kind of skier he was. In retrospect, Sutherland noticed that her questions nearly always dealt with his adventures or competitions.

Surprisingly the topic of his marriage and divorce didn't come up, and whenever he tried to change the subject to her history, interests, or opinions, she managed to turn the spotlight back on him without giving up much. All he learned about her was that she was a nonpracticing attorney who traded securities for a living and liked horse racing, poker, and trips to Las Vegas. It was very late when they teetered back to Bill Jamison's townhouse. She fumbled into her red Corvette, and he flagged a taxi home.

At the cash bar in the Palmer House ballroom, after taking a good-natured ribbing from a couple of brokers about how bad he looked, Sutherland ordered a virgin Mary and surveyed the huge room, looking for Jules Langer. The football-field-sized hall held a couple bars in the near end zone, a podium in the other, and tables set for a few hundred lunches in between. Feeling a tug at his sleeve, Sutherland turned to see Kelly's shining face staring up at him.

"Hi there." He wasn't surprised to see her; she, Margaret Lieberman, and Jules Langer were on the agenda, a forum on preservation versus renovation and new development.

"You must be pumped up," Sutherland said. "Between you and Maggie Lieberman, Jules Langer hasn't got a chance."

"Jules doesn't care. Just wind him up and he can promote his latest dildo all day. And why knock Lieberman? She approved your zoning."

"Unlike some, she couldn't deny the overwhelming logic. She's still a preservationist."

"Let's not go there," she said. "I'm surprised to see you here. It's not your type of thing."

"I need to talk to Jules Langer."

"Haven't seen him," she said, studying his face. "By the way, you look like shit. Major bags under your baby blues—or I should say, reds. Bad night?"

"Bad week," he said, feeling swallowed in her gaze. "Lot of shit."

"You should take better care of yourself." She compressed her lips, her preparation, he knew, for a touchy subject. "Jenny called me again. She wanted to know if I was going to the Mackinac party Friday night. She wanted to come too."

"What did you tell her?"

"I'm doing something else."

"She's way too young for the club party, anyway."

A voice from the podium asked that the group to take seats for lunch.

"Good luck with Langer," he said. "Fight clean."

"Not everything's a fight, you know."

He shrugged and held his hands palm up.

She shook her head and walked to the head table.

*     *     *

During lunch Sutherland poked at his chicken and discussed the real estate market with several bankers, three brokers, and two suburban developers. He was surprised at the fame he'd gained from his battle with the landmark people and the Broadwell deal. Everyone at the table had questions, as if suddenly he was the guru. No one asked him about the discovery of Danny, the event that could change his status from hero of the development community to the object of pity or gloating, depending on one's perspective.

The panelists converged behind a table facing the gathering. Margaret

Lieberman, City Planning Commissioner, launched the program. "Today we're privileged to hear from two distinguished members of Chicago's community, each representing their position on an issue important to everyone here: new development versus preservation of older and landmark buildings. Our first speaker is Kelly Matthews, chairperson of the Landmarks Commission."

The lights were dimmed, and when Kelly moved into the glow of the podium light, Sutherland felt a vestigial twinge of jealousy at others admiring her. A young broker next to Sutherland asked, "Weren't you and her a thing?"

"History," he said.

The broker smiled and turned his eyes back on Kelly.

With color slides she described the city's classic buildings: the Monadnock, The Rookery, the Marquette, the Santa Fe, the Wrigley, and the Tribune. She discussed their architects, design influence, materials, and distinctions. Then she highlighted other buildings, "gems" that over the decades had been razed and supplanted by "uninspired boxes and tawdry designs."

Sutherland observed with ambivalence as Kelly built her case: she was eloquent, but the assumed certainty of her opinions bothered him. The world was not that black and white.

"The last victims," she said, "were the Carson Building, site of Mr. Langer's planned America Tower, and the McCollum Building, under the wrecking ball as I speak. In destroying these structures, we betrayed our heritage, and for what? For an egotistical obsession to build a taller building or to make more money. It's criminal that people without a proper sense of history and beauty have a license to deprive the public of its culture and force it to live with replacements whose only characteristic is newness."

*She's rolling now*, mused Sutherland. If he didn't want to see Langer, he'd leave; he'd heard this too many times before.

Five minutes later, a ripple of polite applause followed her "thank you." The cool response was only to be expected from an assembly addicted to development.

"A real ball buster," one of the developers said.

"She can bust mine any time," another replied.

Sutherland took a deep breath and counted to ten.

After Lieberman's introduction, Jules Langer swaggered to the podium, nodding his acknowledgment to the light applause as if the whole room was his fan club. He fingered his tie knot, cleared his throat, put on his best smile, and began.

"You know my views on this subject. Preservationists are obstructionists, hanging on to antiquated ideas and times while disenfranchising people who want to build a better tomorrow."

Sutherland ate his ice cream, the only food that seemed to go down well. Jules was a hell of a promoter. He had taken his father's company, already successful when he died, and through his connections, chutzpa, salesmanship, and some luck, made himself the big-name developer in Chicago. It had always intrigued Sutherland how a man of average intelligence, by dint of irrepressible ego and a mouth never lacking for words, had pulled it off. He had somehow suspected that some under-the-table shenanigans might have helped.

"These people are driving toward tomorrow through a rearview mirror," Langer continued. "If they controlled our country the way they want to control real estate, we'd all be in horse and buggies, still be running to the outhouse to do our business."

Enough of this. Sutherland folded his napkin, gave the table a good-bye wave all around, and slipped away. He didn't have to stay; he knew where to find Langer after he finished his one-man show.

*    *    *

Langer's limousine was waiting outside on Monroe when Sutherland slid into the backseat. "I'm meeting Jules here," he said to the chauffeur, who looked up, surprised, from his newspaper. "He should be here in fifteen minutes or so. You got the business page?"

"Mr. Sutherland, isn't it?" he said, nervously handing Sutherland the whole paper. "You want a drink? There's cold drinks and hard stuff in the cabinet. Help yourself."

"Don't mind if I do," he said, finding himself a diet cola.

Twenty minutes later Langer opened the door and, seeing Sutherland, looked like he'd just stepped on a rattlesnake. Then, in an instant, his face broke out into a big smile. "Doug. Good to see you."

"I'll bet you are," Sutherland scoffed. "So let's have a talk about the mess our fathers left us."

# Chapter 32

After driving the several blocks from the Palmer House to the Union League Club, Sutherland and Langer sat alone in graveyard quiet in a cavernous room surrounded by heavy draperies, ponderous furniture, and grand portraits. The air hung close and motionless, as if crowded with the ghosts of a century of members. Sutherland broke the silence. "I was interested to learn you tried to buy the notebook."

Langer pinched his tie knot and stared at the ceiling.

"You met Scooch the night he was killed," Sutherland said. "The police know."

Langer 's brow knotted in puzzlement. "How?"

"You were seen. By more than one person."

He pressed his lips together and inhaled deeply through his nose. "So now what? The police think I killed that slimeball?"

"I don't know what they think. But I know the same board members you talk to in Broadwell. If I whisper in their ears, they might conclude that there's something in that notebook you want to hide."

"You don't know that."

"But I do. Your father's activities, along with Sandler, Tunney, Delaney, Gorman—the list continues, and so does the corruption." Sutherland leaned forward and fixed his eyes on Langer's. "What I'm saying, Jules, is two can play that game. You try and fuck up my deal with Broadwell, I'll burn you. Jamison will help me."

Langer's mouth widened, looking insulted. "Me? I wouldn't do—"

"Cut the shit. You tried to stop my zoning, you tried to smear me before I won the Broadwell deal, and you've never stopped trying. Give it up. Your old man was at least as guilty as mine. You're living off what he did and you still have underhanded dealings with those fuckers."

Langer held up his hands in surrender. "Okay, okay. I got you." He messaged the back of his neck with his fingers, apparently in thought. "I gave the greasy prick five grand, and all I got was a promise. He was supposed to call me."

"He was dead a few hours later."

"He said he sent that goddamn book somewhere safe. Does that reporter know where?"

"If so, whatever's in that book will come out. He plans to tie all the names in it to today's players."

Langer's jaw clenched and his face lost some of its tanning-bed color. But he maintained his cool, adjusting his tie knot and taking a deep breath before answering. "There's things I wouldn't want public, but no one's ever got hurt by what I was involved in. My father maybe, but not me."

"Jamison doesn't care. Look what he's said about my father. If I'd known he'd print all that, when Scooch called me, I'd have bought and burned the damn book in a second. Now someone wants it more than either of us. Already killed to get it. A real sick fuck. Cut off Scooch's ear."

Langer pulled himself out of his chair, shaking his head. "I didn't need to know that. Look, I'll lay off Broadwell, okay? But if your buddy the reporter finds that thing, I'll help you burn it."

When Langer walked out of the room, he wasn't the confident man who had delivered his speech an hour ago. His shoulders were slouched, and his steps didn't have the normal bounce. But Sutherland figured he would be his old self in a matter of hours. Langer wasn't going to stop lobbying to win Broadwell, and he wouldn't be deterred from finding the notebook.

*　　　*　　　*

"Did you make out the guy following you?" Sutherland asked Jamison fifteen minutes later on his office phone.

"Ronnie called me, but I didn't see a soul."

"Doesn't that worry you? You're advertising that you know where the notebook is and promising to name names. A few people might take exception to that. Are you still going to see Scooch's aunt about the FedEx package?"

"I can't. I'm still fleshing out the Spanos thing, hoping to get it in tomorrow's edition. Then I'll be working on getting the tax information over the next few days. As soon as Vislowski gives us the aunt's address, Ronnie's going to see her."

"Others might know about the receipt. Aren't you worried?"

"There's no stopping my sister. Nice you're concerned about her, though. The interest's reciprocal."

"What's that supposed to mean?"

"She's asked about you. About your ex-wife. Do you have a girlfriend? Like that. Be careful, she usually gets what she wants."

"Romance is on the bottom of my list right now. You're crazy to let her go to Niagara Falls."

"Like I could stop her? If you're worried, go with her."

*That might not be a bad idea*, thought Sutherland. He could see firsthand what was in it and expunge anything damaging—or burn the thing, if he had to.

"Why's she so determined? Helping you win the Pulitzer?"

"That's only part of it. She'd love to put one over on Vislowski. They worked together when she was with the state's attorney. There's a rivalry there."

"Sounds stronger than rivalry."

"Well," Jamison said, as if thinking, "They went out for a while before she left the prosecutor's office."

"Because too many bad guys get away." Sutherland remembered her tone of disgust when she told him why she'd left.

"She's got an inflated sense of justice. If she can retrieve the notebook after the police failed, it'll be her victory. We win."

*Not all of us*, thought Sutherland. Not if that book implicated his father in a multimillion-dollar theft. Jamison still believed it was pension fund money; he hadn't learned about the skimmed casino cash or the diverted property sale proceeds. Agent Branson evidently hadn't told Jamison when they'd talked.

"I'll give her a call," Sutherland said. "Maybe I will go with her."

"I'm sure she'd love to have you. In more ways than one." Jamison chuckled before he hung up.

# CHAPTER 33

The woman who gazed from the portrait could have been the goddess of melancholy. Even the field of red and white tulips and yellow daffodils that surrounded her couldn't brighten the painting's mood. In her thin hands she held one milky rose, the color of her skin. She shared her twin brother's handsome features, but there the resemblance to Jules Langer ended. He sparkled and smiled while she frowned, her expression on the verge of a whimper. He primped and glowed with confidence and a year-round tan, while she cringed as if light itself was painful. But Jules, admiring his twin's portrait in his living room, saw only her beauty.

The telephone interrupted Langer's worship. He picked up his handset and, taking a deep breath, steeled himself. "Hello."

"Jules, you didn't call me." There was no mistaking Gene Sandler's reedy voice.

"No. I didn't." The fact was he hadn't felt himself ever since learning from Sutherland about Scooch's ear. The news had changed things for him. He had always known that Danny Delaney and his associates, including Langer's father, were guilty of payoffs and other questionable, if not borderline illegal, schemes. There might have even been some rough stuff involved, but Jules's father had kept him insulated from it. Now he was on his own, and up until now, he hadn't realized how dangerous his company was.

"Why didn't you tell me you were meeting with that scumbag?"

How did Sandler know? No point in asking. The man had contacts everywhere. "Because I didn't have time. He gave me fifteen minutes to get there. Anyway, it's a moot point. He didn't have it with him."

Langer heard the snap of Sandler's lighter, envisioned the smoke seeping from Sandler's frog-like mouth, the blotches on the fleshy face surfacing with his irritation, the cigarette held between his plump fingers. The image was enough; he was glad he was on the telephone and not in the same room.

"So the guy didn't have it. How about your meeting with Sutherland yesterday?" Sandler continued. "Does he or his reporter buddy know where the notebook is?"

How did the fat man know Langer talked to Sutherland yesterday? Langer must have been seen leaving the luncheon, because it was unlikely Sandler would talk to Sutherland. The animosity between them was well known.

"I don't know," Langer said. "Anyway, this whole thing's getting to me. You hear about Scooch's ear?"

"He used to box. Not very good at it. What about it?"

"It was cut off. And Gorman. At first they said he was killed by some junkie. Now they're not sure."

"What do you care?"

"What's going on, Gene?"

"You tell me. You're the guy meeting everybody. Did you get rid of the stuff we talked about?" Sandler asked. "Your father's collection?"

"I'll get to it, don't worry."

"Don't fool around, Jules. This is too big to fuck with. Your father knew that—knew how to deal with these things. Just do what I told you. Nothing else."

The phone went dead.

Langer's eyes were drawn again into his sister's portrait. Those mournful eyes, those delicate hands. The thought of her virtual incarceration as Reginald Tunney's wife made him weary. He lay down on the couch with his head on the arm, his gaze fixed on her face. If they could hide together again, like when they were children, they would be safe. Those times in their bedroom closet, holding one another to stop the fearful shaking, humming to drown out their father's alcoholic rants, their mother's mad wails.

Despite the risks, he saw a way to free her. Even if the notebook's contents could be damaging to himself, they posed a far bigger danger to Tunney and Sandler. If Sutherland was caught up in the mess, so much the better. The reporter had hinted that he knew where the book was. Langer could afford to pay him a lot more than he'd earn writing some muckraking column.

\*     \*     \*

When Sutherland replaced his office telephone, it was after four o'clock. For the last hour he had been back and forth with his lender—a struggle he wasn't going to win until and unless Broadwell Communications signed the lease. For several months since Sutherland and Broadwell had signed the letter of intent, lease negotiations had progressed steadily, albeit more slowly than he would have liked. He was too busy to be overly worried; he was consumed with demolition, financing, and design issues. Now negotiations had come to a halt, and he couldn't be sure of the cause. Was it publicity over the alderman and other deaths, fanned by Jules Langer's calls to friendly directors, or did it have to do with Broadwell's rumored financial problems and the SEC's growing interest? Sutherland couldn't affect Broadwell's financial issues, but he might be able to influence how the Delaney story played out.

Until the notebook turned up, Bill Jamison would probably make more accusations that couldn't be substantiated or refuted—accusations that could crater Sutherland's development. How could he put a stop to it? The book itself was in limbo, and Danny Delaney, Miles Langer, Benjamin Gorman, and Bernard Sutherland were dead. Eugene Sandler and Reginald Tunney were the most prominent members of the original cabal. Speaking to Sandler was out. Over the years Sutherland had refused to buy commercial insurance from Sandler or use his office building janitorial services. Sandler's prices were higher than the competition, yet he managed to control the majority of Chicago's real estate business. Sandler's sales pitch was simple: if you need anything from the City or Cook county, and you want to avoid government bureaucratic harassment, you did business with him.

But Sutherland had never had any dealings, positive or negative, with Tunney. He couldn't remember the last time they had seen one another. Perhaps good old Reggie could shed light on what happened during Doug's father's era. He might know about videos and whether money was stolen and, if so, by whom and what had happened to it.

Sutherland picked up the telephone and a moment later reached Tunney's secretary. She was cold and protective, but when Sutherland dropped his name, she put him on hold. After a moment she was back on the line and granted him an appointment for breakfast the following day. "The University Club. Seven thirty sharp. Mr. Tunney doesn't like to be kept waiting."

As he sat staring into space wondering what else he could be doing on the Delaney matter, Sutherland's secretary walked in and placed a message slip on his desk. He lifted the phone and punched in the number.

"Veronica Jamison."

"Ronnie? What's with the formality?"

"People I deal with don't want cute. Reason I called—Billy tell you I'm going to Niagara Falls?"

"Yeah. Find what the police couldn't."

"Idiots," she scoffed. "They believe Scooch's killer took the notebook, so they didn't push the aunt. If it was me, I'd have had a warrant."

"You think sweet talk will work on her?"

"She probably lives on Social Security. I'll buy it."

"Bill's paper pay for that?"

"You kidding? I'll spring for it. Compared with what I win or lose in a day, it'll be peanuts," she said. "Since Billy can't go, he suggested you."

"When?"

"The police asked the Niagara Falls cops to put surveillance on the old lady's house. Stanley Vislowski was vague about when they'll remove it, but we've gotta see her as soon as they leave and he gives up the address. He's being a little difficult."

"I thought you and Bill had some quid pro quo with him."

"When it's in his interest," she said. "I'll get the name and address another way. Then we wait until the police leave. You with me?"

He thought about the Mac race Saturday. He'd never missed it, not once since returning from his wanderings south of the border. This year he could win it. He and his crew had worked hard during the spring and early summer. Tonight was to be their last practice before the start, three hours of sail changes, jibes, and tacks. They would be ready.

"When do you think the police will leave?" he asked.

"No more than a week."

"By then the Mac will be over. I'll keep in touch and meet you there."

"How long is the race?"

"From Saturday, two days, more or less, depending on the weather. From Chicago to the island, 333 miles on the rhumb line. You want to know more, I've got a proposal. There's a party at the yacht club tomorrow night. Drinks, food, a band, sailboats rafted up all along the docks."

"I'm not much into yachting. Seems boring."

"The yacht club's at the foot of Monroe. My boat will be in the slip on the left as you come in. Name's *Circe*. Dark-blue hull."

"Thanks, but—"

"At dinner you said you like horse racing. Tomorrow night will be like the paddock where you see the entries and pick your winners. I'll even have the latest news. I'm meeting one of Danny's old friends tomorrow. Reginald Tunney. I might have something Bill can use."

After a moment's silence she said, "Maybe I will. What time?"

# Chapter 34

The next morning, torrential rain awaited Sutherland outside the front entrance to his high-rise condominium. He searched up and down the street then, looking up, appealed for help from the taxi strobe light pulsing over the lobby canopy. His suspicions could well be true: when it rained, half the taxi drivers stayed home in a perverse and rebellious pact. After waiting fifteen minutes, he gave up and ordered his Jaguar from the valet garage.

Through the downpour and spray from breaking waves along Lake Shore Drive, Sutherland inched south, cursing the water that dribbled on his leg from the leak where the window didn't quite couple with the convertible top. An insult to cap the long night and dismal morning. He hadn't slept at all well, opening his eyes every half hour to curse at the numbers on the digital clock on his bedside table. It must have been four thirty before he dozed off.

He sifted through the events of the last ten days, his thoughts stretched thinly between hope and dread at where this Delaney business might be taking him. Hope that it would all amount to nothing, dread that he'd find a worse truth, one that would sink his project and further implicate his father.

It was a long shot that Reginald Tunney could or would help. He had certainly been around then, part of the Raskoff crowd, in the midst of the city's development and power circle. He'd rubbed elbows with all the players: Danny Delaney, Miles Langer, Benjamin Gorman, Gene Sandler, and Sutherland's father. But Doug Sutherland didn't know how deeply Tunney was involved, because unlike the others, he was never mentioned in the articles about Delaney that he'd read. The man kept a low profile.

Since leaving Raskoff, Tunney had gone out alone to continue what he had been doing: commercial building leasing and management. In fifteen years he had slowly grown his operation into a second- or third-tier Chicago company, managing a few older office buildings in the Loop. As real estate businesses go, management wasn't as flashy as development or brokerage, but it provided a steady, low-risk income year after year. But unless you happened to enter one of the buildings his firm managed and saw its name in the elevator, you wouldn't know it existed.

Entering the University Club's Cathedral Hall, Sutherland spotted Tunney at a corner table. It was an enormous stone and wood-beamed room, a replica of an old English manor. Its Gothic arches and tall, leaded windows reached nearly fifty feet, and high overhead, heraldic crests of America's oldest universities reminded visitors of the Club's roots. Sitting with his morning paper, a waiter pouring coffee at his elbow, Tunney was a picture of the lord of the manor.

"Morning, my boy," he said, setting his newspaper down. "Rotten day."

"An understatement," Sutherland said. As he took the chair opposite, he caught the older man's eyes crinkling in satisfaction as he assessed Sutherland's sodden pants.

Another waiter arrived with a cart and began setting plates in front of Tunney. "I wasn't sure when you'd arrive, so I ordered." Tunney unfolded his napkin onto his lap.

Tunney had a sharp nose, long face, and a large, bony frame under his expensive suit. His skin was webbed with purple veins, and his eyes had a yellow cast around the irises. His manner of speaking suggested he had spent time in England, though it might have been an affectation.

The poached eggs and toast seemed meager for a man several inches taller than Sutherland. It was, because the waiter then cleared room in the center of the table and added a plate of bacon and another of home fries. The aroma made Sutherland's stomach grumble.

But he was here with a purpose and needed to focus. "I'll just have coffee," he said to the waiter.

"Well, my boy, you're getting to be more famous every day. First the fight with the preservationists, now with this Delaney matter. I'm surprised you've got the time to see old acquaintances."

"That's why I'm here. Your acquaintance with my father."

The older gentleman smiled wryly. "If you're looking for a job, there's always an opening for the son of an old friend."

"Thanks, but I've got a full plate right now."

"You certainly do. I should congratulate you on the Broadwell deal. It must have felt good to beat out Jules. He's such a lousy loser."

"It was a tough fight."

"And it's going well? I heard a rumor that there was a bump in the road. Some rethinking going on in headquarters."

What a small world real estate was. Everyone knew someone who was connected to someone else. A few rumblings at Broadwell Communications in New York reached Chicago as fast as wires and satellites could speed them.

"Nothing serious. Langer's still stirring up trouble."

Tunney laughed, a throaty roar that turned a few heads their way from other tables. "That spoiled prick," he said more quietly. "If he hadn't inherited that business he'd be a shoe clerk someplace. I ought to know. I married his sister. Peas in a pod."

The revelation that Tunney and Langer were linked by marriage was news to Sutherland. Then again, what difference did it make? "How well did you know my father?"

"We were associates in some deals," Tunney said between mouthfuls. He ate with the fork in his left hand, tines curved downward, like the British he seemed to imitate. "That thing at the end was too bad. He didn't have to confess. They couldn't have proven it."

Sutherland's coffee arrived and he added cream and sweetener. "No? Then why did he?"

"Who knows? Didn't he explain it to you?"

"I didn't stick around for his excuses. He died before I returned."

"So why the interest now? First Gorman, now me."

"You know I saw Gorman?"

"We talked from time to time. He said you'd called and he was going to meet you. Did he help?" Tunney waited, fork suspended, appraising Sutherland through cool, gray eyes.

"He didn't know about Delaney's notebook. Did you?"

"Not until I read about it." He slipped a strip of bacon into his mouth. It crunched as he chewed. Crisp, the way Sutherland liked it also.

Sutherland sipped his coffee, trying to ignore his growling stomach. "What about the money?" he asked.

"Like you, I read the paper. But then, maybe you already knew."

"No." Sutherland picked up a fork, examined its luster with the careful eye of a headwaiter, and replaced it. The next point was important. "Gorman said you all knew about that money. Why would he lie?"

Tunney seemed momentarily unnerved by the question. He stiffened and stretched his neck, thrusting out his chin as if his shirt collar was too tight. "Lying was an art form with Gorman." He pointed at the bacon with his fork. "Take some. You look hungry."

The conversation was going nowhere. Tunney was fencing, denying any knowledge or involvement. Before Sutherland would admit defeat, he'd try a different tack. "Tell me, Reggie. You must have suspected why I wanted to meet. Why bother if you don't know shit about anything?"

Tunney soaked up the last of his egg yolk with a piece of toast, stuffed it into his mouth, and chewed it as if it were his thoughts. He dabbed his mouth with his napkin and sipped his water. When he looked at Sutherland again, he said, "Curiosity. It's intriguing. What happened to the money? What about those tapes the reporter writes about? Did the feds get their hands on Delaney's stuff, or is it still missing? What do you think?"

"FBI's already come to see me. About money, videos, and that fucking book."

Tunney raised an eyebrow and nodded philosophically. "Why wouldn't they? It seems to me that a man like your father must have left some trail."

"Like what? Crumbs, dollar bills? There's nothing there."

"You're saying you haven't a clue? It's hard to believe."

"Until a week ago, I didn't know the first thing about any of this. That book started it all. I should have bought and burned it."

"Does that reporter really know its whereabouts?"

"He's just selling newspapers." No use adding another hound to the chase.

"More like chumming the water around him, my boy. It's just a story to him, but it's indictments and loss of power and money to others. If he was smart, he'd burn it." Tunney folded his napkin and arranged it neatly on the table. "But you never really answered my question. Why your interest now? Not just because you find a dead alderman in your building. Is it the money?"

If only Sutherland knew for sure. On one hand, he wanted to snuff out any story and repercussions before they derailed his deal with Broadwell. Yet, deep down he had this morbid interest in knowing how involved or guilty his father really was.

Before Sutherland could answer, Tunney pushed his chair back and got to his feet. "If you find it, let's split it fifty-fifty," he said, chuckling. "Find anything else, I'll help you burn it." Then he turned and headed to the entrance, shoulders back and head high, strutting regally, as if he were born and raised in the grand hall towering around him.

# CHAPTER 35

George Spanos was sitting in his Chicago living room with a tall glass of vodka on ice when his cell phone rang. He looked at the caller ID and cursed the day they'd invented the damn things. It was his Chicago public relations manager, Irene Russo. Couldn't she give it a rest? It was Friday night, TGIF and all that. He'd had a long day, visits to union groups and citizen centers sandwiched around a potluck lunch in a Brownville church basement. He needed to rest up for another marathon weekend, including a major fundraiser on Saturday night and a pancake breakfast on Sunday, downstate.

"Didn't we say good evening a few minutes ago in the car?" he said, answering.

"We did, but I've got something new to discuss."

"Can't wait until tomorrow?"

"You tell me. It's a reporter. The one that's writing about the Delaney thing. William Jamison."

"What about him?" Spanos took a large gulp of vodka and steeled himself.

"He'd like an interview, or at least some comments on an article he's running, possibly in this Sunday's *Tribune*."

"Comments? Like what? What's he writing?" the congressman asked, his voice rising.

"Why so excited? It could be good for us. He's asking about your time in the state's attorney's office and what you can remember about Danny Delaney—how well you knew him, and whether you had anything on him. You can build up your anticrime reputation. Like, you were ready to nail him when he disappeared."

"That's it?" Maybe she was right. Even though Spanos hadn't been part of the investigation's inner circle, who could prove otherwise? The lead FBI agent, John Durham, was dead, and fifteen years had transpired. No one would know if he exaggerated his role a little. But there were risks with being associated with Delaney. It could be a trap.

"There was another thing. The reporter asked me if I knew anything about a limited real estate partnership called Park Place III, whether you were ever an investor. It's not on your disclosure statements, so I told him no."

"Jesus H. Christ," Spanos rasped. How did he ever find out about that? The building had been sold years ago.

"Something wrong?" she asked.

"This guy's trouble, Irene. Mucking around looking for mud to throw. I already talked to his editor and told him in so many words that if there were any insinuations, I'd go to their chairman and general manager. They endorsed me for Christ's sake. This guy's a loose cannon."

"I'm sorry, I just thought—"

"Just tell him I'm too busy to comment. I'll see you tomorrow." After he disconnected, he slugged down what was left of his drink and plunked the glass hard on the coffee table.

"Are you all right?" his wife asked as she entered the living room from the kitchen. "Hard day on the campaign trail?"

Spanos turned around in his chair to see her and forced a smile. "Yeah. Scheduled too much and got a little cranky."

"You up for some dinner? I could whip up some pasta."

"Sounds good. Gotta make another call first. Give me a minute."

When she left the room, he walked over to the wet bar and poured himself another three fingers of vodka. After dropping in a few more cubes, he went back to his leather armchair and punched in a private number.

"Governor, how are you?" the reedy voice answered.

"Not good. What are we doing about this Delaney thing? Now the reporter's nosing around me. Asking how well I knew him. He knows something, I'm sure of it. Something in the notebook."

There was silence for a few seconds before Gene Sandler spoke again. "Interesting. And unfortunate," he mused. "So he thinks he's got something."

"He also found out about that building deal you put me into. I didn't want a part of it in the first place. Now it connects me with you."

"And you made money on it, which is what we wanted. It breeds loyalty."

"You don't have enough hooks in me?" Spanos said.

"No worries. That deal was put together after Danny was dead, and it sold a long time ago. History. It's the fact the reporter's asking about you and Danny that's troubling. Very telling."

"What about those tapes he's writing about? Could I be in them?"

"We don't know what Danny taped or how long he was doing it. We were all in his place, one time or another. You too, if I remember correctly."

How could he forget? No matter how hard he tried, it was forever burned into his memory, like the rest of that awful year. "So what are you doing about it?" Spanos asked.

"One step at a time. From what you said, the notebook's more dangerous than I thought, and it's not the only thing the reporter's snooping in. He's trouble." There was pause, and Spanos heard the click of a cigarette lighter before Sandler continued. "You ever hear of an FBI guy named Mark Branson?"

Another name he'd like to forget. "Yeah. He was on the Delaney case. Worked for Durham."

"Use your contacts and call him off. With all the emphasis on homeland security, why's the FBI spending time on an ancient case? Got it?"

"Can do," Spanos said, though he doubted that he had that kind of clout with the FBI. Making a stink about misguided federal priorities would only call attention to what he'd like to bury.

"Next, talk to the *Tribune*. They trying to torpedo their own candidate? We'll work on that from our end too."

"Already on it."

"Good. Meanwhile, keep stumping."

"Wait," Spanos said, summoning the nerve to ask the question. "What's with Delaney's murder? You told me he'd split, taken off with the money."

"It shouldn't surprise a politician, George. You know you gotta tell people what they want to hear."

# Chapter 36

Belowdecks in *Circe's* navigation station, Sutherland was studying weather charts and forecasts for the race's start and the ensuing days when he heard his name called from the dock. *That's all the work for today*, he thought, recognizing Ronnie's voice. He'd finish the course planning in the morning with the latest reports.

With help from three of his crew, Doug had spent most of Friday preparing for the race. They'd moved *Circe* to a temporary slip at the Chicago Yacht Club at Monroe Street, stowed food for ten crewmen, inspected rigging, equipment, and sails, unloaded unneeded weight, and planned tentative routes, subject to the final weather conditions. The remaining preparation would be completed in the morning when the whole crew arrived.

Sutherland stuck his head up through the companionway and saw Ronnie's hair, bright red in the blush of sunset. She stood on the dock wearing a green tennis shirt, white shorts, and a white cotton sweater tied round her neck by the sleeves. He noticed her leather-soled loafers. Right lady, but wrong shoes for a boat.

"Come aboard. But take off those shoes. Slippery," he said.

Ignoring his advice, she stepped through the opening of the boat's lifelines, around the genoa winch, onto the cockpit seats, and down into the cockpit itself.

"What is all this stuff?" she said, looking around her, eyes wide and inquisitive. "More gadgets and whatchamacallits …"

"Standard stuff."

She stopped her gaze on the banks of digital lights on the mast just above the flush deck. "What are all those numbers?"

"Boat speed, wind speed, direction, depth, so on."

"This and this?"

"Grinder and winch. You want it all at once, or a little at a time?"

"Spoon feeding, please; there's too much of it." She touched the chrome finish of the mainsheet winch, seeing her distorted reflection in its mirrored top. "Seriously, this looks complicated. When you said sailboat, I pictured a little …"

"Dinghy?"

"I'm not sure. But this is huge."

"She's only forty-five feet. You'll see much bigger ones here along the dock. Come on below. Careful with those shoes."

"I'll be okay." But two steps down the gangway, she slipped, banging down three rungs on hip and leg before ending in a heap on the cabin floor.

Sutherland bent over to help her and she got up, wincing, eyes wet.

"Damn," he said. "Should've had you sign a disclaimer."

"It's not funny."

"Sorry. Want some ice for it?"

"No," she snapped in a hurt tone.

"How about a beer … drink?"

"Beer," she said, rubbing her leg and hip, grimacing.

He handed her a Foster's from the refrigerator. *Spurns advice and has a temper*, he thought, noting the flush of color recede from her cheeks, her green eyes soften. *Can't fault her looks though.*

She scanned the interior and sipped the foam off the can. "Now this is more like it. More like a house." She wandered to the forward hold and back, registering the details of the custom-built yacht, which Sutherland had bought from Jules Langer. "Rooms, beds, bathroom, and even a kitchen."

"It's a galley, but it works the same." He opened a beer for himself, quickly slurping the spreading spume.

Ronnie sat in the navigation seat and inspected the GPS, radar screen, radios, and personal computer, each built into the instrument panel. "This looks serious. And expensive."

"It was, but not for me. I bought her at a big discount."

"Her?"

"*Circe.*"

"Oh," she said, with a puzzled squint. "Sounds familiar, but …"

"Circe's a Greek goddess in *The Odyssey*. A temptress."

"Oh yeah," Ronnie said vaguely. "That why it's feminine?"

"Most boats and ships are."

"Sure," she said sarcastically. "Another thing men think they own."

"Tradition. No big deal."

"Traditions like that keep women down."

"End of lecture?"

"Done."

"Good, let's go boogie. The band's started." And just in time, he thought.

*     *     *

119

Stretching from the Shedd Aquarium on the south to the two yacht clubs on the north, hundreds of moored sailboats in Monroe Harbor pointed west, into the wind, like an armada advancing through the light chop on Chicago's shores. On the closest can, a classic-lined sloop with a black hull and long fore and aft overhangs reminded Sutherland of his father's *Gabriela*, named after Sutherland's mother. Then his attention was caught by a trawler, a high-bridged cabin cruiser weaving through the moored sailboats looking like an overstuffed turkey among a flight of seagulls. His father had owned a boat like that, but he hadn't much cared for it, only using it for fishing, an occasional cruise, entertainment, or as a race committee boat.

At the club dock, sailboats rocked easily, their pennants drifting in the breeze. When the rock-and-roll band erupted, a charged-up crowd collided on the patio. The annual pre-Mac race party was in full swing.

After a half hour dancing under the rising moon, Sutherland and Ronnie, perspiring and contentedly enervated, strolled along the dock past sailboats rafted four abreast into the harbor.

"These boats are from all over," he said. "Each one will take anywhere from a half-dozen up to fifteen or twenty crew, depending on the size. We work in shifts, nonstop, for as many hours as it takes. Sometimes a couple days."

"You're just sitting there? For days? Talk about boring."

"Not for me. It is for the crew at times, sitting along the rail for hours at a time. But there's always sail changes and storms to keep us busy."

"I'd need more action. Even if I could still trade or place bets through my BlackBerry, I'd go nuts cooped up with nothing but ropes and pulleys."

"Lines and blocks. No ropes on a boat."

"Look like ropes. What's that?" She pointed, smiling at him.

"The main sheet."

"Not a rope?"

"Every rope has a name. Need specificity for communication."

"Specificity's a word should be outlawed at a party. Should stick to four-letter words—like beer. Let's get a cold one."

Ronnie walked ahead through a gap in the crowd, and Sutherland noticed the ugly bruise darkening her thigh from her tumble down the companionway. The anatomical survey, encompassing her athletic legs and rolling hips, inspired him. "You ever been to Mackinac Island?"

"No," she said over her shoulder.

"Why don't you come, after the race. It's a party."

"I've got to be ready when the police lift the surveillance on Scooch's aunt. Niagara Falls, remember?"

"We can go from the island. It's closer."

Before she could comment, Sutherland saw Jules Langer, in crisp white slacks and blue blazer with a billowing navy-blue ascot at his open neck. He would wear a tux to a beach party. Clinging to his arm was an attractive blond in tight slacks, a low-cut blouse, and with a tan that surpassed Langer's. A typical Langer trophy since his well-publicized divorce.

"Doug," Langer said, stopping so abruptly his blond friend stumbled into him. "I figured I might run into you. You got a minute?"

"What's up, Jules?"

"It's about the thing, you know, that we talked about? You hear anything?" His date stood gazing around her, as if the club, the boats, the stars, the moon, everything bored her to tears.

Ronnie stepped forward and said, "Jules Langer, right?" She held out her hand. "Ronnie Jamison. I'm Bill Jamison's sister. The reporter for the *Tribune*."

Langer blinked, and he looked startled. "Oh, nice to meet you." He shook her hand, a wary expression on his face.

"Bill saw you the other night," Ronnie continued. "When you met with the man that got killed. Scooch his name? Anyway, no luck with the notebook?"

"He claims not," Sutherland said. "Right, Jules?"

"What is this?" Langer said, fuming. "An ambush?"

"Take it easy," Sutherland said. "It's no secret, you meeting Scooch. And if you want to know about news, Ronnie's the one to ask."

"So that's how the police knew I'd met with him," Langer said. "Your brother followed me?"

"Followed Scooch," she said.

"The police asked me about it today, but I couldn't help much. Just said that I tried to buy it. Your brother has it or knows where it is."

"He used to," the reporter's sister said. "But with Scooch murdered, it's a dead end."

"His articles say otherwise," Langer insisted.

"He's a good bluffer," she said.

*And she's a good liar*, Sutherland thought as he said, "It may be lost forever. Better for everybody."

"You're probably right." Langer didn't seem convinced, more like disappointed. He turned to his date, who had been standing a few steps to the side, and said, "Sorry, hon. Let's go."

Sutherland scanned the rows of sailboats rafted off the club's dock, but he didn't see Langer's. "How's your new crew?" He'd heard that Langer had brought on several crewmen and a helmsman from an America's Cup team. There were no rules against professionals, and Langer's wouldn't be the only boat using them. But the vast majority of the skippers and crew were amateurs, weekend sailors who did it for the fun, challenge, and competition.

Langer puffed out his ascot with a manicured hand. "We're ready."

"With those ringers sailing for you, why don't you skip the race and wait on the island? Why risk getting wet and seasick?"

"Thanks for the advice, Doug," he said, taking his date's hand. "Come on, Sherry." He nearly jerked the woman off her feet as he tramped past Sutherland and Ronnie into the crowd.

"So he's in the race?" Ronnie asked as they disappeared.

"Big time. A few years back, he spent a fortune on a specially designed boat and still finished near the back of the fleet. He sold the boat to me. I renamed her and have been doing pretty well ever since. He bought an even more expensive one and hasn't done much better. That's why he brought in the pros."

"You expect to win?"

"Good chance. I finished second overall a year ago." It was true, and it had been a real test: trusting his crew rather than micromanaging was new for him. In the past he had lost more than one crewmember by being too much like Captain Queeg or Bligh. He was lucky he'd never had a mutiny.

"Only second?" Ronnie said, disdainfully.

"You make it sound like losing. Three hundred entries. First in my section," Sutherland said, grinning.

"It's still second," she said. "What's so funny? You're laughing at me."

"Maybe a little. You don't know port from starboard, but finish anything but first and you're a loser. My crew could take lessons from you."

"Now you're patronizing."

"No. I could use more competitive attitudes."

"I know all about that. I started tennis at seven. I almost turned pro."

"Almost?"

"Was asked to leave the junior tour. Bad loser." She gulped down the remains from her beer cup. "Now where's that cold beer we talked about? On the way you can tell me about your talk with Reginald Tunney."

"Not much there. He plays it close to the vest. Thinks your brother is playing with fire, pursuing that notebook story. Too many people want those tapes to stay hidden or destroyed. Including him, though he's a good actor, seemingly unworried. Was evasive about the money, wouldn't say who took it or from where. Only that it's still missing." Once again Sutherland stopped himself from mentioning the casino skim or sale proceeds that Benjamin Gorman and Agent Branson had mentioned. If Ronnie and her brother knew about it, it would be in the paper tomorrow.

She stopped walking and faced him. "The money's still missing? After all this time? What else?"

"Just that the FBI doesn't seem as bothered about it as they are the videos."

"So add money to fear of exposure and you have Scooch's and Gorman's murders."

"Remember what Tunney said about playing with fire. Don't get Bill revved up about it. Okay?"

"I hear you," she said, but he didn't believe her. Odds were he'd read all about it tomorrow.

The dock leading to *Circe* was choked with crew and their friends ambling past the sailboats. When they arrived at *Circe's* temporary slip, six of Sutherland's crew, another half-dozen wives or girlfriends with them, were departing with drinks in hand.

"Party's moving on," Sutherland said.

Amidst laughter and hooting, the happy group filed along the dock through the crowd. "See you later, Skip," the last of them called to him.

Just then, a radiant face with chestnut hair appeared in the companionway.

"Kelly," Sutherland said, uncomfortably. "What brings you here?"

Kelly's eyes narrowed as she glanced at Ronnie, then back at him. But the brightness returned and she smiled. "I brought you some good luck presents." She held up a bottle of Dom Pérignon.

She vaulted up the last two steps and handed Sutherland the champagne. He looked down at the bottle. "Thank you, that's real …"

"Just have a sip for me on the island. And the other present," she said, grasping his shoulders and planting a wet kiss on his cheek before he could resist, "is from Jenny. She says have a safe race and she loves you."

Sutherland felt the flush in his face and wondered whether the heat was from embarrassment, irritation, or something more physical. The smell of Kelly's perfume reminded him of old times.

"Make sure you call her when you finish," Kelly said. "She's going to be following you on the race website."

"I will," he said, wondering how he was going to tactfully ease Kelly off the boat.

"Well, I'll be going." She glanced at Ronnie. "I'm Kelly. Nice meeting you, Red." Before Ronnie could answer, Kelly sprung over the cockpit, combing onto the dock, a graceful movement Sutherland had seen countless times before. Singing a final "have a good race," she waved and bounced along the dock onto shore.

He turned in time to see Ronnie following the other woman with an appraising gaze. "Your ex-wife?"

"An old friend."

"Jenny your wife?"

"My daughter. The kiss was meant to be from her."

"You going to open that?" she asked, pointing to the champagne bottle.

"Hell no. It's for the finish line, when we win."

"At Mackinac."

"Yep."

"Will she be there? Your old friend?"

"She does her own thing now. I'll get us some beer."

"That offer still open? About meeting in Mackinac?"

"Don't you want to wait for the results? In case we don't win?"

"Now you're definitely laughing at me." Ronnie placed a hand on his forearm, turning him to look into her eyes.

"Maybe a little," he said, returning her gaze. "How'll you find out when the police give up on Scooch's aunt?"

"I'll check from the island. We'll leave from there."

"Then here's to Mackinac." He raised the bottle.

She rose up on her toes and kissed his cheek, lingering longer than necessary, sending her own scent into Sutherland's nerve center. "That's for winning," she said in a breathy whisper. "Good luck."

He smiled and said, "Careful there. We don't want to make *Circe* jealous."

# Chapter 37

Eugene Sandler eased his massive body into his desk chair and sighed. It was more exhausting every year, the pounds piling on, the cigarettes shortening his breath. Neils, his driver and bodyguard, had left him at the curb, and after climbing the single flight of front stairs to his gray, stone house, he felt his heart racing and his chest about to burst. His onetime doctor's exhortations echoed in his mind like his mother's had years earlier: lose some weight, stop smoking. But his mother was long dead and he'd stopped seeing physicians; their advice was always the same. Eating and smoking were his only physical pleasures. Drinking nauseated him, drugs interfered with clear thought, and sex had never been possible.

In any event, it wasn't anything physical that drove him. His satisfaction came from power, the wielded club over those who thought themselves superior by virtue of their normalcy. If Sandler ever thought of God at all, it was with a bitter memory of unanswered prayers as a boy, of unhelpful priests and unsympathetic nuns. Cheated at birth, rebuffed by the church and heavenly powers, he was justified in making his own rules and scoffing at conventional mores.

From an early age, errant chromosomes had made a typical childhood impossible. He was a hermaphrodite, and the decision that he should be raised as a male was made between his parents and medical specialists. Based upon his ambiguous external genitalia, the choice was tantamount to a coin flip. But gender identification wasn't his only problem. Classmates called him Magoo because of his thick glasses and perpetual squint. His poor eyesight excused him from gym class, thus avoiding further persecution from boys in the locker room and showers.

While his peers were in gym and on sports teams, he concentrated on schoolwork, where he excelled, toiling over his books through Coke-bottle lenses. He learned chess and became captain of the team, joined the debate team, and led the school to win the state finals. Let the athletes and the popular kids have their fun; he was going to own them someday, though it would be a few years before he would learn exactly how.

At the age of thirteen, ninth grade, when other boys began maturing,

Sandler could only look on jealously. In his few visits to the boys' locker room, peeking into the showers, he saw the changes in the others—testicles developing, pubic hair sprouting—knowing he would never experience the same metamorphosis. His parents took him to specialists who prescribed hormones, but nothing worked. He was an in-between, a eunuch, a soprano, a male without *cajones*. His voice would never deepen, he would never sire children, never experience an orgasm. With hormones, he could have grown a beard of sorts, but he declined. The one step he took to hide his condition was voice lessons, learning to force his speech to lower the register an octave. It sounded reedy and croaky, but at least he wasn't taken as a choir boy.

An eye operation had mixed results. His vision improved, but he was left with an excruciating sensitivity to light, necessitating dark glasses outdoors and tinted lenses inside. In his freshman year at the University of Illinois his nickname changed from Magoo to Hollywood. That only lasted until he learned how to earn a fearful respect.

In college he'd studied psychology and management and started a small real estate business on the side. He parlayed a four flat he inherited from his father into two strip malls and a twenty-four-unit apartment building by his senior year. Observing that his classmates were always short of money, he got into the lending business, using some local roughnecks as collectors when necessary. More than one delinquent debtor had ended with a broken arm or thumbs.

Upon graduation he started work for Raskoff Real Estate. It was in this venerable firm that he began learning how the Chicago machine worked, lessons he would later perfect and take to a new level, more daring and corrupt, but with commensurately lucrative results. Old man Raskoff, an old-school grafter, placed boundaries on the company's sleaze. Had he known how well Sandler and the others had perfected the corruption, he would have fired them all. Years after Raskoff died, when the company finally dissolved, Sandler took his connections, insider knowledge, and IOUs and formed his own company. He found there was no end to what greed, extortion, bribery, and threats could accomplish.

For centuries, philanthropy has burnished many a reputation, painted over the tarnish associated with unscrupulous moneymaking. With Sandler in Chicago it was no different. How many charities or nonprofits turned down seven-figure donations in return for a seat on the board, feigning ignorance of the manner in which the money was made? Sandler served on four boards, including an art museum, a ballet troupe, and a symphony. His name was etched on placards recognizing large donors, and an auditorium at his alma mater bore his name. It amused him when he attended galas and openings to have bejeweled women in fancy gowns and men in designer tuxes suck up to him. Some of them whispered about him behind his back, believing they knew some secret about his private life or business. Those who really knew anything kept their silence.

That same silence was even more essential now. This trouble with Delaney's legacy had to be squelched, and it was clear that the starting point was the *Tribune* reporter. Could he be bought? Scared off? Put in a compromising position to be blackmailed into being reasonable? It had worked on others, not the least of whom was George Spanos. In fact the call from Spanos was the tipping point, adding to what Sandler had just learned about that reporter snooping into his accountant's files. It was time to act, to place his opponent in check.

Sandler picked up his phone and made the first of the calls to set the pawns in motion.

# Chapter 38

## SATURDAY, JULY 21

Ronnie Jamison had spent early Saturday morning in her apartment studying stock market charts, researching oil and commodity data, and quantifying gaps between exchanges and countries looking for arbitrage opportunities. She needed to change her luck. After hours of calculations, note taking, and establishing stop and buy orders for her brokers, she switched her focus to the weekend sporting and racing events. But before she could place any bets, the phone rang. Her caller ID indicated it was her brother.

"Billy, what's up?"

"Vislowski called. The Niagara Falls police gave up the watch on Scooch's aunt. Chicago's cops convinced themselves Scooch's killer took the book."

"They're just lazy. He gave you her address?"

"On the condition that if we find it, he gets a copy and some credit."

"You agreed of course, you whore," she said, laughing. "As if—"

"Maybe after I finish with it. Are you ready to go? We can't waste any time. Others might know about the aunt, and I'm meeting with Robert Hurley this weekend. He's nervous about pulling those tax files, so I've got some persuading to do."

"Your seductive powers not up to it? You disappoint me."

"What about you? Is Doug going with you?"

"He's tied up in that race. I'll go alone. In fact, he'd be in the way, want to bury the story."

"I thought you liked him. More going for him than some of your choices."

"What's your point?" she snapped, riled at being reminded of her trail of broken relationships. Her brother knew which buttons to push, especially her history of failed romances, some of them ending tragically. Like her college professor's firing, a law partner's attempted suicide, a judge's divorce, not to mention a few less disastrous endings in between. The breakup with

Vislowski still rankled, and Vislowski wouldn't let the relationship die the death it deserved.

"Sorry I brought it up," Jamison said.

"Just forget it," Ronnie said, willing herself to settle down. Her brother had a point. Sutherland was a step up from Vislowski and the others. Last night at the yacht club party she decided he was something of a hottie: tall, athletic, good-looking. Admitting it to Billy was another matter.

"Doug can help us," Jamison continued. "He's hyper about all this. If this book and my other research dig up more dirt on his father, it could cost him big-time. He acts like he's helping me, but it's just to protect himself and get a jump. Like getting to Gorman before I could. And he's already seen Langer and Tunney and hasn't said much about what he knows. If we stay close, we may learn something."

"So I should stick close."

"Not a bad deal, knowing you …"

"What about the notebook?"

"If you get it from the aunt, send it here. Don't let him see it until I have everything I need."

"He won't be happy if I show up without it."

"If you can't finesse that, you've lost your touch. He's got to protect himself from more bad publicity, and that means being first at getting the whole story. And here's some added incentive: besides the corruption and murder angle, there's still the matter of the money. I'm betting there's no separating the money and Sutherland's father. How's your net worth these days?"

*What net worth?* she thought as she glanced at one of the trading screens on her desk. "I guess I'm going to Mackinac Island after I see Scooch's aunt." Not such a bad assignment, all things considered.

# Chapter 39

On the second evening of the Mac race, thirty hours after the start, the crew of Sutherland's yacht glanced astern to see a storm gaining on them from the southwest. They stole anxious glances at the building clouds, a purple mass climbing, piling higher with each minute. As the daylight faded, they saw the first flashes and counted off until hearing the thunderclap, estimating the ever-closing distance. The weather report called for squalls, but on the lake beyond sight of land, you never knew.

As the dark curtain overtook *Circe*, every few seconds the heavens lit up with myriad jagged lightning bolts, silver daggers slashing into the black lake. In one flash Sutherland made out Jules Langer's boat to port. He had been shadowing *Circe* from the start, which was good news, because *Julia* would owe handicap time to *Circe*.

Expecting the worst, Sutherland decided to shorten sail, and Dirk ran forward with his foredeck crew while others wrestled a reef in the main. When the full force of the squall hit, crew scrambled for handholds as the wind clocked ninety degrees and slammed the boat on its side. The wind speed indicator said fifty knots, but no one needed to look—the whistling rigging said it all. Sutherland saw a flash of yellow in the water to starboard and someone cried, *"Man overboard!"*

"Jesus," another shouted. "It's Dirk!"

# Chapter 40

Night sounds drifted through Robert Hurley's bedroom window. A neighbor's air conditioner, Lake Shore Drive traffic, a faraway siren, a car horn's angry bray.

Bill Jamison heard only his pounding heart and rapid breathing, one rhythm within another. Slumped in post-sexual collapse, he studied the profile of the young man lying beside him and felt a stab of remorse. What was he becoming? What had this obsession for a story driven him to? This conquest hadn't been for love, not even for lust. This time a career-making exclusive was at stake.

He remembered the party where he had met Robert six weeks ago. The loft apartment had been packed, and Jamison hadn't noticed the young man until he'd overheard him say, "I work for Gene Sandler's accountant." Jamison had edged closer in the crowd and listened while the young man lamented on how his acting talent suffered at the hands of blind critics and fickle directors, how his need to pay the rent forced him to find a more conventional job. "But it's so boring. Real estate partnerships, tax returns … boring."

Eugene Sandler's company. Just what he needed, Jamison had thought. A source for linking the takers with the corruptors. Proof that the trail he'd been following wasn't a series of coincidences, that his investigation had uncovered a decades-old conspiracy. He had studied the young man, assessing the anxious eyes, the quivering lips, wondering how he could exploit the insecurity he sensed, while asking himself whether he should. It might be dangerous for the young man, and Jamison would hate himself for stooping that low. But he wanted the story; it promised to be a blockbuster. With Delaney's notebook and Sandler's tax files, the connections would be clear as day.

He swung his legs from the bed and pulled on his shorts. "I'm counting on you tomorrow night, Robert." He sipped from a glass of stale beer on the dressing table and waited.

"Robert, I know you're awake. The partnership files. The tax forms, like we planned?"

"I'm going to get caught," Robert said, his voice muffled by the pillow he was hugging.

"You won't. We'll have them copied and back in the warehouse by next weekend. No one will know."

Robert sat up against the headboard. "You don't know Mr. Sandler. He looks like a big, fat marshmallow but he's smart. And mean."

"How's he going to know? He hasn't caught on to what you've already taken. They probably don't even realize the records are there."

"They're bound to be suspicious. All the time I spent looking. What if someone sees us at the loading dock?"

"For God's sake, nothing's going to happen," Jamison said, irritated. "I'll be there tomorrow night at ten o'clock with the van, and you have the boxes ready."

Robert stretched out again and rolled onto his stomach. Jamison's gaze followed the line of the young man's back to the curve of his buttocks. The white, bikini-shaped cheeks against the long, tan legs. A twinge of excitement pricked Jamison.

"Bill?" Robert said. "I'm scared."

*     *     *

Two hours later, moonlight spilled through the window where Jamison and Robert slept. Out of the quiet the doorbell shrieked, sounding like a school fire alarm. Jamison bolted upright, wondering where he was, what had awakened him.

The bell screamed again.

"It's almost two o'clock," Jamison said to the inert form next to him. "Who is it?"

"The lobby. Ringing the wrong apartment," Robert muttered.

Again the bell raged, this time longer. Jamison stared at the ceiling, cringing at the sound. Robert pulled his pillow over his head. After an excruciating minute, the noise stopped, and the apartment sank into tomb-like quiet. Jamison closed his eyes.

But his drifting thoughts were shattered when the apartment door exploded with the sound of heavy pounding. The caller had gained entrance and climbed the stairs. From two rooms away the door demanded to be opened, booming a bass-drum cadence. It didn't stop.

"Jesus Christ," Robert said, crawling out of bed. He pulled on a short Japanese robe and padded down the corridor to the front door.

"Use the peephole," Jamison shouted after him. He walked to the bedroom door to listen.

The racket stopped, and Jamison heard unintelligible remarks—excited, surprised inflections. Then he heard the security chain rattle, the dead bolt thrown back, and Robert exclaim, "What are you doing here?"

Moments passed. Jamison listened, but the front room was silent.

"Robert?" he called. Nothing.

He pulled on his pants and went down the hall toward the dark living room. "Robert?" He smelled something out of place, something reminiscent of a doctor's office. In the dim light from the street he saw gray silhouettes. A sofa, a table, some lamps, a chair. Then he heard a moan and spotted a body sprawled by the couch. "Robert!"

After taking a step forward, Jamison's arms were pinned and he was slammed to the floor. Knocked breathless and immobilized by the attacker's weight and grip, he felt someone clap a wet cloth over his nose and mouth. This time he recognized the odor. He squirmed and kicked and resisted his hunger for air, but finally he inhaled the biting fumes and fought no more.

# CHAPTER 41

## MONDAY, JULY 23

At nine fifteen on Monday morning, after hours of drifting in the straits, hand-nursing the sails for every inch of forward progress under the long span of the Mackinac Bridge, they heard the gun signaling they'd crossed the finish line. They had five boat lengths on another boat in their class and were only a minute behind another that would owe them at least five minutes in the handicap system. Despite the man-overboard debacle, Sutherland might have still won his section, though not the overall race. The news that Langer's boat, *Julia*, had finished fifteen minutes earlier meant that Sutherland's old rival beat him. Bad luck, or carelessness? In either case, Dirk's ten-minute swim had probably cost *Circe* the trophy.

Sutherland tried to hide his disappointment as high fives, backslaps, and whoops resounded around *Circe*. The beer and champagne that had been on ice were brought topside, opened and, after toasts to the wind gods, guzzled. Tired but high on alcohol, adrenaline, and success, the crew hauled in and bagged the sails, cleared the deck of everything except the mooring lines, and ran up the fore and aft pennant strings of previous regatta wins. When they rounded the point into the harbor, they had their choice of spots on the dock. Only a dozen yachts had finished ahead of them, many of which would be giving *Circe* time. They put out bumpers, secured the bow, stern, and spring lines and, when the last line was made fast, let themselves fall back and relax.

In an attempt to conserve weight and space on the boat, Sutherland hadn't stocked all the booze. Instead he'd arranged for more beer and a case of champagne to be delivered from shore upon their arrival. Cheers greeted the new supply as the cases were wheeled down the dock. Five women followed, waving at their husbands or boyfriends on *Circe*. Behind the line of excited women, looking as if she wasn't sure she was in the right place, stood Ronnie.

"You win?" Ronnie said as two of Sutherland's crew helped her into the cockpit. Someone handed her a plastic cup and flooded it with champagne.

"We won't know until the handicap results are posted," Sutherland said. "We had a little problem."

"What happened? You didn't win?"

"I'd rather not talk about it." He clenched his jaw, remembering the rescue, the seconds ticking by, wondering whether they'd find the man and, after the relief of finding him, knowing they'd never make up the lost time. During it all, a ghost of a memory hit him. Of himself as a youngster, choking on water, sinking under the waves. He'd felt his old dread knot his stomach and gripped the wheel tighter, as if he himself were sinking, not Dirk.

"When will you know?" Ronnie asked.

"Could be a while. Every boat has a handicap based a host of measurements. We give time to some, others give time to us. So, we wait. Meanwhile, tell me about the notebook."

"Done deal. The police removed their surveillance on the aunt and I went and got it." She pumped her fist.

"How much did it cost?"

"Money wasn't the issue." Ronnie blew out a breath and drew her fingers through her hair. "First she handed me the same bull—the package only contained gloves." She laughed. "Great police work. Anyway, the old bat's lonely and would've talked for weeks. After four hours, gallons of tea, hundreds of photographs, a couple thousand dollars, and promises to write always, she still wouldn't give it up."

"What then?"

"I stopped being Miss Manners and threatened to beat the crap out of her."

"You're kidding."

"You think? She had it and I wasn't leaving without it. Broke some china and tore up some photos to show her I was serious."

Sutherland, noting Ronnie's emerald eyes harden in the telling, wondered whether she really would rough up an old woman. "So let's see it," he said, thinking at the same time, *Let's deep-six it, lose it overboard.*

"I sent it to Billy at his office. He's busy getting those tax records."

"You don't even have a copy?"

"You think I'm carrying that thing around? I sent a copy to my apartment. A doorman will sign for it."

"What about the police? Vislowski?"

Ronnie shook her head stubbornly. "Not until Billy's finished his story."

"You and Bill want to join Scooch and Gorman? That book is chum and you're swimming with barracudas."

"Billy will make it clear that it's in a safe place."

"If I'd known Bill was so thickheaded, I'd have never told Scooch to call him."

"Forget it. You're not responsible."

"Did you read it before sending it? What's in it?"

"I reads like a series of transactions and an index to tapes. You know, cash in, cash out, with names, initials, abbreviations, and dates and what looked like shortened descriptions of the purpose. Don't ask me whether Billy can decipher it all. I don't know if there's enough there to make a case in court without the tapes themselves or the author there to explain it."

"What does Bill care? He can make damaging claims, hurt a lot of people while getting his moment of fame."

"Not fair. He's getting records that can connect the activities in the book to these people. Between the two, there's a defensible story."

Sutherland scanned the harbor, the boats, the picturesque town, and the clouds scudding over the fort on the hill. Everything was so beautiful it was hard to imagine anything bad in the world. But there was, and he knew it, and being told he wasn't responsible didn't ease the burden. Nor did feeling that there was something in that book that could ruin him while it was out of his reach.

*     *     *

Sutherland left Ronnie with several of the crew on *Circe* while he went ashore to sign in and report the man-overboard event at race headquarters. She was in the cockpit chatting with two of the crew, Larry and Tom, and she couldn't contain her curiosity. "So what really happened? What was the big problem?"

Larry cast a glance at Dirk, who was sitting on the bow with his wife. Apparently satisfied that he couldn't be overheard, he jerked his head in Dirk's direction and said, "Went overboard at night. Lost his footing during the knockdown. Didn't have his safety line attached. He could've drowned if Doug didn't know what he was doing. Unbelievable."

"He won't talk about it," she said. "Must be pissed."

"He tries not to show it, but yeah," Tom said. "Thing is, it really was a bad storm. Lots of boats dis-masted and others just dropping out. Too much for them."

"We still may win," Tom interjected. "At least our section. Can't blame Dirk."

Ronnie thought otherwise. If someone had cost her a first place, she'd have had his ass. Second place was for losers.

"Got you a drink, I see," Sutherland said, stepping off the dock to *Circe's* deck.

"Well taken care of," she said. "They were telling me about the race. Periods of boredom interspersed with stretches of abject fear with a barf bag for company."

Sutherland laughed and pointed to the two men. "Don't believe these assholes. Make a ripple into a tsunami."

"They were big suckers," Larry insisted. "Couple waves had names."

"How many did-not-finishes?" Tom asked. "They know yet?"

"A dozen so far," Sutherland answered. "Equipment failures, unprepared crew, you name it."

"So what now? Wait around for results?" Ronnie asked. "And where does a person sleep? I couldn't find any vacancies on the Internet or tourist office."

"We rent a house every year. It's crowded, but friendly. Or there's the boat. Grab a sail bag and crash. As for now? The party's just begun."

# CHAPTER 42

## TUESDAY, JULY 24

Sutherland awoke, smelled dead fish, tasted stale rum, and wondered where he was. His head hurt, his bladder throbbed, and his world swayed like a hammock. He wouldn't move—not until he settled the where and how.

On his back, he stared at a ceiling three feet above. He heard screeching gulls and the faint pinging of slapping halyards. In pieces, the memories assembled. *Circe.* Mackinac Island. In a slip in the harbor beneath the old fort. They celebrated their sectional win last night. Ronnie Jamison arrived. It was Tuesday.

He moved his hand and felt warm skin beside him. Slowly lifting his head, he glimpsed his sleeping companion. The orange-red hair splayed across the pillow and strawberry breast peeking from under the sheet brought back more memory. His tumescence welled, but not from libido; he slowly pulled himself out of the bunk and shuffled to the head.

"Morning, sunshine," Ronnie said when Sutherland came out of the head. She stood barefoot in running shorts, pulling a tank top over a sports bra. She inspected Sutherland. "You look like death. How about a run around the island to wake up?"

Sutherland's insides gurgled. "Dying would feel better."

She laughed. "Well deserved. Your whole crew did a commendable job at nautical debauchery."

"An annual rite. I could tell you stories."

"You did. Trying to capture the fort's cannon, the kazoo band through the restaurant …"

"What do you expect? A fleet of sailors on an island with nothing but fudge and quaintness?"

"It's a time warp. No cars, just bicycles and horses."

"Supposed to make it romantic."

"It works. Especially in there," she said, winking and pointing to the aft cabin. "Where's your crew?"

"Must all be at the house. We could've stayed there."

"What can you do there that you can't do here?" she said, smiling. "You up for a swim? Beautiful day."

"I don't swim. Maybe a run, if you take it easy."

"Don't or can't swim?"

"Don't, can't, what's the difference? I almost drowned once."

"You're a sailor," she said. "You just crossed the lake."

"I didn't need to swim, did I? Fear makes for a better sailor."

*     *     *

Two hours later, after a broiling run around the island, a freezing shower in the boat's head, and a breakfast of coffee, donuts, and rum and orange juice, they sat in *Circe*'s cockpit under a sun shade. The air carried drowsy sounds of an idle harbor: flapping pennants, pinging halyards, creaking hulls, a Randy Travis tune, and the occasional cry of a hovering gull. A faint mixture of fish and seaweed floated on a north wind.

"Explain this to me again," Ronnie said, stretching her legs, resting her feet on the opposite cockpit seat. "When I first arrived last night, I'd thought you'd won. Everyone doing high fives, celebrating. Then we find you finished fourth."

"Three boats corrected ahead of us. That's the way it works. Bad part is, they all beat us by less than the ten minutes we lost when we had to rescue Dirk."

"He must feel awful. He should."

"A little rum and you can forget anything. The whole gang's at the party. Interested?"

"Everyone's there?" She stood up and started down the hatch. "Just a minute." Twenty seconds later, she called up from the salon, "You hungry?"

Sutherland stuck his head down the companionway, looked, and blinked. Ronnie stood naked, a bag of potato chips in her hand, smiling up at him— lime eyes, peaches-and-cream breasts, and between her thighs, a handful of cinnamon and brown sugar.

"I read about Circe," she said. "She turned lovers into beasts. Just a thought …"

"Which part are you talking about? The beast or lovers?"

"Are they mutually exclusive?"

*     *     *

Sutherland was on the way back from the committee tent after reviewing the latest race results when he heard his name. Turning, he saw Jules Langer running toward him with a folded newspaper in his hand. He let him catch up and fall in beside him as he continued toward the dock.

"Congratulations," Sutherland said. Langer had finished third in the fleet. Sutherland came in fourth overall but still won first in his section, a different class from Langer's. But Sutherland was sure Langer was there to gloat and rub in his rare victory over *Circe*.

"Oh, thanks," Langer said, catching his breath. "Bitch of a race. I heard about your man overboard. Too bad. We were on the same tacks as you until that happened. You would have beat me."

*Is this the real Jules? Where's the ego, the swagger, the lording it over me?* Sutherland thought. Instead he seemed nervous and reserved. "The breaks, that's all. What's up?" Easily said, not necessarily felt.

Langer blew out a breath. "I've been looking for you. Evidently you haven't seen this morning's paper. It's bad."

"More about Broadwell?" *So that's what Jules is here about.* Not a day went by without new rumblings about the company's questionable finances and edgy management. Now Sutherland would have to listen to more taunts over the possible loss of his anchor tenant.

"There's that, but this is worse, Doug. See for yourself." Sutherland thought he saw Langer's hand tremble when he offered him the paper. "Remember you told me that reporter saw me with Scooch the night he died?"

They had reached *Circe*'s dock and stopped. Sutherland took another step and turned to face Langer. "What about it?" he said.

"Doug?" The call came from Ronnie, below deck in *Circe*.

The voice seemed to disconcert Langer, and he whispered, "Is that his sister?"

"Yeah. Why?"

Langer shook his head nervously and jammed the newspaper in Sutherland's hands. "Read it. Metro section. When you get back to Chicago, call me. I've some stuff to show you." He turned and hurried away as if he was afraid someone might be after him. Thinking Langer's behavior strange, Sutherland wondered whether the man's wits had been scared out of him during the storm, taking his strut and ego with them. He stepped onto the dock, leafing through the paper's sections as he walked. He stopped. The front page of the business section featured the headline:

FEDS ARREST BROADWELL CFO, ALLEGE FRAUD

This wasn't merely more of the same. Smoke had turned into fire, and this blaze could travel all the way to his project. The article was short, probably written at the deadline without time to elaborate and fill in more blanks. Besides the actual arrest, it regurgitated previous news about shareholder suits, dwindling profit, questionable accounting practices, executive departures, director clashes. Now Sutherland would have to try and prevent Broadwell's headquarters problems from changing their plans for Chicago.

Distracted by the Broadwell news, he'd already forgotten Langer's odd behavior by the time he jumped onto *Circe*. As he reassembled the newspaper, he heard a clatter below.

"That today's paper?" Ronnie asked, pointing a potato chip at it. "Hand it here, Billy's story's probably in it."

He passed the paper over, and Ronnie sat in the navigation seat rustling through it, searching. "I can't find his column." Suddenly she stopped and glared wide-eyed at the page. She groaned, then gasped in squeaks, as if she couldn't breathe.

"Ronnie, what?"

Sutherland snatched the paper from her hands and seized both bare arms, shaking her while she gasped convulsively. He held on in anxious bewilderment until she quieted, moaning softly, breathing deeper and slower. Finally she closed her eyes and sobbed.

Sutherland turned to the newspaper, lying open and torn on the navigation table. The article began:

## REPORTER MURDERED IN DOUBLE KILLING
Police discovered the mutilated bodies of William Jamison and
Robert Hurley in a Lincoln Park apartment Monday morning.

"Noooo," Sutherland moaned. He reached to pull the newspaper closer. But Ronnie's hand flashed out, her fingernails biting into his wrist. He jerked away, and her nails raked his skin. Her eyes were green cauldrons, her mouth, drawn and snarling.

"You started this," she hissed. "You killed him; if you hadn't—"

"Wait a minute."

"You did, you did, you killed him," she screamed.

*Calm her*, he thought, placing his left hand on her shoulder. But she caught his little finger and bent it back. He heard something snap then felt the burst of pain just before she cast away his finger and hand like a dead fish. A flood of fire coursed to his elbow and he wanted to strike her, but he bit his lower lip, stopping himself. He tasted blood.

"Someone will pay for this," she hissed, snarling. "I'll see them eat their own liver." She glowered at the newspaper, as if her eyes could bludgeon out the truth.

*     *     *

After gathering her things and spurning Sutherland's offer of help and consolation, Ronnie left for the small island airport in a horse-drawn taxi. Sutherland returned to *Circe*, pulled a bag of ice from the freezer, dropped a handful of cubes into a tumbler of Myers's Rum, eased his throbbing finger into the ice bag, and waited for the world to go numb.

# CHAPTER 43

It had taken the rest of the week for Sutherland, two crew, and their girlfriends to sail and motor *Circe* back to Chicago, making stops in Harbor Springs and Saugatuck on the way. He spent much of the time on his phone to his attorneys to keep posted on the Broadwell situation and to his lenders, architects, broker, and contractor to keep the project moving in the hope that he still had a tenant when the dust settled. After learning that Bill Jamison's memorial service was scheduled for Saturday, they cut the trip short.

Sutherland arrived early for Bill Jamison's memorial service at St. Paul's United Church of Christ in Lincoln Park. He sat in the rear of the chapel recalling events of the last two weeks: images of Delaney's body's discovery, his meetings with Gorman, Langer, and Tunney, and his short-lived fling with Ronnie. Now Bill was dead.

The television, radio, and newspaper media couldn't agree on the story. Fox News theorized that Jamison and Robert Hurley's murders were the result of a love triangle. Several newspapers reported it as a burglary gone bad. Channel Two claimed Jamison's series on corruption and the Delaney discovery were the motives, that someone vulnerable to disclosures killed him along with his news source.

So what did Sutherland think, he who'd suggested that Scooch call Jamison, the first in a chain of events that led to both of their deaths? He wanted to believe it would have happened anyway. Hadn't Jamison already been working on an exposé of Sandler et al. before meeting Scooch? Hadn't his pursuit of acclaim made him reckless?

But Sutherland couldn't acquit himself.

He looked at the tape wrapped around the little and ring fingers of his left hand and thought of Ronnie. She was no help. When Sutherland arrived at the church, she greeted him with detached resentment, her handshake cold and dry. There was no doubt: she blamed him.

The service lasted forty-five minutes. Through the hymns and eulogies Sutherland felt like a trespasser. Afterward, as the assembly spilled into the hallway, he felt a painful grip on his arm and heard a man ask, "Douglas Sutherland?"

Sutherland glanced over his shoulder into brown eyes glaring out of a broad, unlined face. The man was over six feet, had brown hair and a thick mustache that showed flecks of gray. He had the build of a weightlifter who had either put on weight or liked his sport coats tight.

"Yeah?" Sutherland said, jerking his arm free.

"Detective Vislowski. Homicide." His breath smelled of onions.

"You're that friend of Ronnie's," Sutherland said, rubbing away the hurt in his arm. *Strong son of a bitch.*

Vislowski grimaced when he heard Ronnie's name. "Never mind that. I've got a few questions, Mr. Sutherland. Let's go in there," he said, pointing to a door down the hall. Sutherland followed him into the main church sanctuary—long, wide, high, and empty. The detective sat in the closest pew and motioned Sutherland in beside him.

"You buying that love triangle baloney?" Sutherland said as he sat.

"That's what we're trying to find out. Please, just a few questions." Vislowski pulled out his notebook. It seemed to Sutherland that he'd seen that movement in dozens of television detective shows and movies. The inevitable notebook. Did they really take meaningful notes, or was it just a prop?

"Let's see," the detective said, flipping pages. "You were with Miss Jamison when you heard of her brother's death?"

"That's right. We read it in the paper."

"You were together on Mackinac Island? What were you doing there?" he asked casually, as if it wasn't official, just chitchat until he found his place in the book.

"I'd just finished a race."

"Where were you staying?"

"We rent a house, but I stayed on the boat."

"Both of you?"

"It's a big boat."

"Known Miss Jamison long?"

"Couple weeks."

Vislowski's brows bunched into a scowl. "Fast worker."

Sutherland chuckled. "An official comment?"

Vislowski regarded Sutherland with undisguised dislike and then went back to his notes. "Okay, how'd you know this Scooch character?"

"I didn't," Sutherland said. "He called me after we found the body in my building. Told me it was Danny Delaney's."

"Why'd he call you if you didn't know him?"

"He knew my father."

"So he knew your father. Why'd he call you?"

"You'd have to ask him. He just called."

"Veronica … er, Miss Jamison told me you told him to talk to Bill Jamison? Why?"

"He's a reporter. If Delaney was really buried there, he could write about it. That's what got him killed. That, Danny's notebook, and—"

"Not the notebook. Scooch's killer took it."

So Ronnie still hadn't told Vislowski she'd retrieved the notebook. "If not for the notebook, it was for the files Bill and his source, Hurley, were copying from Gene Sandler's warehouse. Or maybe 'cause he saw the guy following Scooch the night he got killed."

Vislowski crossed a leg over his other meaty thigh. It took some effort and didn't look comfortable. "All maybes. You sound like Miss Jamison. Make your theory fit no matter what. It was a pervert murder, as far as the evidence goes."

"If you can't see a connection with Delaney, Ronnie was right: you guys can't find your butts with both hands."

Vislowski's face reddened, his tight collar strained around his swelling neck. "How long you know the victim, Mr. Smart-ass?"

"College. Fraternity brother."

"So you knew he was a fag."

The pronouncement would have stunned Sutherland a few weeks ago, but the news reports had prepared him. After first hearing the theories, he'd reflected on what he knew of Jamison, looking for indications, but he could come up with none. While at college, Jamison dated girls from nearby colleges and even married one of them, though they later divorced. Since then Sutherland only saw him every year or so, and usually accidentally. Even the night he'd seen him leave his apartment wearing black leather clothes, Sutherland had assumed he was playing a role.

"Not really," he said. "Still don't."

Vislowski's mouth twisted into a sneer. He reminded Sutherland of the bully years ago at school who'd given him the black eye. Sutherland had brandished that shiner like a dueling scar; he hadn't backed down to the older boy.

"Open your eyes," Vislowski said. "Your pal hung out in gay bars."

"He was a reporter—did a lot of things for a story."

Vislowski leered. "Like butt fucking?"

"Well …"

"Autopsy says they'd been butt fucking before they died. That some kind of new reporting technique?" Vislowski was enjoying this.

Sutherland shivered. He took a deep breath.

"Still doesn't mean—"

Vislowski smiled cruelly. "The way they were killed, it was a sex thing."

"How about someone making it look like that?"

"You didn't see it. I did."

"Do tell." He took another breath.

"Killer was known by one or both of the deceased. He was let in. Chloroformed them. Tied and gagged them with duct tape. Cut them up. For starters, he sliced their nipples off …"

Sutherland tasted his breakfast bacon, felt it balling in his gut.

"Must've tortured them a long time. Before the other parts, the coup de grâce."

Sutherland swallowed hard, willing his stomach to behave. Parts? Like with Scooch and Gorman: the ear and tattoo. Or Delaney, the tooth?

"Wanna guess what parts?" Vislowski grinned.

Sutherland willed down the nausea. He rubbed his clammy hands on his pants and tried to think logically. "Their fingers smashed like the others?"

The question seemed to surprise Vislowski. He scowled and said, "How'd you know about that?"

"You told Bill, he told me. You see the connection?"

"Hard to prove."

"You can't blame it on some bullshit burglar or sex triangle just 'cause it's easy. Ronnie won't buy it. Neither will I."

"It doesn't matter what you buy."

"Then are we through? I've got to go." The nausea had passed, but he felt light-headed and cold.

"You look kinda green," Vislowski said, grinning again. "Veronica know what a pussy you are?"

Sutherland stood and looked down into the detective's taunting eyes. "You enjoy this? People getting cut up?" He slipped out of the pew into the aisle.

"Perverts like him, I don't mind." Vislowski grabbed the pew back in front of him and pulled himself to his feet. "But speaking of getting cut up, take some advice: stay away from Veronica. She's bad luck."

"I know." He held up his taped finger.

"She'll chew you up and spit you out."

Sutherland nodded. "That from personal experience?" He turned, strode out of the sanctuary, crossed the foyer to the exterior doors, and bounded down the stairs to the sidewalk. He didn't look back, but if he smelled stale onions, he was ready. Even if it meant another black eye.

# CHAPTER 44

Jules Langer sat in his office staring at the two photographs he'd set side by side on his desk. One was of his sister, the other of Jules himself, taken on Mackinac Island as he was being congratulated on his win by the commodore. He should be jubilant. His sister's namesake, the yacht *Julia*, had won its section. The tragedy was that she wouldn't know, being locked up like a prisoner and kept incommunicado by her nurse jailers. So who could he share the victory with? Langer was divorced, and none of the women he was seeing meant anything to him. Other skippers and their crew appreciated the difficulty and importance of a sectional win. They had applauded his win and congratulated him, but it all seemed formulaic, polite, expected, what one did. Ironically, it was Sutherland's sincere handshake afterward that had meant the most.

Possibly it was because of their history. Over the years, nearly every time they had competed, even racing dinghies as kids, the younger Sutherland had beaten him. Their most recent clash, costly and painful, had ended with the loss to him of the Broadwell Communications deal, a tenant that would have kick-started Langer's America Tower.

Earlier, in a less expensive but just as galling offense, Langer had been victim of his own scheming. After suffering a humiliating losing season with his specially designed new boat, he had sold it dirt-cheap to Sutherland— "palmed off the tub" he boasted at the time. In gratitude, Sutherland sailed the "tub" to win the Yacht of the Year Cup the next season, scarcely mitigating the insult by changing the yacht's name from *Julia* to *Circe*.

*Times have changed*, he said to himself. *The curse is over.* He had finished the Mac race ahead of Sutherland, and even though Danny Delaney's discovery had created an opening for Langer's project, it didn't seem as important anymore. The previous weekend's murder of the reporter and his partner had settled it. He sensed there was more drama yet to be played out, and he lacked the courage to face that future alone. If he expected to come out unscathed, or at least in one piece, he had to put his old his animosity toward Sutherland aside. So when Langer called, Sutherland had agreed to meet in Langer's co-op apartment that evening.

His ruminations were interrupted when his phone rang. His secretary didn't work Saturdays, so he glanced at the sender's number and reflexively reached for his antacid tablets. It was Gene Sandler. The reporter's death had made Langer dyspeptic and jumpy, and speaking to the fat man was bound to make it worse.

Sandler didn't waste time. "Did you do what I asked?"

"Up in flames," Langer lied. His father's files were to be the subject of that evening's talk with Sutherland. "Just like your warehouse. The fire was all over the ten o'clock news."

"Shit happens. That's why I'm in the insurance business."

"What was stored there?"

"Records. If the feds get their hands on Danny's tapes it's a matter of time before they have warrants for all of us. You should have got that book when you had a chance."

*So it's still out there*, Langer thought. *The reporter and that other guy are dead, and the notebook still hasn't been found.* "Why are the feds into this in the first place? You'd think this would be a Chicago Police case."

"It was a federal case when Delaney disappeared and Bernard Sutherland drowned. Our favorite mole told me the FBI couldn't figure out what happened. Did Danny renege on his deal and take off with the money? Was he with the fishes? Same thing with Sutherland. Did he split or drown? Where were the tapes he was supposed to deliver? With the appearance of the notebook they're poking around again."

"My father thought the prosecutor working with the FBI took off with the money."

"That was Daryl Anderson. He took off all right, after he realized his insider disclosures to our favorite congressman were about to get people killed, but it doesn't explain what happened to Delaney's tapes, and that's what you should worry about. You joined your father in a couple of those meetings with Delaney."

"Nothing illegal happened that I remember. No money changed hands, just talk."

"But talk can be construed as conspiracy and can connect you to the bigger scheme of things. We have no idea how much or who he taped. If he got some of what went on toward the end with Spanos, we're in trouble."

# Chapter 45

After leaving the memorial service, Sutherland hurried through the rain to his office and let himself in for the first time since he'd left for the Mac race. In his mail he found a registered letter from his lender issuing a deadline for completing the lease with Broadwell. He called Marty Stevens, the point attorney on the lease negotiations, and learned that Broadwell's lawyers weren't returning his calls. "I hear they're circling the wagons or hiding in a bunker," Marty said. "My partner in New York smells blood. The SEC's auditors are like wolves." Marty was a man of many metaphors.

After hanging up Sutherland shuffled through his mail, putting aside the usual invoices, invitations, résumés, and proposals for later scrutiny. With his project essentially on hold, where was the urgency? he asked himself. Besides, crucial as Broadwell's tenancy was for his future, it didn't have the same life-and-death gravitas as the other events of the last few weeks. He loaded a briefcase with the rest of his mail, relocked the office, and drove home.

*    *    *

Half an hour later, Sutherland poured himself a scotch and slumped into the living room sofa. Through the window he could see the traffic on Lake Shore Drive, ribbons of flickering red and yellow in the twilight. In the small island of light from two floor lamps, he took in his immediate surroundings. He had to admit the room was spare, but he liked it that way. The two large abstract oils on either side of his flat-screen TV provided color, and the view of lake and park was spectacular. What else did he need?

The intercom buzzed. Over the malfunctioning speakers the doorman screeched, "*A Miss Jamison is here. Send her up?*" A few minutes later Sutherland opened the door to Ronnie's cheerless face. She brushed past him into the apartment, a flash of disheveled red hair, all business. She wore jeans and a tee shirt and carried a brown leather shoulder bag the size of a small suitcase.

"We alone?" she said, looking toward the kitchen then down the hall.

"Just us."

Her inspection stopped, her eyes fixed on the living room. "You just moving in?"

"Here five years. Why?"

Her frown was half scorn, half pity. Then she shrugged. "Nothing. You got more of that?" She pointed to his scotch.

"Sure."

"What did you do to your hand?"

Sutherland held up his left hand, showing her the pinky taped to the ring and middle fingers. "You did this on the boat."

"Does it hurt? I'm sorry, I don't remember."

"Least of my troubles," he said.

When he returned with the drink, she was gazing out the window. She looked frail, standing alone against the darkness outside—but the ache in his taped finger belied the impression.

He sat on the sofa. She turned to face him.

"Someone broke into Billy's house, but a neighbor called the police before they could do much. From what the police found, they were planning to torch the place," she said.

"So the notebook's safe?" Sutherland noticed fatigue rings under her eyes, a detail he'd missed at the memorial service earlier that day.

"I'd expressed it to his office at the *Tribune*. I've got the only copy." She patted her bulging briefcase and took a deep breath. "I've been busy. Collected Billy's notes and computer files, wrangled some police records, and talked to Craig, the retired reporter who knew Delaney. With what I've got, I could almost finish Billy's story."

"How would it end?"

"I'm still not sure. But I think I know who killed Billy." She sank into the upholstered chair facing Sutherland. "And Billy's editor agreed to let me write a memorial column. I'll finish what he started. Just wait."

"You think Sandler's the guy?"

"Bill's source, Robert Hurley, worked for Sandler's accountant." She slurped the scotch, wiping her mouth with the back of her hand. "Hurley found tax documents going all the way back to Delaney's era. Billy was planning to pick up the files in a van. Sandler must've found out."

"Will the police pick him up?"

"They'll talk to him, but he's too wired. Same old pussyfooting bullshit."

"Can't they search his place? For the files?"

She scoffed, spilling some drink, though she didn't seem to notice. "The files were kept in a West Side loft. It burned down two days ago."

"Taking no chances," he said. "Unlike you. Did it occur to you that whoever killed your brother knows that you went to get the notebook?" He avoided reminding her that Bill had been tortured. "Now the killer thinks or knows you have it. Your item in the paper will confirm it. You really want to keep the police out of it?"

"I'm taking precautions. I'm not staying in my apartment. I've got a hotel room and been spending my time on the Internet and the *Trib*'s archive library. And there's this." She groped around in her bag and, after pulling out and setting aside two stuffed folders, retrieved and brandished a shiny revolver. "Forget the police. They haven't even officially connected Billy's murder to Scooch's and Gorman's yet."

"I met Vislowski today. We didn't get along."

"I'm not surprised."

"He carries a torch for you."

"It's useful sometimes," she said with a tired smile.

Sutherland studied Ronnie as she looked away in thought. After burying her brother just a few hours ago she'd become a woman on a mission. A very determined, unstoppable woman, he decided.

"So now what?" he asked. "What did this reporter, Craig, tell you?"

"Things you probably already know. Like fifteen years ago someone leaks that the mayor's taking bribes. Next thing, your father confesses—takes the blame—and the mayor's off the hook."

"They were good friends."

"After Bernard Sutherland was released from prison, a few weeks before he died, he made five million disappear. Danny Delaney said as much to Sandy Craig, but not for publication. And not from a pension fund like Billy thought."

*Just like Agent Branson and Benjamin Gorman had said*, Sutherland recalled. "What else?"

"A little later, Danny disappears. Then your father's boat is found floating empty on the lake. Never found the body, so authorities assumed an accident or suicide. Fast-forward fifteen years and Scooch, Gorman, and Billy are killed."

"Did Agent Branson tell you about the dead agent?"

"Didn't have to. It was in the papers. A random murder. But I'm not sure how it fits."

*So she still doesn't know that the feds had squeezed Delaney into working with them or that the evidence had disappeared when the agent died.* "How about the prosecutor who disappeared around the same time? Name was Anderson. Branson told me they found him, but then he clammed shut. Got to be something there, or he wouldn't have been so secretive."

"Don't worry, I'll find out."

"Did Bill ever identify the other man outside the diner where Scooch and Langer met? Could it have been Sandler?"

"It was rainy and dark. Billy was so scared all he remembered was the guy was big and white."

"It could've been a hired killer, someone we won't recognize."

Ronnie shook her head. "Too personal. Taking Scooch's ear and what they did to Billy …" She stopped, her eyes focused on the floor in horror, as if she was at that moment witnessing her brother's torture.

"Don't think about it."

"I have to," she said fiercely. "It keeps me going." She looked away, wiping her eyes with the hem of her tee shirt. When she turned back it was with a look of hard resolve.

"Did anyone see the guy at Scooch's hotel?" he asked.

"I talked to the manager yesterday. She's scared to death. Swears she saw nothing. Suggested the fancy umbrella they found under Scooch's bed might've been his."

"What'd it look like?"

"I saw a photo. Kinda like this." She stood, snatched a pen from Sutherland's shirt pocket, and on the cover of a magazine sketched an *L*-shaped umbrella handle, complete with swirls and an almost invisible *R* in the engraving.

Sutherland thought a moment. "Nobody we know. Except Raskoff, the guy some of them worked for."

"Like Sandler. You ever run into him?"

"Not if I can help it," he said.

"The piece I'm writing will shake his tree."

"You're kidding," he said, rolling his eyes. "You've got a gun. Why not just shoot yourself?"

She scowled and shook a fist at him. "Don't laugh at me. And never tell me what to do."

Sutherland stood and walked to the floor-to-ceiling glass. Beyond Lake Shore Drive there was nothing but mist—no lake, no lighthouse, no distant shore. *What a world. People getting killed and others lining up.*

Ronnie joined him by the window. "You're right," she said. "I'd be stupid to admit I've got the notebook."

"Did Bill know you had a copy? If he did, then they know you have it," he said, again avoiding mentioning torture.

"I never got a chance to tell him."

"Do you have it with you? I've only seen Bill's notes."

She opened her portfolio and pulled out several sheets. "Here's the last couple of pages. A quick look, 'cause I've got to get going," she said as she handed the pages to him. "I've got to see a man about some money."

Sure enough, the listings looked like accountant's entries. Starting on the left was a date for each line, multiple lines for each day. Then moving right on each line there was a dollar amount in or out, and names, initials, or abbreviations presumably identifying the source or recipient of the money. The last entry on each line was a reference to a video tape. A few abbreviations appeared: ald. for *alderman*, sen. for *senator*, com. possibly for *commissioner*. One of the last lines, dated shortly before Sutherland's father's disappearance, had the initials BS, the figure five million dollars, and what looked like a long routing and account number.

"What's the matter? You look puzzled," Ronnie said.

"Nothing," the other said, trying to collect himself.

She stepped between him and the window, looking up into his face. "You see it now? It's clear as day."

He stared into the darkness over her head. Only the streetlight glow from below anchored him to the city. "Clear? A perfectly decent man turns crooked? A fearless man commits suicide? For years I tried not to ask those questions, had even fantasized that his only crime had been in protecting the mayor and then failing to face up to his deception and dishonor. I got sucked into this thing with Bill because reporters were making even more serious allegations; federal agents were, too, threatening to screw up my project. I wanted to prove these latest allegations wrong, but I'm more confused than ever. You'd think I'd be used to living with lies."

# Chapter 46

Sutherland had to face it. His father was a worse criminal than he'd thought. Bill Jamison's articles had already suggested his father's involvement, but alone those allegations could still be passed off as sheer speculation. Not to Sutherland. He was convinced that it was in fact his father's initials associated with the five million dollars. If more conclusive evidence materialized, it could sink his project for good, ruling out its development for Broadwell or any other company. As Agent Branson had suggested, any proven link between the missing millions and Sutherland's father could further taint the project and even jeopardize the legality of the trust the elder man had established and thus Doug's legitimate ownership of the McCollum Building. It could tie up his right to title in court for years. So even though Broadwell was currently distracted by its own problems, he couldn't allow more disclosures of his father's culpability. If those tapes still existed, he had to find them first.

*     *     *

At nine o'clock that evening, Sutherland hailed a cab and rode to Langer's apartment overlooking Oak Street Beach. The idea that Langer wanted to see him, wanted to tell or give him something without any catches, didn't ring right. After years of aggressively competing in regattas and, lately, for business, it was hard to believe Mr. Ego was about to be helpful. His worried earnestness when they met on Mackinac Island after the race was the only hint that there was a feeling human being inside that shell.

The doorman, a sleepy man with wispy, white hairs on a nearly bald head, called Langer's apartment, announced Sutherland, and waited, apparently listening. The doorman replaced the phone and pointed to the elevators. "Twelfth floor, A."

The apartment was one of two on the twelfth floor, and before he could knock, Langer, in yellow cashmere sweater and white linen slacks, opened the door. Walking back into the apartment, he said over his shoulder, "You want a drink?"

"If you are," Sutherland said, entering the wide foyer. Its walls were covered with photos and architectural renderings of office and apartment buildings from all over the world. Only a few had actually been developed by Langer, but anyone unfamiliar with his career would credit him with a worldwide reputation. *Pure Langer*, Sutherland thought.

"Scotch, gin, what?" Langer shouted from the living room.

"Scotch."

While Langer busied himself at the built-in bar, Sutherland strolled along the passageway, glancing at the photos, and he nearly tripped over an umbrella stand. His eyes immediately fixed on one of the three umbrellas, the one with the silver handle. It looked similar to the one Ronnie had sketched, the one found in Scooch's room. He held it up and inspected the *R* inscribed within the swirls.

Langer reappeared with a glass in each hand. When he saw Sutherland studying the handle, he said, "I've lost a dozen umbrellas over the years, but never that one. Weird, considering I hated the bastard that gave it to me."

"Who was that? It's got an *R* on it."

"Raskoff. We all got one."

"All?"

"Everyone working for him then."

"Scooch get one?"

"That lowlife? Raskoff wouldn't give him the sweat off his ass. Maybe ten of us got one. Here's your drink." He handed Sutherland a crystal tumbler filled with amber liquid and clinking ice cubes. Sutherland followed him into the living room, reasoning that ten recipients narrowed the suspects. Problem was, you'd never convict anyone for no longer having an umbrella.

Two features of Langer's expensively modern space struck Sutherland immediately. The first was the east wall of floor-to-ceiling windows overlooking the lake and the darkness. From where he stood, nothing could be seen but his own reflection against a black abyss. Perfect if you enjoyed looking at yourself, as Langer certainly did.

The second detail was more intriguing. Dominating the north wall, heavily framed in swirls of gilded wood, was a five-by-seven foot portrait of a woman in a white gown. Her fine nose and slightly receding chin were feminized replicas of Jules Langer's, but her eyes were sad and troubled. To Sutherland, the portrait's size and prominence suggested a curious, if not unnatural, reverence. He remembered that she was married to Reggie Tunney and wondered if Reggie's adoration could possibly match Langer's.

"Have a seat while I get some papers," Langer said.

A minute later he sat down, placed a leather suitcase on the glass coffee table, and took a long drink from his glass. He took a deep breath, looking straight ahead, seemingly making up his mind. This was definitely not the aloof and irrepressible real estate mogul from a week ago. "I've been thinking about this for weeks. I can't keep quiet any longer."

Sutherland's curiosity tingled, but so did his alarms—strangers bearing gifts.

"You know this thing started back when our fathers were alive. In fact, yours might've inadvertently started it all."

Not a propitious beginning. "Mine? How?"

Langer breathed in and out deeply, then he said, "He refined this system to use numbered trusts and layered partnership interests. Partnerships within partnerships make it difficult to penetrate or identify the participants."

"It was done all the time. And it's not necessarily illegal."

"True, it's what the rest of them did with his framework—raised payoffs and corruption to an art form by basing their dirty network around it. Started with apartments and grew into condominiums, offices, and hotels."

"You talk in the past tense. Aren't *you* involved *today*?"

"I'll get to that," Langer said. "Back then I knew a little, even though I suspected more, about what was going on. I was on the sidelines, a new broker working for Raskoff Real Estate. My father ran his construction and development company and mostly kept me out of things. He died not long after your father went missing. Spent his last days in an oxygen tent." Langer breathed deeply again, as if remembering his father's struggles.

"He involved in Danny Delaney's disappearance?"

"Told me he didn't know what happened to him, but he could have been protecting me. What he did say was that Danny was talking to either the state's attorney or the feds. Threatened the whole setup and everyone in it. And here's the thing I didn't know until Sandler let it out the other day. There was someone in either the FBI, the state's, or the US attorney's office who was sabotaging their case, telling the group what was happening. That's how Delaney got found out and the reason he disappeared."

"Delaney, then my father, one right after another. An FBI agent on the case was murdered about then too. What do you know about him?"

"Just that my father said it was a lucky coincidence."

"All the case files and tapes disappeared. You think that mole destroyed them?"

"What do you think?"

"My father was the only one who went to jail. How'd he get singled out?"

"That was at least a year earlier, before the fed's investigation. Up to then he was viewed as kind of a goody-two-shoes. In fact, when he saw how widespread and corrupt it was becoming, he wanted them to stop."

"Honesty or worry about being exposed?"

"I don't know. It didn't matter because someone filmed him in a restaurant with the mayor, and it must have looked bad, because he confessed."

"Why didn't he fight it?"

"He and the mayor were friends. It could've brought him down. It was his idea."

"So let's see," Sutherland said. "My father goes to jail for a year. Comes back, and if you believe what's being said, siphons off a pile of money and commits suicide."

"That's the story anyway."

"And the money? That true?"

"My father thought the feds got the money somehow. Maybe that government insider double-crossed everyone. But the arrival of the FBI agent so soon after they discovered Delaney's body suggests the feds originally thought Delaney absconded with it. Went to Rio or something."

"If my father took it, how would that insider get a hold of it?"

Langer held up his hands palms up and shrugged.

"What do you know about Delaney's tapes?" Sutherland asked.

"They've got Sandler pretty worried. I could even be in a few, but I wasn't involved in anything dirty, so they won't hurt me."

Sutherland took a few seconds to assimilate as much as he could then asked, "Why are you telling this, Jules?"

"Simple. Those tapes are the cause of this killing. I'm sure of it. If the authorities get the videos somehow, or better still, if they're destroyed, the killing will be over."

"And the missing money? Isn't that a motive too?"

"To a lesser extent, I imagine."

"Okay. And ...?"

"Seems to me, if anyone can find either, you've got the best chance. Your father took their money. May have taken Delaney's tapes. I'm giving you as much help as I can."

"What's in that case?" Sutherland pointed to the suitcase on the coffee table.

Langer patted the case and said, "Not Delaney's tapes, unfortunately. When my father died, all his files were moved to his house, the same one my mother still lives in. She had everything dumped in his den and locked it off, as if shutting away all her bad memories of him. He treated her so brutally, I'm surprised she didn't set it all on fire. There's years of shit in there, and what's in that case is only a smattering. It could be damaging to reputations, might cost some aldermen, police, or judges their jobs, but the statute of limitations on that kind of thing is over. Still, Sandler wanted me to get rid of it, so consider it background. If I find anything more, I'll let you know."

"Bill Jamison was out to prove the system still exists."

"Not like it was then. You had Delaney, Gorman, Sandler, Tunney, and my father, a tightly knit group, with their tentacles into a lot of influential people. Now Sandler does his own thing and Tunney his, though their interests often overlap."

"In any event the corruption continues," Sutherland said. "For example, how much of your America Tower equity did you give away to secure all those zoning and height exemptions?"

Langer gritted his teeth, stood, and headed straight to the bar where he mixed an even larger drink. With his back turned, he said, "How do you know about that?"

"Two and two, Jules. I know it wasn't just you and the preservationists who were against my demolishing the McCollum. Nor were you the only one hoping Broadwell would pick your project instead of mine. Your pals knew that they weren't getting any vigorish from me, plain and simple. So they did everything possible to help you."

"With Broadwell in trouble, neither of us won."

"I'll give you another reason your pals didn't want me to succeed. They didn't want the body found. Your associates are murderers, Jules. Maybe they didn't do it themselves, but they're responsible. You must have thought of that."

"Not until recently. I tried to deny it with Scooch and Gorman. Now with the reporter …"

"Who do you suspect?"

"Like you said. Sandler or Tunney is behind it."

"What about you? Are you bulletproof?"

"No. Neither are you."

Sutherland stared at the suitcase. What would the contents tell him? "Okay, Jules. Sandler wants you to get rid of these, you just have." He closed the case, snapped the clasps shut, and stood up, grabbing the handle as he did.

"What will you do with them when you're done?" Langer asked.

"Dunno yet. I'll talk to you before I do anything."

As Sutherland descended in the elevator, he was under no illusion that Langer had been truthful. He welcomed the professed help, as long as it led to the tapes and their destruction. What he couldn't buy was Langer's purported motives. Despite everything he'd said, the old tapes would most likely lead any competent prosecuting team to more recent activities and Langer's downfall. So why would he risk incriminating himself? Was it to bring down the others? Whatever his reasons, in his gesture of assistance, Langer had just put a large bull's-eye on Sutherland's back.

# CHAPTER 47

## SUNDAY, JULY 29

The next morning Sutherland, after a seven-mile run, read the *Chicago Tribune* while drinking coffee and munching on a granola bar, the only semblance of breakfast in the apartment. Local coverage didn't have anything new on Bill Jamison's murder, and Ronnie's memorial piece wouldn't be in print until tomorrow at the earliest. She wanted to include some startling revelation and was still researching to fill in the details.

The business section had another story about Broadwell Communications' problems, this time suggesting that the SEC might step in and that a forced bankruptcy wasn't out of the question. Sutherland could already imagine his lender's frantic messages awaiting him in his office, calling back the demolition loan before the last brick had fallen. It would be another week before he expected the crews to be finished. Where was he supposed to get that kind of money in short order? He'd sworn he wouldn't use his father's trust fund. In theory the demolition loan was to be repaid by the construction loan, but that wasn't going to happen without an anchor tenant and an executed lease.

Scanning the rest of the business news he noticed an item about Imperial Food Products, Inc. They were shutting down their Cincinnati and Minneapolis offices and consolidating them in Chicago. The article didn't say it, but it would mean they would need more space. Sutherland knew the chairman of Imperial and had played squash with him several times. Could they substitute for Broadwell and save Sutherland's ass? It was worth a try, so he called his leasing broker, Frank Mann, at home. Frank told him he was already working on getting in front of Imperial's real estate team and would let him know as soon as they responded. Judging from the article in the paper, they were on a fast track, meaning his project on the McCollum site would be ready if Broadwell did fall through. Langer would be the strongest competition, and Sutherland knew he'd do anything to win this time.

Sutherland was to meet his crew at eleven o'clock for brunch at the yacht club before competing in an informal race that afternoon. On the way out his apartment door, seeing Langer's suitcase where he'd left it by the hall table, he decided to take it down to his car and go through it in his office on Monday. From the size of it, it would take a few hours to sort through, and he didn't want to miss anything.

# CHAPTER 48

## MONDAY, JULY 30

Sutherland's secretary Eileen and Dan Dixon were waiting for him outside his office when he arrived Monday morning. They looked like they were at a wake—long faces, tight mouths, worried eyes. All that was missing were organ music, flowers, and handkerchiefs.

"We just got a fax," Eileen said, holding out the sheet of paper as if it was burning her fingers.

The letter was from Broadwell Communications' legal office in New York. Addressed to Sutherland, its message was short:

> This is to advise you to suspend all activity on our behalf for our new headquarters offices in Chicago. This letter (original to follow) serves as official Notice of Termination pursuant to paragraph XV. A. of our Letter of Intent with Sutherland and Associates dated April 15 of this year.

"Bastards," Sutherland growled. "They really fucked things up, didn't they? Cut some corners, fudge some books, and hope no one finds out." He threw the letter, as if trying to hurl it back to New York. It flipped in the air and fluttered to the floor, where he glared at it, damning its defiance. Dan Dixon picked it up, read it, and sighed.

"That's it then. The fat lady sang."

"What are you going to do?" Eileen asked. "Should I put in a call to your attorneys?"

"Technically we have a deal with their letter of intent, even though the lease isn't finalized and despite what that bullshit letter says. But bankruptcy trumps everything. We may be able to get some damages, but I'm not counting on it." He looked at the papers covering his desk, the spreadsheet on his computer screen, and shook his head. Pounds of plans and documents, hundreds of rows and columns representing fifteen months of his life. Worthless, wasted, futile months. He grabbed his telephone and held it up. "But Eileen's right. I better get my attorneys on board. This could get nasty. Would you excuse me, Dan?"

Dan left and Sutherland spent the next half hour in a conference call exploring his options with his New York and Chicago attorneys. They would file some petitions in New York first thing the next morning. But after that, it was a game of wait-and-see with the feds to see what they were going to do. If all this was ineffectual, after the demolition, his site would be leveled and made into another parking lot. Maybe that was all the McCollum was meant for, his father's poisoned legacy. An empty monument to corruption.

*      *      *

Langer's suitcase lay open on Sutherland's conference room table, its contents spread across the polished surface. Sutherland had spent two hours going through the documents, making notes and comparing dates with what he already knew. There were construction bid submissions, requests for proposals, construction budgets, inspection reports, zoning petitions, all the things one would expect to find in a construction company's files. There were also several business-size checkbooks, letters, and partnership agreements.

On first glance through, Sutherland couldn't help wondering why Langer's mother would save all this stuff if she despised Miles Langer as much as Jules indicated. Maybe she knew he was corrupt and was hoping someday these files would prove it. It took Sutherland a thorough search to begin to see connections. It started with one piece of lined notepaper with handwritten names and dollar amounts. In the left column were the names of construction companies, some of which Sutherland recognized and were still in business. On the right were the dollars, starting from the lowest at the top, $30 million, and increasing to the bottom, $35 million. Langer Construction was the third line down at $32 million.

He looked through ten project proposals until he found the $32 million bid document. It was for the new wing of a hospital. Attached to it was an amended document with a new bid, $29,500,000. Then he opened the checkbooks and found an entry for $100,000 in cash with the notation: bid consulting. Another hour produced three more occurrences of payoffs for bid rigging.

Once he paged through the checkbook he found entry after entry for cash, all of them for slightly less than $10,000 and all of them with the notation "services." Many checks were endorsed by companies or organizations that Sutherland would bet were fictitious.

Setting aside Miles Langer's records for his construction company, Sutherland turned his attention on Miles Langer's first development project by the company his son would inherit. The partnership papers along with the initial accounting records showed that Gorman's pension fund was the lender and that Sandler, Tunney, Delaney, and Miles himself owned the majority equity stake. However, there was a master partnership consisting of twenty limited partnerships, which had contributed one dollar and a promissory note in exchange for a percentage interest in the development. With that master partnership, Langer et al. gave away 20 percent of the development. When the building produced the expected cash flow or was sold, these favored partners would receive a windfall. Next to each limited partnership, the senior Langer had written the name of the person behind the façade, including some of the best known power brokers and politicians in Chicago.

It didn't take a genius to conclude that Miles Langer was dirty and in collaboration with several dozen other figures. *Why keep incriminating records like this?* Sutherland wondered. Self preservation, he supposed. With this information, Miles Langer could take others down with him.

Before replacing the piles of paper into the suitcase, Sutherland reread a letter attached to the development documents. It was a cover letter, conveying the executed agreements to Miles Langer as general partner. There was no denying it any longer. The letter was signed by Bernard Sutherland and dated a year before he'd gone to jail.

*    *    *

Every new disclosure about his father's relationship with Miles Langer and his cronies darkened Sutherland's mood. After years he had come to terms with the one crime his father had confessed to, had learned to live with it, even to forget it. It wasn't denial, it was simply a matter of burying the shame deep and out of sight. Now the five-million-dollar theft and the idea that the old man was an integral part of the cabal had forced his shame out of its hiding place.

Miles Langer's papers laid out how his father's original legal framework had been corrupted into an extensive system of payoffs and kickbacks. Aldermen, senators, representatives, police officials, city hall pols—the list went on. The men at the top seemed untouchable. Sandler as patron of the arts, Langer the flamboyant developer, Tunney the secretive aristocrat. Underneath the shiny patina, people were being bought, robbed, pressured, extorted, and now, even murdered.

The breakfast with Reggie Tunney was still fresh in Sutherland's mind. How blasé he was, seemingly indifferent and unconcerned with the notebook and its implications. His only indication of interest was the supposedly offhand offer to help Sutherland burn the tapes if they were found. Something in that comment now seemed an attempt to disguise real concern. Two deaths later, it might be time to exploit that concern by exploring some ideas about the tapes' possible whereabouts. They would both be fencing, but if Sutherland was lucky, a morsel of truth might surface. It would also be an opportunity to observe Tunney's reaction when he asked him if Gene Sandler had really killed Bill Jamison, as the police were beginning to suspect. It was a lie about the police, of course, but what was another lie in this world of deceit he found himself in?

When she agreed to the meeting, Tunney's secretary acted as if she were granting Sutherland an interview with the president.

# CHAPTER 49

South Michigan Avenue separated Grant Park on the east from a long bluff of offices, hotels, and cultural buildings fronting the park and lake. Reginald Tunney's offices occupied the top floor of one of these structures, a vintage 1924 weather-worn and discolored edifice that had seen its better days.

Sutherland entered the building from the Jackson side entrance and waited for his eyes to adjust to the lobby's meager light. His cursory inspection uncovered more evidence of the neglect he had seen on the exterior—cracked tiles, peeling plaster, unpolished brass, ingrained dirt—signs of a financially strapped or negligent owner. In this case, Reginald Tunney.

Behind the security desk sat a large Hispanic man in a white uniform shirt, eyes down, absorbed in a magazine. Sutherland addressed the short-cropped dome of the guard's head. "What floor's Chartered Associates on?"

The man looked up with indifferent eyes. "Building's closed. They expecting you?"

"Yes. Name's Sutherland."

The guard called a number he knew by heart and after a few words said, "Sign in. Twentieth floor. His secretary's waiting."

Sutherland printed his name and "6:30" under "Time In," while the guard's face stayed buried in his body-building magazine.

On the twentieth floor, the elevator opened to the scowling countenance of a woman in an olive-green dress. "It's after six thirty," she said as if the words gave her stomach cramps.

Sutherland consulted his watch. "Six thirty-two. Guilty."

"You've kept Mr. Tunney waiting."

"He can bill me." Sutherland tried a smile, but the woman didn't soften.

"Mr. Tunney's in that corner office." She pointed, glared, and scuttled to the elevator. Great attitude. She'd last five seconds working for him.

He walked down a corridor to the corner office where he found Reginald Tunney standing by the door in a vested suit. With an expansive sweep of his long arm, he waved Sutherland past him into an enormous office. "Welcome to Chartered Associates, my boy."

From the center of the room Sutherland appraised the antique partners desk, the large Persian carpets covering the marble floor, the framed surveyor's maps on the silk wall panels, and the mahogany wainscoting and trim. A leather couch and chairs, a grandfather's clock, a nineteenth-century transit, and one wall covered in a solid floor-to-ceiling bookcase filled with leather-bound volumes. It looked less of an office than a page out of *Designer's Wet Dream,* if there were such a magazine. "Not a bad workstation, Reggie. All your employees live like this?"

"A holdover from better times," Tunney said, jutting his chin forward, stretching his neck in his odd habit. "You know how it was." As Tunney stepped closer, Sutherland caught a whiff of Scotch.

"Too well." Sutherland regarded the big man standing grandly in the doorway—the paunch pushing at his vest, the ripening bags under the eyes, the veined network on nose and cheeks—Tunney was the putrefying fruit of the real estate booms.

"I've read about Broadwell's problems. Must make you nervous." Sutherland detected a spark of amusement in his yellowish eyes.

"Nothing I can do. My lawyers are on it."

Tunney led the way into the office, sat behind his desk, and motioned for Sutherland to take the chair on the other side. "Bad things seem to go in twos and threes. Your friend the newspaper man got caught up in a love triangle, according to what I read."

"No one believes that. He was killed for what he was investigating. For one thing, your buddy Gene Sandler was in his sights, and that's why the fat shit had him killed. Am I right?"

Tunney arched his brows, as if surprised by the statement. "I thought it had something to do with this notebook and Delaney. But you have a point—there could be another motive, and Gene is a cagey devil. Doubt if it could be proved though."

"I could care less about him. The point is, none of us want the notebook or Delaney's tapes made public. I've learned enough to realize my father's involvement could damage me as well. Problem is, I've run out of ideas. I've been through his stuff and haven't a clue. Where do we go from here?"

Tunney seemed genuinely surprised this time, never expecting this implied offer of an alliance. He thought a moment, leaned forward with his forearms on his desk, and said in a serious tone, "Forget everything but the last two days of his life. That's when he must have made off with Danny's tapes; that's when he moved the money around. The wired money may be lost for good if he didn't keep a record of its routing. But the tapes? Where would you hide them?"

"His house or office would make the most sense. But what was left of the house was torn down to make way for a McMansion, and the McCollum is nearly leveled."

"Doesn't matter," Tunney said. "Both were pretty thoroughly searched by more than one party."

"Who?"

"I'd guess the FBI, since we now know they didn't already have them. As for others, use your imagination," Tunney said, smiling. "Bernard was a shrewd man. He obviously thought of something more clever than that."

"Yet after all this time, you and the FBI come up empty. Why would I have better luck?"

"Maybe you won't. Best thing would be they're lost forever. On the other hand, that notebook could lead to them. Start there."

"I don't have it, and I haven't seen it."

Tunney stretched his neck and peered skeptically. "That friend of yours had it. So where is it now?"

"Beats me."

Tunney nodded, a cynical gleam in his eyes. "I think you do know. Start there, focus on you father's last day, and you'll find those tapes. Once destroyed, you can get on with living." He hoisted his large frame out of his chair and said, "Now if you'll excuse me, I've got an appointment. If I can help with anything, let me know." He held up his index finger to make a point. "Anything."

This man was a criminal, part of an elaborate payoff scheme. Was he also a murderer? A sadist? Whatever the answer, he was stonewalling, and Sutherland had had enough. He stood and stepped to within a foot of Tunney, looking up into the big man's face. His stomach was tightened like his fists, but his words came out calmly. "You said anything? In that case, tell me this. Why would my father steal that money and take those tapes if he was going to commit suicide? What am I missing, Reggie? What aren't you telling me?"

Tunney stared at Sutherland with a look that could have been pity or contempt. "I said your father was a shrewd man, my boy, but he was foolish in a lot of ways. Why did he confess and go to jail? Why did he take that money and then the tapes before choosing to die? Whatever the reason, take my advice and don't be like him."

Tunney turned and walked from the office. Sutherland followed to the door and watched him haul his tall frame down the corridor, stiff-legged, like a former basketball player with bad knees. At the end, he entered a private elevator, presumably to the penthouse. Sutherland remembered an article on Chicago architecture describing how the tower above these offices was designed as a penthouse apartment for the original owner. Now Tunney occupied it, hardly returning to his suburban home where his wife resided with two nurses.

In the lobby below, after signing out at the security desk, Sutherland crossed the terrazzo floor toward the front doors. Hearing laughter behind him, he turned to see a black man with a shaved head and a woman with long, blond hair, both tall, athletic, and dressed in black with shiny, draping chains around their waists. They floated giddily from a rear door to the security desk and asked the guard something.

"Penthouse floor," the guard said, his voice echoing around the lobby.

*Penthouse*? Sutherland thought. What business could those two have with Reggie? Then, when the two turned toward the elevators, he was stunned to see that the man and woman wore leather chaps—with nothing apparent underneath. He couldn't help noticing because their bare buttocks protruded like loaves of bread—his overdone, hers unbaked.

# CHAPTER 50

Ronnie entered Ristorante Volare and stopped by the end of the bar. She ran a hand through her hair and glared across the field of diners like a raptor. Spotting Sutherland in a corner table, she headed straight for him, grabbing the opposite chair and dumping her large shoulder bag beside her on the floor. "Sorry I'm late. I fell asleep right after you called. Haven't had much lately."

"You look it." She wore a short-sleeved shirt and jeans and her eyes were red-rimmed and puffy—hardly the woman he had known before, but what could you expect? "Did you hand in your piece for the *Tribune*?"

"This afternoon. Be in tomorrow's edition. It might already be in the early edition or on the website."

The waiter arrived with the fried calamari Sutherland had ordered before Ronnie arrived. Ronnie picked out a large ring from the steaming pile and bit on it savagely, barely flinching at the heat. They ordered New York strip steaks and beers, hers bloody and his rare, without looking at the menus.

"So what do you have for me?" she asked. He'd called her mobile and found her at her hotel, suggesting that Langer's records might help with her *Tribune* article, intending to trade them for a copy of the notebook. He'd removed the references or papers with his father's name, not wanting to add any more fuel to the bonfire. Ronnie had said that although it was too late to change anything, she still wanted to see what the files contained.

Over their beers and steaks he filled her in on what he'd gleaned from the stack of documents in the suitcase. Everything except the author of the executed partnership agreements: his father. He also confirmed Bill Jamison's belief that the payoff scheme was still being used today and that Langer's America Tower was only one example.

"The suitcase is in my trunk. If you find anything useful, don't mention that Langer was the source."

"Why? He doesn't deserve to be protected from the bad guys. He's as big a crook as the rest of them. You just said so."

"But he doesn't deserve to be murdered for giving me the documents."

"Okay. I'll just compare dates and such with what I have."

"In exchange for a better look at that notebook."

"You saw it last night."

"A glimpse of a few pages before you yanked them away. With a copy I may be able to help."

"No way. The *Trib* is considering letting me work with another reporter to finish what Billy started. He'll share the byline posthumously. Can't let anyone have it until we finish pulling it together."

"You won't give the FBI or the police a copy?"

"They could gag us. Stop us from publishing. Say it would compromise their case. I've seen it before."

"You have a copy of Bill's obit with you?"

"Just a second." She hefted her heavy bag onto the table and rummaged through it, pulling out contents and setting them on a cleared-away section of table: folders, her cell phone, her BlackBerry, two sets of keys, a notebook, and then her gun.

"Jesus, Ronnie, put that away," Sutherland said, turning around to see if anyone in the crowded restaurant was looking.

"Here it is," she said, handing him three folded typed sheets. "Take your time to read it; I'll be back in a minute." She gathered the gun and other items, crammed them into the leather satchel, and headed to the ladies' room with it.

"Jesus H. Christ," was all Sutherland could say after he'd read her brother's epitaph. It started like any obituary with data about his background, schooling, and awards for his investigative reporting for the *Chicago Tribune*. It continued with his age, thirty-six, and his only remaining family being his older sister, Veronica Jamison. It was only in the last paragraphs when it ventured into the cause of death that it became troublesome. After referencing Jamison's latest series of columns on Danny Delaney and his tie-in to recent murders and current-day corruption, she suggested that her brother's death had been meant to stop further probing. By locating Delaney's notebook, Jamison was about to fill in the blanks, but it was his research into Eugene Sandler's activities through one of his accountants that had sealed his fate.

"What do you think?" Ronnie said, plunking her bag on the table and again sitting across from Sutherland. "Did I stir the pot?"

"With nitroglycerine. Will they print it like that?"

"Why not?"

"Sandler's lawyers will come out with guns blazing for one thing. And I thought you weren't going to say Bill knew where the notebook was."

"I didn't say he had it, just that he'd located it."

"This isn't time for splitting hairs. You've just made yourself a target. And because you won't ask the police or the feds for help, you're an easy mark, no one watching your back."

"How about you?"

"Sorry. If you won't share what you have, I'm out," Sutherland said, hoping he sounded convincing. He had no intention of quitting until he had prevented any more negative publicity from surfacing. "I only got involved to stop any of my father's deeper culpability from ruining my office development. With the Broadwell deal as good as dead, it doesn't matter anymore." He pulled out his wallet and placed four twenties on the table. "If you want Langer's files, they're in the trunk of my car. It's across the street. But I have to see that notebook."

The fire in Ronnie's eyes could have singed his hair. She stared at him across the table, breathing heat. "That's it? You'd quit?"

"No reason not to. You're blocking me out, so it's your fight," he said.

"And Billy?" she hissed. "You got him into this and you don't feel any responsibility?"

"I warned him. Like I'm warning you."

"Then how about doing it for your father?"

"He had me fooled for years. In the end, he couldn't even face himself."

"You mean suicide? What if I told you it wasn't?"

"It was either a freak accident or suicide. He was too experienced to fall overboard on a calm night."

"Then you haven't seen the police report." She dug into her bag again, hunted around and, frustrated, gave up, saying, "Damn, must've left it in my room. But I can tell you what's in it. Vislowski found it for me. There was evidence of at least two other people on your father's boat that night. Footprints, empty bottles, cigarette butts. And the boat was torn apart inside, as if someone was searching for something."

Was it possible? Other people on the boat, there to kill his father and hunt for the videos? If it were true, did it change things? "Wait. How could there be others? The boat was found abandoned, empty."

"The report mentioned a big gouge in the fiberglass and a couple ropes that had been attached and cut, indicating another boat alongside. It doesn't take any imagination to figure out he was thrown overboard. That far out on the lake, it was murder."

"Then why …?" But he didn't need to finish the question. It didn't take much to explain how evidence could be lost or overlooked when you have police officials on your payroll.

"See? You've got as much reason as I do. If you don't finish this thing for Billy, do it for your father."

For years Sutherland had believed his father was guilty of attempted bribery and then committing suicide. Now he was learning he was guilty of broader crimes but might have been murdered. Did that revelation change

171

his perspective on his father? Sutherland was too surprised and conflicted to come to any immediate conclusion. He stood and pointed to the front of the restaurant. "Car's down the street. Langer's files for a good look at the notebook. Agreed or not?"

She hefted her case onto her hip and said, "Agreed."

# CHAPTER 51

Ristorante Volare sat on Grand Avenue just east of where it plunges into the darkness beneath Michigan Avenue, The Magnificent Mile. At ten in the evening the neighborhood was a landscape of vacant lots and darkened buildings. They saw no one as they walked south on St. Clair and east on Illinois Street toward Sutherland's car.

The Jaguar sat in the far line of spaces next to an early-nineties Cadillac in a nearly empty lot. From ten yards away Sutherland pressed the remote unit on his key ring. The alarm burped its disarming signal, two short chirps from under the hood.

Sutherland saw a shadow moving near his car. He stopped, pulling back Ronnie by her shirt.

"What?"

"Shhh. Someone's behind the car." They slinked behind a BMW and watched. Nothing.

"I didn't see anything."

"I did. Watch." He aimed and pushed the remote unit again. The car squealed, signaling the alarm rearmed. This time they both saw shadowy movement.

"What now?" she said.

It could have been a bum taking a leak, a car thief, or someone after them for the notebook. Whoever it was had seen them, and Sutherland wasn't taking any chances. He took a deep breath, edged by the BMW's hood, and bellowed, trying to sound like three hundred pounds of muscle. "We see you, asshole. You got ten seconds to split."

They waited, eyes fixed on the Jaguar. Nothing. He whispered to Ronnie, "Let's head back to Volare's, call 911 on our way. Got your phone handy?" She struggled with the clasps to her bag. "Fuck the phone, I'll get my gun."

As she started to dig around inside, the man rose and came charging toward them. He was burly, past forty, and dressed in a golf shirt—hardly a bum or a teenaged car thief. Then another face surfaced in the adjacent Cadillac's front seat.

"Run," Sutherland yelled, turning to see Ronnie franticly groping in her bag. "Come on, no time." He shoved her toward the street and glanced over his shoulder to see the man scramble around the cars, in pursuit. Something was in his hand. It looked like a pipe, and not the kind you smoke.

Sutherland caught Ronnie, who was still rummaging in her heavy shoulder bag, open and bouncing at her hip, slowing her down. Their pace also suffered from leather-soled shoes, alcohol, and a heavy meal, but they were a hundred yards from Volare's, and their pursuers were barely gaining. Home free.

But before they could cross lower Illinois Street, a gray Chevrolet, headlights out and tires squealing, lurched directly in their path from where it sat by the curb. The car blocked their way north; the man on foot approached from behind. They veered left, jumping the parking lot guardrail, racing across the vacant lot to the south toward the river and lower Michigan. Sutherland grabbed Ronnie's arm to support her and speed her along as she wrestled with the bag, her left hand fumbling deep inside. They had no idea where their pursuers were but didn't dare stop.

Running past the *Tribune*'s truck docks, they plunged into the shadows below Michigan Avenue. Finally, less than a block away, they saw the glow of the Billy Goat Tavern, their subterranean refuge.

"Come on, let's sprint for it," he said.

Skidding, scuffling over the uneven asphalt, they rounded the corner. But after ten more strides, they saw the gray Chevy creeping through the underground shadows, headlights still out and chrome grill grinning malevolently. They slid to a stop, looking desperately for a way out.

"Up the stairs. This way," Sutherland said. If they reached the top of the stairs, they'd be in the light and bustle of The Magnificent Mile.

They ran to the stairway leading to the street above and bounded two steps at a time up the stairs, Ronnie leading. She halted abruptly. The first man stood on the sidewalk glowering down at them, breathing in heaves. His pipe was in his hand, hanging at his side.

He rushed down three steps, but Ronnie swung her shoulder bag. The strap broke as it hit him, stopping him momentarily. He raised his pipe, and Sutherland and Ronnie scrambled back down the stairway. There, another man approached from twenty yards away.

Both the path toward the Billy Goat and the stairs behind were blocked. That left the lower level of the Michigan Avenue Bridge, a desolate underpass of girders and shadow. "The bridge," Sutherland said, giving Ronnie a push.

"There's nothing over there."

"That's the point, come on."

The double-decked bridge accommodated two levels of traffic, upper Michigan Avenue in all its brilliance, and lower Michigan like a netherworld beneath. Sutherland saw only tunnel, stretching dark and forbidding before them.   They darted down the bridge's eastern sidewalk, easily outrunning their hunters. But near the other side, their spirits sank. Another man, this one with a baseball bat, stood in their path. The white Cadillac waited in the dimness behind him.

"Should we try it?" she asked.

*Dodge a man swinging a bat on a six-foot sidewalk?* he asked himself. They wouldn't both make it. And surrender wasn't an option. These guys weren't interested in talk. "Over the wall," he said.

"The water?"

"The street." He pushed her toward the railing and massive balustrade separating sidewalk from car lane. Shinnying to the top, one knee up, then the other, they were on top of the girder and between the diagonal beams before the men on the sidewalk closed the gap.

"Fuck," shouted one of the men from the sidewalk on the wrong side of the girders.

"Shit," said Ronnie, pointing to the gray Chevrolet approaching in their lane.

"Over the center wall," Sutherland said. They climbed onto the center balustrade, crawled between diagonal beams, and jumped to the other car lane. Just in time to see the Cadillac approaching. "One more," he said.

Over the last set of girders, scraping hands and knees on the way, they landed on the west sidewalk as the car slid to a halt on the other side. The sidewalk in either direction was clear. If they won the race off the bridge, they might escape.

"This way." Sutherland pushed Ronnie south.

"Why that way?" Her face was black with dirt and sweat, her eyes pained.

"You win, the other way," he said, pushing her north. She sprinted off with Sutherland close behind. Another thirty feet, and ...

Another man, tall and blond, waited at the end, the light from the Wrigley Building glinting on the gun in his right hand. They stopped, turned, and saw another man climb down from the balustrade and plod toward them with bat in hand.

"Ideas?" Ronnie asked, panting.

Sutherland looked over the side at the river below. The thought of dark water swallowing him made his legs buckle. He grabbed the railing and froze. It was drown or face a charging man with a bat, another with a gun. It didn't matter. "You go," he said.

She stared at him in disbelief. "You nuts?"

"Go ahead." He straightened himself, ready to fight both men.

"Not unless you do," she said, turning to face the man with the bat.

Phobia or no, he wouldn't gamble with any life but his own. Before allowing himself more thought, he hefted her onto the railing and, clutching her by the waist, threw himself over. They toppled together over the rail just as the man with the gun reached them.

Falling, Sutherland heard shouts and then echoing gunfire. But sound faded in the shocks of impact and cold immersion. It was like reliving his father's last breaths.

# Chapter 52

Kelly Matthews passed up the building elevator and took the six flights two stairs at a time. It was her way of burning off a few calories and some of the day's tension. She'd had to cut her run short that morning because of an early meeting with her boss at city hall. She strode down the corridor to her condo apartment, unlocked the door, and entered. Seeing the bouquet on her hall table made her smile. After Doug had arrived with flowers that first time, she'd started bringing them home herself. It was a small but pleasing touch to her otherwise perfect apartment. She couldn't name a single flower in the latest bunch, but she loved the way the purple and blue complemented the white and yellow.

Her loft was part of a converted warehouse. She loved the spaciousness, the high ceilings and exposed brick walls, and the south-facing view of the city. It was a practical size for a neat person who disliked maintenance and cleaning. It contained a master bedroom, bath, and walk-in closet. It also had a modern kitchen with adjacent dining area, a den with a second bathroom, and a living room with a large balcony and fire escape.

She threw her purse on a chair, opened the refrigerator, pulled out a half-full bottle of white wine, pulled out the cork, and poured herself a glass. Work had been nothing but meetings, combative discussions, and "cover your ass" positioning. Lunch was an apple and yogurt at her desk with no time to finish preparing for court the next morning. She'd have to do that after her late dinner.

She carried her glass to the living room, kicking off her shoes through her bedroom door on the way, and turned on the television with the remote. Sinking into her Eames chair, stretching her legs over the ottoman, she changed the channel to local news. A shooting on the West Side, a new superintendent of schools, a possible CTA rate increase, yada yada. After a commercial, a few items of national interest, and a few mouthfuls of wine, she was almost relaxed.

About to get to her feet, a breaking news segment flashed on the screen. A reporter was standing on the Michigan Avenue bridge, the Wrigley Building in the background, talking into the camera. Kelly hardly heard the narrative and was about to turn the TV off, but the scene changed to an image of two drenched and exhausted people being dragged from the river and taken to a waiting fire department ambulance. Two details stuck: the face of one of the victims was Doug Sutherland's, and the announcer said that both of the victims had been taken to Northwestern Hospital.

Jumping to her feet, she ran to her bedroom, crammed on her shoes, and grabbed her purse from the chair. Without a second thought she knew she had to go to the hospital. She was going to make sure Doug was okay and find out what happened. Never mind that she wasn't a relative or a spouse. She was his, she was … what?

Driving to the hospital, she had to wonder what their relationship, if any, was now. A few months ago there was no doubt. Lovers, they were gradually getting closer, even though learning consequential details about him was like pulling teeth. He finally told her about his failed marriage to Margo, an insecure and needy woman. Kelly tried to imagine Doug with a needy person and gave up. Just as he had.

He'd been secretive about his father as well. She only knew that he was deceased, discovering that nugget only after they'd been dating for a year. Much later it came out that his mother—his Mexican mother—was still living. His Mexican heritage would never have occurred to Kelly. When they'd first met at that dig in Chiapas more than a decade earlier, the first thing she'd noticed was those startling, blue eyes shining from that deeply tanned face. She'd been attracted to his quiet manner, good looks, and the special feeling she got when they were together, digging side by side or practicing Spanish over *cerveza fría* with Arturo, the head of the excavation. Their relationship at the dig never had time to develop beyond friendship. They both had too many plans that sent them in different directions.

Just at the time when she'd hoped their disagreements over the McCollum Building would be forgotten, when they could see more rationally, these newest revelations complicated matters. The discovery of a dead alderman in his building, resulting in more dirt spread about his father, made getting close to Doug even more difficult. He was even more defensive and secretive.

Where was it going with Doug and her? Not long ago they were getting closer. With a little more time, they might have felt comfortable enough to take the plunge. Now things were out of kilter. She wasn't calling it quits, but she had to make a serious assessment of where they stood. She, like Doug, had married once. Hers had lasted two years before mutual apathy set in. She didn't feel compelled to get married again. Having children wasn't a priority. She was a successful lawyer and could be as independent as Doug.

He was certainly that. He wanted neither to need nor be needed. Could she live with that?

# Chapter 53

**S**utherland sank through darkness to the bottom, where a cave glowed with pale green light. He floated inside. Through the water he saw her red hair—delicate tendrils drifting around her alabaster face like an exotic sea flower. Her green eyes were strained wide and she opened her mouth as if to speak. Instead of bubbles and words, a moray eel inched forward and peered out.

"Ronnie," he cried.

He burst from the depths, hungry for air. His eyes opened into a dimly lit room and he felt a figure near him, a silhouette gripping his arm.

"It's okay, Doug."

He knew the voice, but where was he? What happened?

"It's Kelly. You're in your own bed. You're okay. So's Ronnie."

"Kelly? Ronnie? Good." And he fell back into his pillow and sleep.

*    *    *

When he awoke several hours later, voices droned in another part of the apartment. He stood and walked to the bathroom, recollecting the odds and ends of the night before and how he arrived in his own bed. He pulled on jeans and sweatshirt and walked to the dining room, where he found Kelly sitting with Detective Vislowski at the table.

"What's going on?" Sutherland asked, looking back and forth between them. Seeing him, Kelly smiled. Vislowski inspected him coldly.

"Now I remember," Sutherland said to Kelly. "You got me here in a taxi and put me to bed."

"You were dead on your feet in the emergency room. What was I supposed to do?"

"Undress me too?" He sat down, thinking, *Like old times.*

"Want coffee?" she asked. "I bought some. Only thing in your refrigerator was beer and take-out Thai food old enough to vote."

Sutherland wanted to laugh but a pain in his side made him wince. He nodded to Vislowski. "You're in homicide or something. Isn't this outside your specialty?"

"Seeing if there's a connection."

"Isn't it obvious? How's Ronnie?"

"Sleeping when I was at the hospital. She's okay, they're doing a test for something internal, and she had a gash when they pulled her out. You two are lucky."

Sutherland recalled glimpses, slow-motion images of the fall, the numbing water, the shouts and gunshots. He remembered struggling to the surface, flailing to stay afloat, fighting the old panic. Ronnie must have helped him reach the pilings where they hid, hanging onto slimy concrete until help arrived.

"Catch any of them?"

"One. Man in the Wrigley Building saw you jump and the guys hanging over the rail. Called 911. Squad picked up one who said he was trying to help you out. You recognize any of them?"

"No. I'd remember one or two if I saw them again. How about the licenses, the cars?"

"Stolen. But the suspect's got a record—out to break some bones, is what we figure. Trying to scare you."

"Who does he work for?"

"So far, we don't know. Four, five men—serious stuff, but nothing to connect them with Bill Jamison or the other deaths. Unless you got some ideas."

"Sandler's my bet. The guy whose records Bill Jamison was trying to steal. Now he's after Ronnie because he thinks she's got the notebook. He also owned an umbrella like you found in Scooch's room."

"Veronica told you about the umbrella?" Vislowski said, shaking his head. "Supposed to be confidential, but it doesn't matter. No way to prove it was Sandler's or anyone else's. It was clean, no prints, no nothing. Company that sold them made dozens of them with an *R* on the handle. Their specialty was monograms, any letter you wanted. What about the notebook? She have it?"

"I think it's in her hotel room. Been staying there since Bill was killed. I doubt she wants anyone to know which hotel."

"Just like her." Vislowski stroked his mustache with his thick fingers and shook his head. "I wouldn't be surprised if she went after Sandler herself. She's got a vengeful side that she calls justice. But this time, with her brother's murder, she's slipped off the deep end." He stood up, gulped down the rest of his coffee, set his cup on the table, and said, "Watch her, Mr. Sutherland. Don't let her go too far." He turned and walked down the corridor, his shoes slapping the hardwood floor, the apartment door closing with a click.

Sutherland poured himself more coffee. Kelly regarded him solemnly, appraising him and what she had just heard, her eyes dark with concern.

"Jesus, Doug," she said finally. "What she got you into?"

Sutherland shrugged. "Not my choice. One thing led to another."

"Come off it. No one leads you around."

He sipped his coffee and noticed his hands. The knuckles were scraped and bruised, the palms scratched, a bandage spanned one wrist, and new tape joined his injured pinky to his middle and ring finger. He realized his shoulders ached and his arms hurt. He flexed and rolled his shoulders; he was sore to his marrow.

"You look like you're hurting," Kelly said. "I'm not surprised. The ten o'clock news showed Red and you being hauled from the river. You had her pinned to the side, hanging on to the embankment."

"We were both exhausted. I'm no swimmer. How'd you come to get me?"

"After seeing you on the news I went to the emergency room. Who else was gonna help you? Your ex-wife?"

"Not likely."

"She called here—well, Jenny called for her. This morning. Hope you don't mind, I spent the night on the couch. Anyway, Jenny was worried."

"What'd you tell her?"

"You were sleeping like a rock. But she had some scary news that should make you think twice about what you're doing."

"What scary news?" Sutherland's stomach tightened.

"She was going to stay here last night, like she sometimes does. She let herself in and was playing a video, waiting for you, when she got frightened and took a cab home."

"To Winnetka? Alone at night? Jesus, that girl …"

"Just listen to what's going on around you while you're on this stupid charade," Kelly said, fixing him with a hard stare. "Here's what happened: she heard someone open the door."

"What?" Sutherland tensed his arms, spilling coffee from his cup.

"The door was on the security chain. At first she thought it was you, but when you didn't answer her calls, she put up the TV volume and called the doorman. He came up and took her to the lobby and a cab."

Sutherland bolted out of his chair and slammed his fists on the table.

Now he'd got his own daughter caught up in this. "Sons of bitches! They were looking for the notebook."

"See what I'm saying, you idiot? While you were running around with Red, some thug nearly broke in. No telling what would have happened if Jenny hadn't scared them away." She was nearly spitting now. "So when are you going to stop listening to that redhead and tell me what's going on? Your own daughter, for God's sake."

"Get you involved? I damn near got Jenny hurt. I'm not getting you into this."

"Bullshit." She stood and leaned on the table, her hands balled in fists. She glared at him, surprising him with her intensity.

He shook his head and tried to stare her down.

"I've got all day," she said. "Maybe I can help."

Would she blink? He probed her eyes. Those beautiful eyes. "I don't want you hurt," he said.

"When I was against your project, you said I played too rough. Now you need to shield me?"

It had started with strangers like Danny Delaney, Gorman, and Scooch. Bill Jamison's death had brought it closer—but even Bill was a stranger given everything Sutherland didn't know about him. But the attack on Ronnie and him, and his daughter's close encounter, made it undeniably personal. Why endanger another innocent?

"Stay out of it," he said.

"I thought we were still friends at least."

From the bitterness in her voice and the sorrow in her eyes, he knew she intended to leave. He also knew that if she left, the last vestige of what they had would go with her. A month ago, he would have accepted that. But today he couldn't. "Sit down. It'll take a while."

After he gave her the PG version of events, skipping a few murders and missing body parts, Kelly hung her head and sighed. "Unbelievable."

"I know. Unbelievable."

"I mean *you're* unbelievable. Getting yourself caught up in this. What were you thinking?"

Her comment stopped him temporarily, raising his hackles. "What do you mean? Like I had a choice."

She held up her hands to calm him, cleared her throat, and began. "Let me see if I understand. A dead alderman's found in your building, murdered. A stranger calls you, selling the alderman's notebook, and you send him to your reporter friend, who happens to be working on a corruption story that may be related. You help with his investigations, secretly wanting to control what he writes or even destroy evidence damaging to your father and your project. Right so far?"

"Right."

"The man selling the book is killed, then your reporter friend as well. His sister gets her hands on the notebook somehow and wants what? To continue her brother's investigation?"

"Before Bill was killed, she wanted him to have the exposé he'd been working on and the fame that would come with it. You heard the detective; now she wants justice, which for her amounts to revenge."

"Dragging you along with her. Damn near getting killed and endangering your daughter. Are you crazy?"

"I'm not going along with her. If those tapes show what I think, that my father was guilty of more serious crimes than what he did time for, it could ruin me. Not just my reputation and ability to keep the Broadwell deal or secure an alternative. The title to the McCollum property could be in jeopardy, according to the FBI. I just want the book and everything else destroyed."

"You're willing to risk dying for that?"

"Those guys on the bridge were scaring us, that's all."

"And the person at your door, scaring your daughter to death?"

"She'll have to stay away. I'll tell her," he said, standing up. "You too. I agreed to tell you, but I don't want you getting messed up in this."

"Because you care, or because you don't want someone around telling you what a damn ass you are?"

"A little of both."

# CHAPTER 54

Eugene Sandler finished reading the museum directors' meeting minutes and tossed the folder into his out-basket to be filed. He'd been on the board for five years, ever since his first generous donation. Next year he would be the board president, if Delaney's reappearance didn't cause publicity he couldn't neutralize. That concern wouldn't disappear until the notebook and videos were disposed of for good.

He switched off his desk lamp, sinking the office into twilight, then removed his tinted glasses. Resting his hands on his ample stomach, the front of his white shirt stretched to the limit, he pictured a chessboard and the position of his and his opponent's pieces since his last move over the Internet. His opponent, also a grand master, would have to take his knight with his rook, and in two more moves, Sandler would have checkmate. There was no money at stake, but that didn't matter, winning was enough. To know and outthink another, foresee all the possibilities, defend with skill and attack decisively were the elements that stimulated him. He'd been at the game since he was six and still found it was one of the few things in his life that challenged him.

The tactics he employed to make him rich, powerful, and feared in the practical world were natural derivatives of what he'd learned from chess. Free of the strict rules that governed chess, by overlooking bothersome laws and mores, it became easy to exploit and control the greedy, venal, and weak around him. A fluke of nature had robbed him of a normal life, so he derived his pleasure by bullying, intimidating, and dominating those who possessed what he lacked.

The telephone rang and the security guard in the lobby fifteen floors below informed him that his visitor had arrived. Two minutes later, Reginald Tunney, tall and rigid in his blue three-piece suit, walked into the office, looked around, and frowned. "Jesus, Gene," he said in his nasal baritone. "It's a cavern in here. You're like a mole. Ever see a baby mole? They're pink, like you. They're blind too."

Sandler dug out a Winston from the silver cigarette box on his desk, lit it with a flick of his Dunhill, and said, "Through with the biology lesson?" He exhaled a gray stream in Tunney's direction.

"So where's our boy?" Tunney asked, waving away the smoke.

"He's running late."

"While we wait, let's talk about last night. Who'd you hire, the Three Stooges?"

Sandler tried to contain his pique, felt the heat spreading on his face. "What's the problem? We got the girl's briefcase, BlackBerry, and apartment keys. They weren't to be seriously hurt—just put in check, not mate, while we searched their places. Shooting wasn't supposed to be part of it."

Tunney stretched his neck and jutted his chin, as if his starched collar chafed. "Sutherland's place? Find anything?"

"Someone else was in there." Sandler leaned his heavy torso forward and slipped a meaty hand into his desk drawer, pulling out three keys on a ring. He held them up in the dim light from the street. His company had the janitorial contract for Sutherland's condo building and his office. "We can get in anytime. Meantime, I'm going to feel Sutherland out directly."

"He hates your guts. Will he meet?"

"He's got to be curious about what I know. You didn't help him much, did you?"

"No. But who knows what that weasel Jules told him? So be careful. He's talked to the police and FBI. He could wear a wire."

"Nothing illegal about buying a book, is there?"

"When I saw him, he acted dumb about it. The money and everything else."

The phone rang again, this time the lobby announcing their other visitor. Sandler ordered him sent up and said to Tunney, "Our congressman's pissing me off, the little prick. Fucker's starting to believe his own bullshit." He looked up to see US Representative George Spanos in the doorway. He gave him a cold smile and waved him in. "Come on in, Governor, have a seat."

George Spanos was a handsome man with a stocky build. People said he reminded them of a taller, better-looking Michael Dukakis, one-time governor of Massachusetts. He wore a gray, pin-striped suit, crisp, white shirt, and red tie. He took off his jacket and took the chair next to Tunney in front of Sandler's desk.

"What a night," he said. "A room full of Vietnam vets and another chicken dinner. Then I get another message from Agent Branson. He wants to see me again." Loosening his tie, he continued, "My poll numbers are up and then all this shit with Delaney and Gorman popping up. Bad timing."

"You didn't help yourself with your comments to the press," Tunney said. "Why'd you bring Delaney up in the first place?"

Spanos stared at Tunney and frowned. "It just came out. With Delaney in the news, I thought it would speak to my experience as a crime buster, the anticorruption guy, now when it's all around us. My opponent can't claim that."

"But bragging about putting Bernard Sutherland away, of having Delaney on the hook, of hounding Gorman out of the pension fund? Where did that come from? They have fact checkers."

"I was there," Spanos rebutted.

"So were we," Sandler said. "You were a junior assistant in the state's attorney's office. It wouldn't surprise me if Agent Branson suspected something. What did he ask you?"

"He was polite. Don't forget, I am a congressman and know some of his superiors in DC. He wanted to know what I remembered about our work with Delaney. He saw me in our meetings with the FBI at the time."

"What did you tell him?" Tunney asked.

"Nothing he didn't know. In fact he reminded me of something. Delaney had agreed to hand over his videos taken of meetings in his office. Branson asked if I ever saw them. Were they destroyed with everything else?"

Sandler and Tunney looked at each other for a moment before Tunney said, "We don't know."

"So how do we find them? Through the notebook?" Spanos asked.

"We'll know soon," Tunney said.

"Branson told me the *Tribune* has the original. Any way you can get it first? According to that dead reporter, my name's in it."

"Shouldn't matter," Sandler said. "You could have been meeting with Delaney because of the investigation. It's the tapes that could put us all in jail, including you. Possibly for murder."

"What do you mean?" Spanos blurted. "There's nothing on Delaney's videos about murder. Not when I was there."

"Settle down, Georgie," Tunney said. "We don't know what he recorded. You keep campaigning and let us handle it."

Spanos calmed down but seemed to be mulling a question, his lips tight, his brow wrinkled. Finally he mustered the courage and asked, "These recent murders. Gorman, the reporter, so on." He swallowed, an audible gulp. "You?"

Tunney chuckled. "You'll learn, Governor, just like others before you. Presidents, mayors, doesn't matter—let the people behind you get things done and don't ask."

"But …" Spanos stuttered.

"Those people were trouble," Sandler interrupted. "Threatening a lot of folks, not just us. Fortunately the suspicion's spread all over the place, pointing in all directions. So don't worry, none of this will touch us. We'll be right behind you when you're elected."

Neither Sandler nor Tunney had answered Spanos's question, but he didn't press it. He couldn't have missed the implication behind Sandler's comment—that not only would they be behind him, they would be pulling his strings. Just as they had since the months leading up to Delaney's death.

# CHAPTER 55

"I see you're okay," Jules Langer said, appearing at Sutherland's apartment door. He was dressed in a gray, pin-stripped suit, and his white shirt accentuated his tanned face. Standing nonchalantly with one hand in his pocket, he nevertheless looked strangely awkward to Sutherland, a man in an alien country, not understanding the culture or how to behave. Not surprising, considering that despite knowing each other and competing for years, they were strangers personally. It was only a few days ago that Sutherland had set foot in Langer's home, and now Langer was seeing where his arch-opponent spent his personal time. "From the news reports, I'd thought you'd be in worse shape."

"Disappointed?" Sutherland said, closing the door.

Langer chuckled wryly. "There was a time I'd have been. I warned you we were in trouble."

Langer had called after Kelly left and wasted no time to follow in person. He looked around, as if searching for some connection—an anchor he could relate to. Then, upon surveying the living room, his face brightened. "Moving in? I'll give you the name of my decorator. With that view, this place could be a showcase."

"Thanks," Sutherland said, not wanting to enter the domain of "less is more" again.

Langer looked around the living room, his hand on his chin, seemingly considering the emptiness surrounding the island of furniture. "Yeah," he said. "Real potential."

Sutherland stifled a laugh. "Have a seat and I'll make you a drink."

"No, thanks," Langer said, sitting on the sofa. "Were you hurt?"

"A few scrapes and bruises." Sutherland took a chair with his back to the window, facing Langer. He pushed his hand over his stubble and realized he hadn't shaved.

"And the girl? The reporter's sister?"

"She's okay too."

"The news didn't say. You see the paper?" Langer tossed a folded second section on the coffee table. The headline read:

DEVELOPER AND ATTORNEY ESCAPE
MUGGING, JUMP IN RIVER

Next to the column was a photograph of a man and woman, wet hair plastered to their heads, draped in blankets, and surrounded by police and firemen. Seeing it, Sutherland shivered and said, "I'll put it in my scrapbook. How I spent my summer."

Langer tried one of his salesman's smiles then quickly exchanged it for a worried frown. "They didn't get a hold of my father's documents, did they?"

That explained Langer's sudden interest in Sutherland's well-being. "As far as I know, they're still in the trunk of my car."

"Were your attackers identified? Who sent them?"

"Police aren't saying. And speaking of that, why didn't you tell me there were other men on my father's boat the night he died? His murderers."

Langer looked like he'd swallowed a hair ball, his eyes bulging and his face draining of color. "Are you sure? I mean, about him being murdered?"

"What do you think? The question is who?"

"Not my father. He was sick and wouldn't talk about it. But murder?" Langer squeezed his eyes shut.

"My father was a sailor, Jules, a good yachtsman. He didn't just fall off. Who had the other boat that night?"

"I'll have that drink now," Langer said, loosening his tie, squirming in his chair. "Scotch. Neat."

Sutherland eased himself up, triggering a few twinges of pain. He walked to the kitchen cabinet, grabbed a bottle of twelve-year-old Glenlivet and a crystal glass, and brought them back, placing both on the coffee table. Langer uncorked the top, poured in three fingers, and took a long gulp. He inhaled deeply, exhaled, and nodded, as if to himself.

"I overheard a phone conversation my father had, but I don't know if I got it right." He finished the scotch in the glass and poured a refill. "Whoever it was on that boat was looking for Delaney's videotapes. They weren't sure they were destroyed in the fire."

"Not the money?"

"They thought the money was diverted to the feds. Apparently it wasn't. Otherwise the feds wouldn't be asking about it. An agent came to my office today."

"So if my father supposedly wired the money somewhere secret, how'd they think the feds accessed it?"

Langer swallowed another mouthful of scotch and sighed. "Don't you ever quit? Why do you need to know this shit?"

"If my old man was killed, I want to know who and what for."

"Okay. But this is all secondhand. This insider, the same guy that spilled about Delaney, suspected that your father was Delaney's contact, working with the feds, reporting to the FBI, probably to that guy that got shot."

Was there no end to the surprises his father's past had in store? First a good, honest man, then a briber, then a possible murderer, now working for the feds? Who was that man? And if he was working for the feds, why the fuck hadn't Branson said so from the beginning?

"You mean that's why they killed him? Why didn't that son of a bitch agent tell me?" He glared at Langer. "Why didn't you, asshole?"

"Like I said, I don't know if it's true," he said, defensively.

Sutherland stood, his hands on his temples in total disbelief. "That son of a bitch. Branson made all kinds of insinuations about my father. Guilty of transferring stolen funds, involved in Delaney's death, that he might even have had something to do with that FBI agent's murder." He stared down at Langer. "What was that all about?"

"Ask *him*," Langer said, still recoiling from Sutherland's rant. "All I want is for all of this to end. Did my father's stuff help any? You any closer to finding the tapes?"

"No. But you've just given me a hell of a lot more incentive. If I find those videos, Branson will have to kiss my ass before he sees them."

# Chapter 56

The fourth ring of the phone jerked Sutherland awake.

"Doug. It's Ronnie."

He looked at the clock on his dresser. Almost nine o'clock, but it didn't feel like morning. He looked around, realized he was still dressed, and remembered drifting off after Langer left. It was still evening.

"Someone broke into my apartment," Ronnie said.

"Where are you?"

"Still in the hospital. It could've been any time last night. My neighbor found the door unlocked. She went in to feed my cat and collect some clothes to bring me."

Sutherland sat up, stretched, and massaged his neck. His aches seemed to have multiplied and spread into a pervasive hurt. *How does one get in shape for banging around bridges and jumping into rivers?* he wondered.

"Lost my bag in the chase last night," Ronnie said. "One of those bastards got it. Papers, ID, address, keys, phone, gun. Couldn't make it simpler for them."

"How do you know?" he asked, standing now, looking out his window at the montage of city lights beneath the purpling sky.

"Neighbor found the bag inside. Empty," she said.

"They have the notebook?"

"Dunno. Anyway, it would just be one copy. I left it in a good hiding place, behind a shelf of books. There's another copy in my hotel room. I don't think they'll get that. The room card key didn't have a hotel name or number, and I paid cash using another name."

"With a card, it won't take long to find the hotel and room."

"I'll get it tomorrow. Meanwhile, do me a favor? I can't leave here. I was pissing blood. Go over and see what they took."

"You call the police? Vislowski?"

"Let's keep Stanley out of this. Will you check it out? In the den. Behind the law books on the right side of the bookcase. And pack some clean clothes for me while you're at it. I'm out of here tomorrow, whether the docs like it or not."

*   *   *

Ronnie's neighbor, a young woman as nervous as her frizzy black hair, opened Ronnie's apartment door and scurried away as if the burglar was waiting inside. Looking in, Sutherland understood her apprehension—he saw havoc everywhere. Someone had searched the living room with wanton determination. Oil paintings and sofa cushions along with the contents of every bookcase and cabinet had been strewn on the floor.

Sutherland, surveying the devastation, heard a familiar voice and turned to face Detective Vislowski, entering from the hallway.

"What's going on?" the detective asked.

"Ronnie asked me to come. What's a homicide cop doing at a burglary?"

"A neighbor called 911," he said. "It's easy to beat the burglary coppers. Why are you here?"

"She asked me to see what's missing."

"The notebook, maybe?"

"Show me the den and we'll find out."

"Down the corridor to the right." The detective led the way.

"That a guess?"

Sutherland could see Vislowski stiffen. "Never mind," he said over his shoulder. They walked around the contents of several cabinets, books and magazines emptied across the Oriental carpet.

When Sutherland entered the study, he stopped cold. It wasn't the upheaval that surprised him. The room reminded him of a stock market trading room. Situated on a semicircular desk in the far corner of the room were three flat-screen TVs, two Bloomberg monitors, a telephone headset, and a telephone console with a half-dozen buttons. On the right, between the two windows, was the bookcase Ronnie had mentioned.

"What the hell is this?" Sutherland asked. "A NASA command center?"

"She's a day trader. And gambler. An addict, if you ask me. On football weekends she'll have the TVs set to different games so she can monitor how she sits with the spreads and make betting adjustments."

"I knew she traded, but this is serious."

"She's really hooked. But that's not why we're here. Let's see what's what."

They found files emptied, drawers spilled, books on the floor, and one of the computer screens smashed. A letter opener was driven through Ronnie's face in a photo posed with her now-dead brother. It was obvious she had done some of her research here before moving to a hotel. Around them lay the litter of Bill Jamison's, Sandy Craig's, and Ronnie's notes dealing with Delaney and years of city corruption. Boxes overflowed with newspaper articles and folders bulged with contracts, agreements, and other documents.

"Good thing she took her laptop with her to her hotel," Sutherland said as he retrieved a manila folder from the floor.

"Don't touch that—fingerprints," Vislowski said.

Sutherland frowned at him. "You find any fingerprints at the murder scenes?"

"No, but—"

"You won't here either." Sutherland paged through the folder while Vislowski looked on. Names and photographs floated out like phantoms from the past. One photo captured Phillip Raskoff with Miles Langer, Sandler, and Tunney at a building dedication. Others featured Danny Delaney with Benjamin Gorman, Gorman with the old mayor, Sandler opening his insurance business, Langer forming Langer Development, Raskoff's lengthy obituary, and on and on.

Opening another folder, Doug Sutherland's father's likeness jarred him. The photo appeared in an article on Bernard's disappearance off his boat. The younger Sutherland stared for a long time before Vislowski coughed behind him.

"I thought all this was burned in her brother's place," Vislowski said.

"This comes from Sandy Craig, a reporter from back then."

"Then why wasn't this torched? Why leave all this?"

"I was wondering the same thing," Sutherland said. "Maybe it doesn't matter anymore."

"Or it was a coincidence. Someone else finding her keys and address."

"This wasn't a coincidence." Sutherland walked to the bookcase on the right side of the desk. The shelves were empty, the contents on the floor. In the back of a chest-level shelf was a one-foot-by-two-foot recess with an open door. They heard a scratching sound within, then the door moved and an orange blur streaked from the recess, bounded over the desk, and tore out of the room.

Sutherland leaped backward and was saved from falling when he banged into Vislowski. "What was that?"

"Bridie, Veronica's cat," the detective said, pushing Sutherland away. "She had something in her mouth."

"There's something there too," Sutherland said, looking into the hiding place.

"The notebook?"

"Take a look."

The detective removed a penlight from his jacket and pointed it inside. "We'll see about prints. What's this?"

"What?" Sutherland peered into the recess. He first thought it was an apricot, a dried apricot, shriveled and curled, blackened by age or mold. But it wasn't an apricot, and the realization came with a painful lump in his throat.

"Just when I think I've seen everything," Vislowski said. "That what I think it is?"

"You never found it, did you?"

"Something new every day." Vislowski pushed the door wider with the light until Scooch's desiccated ear could be clearly seen. "Oh no." He jerked his hand back, as if bitten. "What did that fuckin' cat have?" He jumped up and ran out of the room, down the hall, past the bedroom, and into the bathroom. Sutherland followed, not sure why, but not wanting to miss anything.

The cat was backed against bathtub, next to its litter box, its spine arched, its eyes wary. It sidled backward, snarling while holding in its mouth what looked like a shriveled sausage. While swallowing back nausea, Sutherland remembered what the detective had said about Bill Jamison's last moments.

# CHAPTER 57

Sutherland walked up to the FBI offices on South Dearborn, unknown territory for most people and happily so. Despite knowing the downtown landscape as well as most mail carriers, the interior of this building was a total mystery to Sutherland. As it turned out, it would remain so. He heard his name being called and turned to see Agent Branson waving at him from a black Ford sedan standing at the curb. Sutherland had called Branson's cell first thing that morning, and they'd agreed to meet at nine o'clock.

"Hop in," he said. "I've got to go to the airport. Let you off at your office."

Sutherland slid into the passenger seat and closed the door, saying, "I'm going to Northwestern Hospital. Drop me there."

"Something wrong?" Branson asked.

"Ronnie Jamison's there. I'm delivering some clean clothes." He patted the gym bag on his lap.

"I meant your message. You sounded pissed."

"Shouldn't I be? Why are you fucking with me?"

Branson reached for the coffee cup on the console between the seats, apparently playing for time to think. "Okay, I give. What's bothering you?"

"Why didn't you tell me that my father was working with you?"

Branson nodded a resigned affirmation. "Not that straightforward, Mr. Sutherland. Your father was supposedly working with our chief agent, John Durham, the man who was murdered. Their conversations were between them alone, and that's where it gets murky and a lot more complicated, begging some serious questions. Did your father have something to do with Durham's death? Was he really with us, or playing both sides for his own gain? We don't know for sure, and that's why I didn't tell you. It's as simple as that. I'm hoping—and you should too—that the tapes will clear it up for good."

Branson's answer could be nothing more than an elaborate excuse, but

Sutherland felt like he'd encountered another switchback in the road. His father double-dealing? The real question was whether he should believe anything Branson said. "Did you know there was an insider on your team, one who fingered Delaney to his old associates and was reporting everything you and the prosecutors were doing?"

"We found it out too late and John Durham was killed as a result. What else did you learn?"

"You said you found the insider, and apparently he didn't end up with the money. Otherwise you wouldn't be asking about it."

"Forget the money." Branson sipped his coffee. "The *Tribune's* fighting us, but we'll have the original notebook soon. With it, we'll identify all the players in their old circle. It could also lead us to the videos."

Sutherland suddenly remembered something Bill Jamison told him about Scooch and how he'd discovered the notebook. The recollection produced a flash of insight. He said, "Wait a minute. Everyone's under the impression that the notebook will lead to the tapes. But Bill Jamison learned from Scooch that he found it in Delaney's house the night the alderman disappeared and kept it all these years, not knowing its significance. So how likely is it that the notebook tells what happened to the videos? The book wouldn't have a record of what *actually* happened afterward."

The question must have been dead on, because Branson didn't say a word for half a minute while pretending to concentrate on his driving. After clearing his throat, he said, "You're right. It probably won't, but everyone doesn't know or think that. The killer doesn't; otherwise, why is he or they knocking people off to get their hands on it?"

"Anyway, the tapes are over fifteen years old," Sutherland added. "How will they help?"

"If Danny's videos were as good as he led us to believe, his old associates will be sitting ducks. They were careful for a few years after that, but when they thought everything died down, they went back to their old tricks. Real proof of what went on back then will open the door to investigate all the crap they've been pulling lately. We'll have wire taps, search warrants, access to bank accounts, you name it."

"Finding the tapes and them being as good as Delaney promised is a big *if*," Sutherland said. "Otherwise, you still have nothing. Until a few weeks ago this was a cold case. It took finding Danny Delaney's body and Bill Jamison's digging to wake you up. The notebook's appearance is what has everyone scrambling for the videos. Your buzzing around only convinced everyone that the tapes and money were still out there."

"That get you worried? It should. Everyone will presume your father would have told you what he did with all of it." Branson finished his coffee, wiped his mouth with his fingers, and continued, "Here's the thing, Mr. Sutherland. It's a good bet your father left Delaney's place with the tapes and other material the night Delaney was murdered. That was the plan, the arrangement between Delaney and my boss, John Durham. Presuming your father was still on our side, after my boss was shot that night, your father didn't know who to trust in the FBI or police—who we knew was corrupted. So sometime in that twenty hours before he went out in his boat, he stashed the tapes, files, and a slush fund Delaney kept. We can't find it. The men that are after you can't find it. That leaves you."

"That's another detail you forgot to mention. My father didn't expect to die that night, so why would he leave a trail? Why didn't you tell me about the others on the boat?"

Branson slammed his hands on the steering wheel. "Damn it. What do you think this is? Amateur night? I don't have to tell you shit."

"Maybe not, but the same goes for me," Sutherland said, pointing down Michigan to the next corner. "Drop me off at Ohio by the light. And fuck you too."

Instead of stopping at the corner, Branson turned right and pulled over to the curb. After taking a deep breath, he said, "Okay. Forget what I said. What I did and didn't tell you. Listen a minute." He turned off the ignition and faced Sutherland. "As far as we can tell your father planned to disappear for a while, so we figure whatever he did was supposed to be temporary. We know he went to the bank and made a series of wire transfers on that last day, but where would he temporarily stash the videos and Delaney's slush fund?"

"You really think I know?"

"Not yet, you don't. Think on it. His last day. He left his attorney and secretary messages saying he was going to sail somewhere for a while. Before he went, where did he go, what'd he do? Put yourself in his shoes, Mr. Sutherland. What would you do?"

"You got to be kidding," Sutherland said. "His shoes? I thought he was a great man until he was convicted of bribery. Then you come along and accuse him of even more crime and corruption, possibly even murder, conveniently leaving out the part that he worked with you, then you suggest he might've had something to do with your agent's death. You keep me in the dark and expect me to figure out what you couldn't after fifteen years?" Sutherland opened the door, grabbed the gym bag with Ronnie's clothes, and had one foot on the curb before saying, "Like I said, fuck you too."

"Wait," Branson shouted, holding up his hands in surrender. "Sit down a minute. Please."

Sutherland blew out a breath and tried to calm himself. How much more of this guy's manipulation could he take?

"Please, Mr. Sutherland," Branson beckoned. "It's important."

Sutherland sat down and closed the door. "This better be good."

"I shouldn't be doing this, but I'd like to find those tapes and prove your father was totally on our side," Branson said as he pulled an envelope from his inside suit pocket and held it up. "This is an inventory of everything we found on his boat when the Coast Guard towed it in, and what was in his sailboat and his office. Agents followed up on every item, and the results are here too. Dead ends, all of them. There's also a summary of your father's movements during that time, as far as we could ascertain. It didn't help us either." He handed the envelope to Sutherland. "Look this over carefully. You might see something we didn't."

"This mean no more secrets?"

"No more secrets. And to prove it … the reason I didn't tell you about the other boat was because there was always the possibility that it picked him up that night—that he didn't drown but wanted everyone to think he did while he took off with the money. You know they never did find his body, don't you?"

*     *     *

After Branson left him in front of Northwestern Hospital, Sutherland called his office, and Eileen relayed some surprising news—especially surprising in light of the recent events. She told him that Gene Sandler's secretary had called asking if he and Sutherland could meet that evening.

"Tonight?" was all he could utter.

"That's what she said. What should I tell her?"

A trap? After being chased by thugs, seeing Ronnie's place burgled, and barely dodging an attempted intrusion on his own apartment, he was being openly invited to sit down with one of the principal suspects? It was too obvious, and it couldn't be the intent. One way to find out, and Sutherland wouldn't mind confronting the man. He might learn something that would bring him down.

"Tell his secretary yes. But let's meet in Croakie's; it's a bar on Elm."

"I know the place. It's a pit, and always crowded."

"Perfect."

# Chapter 58

Sutherland entered Ronnie's private room to see Vislowski leaning against the wall by the window. His arms were folded across his chest, and his frown said he was clearly frustrated. Ronnie sat on the edge of the bed wearing a blue hospital gown and a scowl. Her right thigh was bandaged, and she had bruises and abrasions on her legs and knees.

Sutherland looked at one, then the other and could almost feel the tension, like inflammable vapor needing only a match. Finally he broke the heavy silence. "Hi. Feeling better?"

"About time you came," she said. "In another minute, I was out that door in this gown."

Sutherland handed her the blue gym bag he'd taken from her apartment. "The detective fill you in on the break-in?" He hoped she hadn't been told what had been left in the notebook's place.

"That's what we've been talking about," Vislowski said.

"It's your damn fault," she fumed at the detective. "You knew they had my keys. Where were the police? If you had the place watched, you'd have your killer."

"What about you?" Vislowski replied, seemingly oblivious to Sutherland's presence. "You and your brother brought this on yourselves. His death, the burglary—your own fault for holding out on us. Keeping that copy, writing about it."

They were Sutherland's thoughts exactly, but he knew better than to say them to Ronnie's face. He watched her jaw tighten, her eyes narrow, her fingers curl into claws. She jumped up and lunged at Vislowski, and before he could fend her off, she raked her nails down his cheek. When he grabbed her wrists she tried to knee him in the groin, but he managed to turn sideways and took the knee in his thigh. Spinning her around, he pushed her onto the bed and landed on top of her, pinning her. She struggled, kicking and squirming, but he outweighed her by a hundred pounds, and finally she calmed down.

"You through?" he said, breathing hard.

"Bastard," she said. "Get off me."

Vislowski got to his feet and backed away from the bed. He ran his hand over his cheek and scowled at the blood on his fingers from where she had scratched him. Ronnie rolled over and sat up, glaring at him. "You finally get it. They murdered Billy for what he was writing, for the book. It's all related, just like I've been telling you."

"I never said it wasn't," Vislowski said, dabbing his cheek with a tissue from the box on the night table.

"You never believed my brother's death was." She opened the bag and pulled out shorts, a green cotton sweater, loafers, and underwear, examining everything as if it might not be hers.

"There's no question now." Vislowski looked at Sutherland and shook his head slightly. He probably hadn't told her about what the intruder had left.

She grabbed her clean underpants, put the left, then the right leg through the holes, and pulled them up under her hospital gown then did the same with the pair of white cotton shorts.

"Unfortunately, believing and proving are different things," the policeman said. "You, of all people, should know that, Counselor."

"If you depend on the fucked-up system."

"Let's not start a pissing match," Sutherland said. They both looked at him, offended, as if he had interrupted their private game. "Whoever killed Scooch burglarized Ronnie's apartment and left the ear. Odds are the same person killed Bill for the notebook, or because Bill saw him the night Scooch was killed, or because Bill was messing in his business. Sounds like it was Sandler's doing. Funny thing is, his secretary called this morning. He wants to meet tonight and I agreed. Unless you arrest him first."

Vislowski, still holding the tissue to his left cheek, said, "We can question him again. It was his accountant's employee that was murdered and his warehouse that burned. But he'll have good enough alibis."

"Same old crap." Ronnie turned her back to both men and pulled the hospital gown off, revealing her smooth, white back. With thumb and forefinger she lifted the white bra Sutherland had brought, looked at it, and returned it to the overnight bag. She picked up the green cotton sweater, pushed her arms through, pulled it over her head, and turned to face the two men again.

Combing her fingers through her hair, she asked, "Can you run me home, Doug?"

"I didn't drive," Sutherland said.

"I'll run you home, Veronica," Vislowski said, buttoning his sports jacket with his free hand.

"Just lend me twenty and I'll take a cab, thanks," she said to the detective. "I've had enough of you today."

"Why don't you face it?" Vislowski said, reaching into his pocket and handing her two tens. "Whoever wanted the notebook is a murderer. Give it up and stay out of it. That goes for both of you."

"What about Billy?" Ronnie said, her color rising again.

"You can't bring him back by getting yourself killed. Or arrested."

"I should forget it? My own flesh and blood?" she said.

Vislowski shrugged and shook his head as if giving in to a hopeless cause.

Sutherland stared out the window, thinking of Ronnie's words and marveling at how they resonated with his mood. "Own flesh and blood," she'd said—the same words he heard seeping from somewhere deep inside. Get the man who disgraced and killed his father. Get Sandler. What held him back? Could he let his father's killer get away with it?

"I can't," he said, thinking aloud.

"Can't what?" Ronnie asked as she reached for the doorknob.

Sutherland blinked from out of his reflections and saw them both staring at him quizzically.

"Forget about it."

# CHAPTER 59

Back in his apartment, Sutherland opened the envelope Branson had given him. Just as he'd been told, it was a detailed printed inventory of everything that had been on the two boats and in the office that wasn't nailed down. Along with the list were eight-by-ten-inch photographs of the boats' and office's interiors. In and around the trawler's navigation station they catalogued: five Great Lakes navigation charts, a plotting compass and triangle, pencils, pens, restaurant menus, two yacht club directories, a pair of binoculars, a set of signal flags, a yacht insurance policy, the boat's registration, a harbormaster directory, a harbor permit, an eraser, a pencil sharpener, a spool of fishing line, a stainless steel cleat, and receipts from restaurants, fuel stations, and marine stores. After each item was the abbreviation *N/R*, which Sutherland took to mean "not relevant," but it was clear from the check marks on the pages of the printed material that each had been scrutinized. The same comment accompanied cushions, a swim mask, swim fins, life preservers, propane tanks, a first aid kit, signal flares, foul-weather gear, a fog bell, a radar reflector, the spare anchor, lines, pillows, cushions, pots, pans, bowls, cutlery, and the list went on.

The items that appeared to have received the most scrutiny were Bernard Sutherland's wallet, checkbook, and several sets of keys, all of which had been found on the trawler. The contents of the wallet consisted of credit cards, a driver's license, an insurance ID card, a magnetic card key for the McCollum Building, his voter's registration, a AAA card, credit card receipts from West Marine and Treasure Island, an ATM receipt, and a parking pass for the yacht club. All were deemed "not relevant."

Someone had tested every key on the four rings to verify the use of each and that none of them led to money, videos, or anything else of a helpful nature. One set fit Bernard's Buick doors and trunk. A ring found hanging in the yacht's ignition lock opened the cabin door and cockpit storage and started the engine. Keys on a chain opened the main hatch and started the diesel engine for the sloop *Gabriela,* moored in a slip a hundred feet away. There were also keys for the dock box and sail locker in the yacht club. The largest ring held two for his house, one for his office desk, another for the file cabinet drawers, and the last for operation of the building's freight elevator. From the comment, "Contents checked, nothing of relevance found," it was obvious to Sutherland that the FBI had been busy in the days after his father's death. The agents had even accessed his father's account information, because every item in his checkbook was checked off and deemed *N/R*.

A second sheet was attached to the inventory. Printed across the top were the words: "Summary of subject's known or deduced movements during last twenty-four hours:"

JULY 14

*Approx. 2200 hrs.* Leaves Delaney's house

*2230 hrs.* Arrives McCollum Building. Record of entry in rear door by magnetic card key. Not seen by security guard in lobby and didn't use after-hours card access to passenger elevators. Must have used his freight elevator key.

*2241 hrs.* Card key entry into subject's office on fifth floor.

*2330 hrs.* Leaves short note for secretary saying he's gone on sailing vacation.

*2332 hrs.* Calls, leaves message for attorney saying will call in a few days.

*Approx. 2400 hrs.* Leaves building (must have used freight elevator; guard and TV monitor didn't record him passing through lobby).

JULY 15

*0026 hrs.* ATM on LaSalle and Lake Streets, three blocks from McCollum, withdrawal, $300.

*0035 hrs.* FIRE reported in subject's house through 911 call by neighbor.

*0112 hrs.* Card access to Chicago Yacht Club at Belmont Harbor parking lot.

*0045–0900 hrs.* Assume subject slept on trawler. Evidence of used bunk found.

*0900 hrs.* Breakfast at yacht club, signs chit.

*0900–1100 hrs.* Dock neighbor states seeing subject working on sailboat *Gabriela*.

*1130 hrs.* Visa card used at Treasure Island—groceries for at least a week.

*1232 hrs.* Visa card used at West Marine—assorted ship's supplies and hardware, including shackle, winch handle, winch grease, snatch block, fresh water tank, bilge pump.

*1325 hrs.* Lunch at yacht club

*1430 hrs.* Meets with First Chicago Bank SVP, uses private office, phone, fax, and Internet for next two hours.. Original deposit in First Chicago Bank, but funds serially wired through three offshore banks to Banco de San José, Costa Rica, which refused to cooperate without the password or account number. No determination made as to whether funds were forwarded or remain with said bank.

*Approx. 1650 hrs.* Informs dockmaster that sailboat *Gabriela* will be out of harbor for a period.

*1700–1830 hrs.* Dock neighbor witnesses subject cleaning and working on sailboat deck. Inspection shows newly installed new winch.

*1830 hrs.* Dinner at yacht club.

*2130 hrs.* Trawler *Gabriela II* seen leaving harbor.

JULY 16

*0530 hrs.* Coast Guard responds to fisherman's report of drifting trawler. No one aboard, and USCG tows *Gabriela II* back to Belmont Harbor.

The final part of the report dealt with his mother, Gabriela Castellano, and Douglas Sutherland himself. Evidently the FBI, after weeks of searching, found Gabriela on a remote Mayan dig in the Mexican state of Chiapas. The narrative stated that she had left the United States fifteen years earlier, abandoning her husband (the subject) and four-year-old child to seek a new life as an artist and sometime archeologist in her native country. There had been no recent communication between the subject and his former wife. Douglas Sutherland, the son, was also out of the country and hadn't been in touch with the subject in more than a year. The report concluded that, given their estrangement and isolation, neither could have known the whereabouts of the money, the tapes, or the subject.

It was true that his father hadn't, and couldn't have, told Sutherland anything at the time. And when Sutherland had reunited with his mother this past year, she'd said nothing about tapes or money, a subject that he was now sure would have come up if she had known.

Sutherland read the material twice, made himself a cup of coffee, and read it again, trying to do what Branson had suggested: put himself in his father's shoes. Was there something on that inventory list or chronology of movements that told him anything useful? There didn't seem to be any obvious detours that would imply where he might have stashed the videos. Whatever he did with them was accomplished somewhere and sometime in the sequence recorded on those pages. The items left behind on his boat and what he'd purchased that day didn't help, but at least they were consistent with his activities. Everything appeared as if he was preparing for a passage on his sailboat. But then why was he offshore on his cabin cruiser, the trawler *Gabriela II*, when he drowned? He must have been forced to go.

He set the pages aside and sorted through the photos. It was obvious that someone had thoroughly searched both boats and the office before the pictures were taken. The FBI? Whoever it was had spilled the desk drawer's contents over the surface. He had already seen most of the items in the package Jenny had brought. But the photos also showed an issue of the *Chicago Tribune* open to an article entitled: "Law Firm Seeks Twenty Million for Tunnel Flood Damages."

Sutherland leaned back and envisioned himself sitting at his father's desk. On his desk, among the papers and office paraphernalia, was the article about the 1992 flood of the old coal and freight tunnel that used to service Chicago's Loop office buildings. Maybe he glances at the caption and remembers his forays into the network of narrow tunnels with his son in an attempt to cure the boy of his phobia. Coal was once delivered through that tunnel to the McCollum's lower level and possibly he recalls the boy playing in the subbasement, hiding in the locker room where the maintenance men changed. The lower levels had been blocked off and unused since the flood, and the freight elevator provided the only access, limited to those with a key.

According to the FBI's report, his father had taken the freight elevator, not stairs or the passenger elevator that night. Before leaving the building, did his father go to the subbasement?

# Chapter 60

Croakie's was filled with an after-work crowd stoked up on a Cubs baseball game, beer, and tequila. Sandler didn't like the place, didn't like any bars, in fact. Another setting for the other world to indulge their habits of watching sports, consuming alcohol, and partnering up for sex. None held an interest for him, professional sports was a caldron of overpaid thugs and lowlifes, alcohol made him sick, and sex was impossible. At least Croakie's was dark enough to hide the dirt on the floor, though he'd had to send his cola glass back in exchange for one without lipstick on the rim. Chicago's smoking ban didn't seem to carry much weight here either. Neither the bartender, waitress, or table neighbors said a word when he lit up.

Sutherland was late, and Sandler was getting hungry. Better judgment aside, he ordered a plate of french fries and miniature hamburgers. While he waited, he recalled the few times he had met the younger Sutherland: once or twice when his father was alive, and then recently, when he'd tried to coerce Sutherland into buying commercial liability insurance. Sutherland had vehemently declined despite the customary pressure and threats, and in the end, Sandler let it go. Sutherland's defiance could be a signal that his father had left something that could be used against Sandler if pushed too far. It irked him all the more, because in his mind men like Sutherland, possessing everything Sandler didn't—looks, women, and health—didn't deserve any slack.

# CHAPTER 61

Sutherland entered the bar with more than a little apprehension. Eugene Sandler was one of the most influential men in the county, having his hooks into politicians, bureaucrats, and businessmen and a near monopoly on the real estate insurance and janitorial business. As deal broker and dispenser and extractor of favors, he was not merely the grease, he was a large part of the machine.

All that was by the way. What concerned Sutherland was that the fat man was very possibly guilty of murder. His father's, for one.

Winding his way past the bar and between the tables, he spotted Sandler sitting alone. A pink-faced Michelin Man, Sutherland decided. A noxious combination of cologne and smoke greeted him at the table. Sutherland pulled out his handkerchief, stifled a sneeze, and nodded a hello. Sandler nodded back and asked, "What are you drinking?"

With those few words—the reedy tones of a bagpipe—a flood of bad memories rushed out. Threats that Sandler would bankrupt Sutherland if he didn't contract for his insurance and janitorial work. For a while, Sandler made good on his threats, using his influence to block financings, delay zoning hearings, and pressure building inspectors to paper him with phony violations. He'd made success difficult, but the challenge of defeating Sandler had made Sutherland fight harder.

Sutherland glanced at Sandler's side of the table, which was crowded with a ketchup-stained plate and an empty glass. "A draft. Anything."

Sandler raised his right arm and from somewhere about the barroom's shadowy fringes a Rubenesque woman in a short skirt jiggled over. "Draft and another Coke." The waitress left, and Sandler said, "I saw your picture, being hauled from the river. City's not safe for anyone these days."

"Benjamin Gorman and Bill Jamison would agree. Delaney would too, not to mention a few others."

"A regular crime wave." The fat man dropped his cigarette into his empty glass.

Sutherland studied the man, how he sat there as if guiltless of what he certainly had a hand in. A lifetime of corruption capped off with a few deaths, and he looked as benevolent as a Buddha statue. Would he be so self-confident after a sound beating? "So? What's on your mind?" Sutherland said.

With his napkin, Sandler wiped a trickle of sweat running down his pink cheek. "You're friends with the woman. The sister of the reporter. She has the original notebook or implies she has. A simple business deal. Strictly legal."

"Copy in Miss Jamison's apartment not good enough?"

"The original's all I care about. And of course Delaney's tapes, when you find them."

"Why do you think I can find them? You couldn't, the FBI couldn't. It's not like he left a message for me. He didn't expect to die that night. You of all people know that."

"A real tragedy. We may never know," Sandler said with a smirk. The waitress delivered their drinks, barely stopping as she hurried to the next table. Sandler flicked his Dunhill lighter, puffing life into a new cigarette.

Sutherland took a long swallow from the beer, restraining the impulse to douse out the cigarette with it, along with the fat man's arrogance. Instead he said, "My father, along with Delaney and his tapes, were going to bring you down, so they both were killed along with the FBI agent. The feds will have the original notebook by tomorrow. Only a matter of time."

Sandler's fleshy lips tightened, his cheeks flushed. He leaned forward. "How long you lived in Chicago? That notebook won't mean shit. And Delaney's tapes are too old to hurt me personally."

"Then why do you care?"

"Find them and I'll tell you. After they're destroyed. I'll pay big for them. Big. And for the record, you're wrong about me killing your father."

The denial stopped Sutherland cold. He stared through Sandler's glasses into his eyes, looking for the truth or the lie, but saw only a glint of malicious mischief. Finally he said, "Then how about Scooch, Gorman, and Jamison? A new Jack the Ripper?"

"Like I said." Sandler smiled slyly. "It's a dangerous city."

"Well Jack's getting careless. Leaving souvenirs like Scooch's ear in Ronnie Jamison's burgled apartment."

Sandler was about to take a drag from his cigarette but he blinked, paused for a moment, and put his hand down. Shaking his head as if disappointed, he said, "That was really stupid, wasn't it?"

"Sick, more like it. And murder's not the same as old tapes."

"What's your interest in this, Sutherland? The money?"

"I want some tattooed, muscle-bound inmate to make you his bride."

Sutherland watched red blotches flower on Sandler's cheeks, suffuse into his jowls.

"You little shit," Sandler croaked, coughing out smoke. "You're a pimple in this town. What can you do?" He dropped his cigarette on the floor, pulled a handkerchief from his breast pocket, removed his glasses, and wiped his eyes.

"I don't have to do squat, Gene. Before your warehouse was torched, Jamison and Hurley copied enough documents to shed light on today's kickback games. It'll be like dominos. Your goons from the other night will make a deal. Jules Langer will turn on you, then police officers, inspectors, aldermen, judges, state commissioners … a lot of names in that book, lot of bullets. Too many for your fat ass to dodge."

Sandler coughed again. Unable to speak for his hacking, he raised his left arm and slammed it on the table. His glass fell over and cola ran off the edge. People nearby stopped talking and cast wary glances at the large coughing man.

Relying on discretion over valor, Sutherland stood quickly and strode toward the door. But jostling his way around the bar, he thought of the darkening street outside and wondered if Sandler had come alone. He elbowed his way into the bar crowd, out of sight, and from there he watched Sandler pushing his way through, like an angry rhino. In his wide wake was a very tall blond man with short hair, the man with the gun he'd seen on the bridge right before he jumped.

# CHAPTER 62

Fifteen minutes later the taxi left Sutherland at the front door to his condo building. He was retrieving his mail from his box in the lobby when someone tapped him from behind, startling him. He spun around and jumped backward, banging into the wall of mailboxes. "Whoa. Don't do that," he snapped.

"Sorry," Ronnie said, holding up her hands. "What did he say? You learn anything?"

Sutherland gathered his wits, grabbed the rest of his mail, and locked the box. "How long have you been here?"

"Half hour. Well?"

He started for the elevators with Ronnie following. "Something strange is going on."

"Go on," she said.

"I'm not sure he's responsible for breaking into your place. He seemed genuinely surprised about the ear. If true, it means he didn't kill Scooch. He also categorically denied killing my father. Not that I believe him."

"He wouldn't admit it."

"But here's the other thing. His sidekick tonight was one of the guys after us that night. Real tall. Could be the guy your brother saw outside the diner watching Langer and Scooch."

They exited the elevator and walked to Sutherland's door. Inside he led her to the dining room table, where she sat silently, seemingly thinking.

"Something to drink?" Sutherland said on the way to the kitchen. He didn't get an answer, so he filled two glasses with ice and water from the tap and returned to the dining room with them.

Ronnie looked up as he set the glass before her and said, "I don't care what you think; he's our killer."

A phone rang, and she dug into her shoulder bag and pulled out her cell phone. While she talked, Sutherland went to his den and checked his messages. His attorney had called, explaining that there was nothing they could do about Broadwell until the bankruptcy judge assigned a trustee.

Not what Sutherland wanted to hear. When he returned to the dining room, Ronnie was standing, one hand in her bag.

"That was Agent Branson."

"I thought I was the only one he hassled."

"Wants me to give you the notebook copy. He's convinced you can find the tapes." She pulled a folder from her bag and handed it to him. "Here it is. Where's Langer's stuff?"

"Still in my trunk. I'll tell garage valet that it's okay for you to take it."

"I asked Branson about Sandler and he gave me the same bullshit as Vislowski: they need more evidence. But the bastard *will* pay. He's not walking away." She stared at him, emphasizing her point, then pulled out a pistol from the bag. "Had to get this to replace the one they took. I hope that fat shit and his buddies come at me again."

"Just as likely to come after me. As if I've got a map to Delaney's stuff." He had no intention of disclosing the information Branson gave him or his theory about the subbasement yet. It was his best guess, and if the tapes were there, he needed time to review and screen them first.

"If you found the stuff, what would you do?" Ronnie asked.

"Go through it and destroy anything harmful to me or my father. Other than that, hand it over to the police or feds."

"And the money?"

He'd never thought about that eventuality. In his mind the money had always been lost. "I'd have to think about it. It's dirty money. But that doesn't mean it's finders keepers."

"You wouldn't keep it as compensation? They killed your father. My brother."

"So we should keep it? I doubt the feds would agree. Anyway, it's a moot point unless it's found."

"Even so, don't forget, you did get Billy into this."

"That dog won't hunt, Ronnie. He was already deep into it before I had anything to do with it."

"You helped him. You had questions about your father."

"Still do. Who was he, what was he?"

"At least you know he didn't commit suicide." She stuffed her pistol in the bag and stood. "You've got just as much reason as me. Get yourself a gun, son."

As he watched her close the door behind her, he wondered if she was right, whether he'd have to make his own justice.

# Chapter 63

After all the buildup, including everything that had been written and speculated upon, finally having a copy of Delaney's notebook pages in his hands was anticlimactic. It merely was an expanded version of the pages Sutherland had already seen, the few pages Ronnie or Bill had shown him or described. It consisted of thirty-some pages, ten to fifteen dated entries per leaf, each with one or more names or initials, sometimes an abbreviated subject and/or dollar amount, and a reference number, presumably designating the tape of the meeting.

Sutherland scanned through the pages, occasionally recognizing a name or building address, while taking an informal survey of the frequency of the participants' appearances. Just as Bill Jamison had surmised, the core of the circle included Gorman, Delaney, Langer, Tunney, and Sandler. Other notable attendees included the former mayor, the police commissioner, other aldermen, inspectors, state legislators, the former governor, county officials, and the current front-runner to be the next governor, George Spanos. Sutherland's father's name didn't appear in Delaney's meetings until after he was released from prison. It appeared next to the $5 million entry and a few days later as the last entry in the book, dated the night Delaney disappeared. Next to the date was: BS & DD's confession, 200K Vol. XXX-7.

# CHAPTER 64

The telephone handset was lost in Sandler's meaty hand. He punched the digits of the private number with the eraser end of a pencil, pulled on his cigarette, and counted the rings while he waited for Reginald Tunney's baritone: two, three, four ...

"Yes?"

"I saw Sutherland," Sandler said in his reedy voice.

"How did the direct approach work?"

"It didn't." He smashed out his cigarette. His desk lamp was off, and he removed his glasses. Sitting in the shadows of his office, with the glow of Michigan Avenue below, he had all the light he needed to see the copied pages of Delaney's notebook on his desk. He'd been through it several times and seen enough references to his meetings with Delaney to lose his confidence in his immunity. Worry made him hungry, and he frowned seeing that the bowl of cashews on his desk was nearly empty. He scooped out a handful and stuffed it into his mouth.

"Is that all?" Tunney asked.

It took a few seconds to chew and swallow before Sandler answered. "He's on a mission, the prick."

"What's he want?"

"He wants to nail us." His and Tunney's offices and phone lines were swept weekly for microphones, so Sandler wasn't overly concerned about unwelcome ears.

"That bitch too?"

"I'd guess." He lit another cigarette and let the smoke leak from his mouth slowly, holding on to the bite in the taste.

"You review the item?" Tunney asked. "You believe that cocksucker? All those meetings in his office? I counted five times."

Sandler glanced down at the pages of Delaney's notebook he'd marked up. His name appeared seven times in the year before Delaney died. Each entry was dated with a subject and, in some cases, dollar amounts. After each notation was a number, presumably designating the missing tapes.

"Sutherland said the FBI will get the original soon, so let's face it. If it's published, some of our favorite officials will be embarrassed, may even get hurt. We knew that as soon as that reporter wrote about it. But is it actionable?"

"Without the tapes, no," Tunney said. "Even the ones with Spanos. He was on the prosecutor's team, so theoretically he had reasons to meet with Delaney when he was finking for us."

"And there's nothing in this book to lead anyone to the tapes."

"Nothing I can see. So what do we want to do?"

"Wait and listen," Sandler said. "The walls have ears." Tunney already knew that Sutherland's office and apartment had been bugged.

# Chapter 65

The next morning, Sutherland woke fixated on one idea. Before he even put on the coffee, he headed to the den and reread for the umpteenth time the information Branson had given him about his father's movements and the contents of his trawler. Ten minutes later, convinced that his previous suspicions warranted exploration, he picked up the phone and punched in the cell number of the demolition foreman on the McCollum site. Jack had just arrived at the construction trailer when he answered.

"Got a couple questions for you, Jack," Sutherland said after saying hello. "How much left to tear down?"

"Just a pile of rubble now. Another week to haul it off."

"The basement blocked off?"

"Yeah. Dig it out later when you do the foundation."

"No way in? How about the subbasement? Is it filled up too?"

"I don't think it's filled, but there's no way you can get in. Why?"

"Nothing. Thanks."

\*     \*     \*

He really didn't want to call her. The other day, when he awoke to find her in his apartment, he'd felt himself pulled into her gravity again. The pain of her campaign to stop his project hadn't abated, yet neither had the memories of their better moments. Could he trust himself?

He reached her in her city hall office, and when she heard his voice, her surprise was blurted out in a concerned reflex. "You okay?"

"I'm fine. Got a question—a favor, actually."

"Really? That's a new side of you."

"Yeah, I know. But here it is. Can you get me into the tunnel? The one that runs through the Loop, the one that flooded?"

Seconds went by, and when Kelly answered, she sounded worried. "Are you sure you're all right? Why would you … why do you think I …"

"The coal tunnel. The City owns it, controls it. You told me once that your department negotiated the legal terms for the fiber-optic people and the cable TV companies to use it. You must know someone that has access to it. I need to get in there."

"Where are you?"

"At home. Heading for my office as soon as I shave and get dressed."

"I'll meet you there in an hour. You're off your rocker, Douglas Sutherland."

*     *     *

"You're asking the impossible," Kelly said an hour later in his office. "Permission to access the tunnel must go through the Chicago Department of Transportation. There's pages of forms and waivers enough to choke a horse. Frankly, it's a waste of time. There's nothing to see anymore." Sitting facing Sutherland at his desk in his office, Kelly stopped to sip from her coffee. "So why in hell do you want in there?"

"Can you get me in?"

"Why, Doug? Answer me first." As usual when she went to work, she was dressed professionally, ready for any situation. Today she had on a light-green jacket, silk blouse, and dark-green linen slacks. To go along with her attire, she wore her all-business face, and Sutherland knew from experience he wasn't going to easily win an argument.

"It's a long shot," he said, leaning forward, elbows on his desk. "If my father took anything from Delaney's place, he had a day to do something with it. The FBI know he went to his office in the McCollum and then to his boat. He couldn't go to our house because it was burning. So where would he hide it?"

"Logical place, the McCollum. His office."

"FBI searched it back then. And if he had other hiding places, the items would have probably been discovered in the ensuing years."

"If not, it's too late now."

"Except for one place. The McCollum's subbasement. It's been closed off ever since the tunnel flooded in 1992. But, owning the building, he had access and used to take me into the tunnel from time to time. Our secret adventure. I think he was trying to cure me of my fear of places like that, but I was always scared to death."

"What makes you think he would've hidden something there?"

"Couple reasons. First, we're out of other options. The FBI traced his movements, they searched the building and his boats and everything he

216

touched but found nothing. He was in the McCollum that night, in his office, probably wondering what to do with the stuff he took from Delaney's after his FBI contact got killed. He'd used the freight elevator in, and here's the thing: that elevator is the only access to the subbasement. At that time, no one went there; it was off limits because of the flood damage. Still was before we tore it down."

"But you're guessing. The FBI didn't check it?"

"Why would they? After the flood receded and repairs were made, it functionally didn't exist. The boiler, electrical boxes, locker room—everything was moved or replaced elsewhere in the building. Nothing of value remained; it was a landscape of debris, and the last I looked, even the elevator's keyhole for the subbasement was covered over. Without consulting a building blueprint, you wouldn't know it was there. Now, with the building leveled to the ground and filled with debris, the only way to access the subbasement is up from the tunnel."

"And you've actually been in there?" she said. "I hear it's dreadful."

"It's been eighteen years or so, and I can't say I'd look forward to going back. You need boots. It's only six feet wide and maybe seven high, and sometimes you have to duck under the conduits that the telecommunication companies strung up."

"Rats?"

"Not since the flood. All entries to the buildings have been blocked, so there's nothing for them to eat."

"If entries are blocked, how will you get in?"

"My father fixed it so even though it looked like it was still sealed, there was a watertight door he could open. I'm hoping it's still there and works."

"And then? If you got in?"

"I'll look around. See if he left anything there." Sutherland leaned back, put his hands behind his head. "So. Can you get me in? There's an entrance below city hall."

She shook her head, a look more of disbelief than of refusal. "Why not let the police or FBI do it? Why you?"

"It's a long shot, it'll take too long, and besides, I want to see the material first. If there's anything damaging, I'll excise it before handing it over."

Kelly took a deep breath and exhaled loudly. "I think I liked you better when you were afraid of places like that. Couple years ago you'd die before going into a tunnel."

"You know the story: at the age of four I was locked in a dark closet by a stranger. Learning the origin of a phobia helps … some."

"Okay, I'll see what I can do. Under one condition."

"Shoot."

"Call me crazy too, but if I can get you in, I go with you."

Sutherland didn't want to say it, but he'd welcome the company. Though close and dark places didn't evoke the same level of terror they once did, thinking about going into the tunnel, he still felt a heavy weight of dread.

*    *    *

Later that day in his office Sutherland was about to call his New York attorneys when his cell phone rang. It was Kelly calling from her office and before he could say hello, she said, "You owe me big-time, tunnel boy. The head of the Chicago Department of Transportation is on vacation, and it's a good thing. He's an ass. But Mick, his assistant, isn't too smart. I told him the City's legal department, which is me, needs to take an expert into the tunnel to document any new perils for the legal waivers. Tomorrow morning soon enough for you? The department head is back next Monday."

"Great. What do I do?"

"Look like an expert. Boots, flashlight, helmet, clipboard."

"My foul-weather boots from the boat okay? I've got plenty of construction helmets and lights. You need anything?"

"My boots are still on *Circe*," Kelly said. A subtle reminder of all the racing and cruising they used to do together?

"I'll pick them up this afternoon."

"Meet me outside the Randolph Street entrance at eight. You got a badge, nametag, or something?"

"I've got a shirt with a construction company logo on it. And Kelly … thanks." He hung up admiring Kelly's creative subterfuge but worrying about how he'd feel once he stepped into the tunnel again, this time without his father to hang on to.

# Chapter 66

**FRIDAY, AUGUST 3**

Carrying a clipboard and laden with an overlarge backpack containing his and Kelly's boots, two flashlights, and a jacket, Sutherland waited by the north entrance of the city hall building until he saw Kelly wave from inside the revolving doors. He wore his construction helmet with headlamp, a denim shirt with a Walsh Construction crest, and khakis, knowing that he'd have to trash the pants after climbing around the tunnel and subbasement.

Kelly Matthews nodded her approval when he entered. "Very consultant-like. Why the big backpack?"

"On the assumption we find something."

"Okay. Mick is waiting for us by the tunnel entrance, a few flights down. He's got a tunnel map. Do you know where you're going?

"I found a map on the Internet. We take the first branch to the left, then it should be about two blocks on the right."

"You're sure you want to do this? I know how you used to hate these kinds of places. You over it?"

"We'll see. Let's go," he said.

They descended a flight of stairs, passed through two sets of doors, and climbed down another stairway where a man in a blue polo shirt was waiting. Mick was, in fact, a Mick, an Irish American. Judging by his accent he probably lived in Bridgeport, the old mayor's neighborhood. Aged about fifty, thirty-five of those years were spent in and around taverns, if his red nose and beer belly were accurate indicators.

"How long youz be in ner?" he asked, his cloudy eyes avoiding Sutherland's and Kelly's. "Do I gotta wait?"

"Not as long as we can get out," Sutherland said.

Mick led them down a corridor to a door that looked like bank vault. By now they were forty feet below grade, maybe thirty below the level of the Chicago River. He opened a small peephole, making sure that the river hadn't flooded the tunnel like it had in 1992, forcing half the Loop out of business for weeks as the water level rose into the subbasements, shorting electrical circuits and snuffing out boilers and furnaces.

"All clear," he said, opening the vault door. A draft of cold, fetid air met them, a breath of a bygone age.

Boots, jackets, helmets, and headlamps on, flashlights in hand, Sutherland led as they ducked through the door and found themselves in a small alcove ten feet from the main tunnel. The grade sloped down a few feet, and when they reached the bottom, they pointed their bright beams left and right into a long, narrow nothingness. As long as he had adequate light, he'd be okay, he told himself.

"It's cold," Kelly said. The temperature had to be less than sixty degrees. "And creepy."

"Imagine how I felt the first time. I was seven or eight."

"It stinks. And you know we're standing in water?" She pointed her light at her feet, illuminating three inches of still water that lay along the center.

"That's why you're wearing boots. Come on, to the left." Sutherland started off, sloshing through the water, sweeping his light beam as he went, looking for the low-hanging conduits he was warned about.

"Are there still tracks under this water?" she asked from behind.

"In some places. It was two-foot gauge; the coal cars had to be narrow to pass through. It's only six feet across, and then they had to fit into the elevators to take the coal into the buildings and the ashes and clinkers back down."

"You sound like a tour guide."

He laughed, and the sound echoed along the space. "I just read up on it. Ask me anything. Started in 1906 by the Chicago Tunnel Company, abandoned in 1959, flooded in 1992, operated on electricity, all the rock and earth removed to dig it ended up in-fill to build Grant Park, now owned by the City and used by utilities. Anything else you'd like to know?"

"Yeah, whose idea was it? Got to be an easier way."

"That's why it's abandoned. Here's where we bear off," he said, pointing his light beam into the darkness where the tunnel arced left. "Not far from here."

"How will you know?"

"I'm counting paces. And maybe there's still an address."

There was. "McCOLLUM." A nearly indistinguishable name on a rusty placard. A rail switch would have been here, allowing for the narrow-gauge cars to shunt into the short spur leading to the building's elevator. They sloshed into the passageway up to a steel door with a crusty padlock. Coming up from behind her companion, Kelly shined her beam on the lock.

"Don't worry, I have a key," Sutherland said, shrugging off his backpack.

Unzipping it, he retrieved a two-foot-long crowbar, which he wedged under the hasp. It took several attempts throwing all his weight at it before it gave with a shriek and a bang.

"Nice key," she said. "As an attorney for the City, I did not see that."

The door opened outward, he supposed in order to make it more difficult for another flood to gain access. Again he needed the crowbar, and with Kelly's help pulling, the door gradually creaked open, revealing an empty cavity that used to house the elevator. The scrappers had removed all the cabs when the tunnel operations ceased, leaving a ladder as the only way up.

"You'll need these." He handed her a pair of work gloves before putting one on his right hand. His taped left hand would have to remain bare since his taped fingers wouldn't fit.

The ladder was steel, running up the side of the shaft where the elevator had hung before it was removed. The rungs were grimy with dirt, grease, and coal dust, which stuck to their fingers like gunk. At the top, they were in a large room with two chambers, one where the coal was stored; the other, the ashes. The skeletal frame of a conveyor belt angled up to the next level where the coal furnace and boiler had been. An iron stairway running upward awaited them between the chambers.

They trod up the steep stairs, one hand on the handrail, the other pointing the flashlights into the black, still air. The next level contained the wreckage of what used to be a building engineer's office, sleeping quarters, and locker room. It hadn't been used since the tunnel flooded and the building's entire electrical, HVAC, and mechanical operation had had to be relocated and upgraded.

"Here's where the fun starts," Sutherland said. "Like an Easter egg hunt. If it's not here, we're done. We can't go any higher; it'd be blocked off by the demolition rubble. You can start with the lockers, there. I'll try the storage closets. If anything's locked, we'll use my key."

The entire area took up only a small portion of the building's footprint, so he had figured the search would only take fifteen minutes. But there was wreckage everywhere—desks, benches, cots strewn and piled. On the walls were cupboards, lockers, storerooms, and a broken commode. He had to push aside chairs, tables, and a fallen partition to access some of the cubbyholes, all the time listening to Kelly's grunts and expletives as she tripped or bumped into something.

"Ow," she cried. "I just bashed my shin. Any luck?"

"It's always in the last place you look," he replied. "Wait!" At first he wasn't sure what he was looking at. He squatted down to peer inside a mop closet, sending up a cloud around him. Sitting upright and covered with a layer of dust that almost concealed the handle was an object the size of an airplane carry-on bag. Dragging it out, he shouted, "This may be it."

It was a leather legal document case with two clasps. Kelly shined her light on it while he snapped the clasps and opened it slowly, trying not to kick up more dust. "Whatever it is, it's wrapped in plastic. And this is my father's document case. See his initials?" He tore open an edge of the plastic far enough to see in. "Tapes. Videotapes." He wanted to whoop. "We got it."

"And I thought you were crazy," Kelly said. "Can we leave now? This place is creeping me out."

"Not as much as it is me, but let's see if there's anything else first. I never want to come back."

They spent another five minutes searching the spaces they hadn't already delved into and found nothing of value.

"That's it then," Sutherland said. "Help me put this case into my backpack, and let's go."

They were climbing down the iron staircase when Kelly whispered, "What's that? Did you see it?"

"I think so. A light from below, in the tunnel." He stopped three steps from the bottom and whispered. "Someone might be down there. Turn out your light."

In ink-black darkness now, he scanned the two chambers then focused where he knew the shaft with the ladder they'd climbed would be. Nothing. Not a hint of light, not the faintest glow. And silence, except for their controlled breathing. They stood that way, Sutherland two steps below Kelly on the metal stairway, in the dark, afraid to move, uncertain as to who might have followed them and reasoning that it probably wasn't a friend. Mick had been warned to keep their visit strictly confidential. Had someone overheard Sutherland's plans, maybe by planting a bug or a phone tap?

As the seconds crept by, Sutherland felt the darkness closing in around him and the old anxiety returning. His throat was tightening and he had trouble getting a full lungful of air. The only thing holding him together was Kelly's firm hand on his shoulder. Then the elevator shaft was lit up by a flashlight beam sweeping the walls from below. Someone was checking out the ladder.

"Now what?" Kelly whispered.

Whether it was the light beam splitting open the darkness or the threat the new arrival posed, Sutherland was wrenched out of his mounting panic. He had to act fast. Finding Kelly's hand, he led her down the last few steps to the narrow passage between the coal and ash chambers on either side. With Kelly following, he maintained hand contact with the stairway and felt around and under it into a small alcove. "Stay here," he whispered while taking off his backpack. "I'm going back up to leave a light on there. Whoever's down there will eventually lose patience and climb up. He'll see the light above us and keep climbing so we can escape. I'll be back in a sec."

He felt his way up the stairway, turned on the flashlight, and left it on the floor so that it was clearly visible from the level below. As he descended again, he realized that as soon as their visitor saw it there, he would recognize the deception and be right behind them. To avert that scenario, Sutherland knew what he had to do.

Five minutes passed while they waited in the semidarkness under the metal stairway. Through the openings between the rungs they watched the light intensify from below. Finally a flashlight appeared and a shadow followed it over the lip of the elevator shaft. The light beam swept from side to side, pointed into the coal storage chamber, the ash chamber, the conveyor, and then the stairway. Sutherland and Kelly held their breath and pressed themselves into the wall, out of the light beam's reach.

The figure walked toward the stairs and started to climb. Sutherland tensed; he knew he had to time his action perfectly. Just as the shadow's right foot touched the fifth step, before weight was fully on it, Sutherland lunged. From under the stairway he reached between the treads, grabbed the ankle in the crook of his arm, and pulled. It was a man's voice that cried out, but the yowl was cut short when his head hit the floor.

Sutherland turned on his headlamp and Kelly her flashlight, both of them scurrying from under the stairs to hover over the fallen man. He was dangling upside down on the stairs, his lower leg bent awkwardly between the treads, probably broken. His head was on the floor, mouth agape, eyes wide and unseeing. Kelly bent down and felt the carotid artery and held her ear near his mouth. "He's alive," she said. "Out cold though."

He was an African American in his twenties with a fullback's build and shaved head. The expensive clothes he wore—silk tee shirt, linen pants wet to the knee, and water-soaked Italian loafers—weren't meant for tunnel diving. The gun stuffed in his waistband was nickel plated and semiautomatic. Kelly jerked it out and handed it to Sutherland. He looked at it and shoved it into his jacket pocket.

"Who is he?" she asked, checking for a wallet. "Ever see him before?"

Sutherland studied the face. The harsh light of his headlamp and the unconscious man's gaping mouth made it difficult, but there was something familiar there. Kelly found a wallet and said as she fingered through it, "Not much here. Lots of money and a few credit cards. I was hoping there wasn't a badge. Wouldn't have been a good thing."

"We'll send the police and an ambulance as soon as we're out," he said. "I'll retrieve my light, and let's go."

223

With his backpack on again, they climbed down the ladder to the tunnel level and were about to leave the McCollum's rail spur when a female voice shouted, "Stop there." They turned, and before they could see the speaker, a bright light came on and blinded them. "Turn off those lights. I've got a gun."

They did what she ordered and shielded their eyes while trying to get a glimpse of the speaker.

"Where's Choc?" she said.

"Who?" Sutherland said.

"Chocolate. What you do to him?"

"Up there." Sutherland pointed. "Needs an ambulance."

"You got his gun? Set it down and slide it here."

Sutherland obeyed, saying, "What do you want? We really should get him help."

"Fuck him. What's in your pack? Take it off and show me."

Sutherland eased out of the backpack and dropped it heavily on the ground. He unzipped it and lifted out his father's case, leaving the crowbar inside. The woman inched closer, her light focused on the case, her other hand holding what looked like a twin of Chocolate's gun.

"Open it," she said, moving closer still and squatting in front of the document case.

Sutherland feigned an attempt to open the clasps then said, "I think we need the key. Kelly, can you find it in the backpack?" Continuing to fiddle with the clasp, he watched as Kelly dug into the pack. Waiting until she'd grasped the crowbar, he drew the woman's attention by saying, "Ah, there it is," and both clasps clicked at once.

As he folded back the flaps, he heard a whoosh, saw the rising arc of the crowbar, heard it smack into the woman's forearm, and watched it continue its sweep up to her chin. The gun flew into the darkness, and the blond flopped flat on her back.

"Wow," was all he could say. Then, "I've seen her before," he continued, looking down on the unconscious woman. She was blond, with a well-proportioned, muscular body, easy to notice since she wore only a singlet, designer jeans, and sandals. Like the man, she wouldn't be wearing those shoes again. "I saw them both going up to Tunney's apartment. He must have sent them to follow us."

"But how did he know?" Kelly was checking the woman's life signs.

"Only thing I can think of is that someone bugged my phones or apartment. Maybe office."

"She's alive, but out. I whacked her pretty good. No ID."

"Let's take the guns and get out of here. Send cops and medics."

They left the blond woman on her back beside her flashlight and headed down the tunnel. As they approached the city hall entrance, they heard shouting. "Help. Someone help me."

The man didn't come into their light beams until they arrived at the entryway. Mick was standing inside the heavy vault door with one arm overhead, handcuffed to a conduit above. "Finally," he sighed when he saw them.

"No one's going to hear you through that door," Kelly said. "Is it locked?"

"I warned them, so they left it part open. I've been here half an hour. Who were those two? You see them?"

"They need an ambulance and the cops. We'll get them, and they can unlock those cuffs," Kelly said.

"Hurry up," Mick said, "or I'll wet myself."

At the top of the stairs at ground level, Sutherland's PDA buzzed, and he pulled it from his pocket and listened. After a few seconds he said, "Sorry, I've been out of touch. Good job, Frank. Let's meet in my office in an hour to prepare. Call the architects and see if they can join us. Let's say eleven o'clock."

He turned to Kelly, "That was Frank Mann, my leasing agent. We have a meeting with Imperial Food Products' real estate committee this afternoon. I've got to run home and change. I'll stash these tapes in the meantime. Can't be in my place or the office. Not yours either. Next, we find someone who has a cassette tape player. I got rid of mine years ago. Do you have one?"

"Uh uh. A neighbor does."

"I don't want anyone else involved until I see them." He checked his watch, frowned, and said, "Can you call the security guys and ambulance? Handle the questions? I'll call you."

"Leaving me to clean up the mess we made? Thanks a lot."

# CHAPTER 67

After leaving Kelly at city hall, Sutherland took a taxi to his condominium building, wanting desperately to see what the videos contained but knowing that he'd have to postpone his viewing until later. With Broadwell Communications all but out of the picture, Imperial was his last hope to save his development. Frank Mann deserved a medal for getting his foot in the door. Presenting to a relocation committee was just the first step, and if they didn't get past that initial screening, there was no second chance. Their meeting was at three o'clock that afternoon, not much time to prepare for such a critical presentation. It meant revising and tailoring the PowerPoint presentations he and his architects had made to Broadwell, a task that had to be completed in a few hours. It could and would be done.

In the meantime, what to do with the tapes? After his daughter had interrupted someone from entering, and having been followed by the couple in the tunnel, Sutherland no longer trusted the security of his apartment or phone. Walking into the main lobby, he had an idea. He took the elevator to the lower level of the building. A corner of the basement was dedicated to storage, with a cage for every owner. To prevent someone tracing his name to the hiding place, he stashed the case in a random, anonymous unused cage and secured it with the lock from his own allocated storage unit. Satisfied that the videos would be safe until he could find a cassette player, he rode the elevator to the twentieth floor, showered, dressed, and headed downtown to meet his team.

*     *     *

George Spanos sat in the backseat of his campaign SUV reviewing the lines he was supposed to speak to the crowd his advance people had bussed in for his arrival in front of the Capitol building in Springfield. Next to him one of his speechwriters tapped away at her laptop, working on revisions he'd made to the closing remarks. The teachers that awaited him were worried about their pensions, their tenure, and their salary increases, and he would assure them that, as governor, he would protect them to the death.

His private phone rang, and as expected, he was greeted by a familiar voice. "George, remember our conversation about your meetings with the alderman? The ones the newsman wrote about from Delaney's notebook?"

Not exactly an ideal topic to discuss five minutes before an important speech. "I remember," Spanos said.

"We've seen the notebook and your name's in there for two meetings. You remember them?"

"Shit," he said. Of course he remembered them. Meetings with Delaney and his cronies in his smoke-filled office. Wondering the whole time if he'd been followed there, worrying that he'd be discovered as the mole on the prosecutor's team. How could he forget?

His speechwriter stopped tapping, glanced at him, and continued typing, by now accustomed to his language.

"I agree," the caller said. "The FBI may have the original by now, so you've got to be prepared with your story. You met with him because it was part of the prosecution's strategy to pressure him to help. Our names are there too, so you can say Delaney introduced you as a new assistant or something. Beyond that, you can claim confidentiality or a hazy memory. Work on it and call me back."

"What about the videos? No way we can bluff those."

"True. You'd be out of the race, and so would our investments. You don't know how many millions are at stake. Which reminds me, next time some reporter asks you about your views on a new airport or casino, hedge, equivocate, lie—anything. Be a little negative on both subjects. Your opponents are about to come out with some nasty ads accusing you of being in bed with some secret investors. Nip it in the bud."

"Got it. But what about the tapes?"

"Just do as you're told, Governor. We'll handle the heavy lifting."

Do as he's told. That's what they'd been saying for over fifteen years. Ever since they videoed him in that honey trap.

# Chapter 68

It was almost seven o'clock that evening before Sutherland left his architect's office. After their presentation to the five members of Imperial's relocation committee, he and Frank Mann joined his architects at their studio to discuss the design changes needed to win the Imperial's business. They expected to hear by Monday whether they had made the cut, giving them the go-ahead to present to the chairman. They were optimistic and wanted to be ready.

After leaving the architecture team to the details, Sutherland returned to his office to revise some project cash flows, consult with his attorneys about the Broadwell bankruptcy and his rights to freely pursue Imperial, and talk to two California banks about a construction loan. A long day, but at least it held several encouraging results. Until he hung up his phone for the last time, he'd had no time to dwell on his father's or Bill Jameson's murder, and where this chain of death was taking him. But when he closed his office door behind him, his focus totally changed. He stopped being a real estate developer and returned to his role as amateur detective. Even though it was late and he was tired, he wanted to see what Delaney's tapes had captured, which meant finding a video player that accepted the outdated protocol.

Kelly's mobile number was still in his PDA call list, and as he retrieved it he wondered if he'd always known he'd use it again. She answered, and he asked her if she'd found a player.

"My neighbor has at least a hundred VHS movie tapes, so she still has a player. When's the first viewing?"

"Tonight, if you can bring it over. We'll watch them in the building's party room. I don't trust the security of my place after being followed by those two today."

"Why not my place?" Kelly said. "They wouldn't know about me."

"Let's keep it that way. And could you stop on the way and pick up some takeout? I'm starved."

\*　　\*　　\*

Sutherland's apartment door closed behind him with a cold echo in the marble foyer. He groped for the light switch and turned it on, but the overhead light didn't work. Only a gray dimness suggested the living room and the darkening evening beyond. "Damn," he said, dropping his keys with a clatter on the hall table, easing along the wall into the living room.

He stopped.

An alien smell teased his nostrils and he sneezed. Stifling another sneeze, he found and flipped the living room switch, and two floor lamps cast their glow through an empty room. Nothing there.

He inhaled, appraising the offending scent as he looked around. One of his daughter's surprise visits? The cleaning lady? Maintenance man? But after another sniff, recognizing the smell as cologne, he knew it was none of them. His instincts screamed for him to get out of the apartment—fast. Pivoting, he strode toward the door, and seeing the intercom on the wall, some defense mechanism told him to press the buzzer to the doorman's desk in the lobby. This was his customary signal that he was coming down and wanted the parking valet to bring his car to the front.

"Stop." The voice was deep and throaty. Sutherland turned his head just in time to see a shadow moving into view from the dining room. In the faint light he recognized the blond man as one of the gang that had chased him on the bridge, the guy he'd seen the other night with Sandler. The gun he held in his gloved hand was pointed at Sutherland's chest.

"This building very strong," the man said in stilted English. "If I shoot, nobody will hear. Sit." He pointed to the leather sofa facing the window.

"I'm expecting someone," Sutherland said, backing toward the door.

"Touch the door, I shoot."

Sutherland stopped, thinking, how many were dead already? What did this guy have to lose? "Okay, I hear you. What do you want?" He inched away until he reached the couch and sat on the edge, every muscle tense. The man circled the couch and stood behind Sutherland, just on his right. He was at least six foot six and solid, with light-blue eyes, short, blond hair, and a slightly crooked nose. The blue, silk shirt he wore was halfway unbuttoned, revealing several thick gold chains and a smooth, hard chest.

"I search your desk room. Where you hide?"

"I don't have it. Never did. The FBI probably does. Leave and save yourself the trouble." Turning his head, Sutherland could see the man's gun hand flashing toward him in an arc. He felt a sharp pain on the side of his head and was knocked sideways on the couch.

Sutherland righted himself and massaged his ear and cheek, feeling the blood dribbling down his neck. After a deep breath, waiting for the pain to abate, he said as calmly as his nerves allowed, "I don't have it; your boss took it from the woman's place. The FBI has the original. You're wasting your time."

This time the blow hit him in the back of the head, a punch, knocking him to the floor. "Not book. I want tapes."

On his back, Sutherland propped himself up on both elbows, looking up at the man, who had come around the couch and was towering over him. *Shit, does he know I found the tapes, or is he just guessing?* He watched as the man pulled a cigarette pack from his shirt pocket with his free hand, flicked out a filter-tipped menthol, replaced the pack, took his lighter from his pants, and lit it. Exhaling smoke in a slow stream, he said, "On stomach."

Evidently Sutherland didn't move fast enough, because the man kicked him in the shoulder. "Stomach," he repeated.

Cringing from the pain, Sutherland didn't need another prompt. He rolled over, and the man took a step forward and dropped one knee in the center of Sutherland's back, forcing the air from him in a grunt. He couldn't move, could barely breathe, and he thought his ribs must be broken. Then from the corner of his eye he saw the cigarette hand descend slowly, carefully, as if performing a delicate operation on Sutherland's neck. And when the pain came, it wasn't with a violent stab—he felt pressure, then nerve-searing fire accompanied with the smell of burning flesh. He clenched his teeth, sucked in a scream, and groaned while white light ricocheted through his head, blinding him, blocking thought.

With a final thrust, the man ground the cigarette into Sutherland's neck and heaved himself to his feet, forcing another groan from Sutherland. "You tell me now."

Sutherland took a deep breath, trying to disperse the white dots that blurred his vision. He struggled to one knee and wiped his teary eyes with his shirtsleeve then tested the burn on his neck with his hand and flinched. He looked at his fingers; they were covered with a red-black goo. The man stood over him, staring coldly, waiting.

Sutherland pulled himself against the couch and tried to clear his vision, tasting the blood trickling in from his cheek. He needed time to think, because even if he gave up the tapes, odds weren't good for staying alive. The body count was clear evidence of that. He held up his hand and said, "Okay." His mind was still reeling, clumsily seeking a ploy, something to give him time. But for what? The man had a gun.

"Where?" The man said. "Show me."

Having signaled for his car, Sutherland knew that if he didn't come down within a few minutes, the doorman on duty downstairs would call back on the faulty intercom to check on him. Would that give him a chance? He needed time, a weapon, a diversion. Then he remembered that Kelly was coming over. He didn't want her in the middle of this. He had to end this fast. "Downstairs. In my car."

Without preamble the man fired his pistol. With a flash and a crack, a hole appeared in the hardwood floor next to Sutherland's knee. "I look in car this afternoon when garage man take cigarette."

"All right, all right," Sutherland said. "I'll show you. We need to go to the den first."

"I already look there."

"We need the key to my storage." Sutherland pulled himself up, wondering what he was going to do, slowed by the aches from his dive in the river and throbbing where the gun, fist, and kick had struck him. While he gained his balance, he watched the man with blurry curiosity. The man squatted and retrieved the cigarette butt recently fused to Sutherland's neck, placing it carefully in his pants pocket. Removing the evidence. No question about it, the intruder intended to kill him.

They walked toward the den, Sutherland shuffling and gathering his wits, the man steps behind. Passing the intercom, Sutherland stared at it, wondering how long it had been since he'd signaled the doorman, willing the box to speak, to shriek. If that didn't work, he'd have to lead the man down to the storage cages and hope the doorman would suspect something when they passed through the lobby.

"You kill Bill Jamison?" Sutherland asked. "Or the guy called Scooch?" This man looked too young to have been around to kill his father. In any event the man didn't answer, just gave Sutherland a shove.

The lights were on in the den, drawers were pulled out, and papers were all over the floor. On the desk, in a box, lay the mail and other papers Sutherland's father had left in his office. The younger Sutherland sifted through his memory for anything useful in that pile, something on the bookshelves, a ruse to distract the big blond for a few moments. Seconds was all he would have. He eyed a yacht trophy on the shelf on his right. It was a first-place cup, eighteen inches high and seven pounds of silver plate and lead. A formidable weapon, if only he got the chance. Time. What was taking so long with the valet and doorman?

"Where is this storage?" the blond demanded, jamming the barrel hard into Sutherland's ribs, nearly knocking him off his feet.

Evidently neither he nor Sandler had considered a storage unit. Rather than tell the blond about the apartment building's cages, why not the warehouse where he kept his old junk? "Down the street," Sutherland answered.

After another jab with the barrel, the blond said, "You lie."

In a desperate attempt for time, Sutherland said, "Really, I'll show you an invoice for the warehouse. It's there on the desk. It's called U-Storage and it's down the street. Look." He pointed at the pile of papers and stepped out of the way, toward the bookcase, allowing the man room to walk to the desk and at the same time giving himself a reason to be closer to the trophy.

Just as the man bent over the desk, the intercom buzzer by the den door shrieked, followed by a deafening, crackling voice filling the room. *"Mr. Sutherland, Mr. Sutherland. Your car is ready."*

The man spun toward the ear-splitting screech, his gun ready and pointing. Sutherland clasped the trophy handle and whirled toward him, following the big man's movements as if in slow motion—saw him facing the intercom, then turning in time to see the flash of silver approaching, his eyes widening before the blow. The trophy's heavy base smashed into the man's temple with a wet clunk, sending blood splattering and his body crumpling to the floor. The gun crashed against the desk and onto the carpet.

Sutherland's momentum threw him against the wall. When he turned and got his balance, he saw the man struggling to his knees, his hand pressing his temple, his eyes dazed. Sutherland dove for the gun, grabbed it, rolled over, and looked up to see the man teetering to his feet while fumbling in his pants pocket. The attacker pulled out a switchblade, flicked it open, and lurched forward. Sutherland found the trigger and fired just as the man lunged.

The gunshot wound doubled him over, and as he grabbed his stomach, he toppled onto Sutherland with his full weight. When Sutherland opened his eyes a moment later he was staring into the blond man's face, eyes closed and jaw clenched in pain. He watched the blood pulse from his temple, heard the labored wheezes, and thought he should be calling an ambulance. But he didn't move, didn't try to move the dead weight off him; he only laid back wondering where this left him, briefly thinking it was over, then realizing it wasn't.

The silver trophy rested next to him. One of the two handles was broken and bent, and red droplets flecked the shiny surface. Freeing his right hand, Sutherland turned the cup over and read the inscription:

FIRST PLACE
*CIRCE*
DOUGLAS SUTHERLAND
D-Day Regatta

The Allies' assault on that historic day had changed the course of a world war. Before closing his eyes again, Sutherland hoped that the D-Day trophy was an omen.

# Chapter 69

Finally everyone was gone. The ambulance crew wheeled away the blond man, leaking life in sputters like a punctured inner tube. The police photographers snapped their final picture, the technicians put away their evidence cases, an EMT attended the last of Sutherland's injuries, and the detectives closed their notebooks. Sutherland and Kelly sat on his sofa with mugs of coffee.

"How do you feel?" she asked. "You look like a punching bag."

He touched the bandaged area where the gun bashed him. The cigarette burn still throbbed, and his ribs ached. "Like I've been run over by a truck."

"You could've given them to him."

"No I couldn't."

"Because you're stubborn."

"Because he would have killed me anyway. Just like they did Bill Jamison and the others. So would those two in the tunnel. You think if we handed the tapes to that blond bitch, we'd be alive now? She didn't give a damn about her injured buddy. You're not having remorse, are you?"

"I hit her pretty hard. She may not recover."

"If you hadn't whacked her, we'd still be down there. Believe it." Sutherland leaned forward to set his cup down and grimaced with a twinge of pain. "When did you get here? You hear the shots?"

"Far as I know, no one heard gunshots," she said. "I must have arrived ten minutes afterward, and doorman was worried because you weren't answering. I let myself in, called out, and wandered to the bedroom. I expected to find you taking a nap or in the shower. When I peeked into the den, the two of you were sprawled on the floor, bleeding and unconscious. After I called 911, you opened your eyes, blinked, and looked at me with a dazed look, like to say, what happened?"

"He hit me pretty hard a couple times."

"Did they tell you they found two bugs?" Kelly asked. "I asked them to check. They brought in some kind of gizmo. One in the phone, the other in the light over the dining room table."

"That's how they knew about the tunnel," Sutherland said.

"I'd call the locksmith to change your locks first thing tomorrow."

"Should have done it when they scared Jenny."

"So now what?" Kelly asked after finishing her coffee, setting her cup on the table. "You think this is over?"

"Why? Because Sandler's man is out of the way?"

"And those two in the tunnel."

"So they'll give up? I don't think so."

"Neither do I. They'll figure you found the tapes."

Still no answer on who Scooch's and Jamison's killer was, though the tall blond, under orders from Eugene Sandler, was a good candidate. No further on identifying his father's killer or killers, who had forced themselves onto his boat that night. And finally, to Branson's and now his own quandary, still no answer to which side of the law his father had really been on.

Sutherland felt like he'd been in a stupor for hours, but the strong coffee was having its effect. He noticed Kelly's clothes for the first time, a light-green silk blouse and white slacks that molded to her contours like smooth frosting on cake. "How'd you end up here?"

She kicked off her loafers and curled her legs under her. "You called me, remember? Bring the cassette player, some takeout? You hungry? Pad thai."

"How'd you get in?"

"My keys."

"I thought you threw them away."

"A sentimental optimist. Good thing too. You were lying there bleeding. So was the other guy. Did he really shoot at you?"

Sutherland pointed to the hardwood floor where the police had dug out the lead. "He was making a point."

Kelly's concerned eyes warmed him, like the old days. Sutherland breathed in deeply and exhaled. "You want more coffee? I'll tell you the rest if you bring me a dish of the pad thai."

*　　*　　*

Twenty minutes later the strident buzzer sounded, and Kelly got up to answer it. It was the same redhead as the other night, the doorman rasped over the faulty intercom.

The redhead looked much better than she had when Sutherland left her at the hospital. Color was back in her cheeks, and for the first time that he could remember, she wore lipstick. Seeing Sutherland's bandaged face, Ronnie reached up and almost touched it with the palm of her hand. "Two times in a week. You okay?"

"Yeah. What brings you?"

"Stanley heard about it and called to tell me," Ronnie said. "I called and got no answer so decided to come over."

She followed him into the living room, where Kelly lounged on the sofa with a coffee cup in her hands. Her shoes were on the floor and her legs and feet were curled to one side on the cushion.

"You remember Kelly?" Sutherland asked Ronnie. "You met on my boat before the Mac race."

Ronnie scanned down Kelly's figure and assessed her comfortable pose. Her lips tightened and she said, "Right."

"Please accept my sympathy for your brother," Kelly said.

"Thank you," Ronnie muttered. "Stanley Vislowski said you were here the other day, too. Kind of a fixture?"

"Used to be," Kelly said.

Still standing, Ronnie turned to Sutherland and asked, "Is it true? The guy from tonight works for Sandler?"

"I saw them together the other night."

"So Sandler's the one," Ronnie said. "Tell me what happened."

"Have a seat." For the second time that evening Sutherland said, "Want some coffee? I'll fill you in."

*　　　*　　　*

It took ten minutes to finish his account of what happened that night, being careful to omit that they had found the videotapes earlier that day. For a minute they all sat around the coffee table in the living room, Ronnie staring out of the window at the high-rise lights on the other end of the park, Kelly sipping coffee while she sifted through the material Sutherland had shown her from his father's office, and Sutherland looking at his watch and trying to stay awake.

As if she was still piecing together a puzzle, Ronnie shook her head, her brow furrowed. "Sandler's gofer was after the tapes, you said. Not the notebook. That means he must have my copy. So Sandler either killed Scooch and my brother or ordered it done."

"He gets my vote," Sutherland said. "Gorman, Delaney, and my father too."

"Can I point out something?" Kelly said. "Delaney's and all the recent murders had similar MOs. But the guy tonight is in his midtwenties, too young to have killed Delaney or have anything to do with your father."

"Maybe so," Sutherland said, his fingers massaging his temples, still a bit muddled from the attacker banging on him. "But here's the other thing. We think Bill's killer was let into Robert Hurley's apartment. So Hurley or Bill probably knew the killer. Sandler was Hurley's boss. Maybe Bill or Hurley knew my attacker too."

"Or he and Sandler were together," Ronnie added.

"Wasn't your brother found in a walk-up apartment?" Kelly asked. "Fourth floor?"

"So?" Ronnie snapped.

"I've seen Sandler once or twice," Kelly said. "He's morbidly obese. It would take him half an hour to climb those stairs. Here's another idea." She looked uneasily at Ronnie. "Weren't the victims gay? That's the police theory, anyway."

"What's your point?" Ronnie said, glaring.

"When Reginald Tunney came to a meeting at city hall, one of the lawyers on my staff recognized him. Said he's seen him in a gay bar in Boystown a few times. Even with the shades, leather, and earring he apparently sports in Boystown, he's hard to mistake."

"Oh come on," Ronnie scoffed. "He's been married to Jules Langer's twin sister for fourteen, fifteen years. I just uncovered their wedding announcement."

"Doesn't mean anything," Kelly countered. "He's never seen with his wife. Word is she's mentally ill and he married her for her money. Odd guy too. He practically broke a reporter's arm for trying to take his picture in city hall."

Ronnie stood up, her hands clenched in fists at her side. "Damn it, Doug ..."

"Take it easy," Kelly said. "Just trying to help."

"I still lean toward Sandler," Sutherland said, "but Kelly's got a point." He remembered the man and woman in the tunnel, the same ones he'd seen in chaps heading for Tunney's penthouse the other night. "Ronnie, when the police checked on Bill's habits and haunts at the gay bars, did they ask about Tunney?"

Ronnie retook her seat and said, "I doubt it."

"If he did frequent those places and knew Bill or Hurley, he could've been let into that apartment."

"Wasting your breath," Ronnie said. "Vislowski and López are over their heads. They won't even go after Sandler or Tunney. Too many friends in high places. They gutted my articles in the *Tribune*. The request, or demand, came from George Spanos, who just happened to be one of the last names in Delaney's book, even though I never claimed it was the same Spanos. The paper's endorsing him for governor."

"Spanos has ideas for gambling casinos along the Chicago River,"

Sutherland said. "What do you bet that Sandler and the others own property or options there?"

"They do," Ronnie said. "Sandler, Tunney, and a string of familiar names. Even your buddy Langer. In addition, Spanos supports the new airport, and guess who owns land around it."

"So it's not just fifteen-year-old videotapes or the five million that's attracting the killers. Between the airport and casinos, there's tens—no, hundreds of millions at stake hinging on Spanos getting elected."

"With Sandler and Tunney as major backers," Ronnie said.

Sutherland looked at his watch, yawned, and said, "It's been a tough night. Time to hit the sack. You mind?"

"One last thing," Ronnie said, standing. "Did the guy tonight say why he thought you had the tapes?"

"He, or whoever sent him, had to be getting desperate. Just taking a chance," Sutherland said, wondering whether Vislowski would have learned of the pair who attacked Kelly and him in the tunnel. Even if he knew about it, he couldn't be sure the tapes had been found, and Sutherland wasn't about to tell Ronnie, the police, or the FBI yet. Not until he'd had a good look himself. "It didn't seem to matter. He was going to kill me even if I had them and gave them up."

"What's another murder to those bastards?" Ronnie said. "You were lucky. What's all that?" She pointed to the coffee table where Kelly had been sifting through the papers and other material from Bernard Sutherland's office.

"Useless, really. Stuff my father left behind. Bills and statements from his office."

Ronnie leaned over and spread the envelopes and bills to view them better. "Too bad they never found him. Might have had the answer in his pocket."

"Keys and wallet were on the boat. The FBI checked years ago and got nowhere. Here's the list of everything they found," Sutherland said, handing her the inventory sheets and photographs Branson had given him.

Ronnie scanned the list Branson had provided. "Can I have a copy of this?"

"I'll make you one." Kelly stood and took the list from Ronnie. She padded in her bare feet down the corridor and disappeared.

While she was gone, Ronnie said, "Wasn't she the head of the preservationist group that fought you on your development?"

"Why?"

"Sleeping with the enemy, is all."

Sutherland didn't comment, and Kelly returned, shaking her head. "You'll never get that blood out." She handed the copies to Ronnie, saying, "I told him he should have gone for hardwood."

As Ronnie made her way toward the door, Kelly held Sutherland back and said, "Doug, wait. I've got to talk to you."

"You coming?" Ronnie said, holding the door.

"I'm staying a moment, go ahead," Kelly said.

Ronnie chuckled with a smirk. "I see. Have a nice night you two."

After the door closed, Sutherland held up his hands and said, "Kelly, I'm in no mood to—"

"Just listen. I've got something to show you." She walked to the couch where she was sitting before and held up the stack of mail left by the elder Sutherland. "You ever look through this?"

"It's just some bills he left in his office. I assumed they were paid and never really looked at them. Why?"

"A Visa invoice dated before his death. Since the remittance envelope is still there, I assume it was unpaid when he died and paid by the estate."

"What's your point?" Sutherland said, getting impatient. He had a headache and wanted to sleep.

"There's a couple purchases he made, but the bill didn't come until after his death."

"And?"

"Did you know he bought a thirty-gallon freshwater tank from West Marine?"

"It's on the FBI list. He owned two boats."

"The date of the purchase was the day he died. What does that say to you?"

"He didn't expect to die. Now let me go to bed."

Kelly smiled, teasingly. "Speaking of which, you slept with her, didn't you?"

"Huh?" *Where did that come from*? Sutherland wondered.

"Come on, it's obvious," Kelly said. "The tension, the way she acts toward me. Jealousy. You dump her or something?"

He felt like he'd been ambushed for the second time that night. "Seems to me, you're the one jealous."

"Just making an observation."

"Truth be told, ever since her brother got killed, she's a different person. Mr. Hyde now. She's scary."

"Maybe she was always like that."

# Chapter 70

## SATURDAY, AUGUST 4

Sutherland didn't wake until after nine the next morning. After his second cup of strong coffee, finally awake enough to think logically, he called the locksmith, who said he could be there in half an hour. While he waited, he made a phone call to his lead New York attorney at home about the latest Broadwell status and another to his architects who were spending their weekend making changes to his building design.

An hour later, his business taken care of for the time being and the locksmith finished installing a new dead bolt, Sutherland went to the basement, retrieved the case with Delaney's videotapes, and returned to his apartment. Kelly had left him her neighbor's VHS player the night before, and it only took him a few minutes to connect it the flat-screen TV in the living room. It was ten thirty, and he was about to open his father's document case when Kelly called. She was outside his door and had just discovered her keys didn't fit the new lock.

"Just in time for the movies," he said as he opened the door for her. She was in her city-hall-attorney pant suit, apparently coming from a Saturday morning meeting in her office. If the boss called a meeting for midnight on Christmas Eve, one had better be there, she'd once said.

"X-rated?" she asked.

"Let's see," he said, leading her into the living room.

His father's document case sat on the floor, with everything in the plastic bag it had been stored in for fifteen years. Knowing that fingerprints could be important evidence to verify the provenance of the tapes, Sutherland slipped a glove on his right hand, the tape on his fingers making it impossible to fit one on his left. After clumsily unwrapping the plastic with his one gloved hand, he retrieved each video cassette, each the size of a paperback book, and stacked them on the coffee table in numerical order. There were thirty in all, and after a closer look, he said, "Are these VHS? They seem different from what I remember."

Kelly leaned over the table and squinted at the nearest cassette. "Philips Grundig, Video 2000. Definitely not VHS or Betamax. Damn."

"Never heard of it," Sutherland said, trying unsuccessfully to fit the tape into the VHS player. "We're screwed. Gotta find a player for this cockamamie brand. Any ideas?"

"A used electronics store, if we're lucky. I can check around."

He reached into the plastic bag again, retrieved a wallet-sized plastic object, and held it up. "Is this what I think it is? A hard drive?"

"How would I know?"

"It is. I saw them remove one like it from one of our old desktop computers at the office. That was years ago, but the computer's still in the office storeroom where we keep all kinds of obsolete crap. Maybe this will fit; it was an old HP, same as this. Care to join me in my office? It's Saturday, so we'll have the place to ourselves."

A half hour later, having replaced the tapes in the storage cage in the basement, they were downtown in Sutherland's office. It took three trips to haul the old CPU tower, monitor, keyboard, and mouse from the storage room and set it up on a desk in a vacant cubicle. After another fifteen minutes, they had figured out the cable connections and installed his father's hard drive, using the wire coupling in the CPU.

"Here goes," Sutherland said, powering up the CPU and monitor. Immediately the computer started to make promising sounds of booting, and in a few seconds a screen appeared with a prompt for a maximum eight-digit password. "Great," he grumbled. "Of course he'd have one."

"Ideas?"

"He named his boats *Gabriela*, after my mother." He keyed the name in and was scolded with the message, "Incorrect Password." Then he tried "McCollum," with the same result. After typing "Sutherland," the screen went blank.

"Know any hackers?" Kelly asked.

"No. You?"

"I'll bet the FBI has a few," she suggested.

"I want to see all the tapes before I let them try. I'm busting to know what's in those things, and it's only a matter of time before another shoe drops."

"What do you mean?"

"Like we were saying last night, this isn't over."

# Chapter 71

It was the first morning Ronnie Jamison had spent in her own apartment since her brother was killed and she'd moved into a hotel for safety. With the notebook stolen and in the hands of both the murderer and the FBI, she didn't see the point of hiding any longer. She didn't have anything uniquely valuable, nothing to make her a target. Even her attempts at pursuing her brother's investigative reporting in the *Tribune* had been squelched, presumably by the important people that she'd threatened to name.

Her cat was the only part of her homecoming that was welcoming when she'd entered. While Bridie rubbed against her shins, she surveyed the mess made by her intruder. Cleaning up would have to wait; for now she had to assess her financial situation. Fearing the worst, she turned on her Bloomberg monitor and flat-screen TVs, all tuned to her various trading and sports channels. A quick scan of the numbers and scores conveyed the bad news.

She'd suffered a disastrous few weeks. For years she'd skated on the edge, leveraging herself to the hilt, and won. But the recent market correction had caught her unprepared, leading to margin calls from two brokers. And whereas she normally batted 70 percent on her sports wagers, at 30 percent she owed her main bookie more than twenty thousand for her bets on the previous week's baseball games. Totaling it all up, margins calls and all three bookies, she couldn't cover what she owed without liquidating her trading portfolio. The recent real estate slump had squeezed out all the equity in her condo, and whatever she'd receive from her brother's piddling estate would have to wait for probate, a process that could take years.

Looking back, she reasoned the slide had started when she lost her focus, getting too caught up in Billy's investigation, hoping to secure the story that would make him famous. Then his death had turned a mere distraction into an obsession for revenge that had preempted her strict regimen of thorough market and sports research. She couldn't blame Billy—everything she'd done and would do was for his benefit. He deserved recognition for what he'd started and retribution for his death. Blame for her financial setbacks fell on the targets of Billy's corruption investigation and on his murderers.

After she placed sell orders for her health care stocks to cover the margin calls, Ronnie shorted a few tech stocks with the hope that the market wouldn't rally. Pulling the last twenty thousand from checking, she arranged to pay off her broker and place a few bets on the horses and baseball games. Seeing justice served was bound to bring back her mojo.

Distress over her bad luck still on simmering in her mind, she forced her attention on the inventory list the FBI have given Sutherland. She read it three times, checking what was found on Sutherland's father's boat against the summary of his last day's movements, trying to find something that stood out, a clue that the FBI hadn't seen or followed. Where had he hidden the tapes? And if the last entry, the 200K, in Delaney's notebook meant cash, where was it? And what about those millions he wired somewhere?

As she went through the list, her current financial status still rankling, she realized that the tapes had taken on a new significance. Not only could Billy receive the recognition he deserved, she could be compensated for his loss, a thought that had recently assumed a great deal of urgency.

She checked off the items on the list, the purchases, the FBI findings and grew more frustrated with each pass through. Finally, after two hours, she concluded that the only hope of finding the hidden tapes or money resided in the water tank Bernard Sutherland had purchased, which was mentioned in the report but never cited on the list of items found. What had happened to it? How many tapes, or how much money, would it accommodate? As much as the FBI report had the appearance of thoroughness, they had either overlooked it or failed to document their findings. With everything Ronnie had at stake, she didn't intend to assume the latter.

One comment in the FBI chronology was both intriguing and maddening. It was the short reference seemingly closing out the issue of the funds that had been wire transferred shortly before Delaney and Sutherland disappeared. The text read: "Original deposit in First National Bank of Chicago, but serially wired through three offshore banks to Banco de San José, Costa Rica, which refused to cooperate without the password or account number. No determination made as to whether funds were forwarded or remain with said bank."

Reflecting on the possibility that $5 million could be waiting for an account number was enough to make Ronnie cry. "A fucking number and a password," she said aloud. "What idiot doesn't write down the fucking information that leads to a small fortune?"

# CHAPTER 72

Sutherland and Kelly sat in his living room grousing over their failed attempt to view Delaney's videos or tap into his hard drive when his cell rang. It was Mark Branson, and as usual, he wasted no time getting to the point. "I just got the word on your attacker in the hospital. Uses the name Neils Swenson, but it's probably fake, and he's probably here illegally from Finland or somewhere. Homicide thinks they can tie him to at least one of the murders."

"Is he talking?" Sutherland asked.

"Not yet. But we know he works for Sandler."

"Can you arrest him?"

"Sandler? We're working with your police on that."

Sutherland could imagine Ronnie rolling her eyes, saying, "Same old bullshit."

He said, "How much longer before you haul in the whole bunch?"

"Now that we picked up the notebook from the *Tribune*, we're closer."

"Why's that? I've seen it, and it's not like it has an *X* marking the spot Delaney's stuff was hidden. You won't get far without the videos and whatever else he left."

"It's a start, and it implicates your father, so don't be a smart-ass. It names the bank where your father first wired the money. We knew that much, but he moved the money from one offshore bank to a few others and we lost the trail. Anyway, the videotapes are more important. Any luck with that inventory I gave you?"

"Still racking my brain." It wasn't really a lie; even if it was an evasion, turnabout was fair play. The agent hadn't been any more open with him. "I do know he was murdered, and the killers had their friends in the police bury the evidence. The same police that can't seem to arrest anyone for multiple murders."

"You know what Vislowski says about that? Alibis. Sandler with Representative Spanos. Tunney with his wife and her two nurses."

"What's Spanos's story?"

Branson was silent long enough for Sutherland to think he'd hung up, but finally the agent said, "Spanos was part of the prosecution team for Delaney's pending plea. Worked for Daryl Anderson, the attorney that went missing. I still wonder about him. Just like I wonder about your father. Gotta go. Keep me posted."

Before Sutherland could object or challenge Branson, the phone went dead.

*     *     *

Two hours later, Sutherland paced his apartment living room contemplating what he'd recently learned, trying to ascertain his father's true character. The nature of Bernard Sutherland's ultimate allegiance—to the criminals, the FBI, or neither, which was what Agent Branson was implying—worried itself in his mind like a pernicious worm. Just as did the true identity of his father's murderer.

There were no unexpected fingerprints on the boat. No CSI-type analysis. Motive? The racketeers had discovered his father had taken their money and learned he was scheming with the FBI to put them in jail. But there was no certainty that the same person or persons murdered his father and the recent victims. Any one, or none, could be guilty of all, some, or none of the murders, and it seemed the police and the FBI were no closer to sorting it out sufficiently to indict. One hope was for Sutherland's blond attacker making a deal and spilling Sandler's role. Another was determining whether Tunney knew Jamison or Hurley from one of the gay bars, which could explain how he would have been let into Hurley's apartment. Then there was the black and white couple in the tunnel. Tunney again.

Sutherland reflected on his meeting with Tunney, trying to recall if there was anything in his office that could shed light on a darker side of his personal life. Had there been any telling photos or mementos on his desk or book shelves? Replaying his visit in his mind, Sutherland couldn't remember seeing a single photo in that office, not even one of Tunney's wife. And Sutherland knew very well what she looked like; her huge portrait dominated Jules Langer's living room.

*Interesting*, Sutherland thought. *The bond between Jules and his sister seems a great deal stronger than between Tunney and Julia. Langer even named his sailboat after her. Wouldn't Julia, his twin sister, confide in a brother who was so close? Especially if she knew something disturbing in her husband's affairs?* Coupling that question with Sutherland's disbelief that Langer's father hadn't told Jules more, it was a good bet that Jules wasn't being honest with him. Time for another visit.

*     *     *

The condominium doorman recognized Sutherland but insisted on calling Langer before buzzing him through the lobby door. When he reported that Mr. Langer was busy, Sutherland grabbed the phone from his hand and barked into it, "Jules, see me now or your father's transcripts will be in the FBI's hands by tomorrow morning." They might be anyway if Ronnie gave them up after going through them. But at this point lying to Langer was like robbing from a thief.

"Let me talk to Max again. I'll tell him to let you in," Langer said.

Minutes later, when Langer saw Sutherland's face, the gauze, tape, and swollen eye, he nodded and said, "So it's true about Sandler's bodyguard. I warned you." Then walking back into the apartment he said over his shoulder, "You want a drink?"

"No thanks."

"How is he? Neils or whatever he calls himself?" Langer asked as he busied himself at his wet bar.

"Hanging on, last I heard."

"Should have been Sandler. World would be better off without him. An evil man." Langer took a thirsty gulp of what looked like dark rum in an old-fashioned glass.

"You're not exactly a saint, Jules."

Langer considered him over the edge of his glass. "Let's sit down."

They sat facing each other, Sutherland on a soft couch, Langer in a leather chair.

"You know why he came after you?" Langer asked.

"The notebook, the money, Delaney's videotapes—what's it matter?"

"You have the notebook?"

Sutherland studied the other man, wondering how much to tell him. From his behavior over the last few weeks—first avoiding him, then questioning him, agreeing to help, and finally warning him away—Sutherland guessed that Langer didn't understand everything himself. In any case, what choice did Sutherland have if he wanted information about Tunney?

"Yes, and so does whoever killed Scooch and Bill Jamison. Someone broke into the reporter's sister's place and left Scooch's cauliflower ear—and parts of the murdered reporter that I won't mention. Is your brother-in-law capable of that?"

Langer grimaced and took a drink. He swallowed several times, as if the liquid wouldn't stay down. "He's capable of anything."

"What about your sister?" Sutherland said, indicating the portrait with a glance. "She must know something. Don't you talk to her?"

"Not lately."

"I hear she's ... ill."

"She's not sick." His voice cracked as he glared at Sutherland. He turned to gaze at the portrait. "She's delicate. Now she's practically in jail. Two nurses round the clock and drugged senseless. He used her, spent every penny she inherited from our father, and constantly humiliates her." He turned back to Sutherland, his eyes blazing. "Behind that urbane manner is an animal. Used to bring his perverted sex partners over and make her watch."

Sutherland was stunned. Langer, normally so inflated with arrogance and self-confidence, was angry to the point of spitting. Or crying, for moisture was gathering in those blue eyes.

"A murderer too?"

"Could be," Langer said, his head hanging. "He wanted to kill Danny. Maybe he did."

"You know that? How?"

Langer sighed, his shoulders bent over as he held his drink with two hands. Finally he looked up at Sutherland and said, "Wait here. I'll show you."

# CHAPTER 73

Eugene Sandler removed his tinted glasses, set them on his office desk, and leaned back heavily in his chair. He pinched the bridge between his eyes and sighed. Tired. Angry. Worried. Neils, his driver and bodyguard, was in the hospital and under police guard. It had gone terribly wrong, and Sandler couldn't understand it. His man had never failed before, had always executed faultlessly, an unquestioning and disciplined chess piece, a product of strict mercenary army training. How Sutherland could have stopped him was impossible to fathom.

After learning of Neils's failure, Sandler felt like the clock was running. It was his move, and he had no strategy. Even though Neils never used his real name or carried ID or had been arrested in the United States, sooner or later the police would connect him to Sandler. Combing his fleshy fingers through his thinning blond hair, Sandler tried to work out the odds of Neils talking. It would depend on what they charged him with and whether he would be offered a deal. Sandler's calls to his police contacts hadn't been able to help. Give him time, one officer had said. He'd get back to him in the morning.

They'd hoped that by pressuring the *Tribune* to give up the story, the whole thing would die a natural death. But the FBI agent was still sniffing around, and Sandler no longer had any decent clout in the Bureau. Congressman Spanos had sent out feelers through his Washington connections but was afraid to be too obvious. One of their friendly officers in the Chicago Police Department had attempted to keep a lid on the investigations, misdirecting linkage between Delaney, Gorman, or Scooch with the reporter's death and his stories. It had worked to a point, but coincidences could only be stretched so far. Sandler felt like he was being squeezed. He had been able to work behind the scenes for too long to be the center of suspicion.

In conversations with Congressman Spanos and Reggie Tunney he was at a loss to explain Neils's botched job. The reality was that the videos were still out there, the threat hadn't been averted. Tunney, impatient for results, informed his two cohorts of his latest plans to acquire and eliminate the tapes. One approach would involve a friendly judge, while another would be more expensive—but what was a million in the scheme of things? Sandler agreed to both strategies, deciding at the last minute not to mention the dubious proposal he'd received to sell him the videos. On the off chance the offer was genuine he'd agreed to meet the supposed seller, but he wasn't holding out much hope.

Hungry, he had another reason to be irritated at the loss of his driver, bodyguard, and general problem solver. Neils would normally bring him an after-dinner snack at this hour, a hero sandwich with french fries, or a pizza from Pizzeria Uno. With him in jail, Sandler would have to go home and rely on whatever his housekeeper could put together on short notice.

He dialed his home number and was sent to his voice mail. Odd. It wasn't unusual for his cook to be gone at nine thirty, but Rita, his housekeeper, had her own rooms in his house and wouldn't be in bed so early unless she was sick.

At that hour, his office staff and the cleaning crew were long gone, leaving no one to drive him the six blocks to his house on Astor. He'd have to take a taxi. After closing and locking his office, he took the elevator to the lobby, said good night to the security guard, and hailed a cab at the curb. Ten minutes later he lumbered up the steps to the porch of his hundred-year-old gray-stone house.

Still breathing heavily from climbing, he unlocked the door, opened it, and noticed a note hanging on the hallway mirror. It was from his housekeeper, saying that she had a family emergency. Why hadn't she called him? Now he had to fend for himself, scour the pantry and refrigerator for something that didn't require preparation or call for a pizza delivery. Opting for the delivery, he walked through the living area to his home office and the phone. The room was dark, with only the light from Astor Street illuminating the room with a faint glow.

Before he could dial, Sandler heard a sound from the living room. "Rita, is that you?" he said, peering in the sound's direction. No one answered. Had he imagined the noise? He heaved his weight out of the chair and had circled to the front of the desk when a silhouette stepped into the doorway in front of him. Framed in the light behind, the figure appeared featureless, a dark shadow, uninvited and menacing.

"Wha? J-Jesus," Sandler stammered, feeling his heart leap. "You scared the shit out of me," he said after recognizing his visitor. Taking deep breaths, he leaned heavily against his oak desk, calming himself with his hand on his chest. "Did Rita let you in? I thought we were on for tomorrow."

His visitor remained in the doorway, holding a leather case, as if waiting to be invited in. Noticing the case, Sandler was pleasantly surprised, thinking the situation wasn't that grim after all. He hadn't been overly optimistic, but if that case contained what was promised, everything could be resolved swiftly. Pushing away from the desk, he pointed and said, "There's a chair in the corner. Show me what you've got, and maybe we can get put this thing to bed."

# CHAPTER 74

For fifteen years Miles Langer's secrets lay hidden in a safe-deposit box accessible only to his son, Jules. Now the metal box sat on the coffee table between Sutherland and Jules like the magic lamp ready to be rubbed.

They pulled closer to the table, and Langer inserted the key and opened the black box. He withdrew and unfolded the dozen handwritten pages and handed them to Sutherland.

"He wrote this when he was in the hospital," Langer said, handing the sheets to Sutherland. "He was dying."

It took Sutherland fifteen minutes to read Miles Langer's chronicle, a combination of confession, apology, and defense. His notes started by describing the background of petty graft and corruption, cash payments, and favors, which was the norm during the period twenty years ago. Then Sutherland's father came along and innocently changed it all. As one of Raskoff's attorneys, Sutherland established a number of trusts and partnerships for owning offices, apartments, and hotels. All perfectly legal and fairly common. But Sandler and Tunney, who were at Raskoff Real Estate at the time, saw these trusts as vehicles for expanding their influence. In collaboration with Gorman, Danny, and Miles himself, they did so. They now were able to pay their bribes and kickbacks with hidden ownership in these partnerships. After a few years, Sutherland discovered the illegal usage of his arrangements, and he urged the group to stop. But the system was too lucrative.

Then something serendipitous happened. Sutherland was filmed handing his friend the mayor an envelope in a local restaurant. At the time the mayor was trying to clean things up, and the newspapers were all over the issue. To save his friend, Sutherland pleaded guilty to attempted bribery and served a year's sentence. The mayor survived with little more than a red face.

When he was released, Bernard Sutherland resumed his old functions, but after losing his law license, he kept a lower profile. Then, months later, everything changed nearly overnight. Miles and the rest of the grafters learned that Danny Delaney was talking to the feds. Then Delaney and Sutherland diverted a large percentage of a property sale that was intended for distribution to the many "partners." Delaney disappeared, and Sutherland went missing from his boat. Miles was on his deathbed but he'd heard that Gorman had searched Delaney's office for the meeting tapes. He found a few odds and ends, but the majority of the recordings were gone, presumably taken by Bernard Sutherland. Since the feds never followed up, it was assumed they never got their hands on them. The matter ended with Langer's cronies believing the feds had the money, but no incriminating tapes. Miles must have died shortly afterward.

Finished reading, Sutherland sat back and massaged his temples. When he looked up, he was Langer staring at him, nursing a second drink. "That was my old man. Piece of work, right?" Langer said. "What he didn't admit was that he was a cruel, wife-beating, drunken bastard."

"He doesn't mention how my dad died. Did he know my father wasn't alone on his boat that night?"

"You're sure about that?"

"Positive. What do you think? Sandler kill him? Tunney?"

Langer shrugged. "Or someone working for them. Can you imagine that fat-assed Sandler floundering around on a boat?"

"Doesn't Tunney talk to you? You're part of the same cabal. And in-laws."

"A sensitive issue, so on the occasions we do talk, it's all business."

"If you broached the subject of the notebook, the tapes, the money, and the murders? What would he say?"

"Drunk, he could say anything. Scares the shit out of me."

"That's the answer. You have some drinks while you record him blabbing."

The blood drained from Langer's face, and he seemed to shrink into the couch. "The guy's violent. You wouldn't believe the stuff my sister told me."

"How else can you help her? He's got to be put away, and as it stands, he's getting away." Sutherland glanced inside the metal box and noticed a video cassette at the bottom. "What's that?"

"I found that among my father's stuff. Probably his last video. He destroyed the rest when he wrote that letter you just read."

"Have you seen it?"

"I don't remember. That's all I'm saying."

From the bottom of the box, Sutherland picked up a velvet ring case and looked at Langer for an answer.

Langer frowned. "You might as well open it. Someone sent that to my father. A present. Maybe a warning. He never told me who the sender was. I hoped he didn't know."

Sutherland removed the ring case and flicked it open. There it was. Propped inside was a graying incisor with a gold backing, all its luster dulled.

He recollected the gap in the mouth grinning at him in the ruins of the McCollum Building.

Sutherland tried to imagine the murderer bent over the screaming Danny, pulling out his tooth, crushing his knuckles with pliers. Such a man could easily hurl someone from a boat.

"Don't try to stop me," Sutherland said, grabbing the tape cassette and Miles Langer's confession. "I'm taking these. You can keep the tooth."

# Chapter 75

"I didn't believe you could pull it off," Gene Sandler said, greedily eying the leather case in his late-night visitor's hand. "Set it on the desk and let's take a look." If the case contained what he'd been told, his concerns about Neils and what he might spill to the police would suddenly become trivial. The airing of Delaney's videos, the principal threat to Sandler and his associates, would be avoided.

He stood to the side, watching eagerly as the clasps were snapped open and the top flaps pulled apart. But as the gloved hand withdrew a large pair of pruning shears, he felt the hot stream of his own piss streaming down his leg and burning bile climbing his esophagus. Seconds passed, his eyes transfixed by the shears, his mind racing, movement seeming impossible. The visitor said nothing, merely opened and closed the shears as if testing them for efficacy while Sandler looked on in terror. Seemingly satisfied that the shears would fulfill their intended purpose, the caller placed the shears on the desk and retrieved a pistol from the case and pointed it at Sandler.

Barely able to move, Sandler raised his left hand, pleading. "Please," he whimpered. It wasn't his reedy growl that came out this time; it was a squeal, a boy's undisguised falsetto. "We can work this out."

A sharp crack split the air, and Sandler felt his right knee give way. He tumbled to the carpet, groaning, the pain momentarily blocking out the fear. Through tearing eyes he watched as the dark stain soaked through his gray pants. It couldn't be happening, it had to be a nightmare, but no dream could hurt like this. He groaned, reached for his knee and, touching it, recoiled and passed out.

Minutes may have slipped by, possibly longer, but finally the pain and his moans brought him around. Opening his eyes, he could see he was on the floor. Lifting his head, he saw the shadow standing over him. Another shot broke the silence, and he felt the bullet slam into his lower gut, penetrating like a hot harpoon into blubber. He curled into a fetal position and lost consciousness again.

When he came to, the figure was leaning over him, gripping his left wrist in a gloved hand. He heard a crunching snap followed by a searing pain, and through his tear-filled eyes he saw his own pinky and diamond ring dangling from his attacker's fingers. Swallowed in a flood of pain, Eugene Sandler barely heard the words the shooter uttered before the last shot drilled into his forehead.

# Chapter 76

Sutherland's phone was ringing when he walked into his apartment at seven the next morning after a five-mile run. Dripping with sweat, he picked up and heard Agent Branson's voice against a background of noise.

"I'm in the airport. Washington. Only got a minute," Branson said. "Where were you last night around nine?"

Holding his phone, Sutherland walked to the bathroom, grabbed a towel, and began mopping his face while he answered. "With Jules Langer until ten. Why?"

"In a minute," Branson said. "Just got off the phone with the CPD. Like pulling teeth, but they finally told me that the guy that attacked you in your place wasn't lawyering up. He wants a deal. He admitted chasing you on the bridge and following Jamison and Hurley, but he swore he didn't kill them."

"What do you expect him to say?" Returning to the kitchen, Sutherland poured a glass of water from the tap.

"Says Sandler didn't either. That he overheard Sandler giving someone on the phone the directions to where to find them—Jamison and Hurley. But it wasn't Sandler, and he says he can give us the precise time Sandler talked to the killer so we can check his phone records and discover who he gave the orders to."

"That's not proof. Secondhand, hearsay."

"But here's the kicker—"

"The guy's playing the system," Sutherland interrupted.

"Here's the kicker. Sandler was murdered last night."

Sutherland almost choked on a mouthful of water. Stunned, he stumbled to the dining room and slumped onto a chair, speechless. Sandler? Number-one candidate for the killer-of-the-year award, just another victim?

"You there?" Branson asked.

"I'm here. How?"

"Shot. In his home. His housekeeper had been lured out of the house by a bogus call from the hospital saying her mother was in the ER. She was cold-cocked when she was locking the front door. I'm telling you this because someone's getting desperate."

"Aren't many *someones* left. Tunney? Spanos?"

"CPD will interview them this morning, but you know …"

"Langer and I are clear, anyway. That why you asked where I was?"

"Just curious," Branson said.

"Wait. Sandler was shot? That doesn't sound like the other murders."

"In one way it was. Sandler was missing his diamond pinkie ring. Along with his pinkie."

*     *     *

While Sutherland showered, he thought about the tape he had taken from Langer the night before. It was VHS, so he could view it with the player Kelly had borrowed from her neighbor. She had also left him a message last night that she'd found an old Philips Grundig machine for Delaney's tapes in a used equipment store on Milwaukee Avenue and that he owed her fifty bucks. She planned to drop it off that morning before she went off to meet her aunt for Sunday brunch.

Ronnie phoned Sutherland just as he was getting out of the shower. She was in her car on the way over to his apartment. He had time only to brush his teeth and throw on pants and a shirt before she arrived. When he opened the apartment door, she rushed by, looked around for signs of anyone else, and stood in the living room facing him, shaking her head.

"You won't believe this," she said. "You got any coffee?"

*She already seems wired; why she need coffee*? he mused. He pointed to the dining room table. "Have a seat, I'll make it."

Instead she followed him into the kitchen, talking rapid-fire. "Sandler's dead and the guy that broke in here woke up and wants a deal."

"I know. But he's saying Sandler's not the guy that killed Bill."

"Huh, what?" Ronnie sputtered.

Sutherland scooped ground coffee beans into the filter and turned on the machine. "I got that from Branson. He called fifteen minutes ago."

"He's saying Sandler didn't kill Billy?" she said, sitting down as if her knees had buckled.

"That's what Branson said. But obviously one of Sandler's cohorts didn't trust him. Tunney, Spanos, the Joker—who knows? We should be happy, in any event. He had a hand in both Bill's and my father's death, whether he was there in person or not."

"I can't believe he wasn't the one," Ronnie said, running her fingers through her hair, a puzzled frown on her face.

"I thought so too, but it doesn't mean he wasn't. Just that there's another murderer out there." Sutherland looked at his watch. "It's kinda early. You could've called first."

"Couldn't sleep. Where'd your father's boat end up?"

"Huh? Why do you care? If you think there's anything there, you're wrong."

"Just the same …"

"Somewhere on the lakes. It was sold before I returned. It'll be registered with the Coast Guard, but you're wasting your time."

The doorbell rang, and Sutherland opened the door for Kelly, who was holding a tape player in both hands. "Do I smell coffee?" When she saw Ronnie, she said, "Oh. What's up? Something happen?"

"Put that down on the table," Sutherland said. "Coffee's ready. We just learned that Sandler's been shot. He's dead."

After setting the player down, Kelly came into the living room and said, "Whoa, Nelly, that's hot news. Any suspects?"

"Your guess."

Ronnie stared at the machine Kelly had set on the table then glanced at the VHS player that sat on the floor, the one Sutherland had connected to the TV the morning before. The wires leading to the wall-mounted flat-screen looked temporary, and Sutherland realized that the success of his and Kelly's trip into the tunnel was about to be revealed.

"What's with the old cassette machines?" Ronnie predictably asked, a curious expression on her face. "You got a porn thing going on? Some family movies?"

Kelly looked to Sutherland for a comment, her expression asking, "What now, boss?"

When Ronnie realized the truth, her face lit up with excitement, then rage as she jumped up and shouted in Sutherland's face. "You found them, didn't you? Delaney's videos. You weren't going to tell me, you bastard." She hooked her fingers into claws and swung at him, just as she had done to Vislowski days before.

Sutherland saw it coming and jerked backward on the sofa, making her miss. He grabbed her arm as it passed and forced it behind her back. "You fucker," she screamed as she was pressed down on the sofa cushion.

No one moved for a full minute. Kelly hovered over Ronnie, ready to help Sutherland keep her subdued. Sutherland leaned his weight on Ronnie, still holding her arm in a hammer lock. Ronnie, face down on the sofa, had ceased resisting.

"Are you through?" Sutherland asked.

"You bastard. Why are you holding out on me?" Ronnie asked, almost in a whimper. "I'm on your side, remember?"

What was the use? Disdaining authority as she did, she could at least be trusted not to inform Vislowski or Branson. "I'm not holding out. We haven't seen them yet. For all we know, it's all garbage."

"I'll bet."

"It's true. You'll see in a minute if you calm down. Okay? You going to be nice?"

Ronnie nodded, and he released her, moving away just in case. She sat up and rubbed her arm then said, "You didn't have to do that. I wouldn't have hurt you."

"I've got this bandaged finger that says otherwise. Now let's all be calm and see what we've got. I'll go get the tapes. Meanwhile, no fighting, ladies."

# CHAPTER 77

Sutherland returned from the basement in five minutes with his father's legal case, which held the videos. He immediately felt the chill between Ronnie and Kelly. It appeared as if neither had spoken in his absence.

After pulling on his right-hand glove again, Sutherland laid out the tapes on the coffee table. Consulting Delaney's notebook, he pointed to the last video. "Let's start with this one. It's the final entry, and my father is mentioned in it. Help me hook up that Philips Grundig machine you brought."

The video was in color and clear. According to the notebook, the section with Sutherland's father was the seventh scene on the tape. He fast-forwarded, stopping at intervals to see what was recorded. Images of Delaney in what must have been his home and his downtown office appeared with various people, some of whom Sutherland recognized. One scene included a developer he knew, another a lawyer specializing in zoning issues, another the head of a local union. In one scene, a pair of visitors handed Danny an envelope. These tapes were priceless, and he hadn't even started. What would his father's part show? He forwarded until he found it.

Danny, sitting at a round table, faced directly into the camera as he spoke. The rings under his gray eyes suggested he hadn't been sleeping well, and there was a slackness in his once smooth and handsome face. His wavy silver hair was combed straight back, and his half-glasses hung on a chain around his neck. But the starched white shirt, tight tie knot, and dark-blue double-breasted suit were clear statements of Dapper Danny's sartorial pride. "My name is Daniel Delaney, alderman of the First Ward in Chicago. I'm recording this from my home on the eve of my surrender to the FBI." Delaney went on to state the date and time of the recording, holding up a copy of that day's *Chicago Tribune* while he spoke. "With me is Bernard Sutherland, who has been working with the FBI for … how long?" From the edge of the screen, Sutherland's father, dressed in suit and tie, came into view, sitting down next to Delaney at the table. "Two and a half years," Bernard Sutherland said. With his blue eyes, dimpled chin, and sharp nose, he was an older, though paler-skinned template for his son, who looked on in astonishment.

"Two-plus years," Delaney repeated.

Sutherland paused the tape and stared at the static frame. Years? He turned to Kelly. "Did I hear right?"

"You knew he was working with them. Branson told you."

"It doesn't make sense," he said. "Two and a half years puts it before he went to jail."

"Let's see the rest," Kelly said. "Maybe it'll get clearer."

Sutherland started the tape again. Delaney continued, this time reading from a page he held in both hands. "Tonight, I am handing over three years of audio- and videotapes I secretly recorded in my office and home. They were taken of meetings I had with various individuals over matters of zoning, development, permits, investments, loans, gambling, protection, intimidation, extortion, and more. I know that these tapes will incriminate me." He attempted a strained smile, and a glint showed from light reflecting from the edge of his left-front tooth. "More importantly, they will incriminate city, county, state, and federal officials, union leaders, lawyers, police, developers, Republican and Democratic party leaders, and ordinary businessmen and women. I taped them out of self-protection, as a defense against others blackmailing, pressuring, or extorting me. And I must confess, I made these tapes as a weapon."

"Do you believe this?" Kelly said, shaking her head.

"No wonder people murdered for this," Sutherland said, looking for some acknowledgment from Ronnie. She didn't return his glance, her gaze fixed on the screen.

Delaney continued. "Mr. Sutherland is delivering these tapes to FBI agent John Durham in return for protection from a group that wants me out of the way. I attest that these tapes are authentic. Additionally, a week ago Mr. Sutherland saw to it that five million in illegal proceeds from a building sale, intended for a secret offshore account, were diverted to the government. I've documented and indexed all of these transactions in this notebook." Delaney put down his script, pulled a notebook from his inside suit pocket, and held it up. Then he placed it on the script and looked at Sutherland's father. "Oh, and Mr. Sutherland is also taking in the money in my … errr … working fund, a couple hundred grand or so. And that's all of it. I'll turn the thing off."

He stood and left the picture, leaving Sutherland's father alone to say, "Call it what it was, Danny. A slush fund for payoffs."

From off camera came Delaney's voice. "Right. Slush fund." In another moment, the screen went black.

The three of them were speechless, staring at the TV. Sutherland felt as though years of toxic resentment were boiling up from deep within, wanting to explode. The shame he'd felt, the disrespect for a man that he'd once admired—all of it was based on deception. Why keep it a secret? Why didn't someone tell him? Why let him believe the fabrication?

"This is a bombshell, all right," Ronnie said, finally coming out of her sulk. "If what he says is true, it's enough to cause an earthquake here. If I hadn't seen it, I wouldn't believe it."

"If what's true?" Sutherland said, still trying to digest the news about his father, unable to think beyond its significance.

"About who he recorded and the criminal implications," Ronnie said, getting more excited by the second. "Let's look at this one; it's got Tunney, Sandler, Miles Langer, and Spanos together. See if this Spanos is our favorite congressman. It's the second-last tape, third scene. Dated about a month before Delaney disappeared."

Glad to divert his thoughts from the emotional haymaker of the last scene, Sutherland ejected the tape cassette and inserted the requested video. Fast-forwarding, he found the third section and pushed *play*. This time, Delaney had his back to the camera. Facing it were Reginald Tunney, Gene Sandler, a pale-as-death Miles Langer, and a younger version of Congressman George Spanos. "That's our boy," Sutherland said. "Front-running candidate to be our next governor. He was a lawyer working in the state's attorney's office back then. Let's see what he's doing with these sleazebags."

For the first few minutes of the meeting, the five of them chatted about the crappy weather, the Cubs' losing opener, and the Chicago Bears' mistake in not picking a QB in the draft. Finally Tunney turned to Spanos and said, "Okay, George. It's your show. Tell them what you told me."

Spanos took a deep breath and began. "Couple months ago the FBI brought in a new guy. Name's John Durham, and he specializes in corruption investigations. You read about the big case in Philly? That was him. He set up a team here with a war room and staff from the FBI, federal prosecutors' and state's attorney's offices."

"That's nothing new," Delaney said. "Tried it before. Nothing happened."

"Yeah, but here's the thing. They assigned me part-time to some research and documentation. I don't sit in many meetings, but I hear and see things. They've nailed someone and he's turned. He's helping them build their case."

"Against who?" Sandler said.

"Your names come up with a few more. High profile."

"Who is the bastard?" Delaney hissed. "Cut his balls off."

"They use a code name: Rex," Spanos said. "Rex says this, Rex's got that, you know. For some reason, I think he might be a cop or someone on the mayor's staff. But that's just my gut."

Sandler, turning red, yelled in his reedy screech, "Why didn't the commissioner tip us? What are we paying him for?" Before anyone could answer, he continued, "We've got to smoke this stoolie out. Snuff him. George, you got to find him. Get his name. We'll do the rest."

"I'm trying, but I only have limited access."

"He's right," Tunney said. "Our boy's got to be careful. And so do we. We start by Georgie getting us the names of the people on the team and we find a weak link. Gambling, women, drugs. Create one if we have to, like we did with you, remember, Georgie?"

"You never let me forget," Spanos said, his eyes cast downward to his clenched fists.

"What do you think, Miles?" Sandler said. "You like anyone as the stoolie?"

Miles Langer coughed out several wet, gravelly sounds before answering. "They've been after Gorman for years. Could've got enough to turn him."

"I don't think so," Sandler said. "Reggie's right. We gotta find someone else inside and squeeze out the bastard's name." Sandler turned to Spanos and pointed a stubby finger in his face. "Georgie, we're counting on you. Get us all the investigator's names. Can you do that?"

George Spanos frowned and nodded. His eyes were downcast, like a puppy that had been told to sleep outside.

The screen turned to snow, and Sutherland pushed *stop*. "So that's how he rose like a rocket, the weasel," Sutherland said. "Had that whole corrupt machine pushing him. Went from there to state senator, to congressman, and now wants to be governor."

"Not after the public sees that," Kelly said. "Be running for king of the cell block."

Ronnie shook her head, sadly. She turned to Sutherland, her eyes moist and lips trembling, and said, "Billy should have been here. He deserves a prize for this."

"He sure didn't deserve to die," Sutherland said. "But now we know why he was killed."

Ronnie wiped her eyes and collected herself. "How long have you had them?"

"We found the tapes two days ago, but we didn't have the right machine to play them." He told her about the tunnel, the discovery, and the attack by the black and white couple. "I didn't say anything because I wasn't sure what we had, if anything at all. I haven't told anyone else."

"Except your old flame." Ronnie glanced quickly at Kelly. "Or is it just flame?"

"I wouldn't have gotten into the tunnel without her. Besides, she cold-cocked the blond who was about to shoot us."

Ronnie rolled her eyes, unimpressed. "Delaney mentioned his slush fund. Couple hundred grand. Was it there too?"

"Just my father's case full of tapes, some files, and a hard disk. I haven't had a chance to get to them except today. We looked everywhere, but no money."

"So it could be on your father's boat," Ronnie said.

"It was searched back then. You saw the FBI report."

"Yeah, supposedly. What's this?" Ronnie asked, holding up the VHS tape Sutherland had taken from Langer the night before. "It's not the same kind."

"Jules Langer's father made it, the last tape before he died and the only one Jules saved. It's dated a few days before Delaney and my father's disappearances."

Sutherland exchanged the cassette players, inserted Langer's tape in the VHS machine, and started the tape. It was black and white with a crisp picture, and the scene was a conference room, one that he didn't recognize. Miles Langer was in profile, this time with a plastic tube running from his nose to an oxygen tank lying in the adjacent chair. Around a rectangular table sat Gorman, Tunney, George Spanos, and Alex Rodriguez, the former police commissioner. There was no chitchat or eye contact; everyone seemed to be deep within themselves. Then Gene Sandler appeared at the door, shuffled his heavy mass to the table, and fell into a chair. He looked around the table and said, "What have we got? Why we meeting here? Where's Danny?"

"That's why we're here," Tunney said. "Our plan paid off. Tell them, my boy."

Spanos cleared his throat and swallowed hard. "One of the team on the investigation is Daryl Anderson, an assistant state prosecutor. After I mentioned that to Reggie, the police found him passed out in a prostitute's hotel room with drugs all around. As prearranged, we got the police to forget the incident." Spanos nodded at the commissioner and gave him a weak smile. "Anderson, showing his appreciation and fear that the tapes we had might be disclosed, unloaded a lot of stuff on the investigation. I don't think he realized what I'd do with it."

"Get to the point, damn it," barked Sandler. "Who's the traitor?"

"Danny," Tunney said.

"Fuckin' impossible," Gorman said. "I don't believe it."

"He's turned," Spanos said. "They had him on film. Solid."

"How?" Langer said between strained breaths.

"That's what Anderson didn't know. Maybe another stoolie."

"Two of them? We gotta find the bastard," Sandler said, turning purple. "George, work Anderson some more. We need that other name. They're both as good as dead."

"What about the evidence they've collected?" Gorman asked.

"It's in their so-called war room," Spanos said. "A warehouse on the West Side. A fort."

"Can you get in?"

"You need a card and the code. Only a handful have them. On top of that, John Durham, FBI head of the investigation, has a lockout key."

"Anderson have the code?"

Spanos nodded.

"There you go," Tunney said. "Get it. Pay him off if you have to. Whatever he wants. We'll have to take care of this Durham too, fuckin' bastard. You'll have to help with that, Georgie. But I'm going to personally take care of those stoolies." Tunney turned to Sandler and said, "Comments?"

Sandler examined his diamond pinkie ring, polished it on his lapel, and said, "I want to be there when you do." The meeting concluded when Tunney stood and announced they'd get together in three days.

Sutherland stopped the tape and said, "The Daryl Anderson that Spanos talked about disappeared a few days before Danny was killed. Agent Branson told me the FBI found him, but he didn't tell me whether he was alive or dead. Durham was killed the night before my father disappeared."

"Your father could be the other so-called stoolie," Kelly said. "He must have trapped Delaney."

"And Tunney killed him for it," Sutherland said. "We've finally got him."

"How?" Ronnie said. "All we have is a conspiracy. You'll never convict him for murder on that. And what about my brother?"

"This is scary," Kelly said. "We've got hours of tape that could ruin dozens of people, put some in jail for a long time. If Tunney sent those two after us in the tunnel, he may know we have the videos. We've got to turn them over."

"Why so fast?" Ronnie said. "Think about it. This is too good to just hand over."

"Besides," Sutherland said. "After seeing those tapes, I don't trust anyone. Is the new commissioner still on their payroll? What do you think, Kelly? Ronnie?"

"Never know who in the department those guys bought," Ronnie said. "Branson's another matter. He's been telling everyone that he's part of a big investigation, on the verge of all kinds of indictments. Stanley did some checking and so did I. No major FBI investigation. No federal or state prosecutors. Just Branson. He doesn't even work in the Chicago office anymore."

"Son of a bitch," Sutherland said, remembering the day he was supposed to meet in the FBI's Chicago office, how Branson had driven up and they'd driven off in his car. "He's had me on a string."

"Not just you," Ronnie said. "What's he after? The money?"

"Who knows?" Sutherland said. "I thought he was just after whoever killed his boss and screwed up their investigation."

"We don't know that," Ronnie said.

"Look," Kelly said. "Whether or not there was a major investigation before, with this material, there'll be one. It's got Tunney and Spanos conspiring murder. Might not get a murder indictment, but it'll sure get things rolling."

"True," Sutherland said. "And there's probably more ammunition on the other tapes, but it will take hours of viewing to find it."

The three of them sat in silence for a moment, staring at the blank TV screen. Finally Sutherland said, "Okay, here's what we'll do. First we need a DVD recorder to burn copies of that VHS and some of these others, depending what's on them. Until then, we do nothing."

"Wait a minute," Ronnie said. "Before you start giving them away, remember—this is my brother's story. I'm not going to be left out."

Kelly stood up, looking at her iPhone. "Yikes, it's late. I've got a brunch with my aunt. Gotta go, call you later. You haven't told me everything about Langer last night." She picked up her purse and hurried out of the door.

It took a moment before Ronnie said, "What else happened with Langer? Something besides the tape?"

Over more coffee Sutherland related the previous night's conversation with Langer. When he mentioned his plan to wire Langer up, she laughed. "You want Jules to trap Tunney with a recorder? Why waste your time? You'd never get a court order on what we have, and it won't be good in court."

"But I may find the truth about my father. Billy too."

"From what you told me of Langer, I'm surprised he'd do it."

"He didn't exactly warm to the idea. He's always been a blowhard and a braggart, now we'll see what he's made of."

"Spineless," she said. "Call him. It's his own twin. Shame him into it."

"Sandler's murder will put him over the edge. But here goes." Sutherland picked up the receiver, and Ronnie picked up the wireless extension to listen to both sides of the conversation.

When Langer answered and heard Sutherland's voice he blurted, "Now Sandler's murdered. Do it yourself if it's so easy."

"What about Julia? Your brother-in-law may be the murderer."

"Looking more and more like he killed your father too. You want to get even, I'll help you. I've got the keys to his offices. Julia had them copied for me years ago, before he had her drugged up. With the keys you can get from the garage to the office and penthouse without the guard seeing you. Once you're there it's up to you. Do whatever you want, but that's all the help you'll get from me. Stop by my place this morning and I'll give you the keys."

When Sutherland replaced the phone, he saw Ronnie pumping her fist in a victory gesture. "All right," she said, her eyes radiant.

"What are you celebrating?"

"Now you've got a way in."

"I don't trust Langer. He probably planned on shooting the bastard when he had those keys made. Before he lost his nerve."

"It takes some big *cajones*. You got them?"

"Not for murder."

"Then just record what he says with your phone."

"I have to find a way to see him first. He may be a mite pissed off about having his black and white playthings put out of commission."

# Chapter 78

George Spanos pushed his breakfast plate away, the scrambled whites and plain wheat toast untouched. Reading the latest news on his iPhone, he felt the pressure build in his chest, the squeeze rise in his throat. The headline said it all:

INSURANCE EXECUTIVE EUGENE SANDLER MURDERED

What was happening? A month ago there was nothing but sunshine and clear skies ahead. On top of the polls, endorsements piling up from all directions, he was a shoo-in to be elected governor. A day at the beach. Now he felt buried in the sand, the tide slowly creeping in. First the notebook appears and the reporter speculates that he was the Spanos mentioned in it, that he was associated with the corrupt Delaney. Then Gorman is murdered, followed by the reporter's death, and now Sandler's. Hovering menacingly over these events was the real possibility that Delaney's tapes could be found and publicized—and worse, that they would include a star performance by Spanos himself. Finally, although he'd pretended that this sponsors were no more corrupt than most, the truth that they were murderers could no longer be denied. They had killed Delaney, though the details, even the truth itself, had never been discussed with him. But since he had played a part in fingering Delaney as an informer, he should have known that the alderman hadn't absconded with the tapes, as he had been led to believe.

It was too early for the police to speculate on Sandler's murderer's identity or motive. A man with Sandler's unscrupulous methods had plenty of enemies, but it was natural for Spanos to think that the death was related to Delaney.

Alarming as it was, there was a positive side to Sandler's death. Spanos had detested the fat man, and with good reason. Though he'd aided Spanos's rise in political stature, from a mediocre attorney to a candidate for governor, he'd also been Spanos's tormentor for fifteen years. By arranging for him to be drugged and then videoed in a compromising situation involving a prostitute and cocaine, Sandler had blackmailed him, forcing him to inform and be a mole inside the federal investigation on Delaney and his entire circle of influence.

The memory of those days fifteen years ago still caused a shudder. He'd been all nerves, hardly able to think, following mindlessly what he'd been ordered. After he'd identified Delaney as the stoolie, trapped and blackmailed Daryl Anderson into spying, and unknowingly given away John Durham's itinerary the night he was murdered, Spanos was further coerced into participating in the FBI office break-in, carrying away damaging documents and setting fire to the rest. Finally, after years of suffering, he was free of the fat man's manipulation.

Spanos cast his gaze around the restaurant in Michigan Avenue's Ritz Carlton Hotel and felt a pang of anxiety. White tablecloths, sparkling glasses, shining silverware, heavy drapery, plush carpet, elegant waiters—this was the world he had lived in for years. Was this good life going to continue? What if Sandler had made an arrangement for the compromising tape of Spanos and the hooker to be made public in the event he died unnaturally? What if Delaney's tapes were uncovered and disclosed, proving to everyone that the aspiring governor was a spineless puppet? All these what-ifs, and yet nothing he could do to stop the outcome. Or was there?

Could he suppress the publication of those tapes, if they were found? He had friends on the bench, judges who owed him and his associates. Puppets like him who were elected or appointed to do what they were told, some of them being blackmailed, others simply venal. Why couldn't he get a court order to confiscate and keep the tapes out of circulation? With the first hint of the tapes' discovery the court officials could swoop in and take them before the police, FBI, or state's attorney could react. End of problem.

He picked up his cell phone and keyed the speed-dial number for Reginald Tunney.

*     *     *

Tunney replaced his phone handset and breathed deeply several times, trying to put this latest conversation out of his mind. Talking to that whiner Spanos was never a thrill, but lately he'd become a veritable pain in the ass. George Spanos owed his entire political success to Sandler and Tunney. He would be a complete nobody without their influence and money, and now he acted as if he'd done everything on his own and that the looming problem of Delaney's tapes threatened him alone. The fact was, no one knew what that cocksucker Delaney had recorded in the last year of his life. Imagining the worst, they could all be brought up on conspiracy, a charge that Tunney felt confident he could defeat given his contacts. But it could cost Spanos the election, and Tunney and the others would lose millions because Spanos's opponent was against the latest proposed downtown casino and new airport.

Tunney took off his suit jacket, hung it on the back of his high-backed leather chair, and poured himself three fingers of scotch from a bottle stored in his credenza bar. After plopping a few ice cubes into the crystal glass, he sat down, swiveled around, leaned back, and put his well-polished oxfords on his antique desk. For a long time he stared at the ceiling, trying to drive out all negative thoughts while he sipped absently on his drink. Finally, he admitted to himself that the peace he sought wouldn't come, that the momentum of events was creeping up on him. It was as if Delaney was back from the dead, or was a ghost haunting them. It should have been over that night in the factory where the plaster molds were made.

That was the last day of Delaney's life, and they all were there. It had to be that way; otherwise those absent could claim innocence and have too much leverage over the actual executioners. Gene Sandler was fifty pounds lighter then but still a lard-ass on the way to hippo-like proportions. Benjamin Gorman went through half a pack of cigarettes on the sidelines, watching gleefully and cackling insults. Miles Langer was in his wheelchair breathing from an oxygen tank, croaking out abuse whenever he summoned the energy. Commissioner Rodriguez helped Tunney subdue Delaney while Sandler weighed him down.

Tunney kept the satisfying work that followed for himself, though it had been Sandler's idea to bury the alderman alive after they had tortured him for what he knew. Bad luck that Bernard Sutherland had already left Delaney's place with the videos and cash. They had planned for him to occupy the twin column. Sandler loved the irony of it. Both columns were intended for the McCollum lobby, Sutherland's own building.

George Spanos had other duties that evening so he was excused from witnessing the execution. It was probably better that way; he wouldn't have had the stomach for it. Besides, after Tunney killed the FBI agent, Spanos's job was to clean out the prosecution team's war room and set it on fire.

Now the prick was acting like he was some innocent dragged into the fray. How easy he forgot how he set the whole chain of events in motion by ratting out the government.

Tunney polished off his scotch and refilled his glass, reasoning he had to assume Sutherland had discovered the tapes. The black and white tag team he'd sent after him might know for sure, but they were in custody, and the attorney he'd hired for them hadn't talked to them yet. Though Tunney would have enjoyed ending this thing with Sutherland and that red-headed bitch personally, acting alone, he had to rely on more subtle means. For once Spanos was right. He picked up his phone and dialed his favorite judge.

# Chapter 79

Jules Langer sat in his apartment nursing a Bloody Mary. The day so far hadn't gone well. Earlier, he and his team of brokers, architects, and engineers for his America Tower had made their final pitch to Imperial Food Products' relocation committee and chairman. It had been well rehearsed and had taken place in Langer Development's conference room in front of the sculptured model of the proposed building. The architects made an impressive presentation, highlighting the high-design features, spatial efficiency, and quality materials. The engineers discussed the energy efficiency and comfort level that the mechanical systems would deliver.

But when it was Langer's turn, he had difficulty with his lines. He'd written and perfected the script himself, had delivered it flawlessly a dozen times to prospective tenants in the previous months, but that morning he'd stumbled from beginning to end. His thoughts were blurred, his mind a jumble of images of America Tower crumbling along with his reputation when the whole truth came out.

There was no stopping the full disclosure now. He had knowingly helped it along, handing over his father's files to Sutherland. At the time he'd reasoned that if bringing Sandler and Tunney down meant he'd be incriminated as well, so be it. Better to be charged for payoffs and minor corruption than a coconspirator or accomplice to multiple murders. Underlying the legal motives was the burning hope that with Tunney convicted and incarcerated, Julia would be free. Now, after Sandler's murder, Tunney's guilt stood out like a wart on a beauty queen's nose.

As it turned out, Langer's dismal presentation hadn't mattered. The conference room went silent, and the faces of the Imperial Food Products audience grew stern and disbelieving when the conversation moved to the proposed rental rates, tenant improvement allowances, and free-rent concessions. The final words of the real estate director on the way out said it all: "You are 20 percent more expensive than your competitor. I'm sorry, but we don't need nor will we pay for a gold-plated palace."

And who was America Tower's primary competitor but Doug Sutherland. The same man who had beaten him out for Broadwell Communications was about to do it again. Langer blew out a breath and sighed. While it rankled that his archrival might gain the prize, it was becoming apparent that America Tower would never be built. Without a miracle, and Langer didn't believe in such things, in the months ahead he would be investigated, indicted, and possibly even convicted. If so, and if he was lucky, he might get off with a short-term sentence or even probation. But his reputation and his company would be ruined, putting an end to thoughts of new construction.

His drapes were drawn and the living room where he sat was deep in shadow, consistent with his mood. A single ceiling spotlight highlighted his sister's portrait. Glancing at it, the image of her being forced to witness Tunney's sexual depravities brought up a surge of acid from his stomach. *The man doesn't deserve to live*, Langer thought as he chewed on two antacid tablets, washing them down with his Bloody Mary.

And what was to become of her? She had no inheritance left; Tunney had made sure of that. For years she was kept as a way to extort money from Langer, though that hadn't helped her well-being. She was a prisoner, pure and simple. How many times had Langer run through his alternatives for freeing her? After futilely offering more and more money, it was clear that Tunney preferred to torment Langer by continuing his sadistic hold over them both. The only answers remaining seemed to be Tunney's death or long-term incarceration. The tape Langer had given Sutherland would ruin Spanos's campaign, costing them their investment in land around the planned casino and airport, but would it be enough to convict Tunney of murder? If only Langer could trust his nerve for that one second it took to pull the trigger.

The doorman rang. There was a messenger downstairs to collect a package for a Mr. Sutherland. Langer went to his desk drawer, gathered one of his two sets of identical keys to Tunney's building, and dropped them into a letter-sized envelope for the doorman. So Sutherland was going to use the keys and confront Tunney. Was he going to use a tape recorder or a gun? He had motive enough—did he have the stomach?

Imagining what Sutherland's visit to Tunney's might be like, Langer had an idea that made him grab the telephone and press Tunney's speed number. He would go see him before Sutherland. If everything went as he hoped, one way or the other, the confrontation between Sutherland and Tunney could free Julia for good. It didn't matter whether Sutherland was executioner—or victim.

# CHAPTER 80

Imperial Food Products had called Sutherland's office late that morning saying that his company had passed the first test. The relocation committee had been impressed with Sutherland's proposed development on the McCollum site and wanted another presentation. This time it would include their requested modifications, and this time the chairman would attend—a good sign. A decision would be made in several weeks, the implication being that the Sutherland team's next proposal and presentation would be critical. It meant all hands on deck.

After a long conference with his architects and leasing team, Sutherland caught a cab back to his office. In the taxi he consulted his phone messages and thought he recognized a number, but he couldn't exactly place it. When he passed Eileen, his assistant, she looked up and smiled. "You've been summoned."

"Summoned? As in, subpoena?"

"Almost, at least that's what it sounded like. Reginald Tunney's secretary called to set up a meeting. Tomorrow evening at eight thirty. Sharp. She sounded like a real ogre."

"Really?" Sutherland had been wondering how he was going to wrangle another meeting with him, and then the bastard surprises him and makes it easy. Maybe too easy, but at least he didn't have to sneak in the back door, as Langer suggested.

"Should I call her and tell her no?" Eileen asked.

"Why say no?"

"That's the other message. Your daughter wants to go to the Cubs game tomorrow. You're to call her back."

"Call the ogre and tell her eight thirty's fine." Tunney must realize he was a prime suspect now, yet he wanted to talk.

Before Sutherland could ponder further, Eileen poked her head in and said, "It's your daughter on the line. The Cubs game, remember?"

He picked up the phone. "Daddy? Are you all right?"

"I'm okay, why?"

"Kelly told me you've got a black eye or something."

"Just a few bangs. What's up with you?"

"We wanted to take you to a Cubs game, like tomorrow?"

"Can't, honey. Got a meeting."

"Like a date?" she asked. "With that redhead?"

"A meeting with a man. What do you know about a redhead?"

"We saw you on TV when you were in the river with her. Veronica somebody. Mom said she looked like a slut, but Kelly said she was pretty."

No surprise that his ex-wife would take the low road, but Kelly's comment wasn't expected. "You talk to Kelly about her?"

"We talk about a lot of stuff." There was silence for a moment, then, "Dad? Kelly still likes you. I can tell."

"That's nice, Jenny. You have a good time at the game; I've got to go." He hung up.

Now that he had a meeting with Tunney, he had to plan his approach. How was he going to get him to open up? His thoughts were interrupted by Eileen again. "Miss Matthews is on the phone. She sounds angry."

"Okay, Doug. What's going on?" Kelly said without preamble when Sutherland picked up. "And don't tell me, nothing."

"What?"

"The ball game, that's what. What's so important that you can't spend an afternoon with your daughter? It's her birthday."

*Oh shit.* Why hadn't he remembered? So immersed in the McCollum development and Delaney's legacy that he lost track of the only part of his marriage worth anything.

"You forgot, didn't you?" Kelly said.

"What time's the game?"

"Three o'clock. So call her back and say you'd be happy to go. Fourth-row seats, first base. I'll buy the beer."

"I thought it was a night game. Okay. I'll call her." No reason to tell her that he planned to see Tunney afterward. He knew how that conversation would go.

"Did you decide what to do with Delaney's tapes? You can't hang on to them; they're too important. And dangerous."

"I've got a few copied to DVD, but I haven't seen them all, so I haven't had a chance to do anything yet. I'm going to play a few more this afternoon. I'll let you know."

\*     \*     \*

Later that day, Sutherland left the office for home, planning to spend the afternoon and evening viewing Delaney's tapes. He had just left his car with

273

the condominium's valet when his iPhone sounded. It was Agent Branson, and it sounded like he was in his car somewhere. "Sutherland? Anything new?"

His voice reminded Sutherland of how the agent had deceived him, had led him to believe there was a major investigation under way, had withheld the truth about his father's allegiance and involvement. He wasn't in the mood to be civil.

"Nothing new, things are peachy here. Terrific."

"Then you've had some luck?"

"Like I said, things are great. How's it shaking at your end? The big investigation steaming along? Getting ready to haul in all the bad guys? Warrants and indictments flying all over town?"

After a long silence, Branson said, "What's with the sarcasm?"

"I'll tell you. There's no investigation team, no prosecutors or agents working with you. You're not even assigned to the Chicago office. What are you up to?"

More silence, then Branson said, "So you know about that?"

"You've been fucking with me all along. So buzz off." Sutherland hung up and walked into the building lobby, feeling better already. He was opening his mailbox when the phone sounded again.

"Don't hang up," Branson blurted immediately. "You're right and I'm sorry. Just listen a minute. I can explain."

Sutherland pulled a few bills and a magazine from the mailbox then closed and locked it and walked to the elevator before answering. "You've got a minute. Get going."

"When Delaney's body was discovered, I couldn't get anybody's attention in Chicago or Washington, so I was on my own, hoping to get some traction. You blame me? They killed John Durham, my boss, an agent of the FBI. They fucked up our case. Now we've got something and we can put them away. They're vermin, all of them. You blame me?"

"Why the deception? Why didn't you tell me my father was working for you all along?"

"I did tell you."

"Not that he was under cover for you or the prosecuting team for two and a half years. Since before he went to jail. That his confession was a farce, a trick."

"Now wait a minute. I came onto the team late. All I knew was he was supposed to turn Danny Delaney for us. That got screwed up, the tapes and money were gone, and we had questions about him ever since. But this other thing? I don't know anything about what went on with the mayor and jail. And anyhow, how do you know this?"

"Never mind."

"You found the tapes, didn't you? Just as I suspected, and the reason we need to talk."

"No we don't. You already conned me enough."

"This is different. Listen. I've been given a heads-up by our Chicago office. They got a tip from a judge who they have a line into. Someone else, someone with a lot of influence, knows you have the tapes."

"They're guessing. Just like you."

"Guessing or not, you may get a court order soon to give them up or face a contempt charge and jail. They're trying to bury the whole thing."

"Who's doing this? Tunney, Spanos, who?"

"Why do you say Spanos?"

"You said you had doubts about him, didn't you?"

"Yeah. He was there back then and I didn't like the vibes."

"At least you were right on something."

# Chapter 81

Inside his apartment, Sutherland finished his third cup of coffee and ejected the last of the Delaney tapes he'd viewed that afternoon. There were still more to play, but what he'd seen so far was enough to convince any jury that Chicago and Illinois were cesspools of sleaze. The one positive note to emerge was the last tape showing Delaney's confession divulging Bernard Sutherland's long-term cooperation with the FBI. Doug had found nothing that could incriminate or cast a negative shadow on his father, so it was clear that this record of systemic corruption had to be aired.

Consulting his yacht club directory, he found the number for Andy Domingo, the five o'clock anchor and investigative reporter for ABC and a sailor Sutherland knew from racing. When Domingo answered, Sutherland identified himself and asked, "You interested in a scoop?"

"Something more on Delaney or Sandler?"

"Meet me at the yacht club after your newscast this evening and I'll give you a blockbuster."

"I have a dinner date with the wife and friends. It can't wait?"

"If not you, Channel 5. I'm doing you a favor. You decide."

"Okay. Seven thirty okay?"

"See you there."

Hanging up, Sutherland called Kelly at her office. When she answered, he said, "I've made up my mind on the tapes."

"Have you seen the rest of them already?"

"Only three hours of them, but enough to make you sick. Give me the number for your friend who writes for the *Sun Times*."

# CHAPTER 82

"**W**hy are we meeting here?" Andy Domingo asked as he shook hands with Sutherland at the bar of the Chicago Yacht Club. He was medium height with handsome, dark features, slick, black hair, brown eyes, and a bright, toothy, photogenic smile. Sutherland noted that he hadn't washed off all of his caked-on TV makeup.

"We're going to my boat to do this. I've got a DVD player on board. As soon as Matt Germaine arrives."

"Germaine from the *Sun Times*? I thought this was going to be a scoop."

"You get the opening round, the kickoff. He gets the in-depth. Way too much material to get into a spur-of-the-moment news show. You can air it tomorrow night at nine o'clock with more background in the next day's paper."

"I'm not on at nine. Just five. And the late news is at ten."

"Then you'll have to have a special or a bulletin. It's nine o'clock or it won't be a scoop." Sutherland wasn't about to risk changing the meeting time Tunney had chosen. It might be then or never to get his answers.

"Man, you're not making it easy."

"Wait until you see. You won't want to miss this."

A large man with a head of curly blond hair and a bushy beard entered the door and was looking around, trying to find someone. Sutherland thought it might be Germaine and hailed him, quickly discovering he was correct. After introducing himself and Domingo, Sutherland said, "First, some ground rules. Everything I give or tell you has to be from an anonymous source until I say otherwise. I'm trying to run a business, and I don't want my name in the same sentence with some of types we're going to talk about. Can we agree on that?"

They both nodded and Germaine said, "As a general rule, that's not a problem. Is there a second source if we need a confirmation?"

"More than one. So let's get some sandwiches to take to the boat. It's going to be a long night."

Ronnie Jamison stared at the MapQuest screen showing the directions to Harbor Springs, Michigan, and the location where she could find Bernard Sutherland's former trawler. The round trip would take the better part of a whole day. She had done her homework, consulting with a local yacht yard, and determined that it would have been easy for Sutherland's father to replace one of the boat's several water tanks with a sealed-off tank in such a way that no one would miss the lost holding capacity. The FBI, or even a new owner, might never realize the difference. They could draw water from the taps or shower, refill the tanks, and never be the wiser.

Ronnie realized it was a long shot, its pursuit an act of desperation. But she *was* desperate. She looked at the spreadsheet on her computer screen and wanted to scream. Another day of losses, this time enough to wipe out what she'd borrowed through her bookie. A bet on a pending merger between two energy companies had gone bad when the European Union had nixed the deal at the last minute, costing her $50,000. Her immediate chance to repay what she owed was in beating the line on her bets for the weekend's preseason games. But her larger hope was in finding the money Sutherland's father took from Delaney. With that two hundred thousand and a little luck she'd be able to pay off her IOUs and meet her margin calls. And if she could locate the elusive account holding the missing millions …

Would she split that money with Sutherland? Why? It was *her* brother who'd died uncovering this conspiracy; it was her Billy who deserved the credit and compensation for the sacrifice. Yet Sutherland had Delaney's tapes and was planning to see Tunney the next evening. With a casino and an airport deal at stake in the gubernatorial election, Tunney could afford to pay megabucks to have the tapes destroyed, a fact that hadn't been lost on Ronnie. Selling the damned originals might be the easiest answer to her own problems. They were hidden somewhere in Sutherland's building's basement, but where?

She'd feel him out the next day. Drive him to Tunney's and wait for him, make sure she stayed tuned in. She had to see this thing through to the end. If Billy hadn't been tortured and killed, driving her to distraction, she wouldn't be facing this financial abyss. It was no longer enough to see that those responsible paid the mortal price. She must be compensated in full.

# CHAPTER 83

It was one in the morning before they finished going through five of Delaney's tapes and Miles Langer's VHS video. Andy Domingo and Matt Germaine had been scribbling feverishly while the tapes ran, barely touching the sandwiches and soft drinks they'd brought from the club. When exhaustion won over their intense interest, Germaine held up his hands and said, "Guys, I'm wrecked. This is unbelievable, but I need to get some sleep if I expect to write this up."

"One more thing," Domingo said. "Who was the other guy on Langer's video?"

"He was the police commissioner back then," Germaine said. "Rodriguez was his name. Retired two years ago. The current commissioner was his right hand."

"That's why I didn't want to hand these over to them," Sutherland said. "So what do you think?"

"A bombshell," Germaine said. "Let me ask you, why me?"

"Kelly Matthews trusts you and you're with the *Sun Times*. The *Trib's* already tried to kill the story. You got enough for now?"

"Plenty," Domingo said. "I'll call a meeting for first thing with the station manager and attorney. Clear this with them."

"I'll do the same with my editor," Germaine said.

"Do you have to?" Sutherland asked as he replaced the DVDs into his briefcase.

"You kidding? Spanos is a congressman, a candidate for governor," Domingo said. "This will sink him."

"Exactly," Sutherland said. "Just what he deserves. And I'll tell you guys this. If your bosses nix the publication, you lose. This will be on YouTube before you can say, 'I just lost the scoop of the year.'"

# Chapter 84

The Cubs beat the New York Mets five to two, a birthday present for Jenny, who was developing a passion for the team and a crush on the second baseman just up from the minors. Kelly bought her a gift for Sutherland to give her, a Cubs uniform shirt with the new player's name and number. Before the game, Sutherland couldn't have named a single player, but Jenny could tell him their batting averages without looking at the scoreboard. Sutherland had tried his best to be the good father and fan, cheering side by side with Jenny and Kelly, booing the ump's calls, and standing to sing during the seventh-inning stretch. But he couldn't stop envisioning the meetings that Domingo and Germaine were having with their respective media bosses. If the story wasn't aired when Sutherland met with Tunney later that evening, he would have no teeth to tease out the truth.

Finally, when they were walking to the El stop from Wrigley Field, he received a text message from Andy Domingo. "Still waiting for approval. Meet me at station ASAP."

He apologized to Jenny and Kelly, explaining that he had to skip the dinner they'd planned together. When Kelly took him aside to ask what was more important than his daughter's birthday, he showed her Domingo's message. "Let me go with you," she said. "I was there when you found the tapes. It might help making the case."

He agreed reluctantly and arranged for Jenny to take a taxi to her friend's apartment in the Gold Coast, where she was to spend the night. Then he and Kelly took the CTA train to ABC's studio on State Street.

They were ushered into the station's executive conference room to the sight of five men and two women staring at Miles Langer's DVD on the flat-screen TV, paused with George Spanos in mid-sentence. The only face in the room Sutherland recognized was Andy Domingo's, who introduced Kelly and him to the station manager, his assistant, the news editor, the producer, and two attorneys, none of whose names Sutherland could remember a minute later. Four other DVDs lay on the conference table, along with the remnants of a takeout plate of deli sandwiches. The expressions on the faces showed frustration and fatigue.

"Where are we?" Sutherland asked. "There a problem?"

After several seconds of silence, one of the attorneys, a man, spoke up. "It's a question of context, Mr. Sutherland. There's no date, no reference to what went before."

Sutherland pointed to a copy of Delaney's notebook and said, "In Delaney's last tape, Delaney's holding a newspaper with a clearly visible headline. And look at the notebook. It's chronological, with the notebook listing each tape and the date. A few days before Delaney was killed, George Spanos was spilling confidential information, getting his marching orders like a well-behaved puppy. Then he outs Delaney and gets more instructions, this time to find the other man working for the prosecutor team: my father. What's so hard to fathom? We know when Delaney died. We know when Miles Langer died. Isn't that enough to confirm the dates?"

"How can we be sure they're authentic? Their provenance?"

Sutherland felt his cheeks getting hot, clenched and unclenched his fists under the table. "Look, I gave Andy the whole story. The FBI can substantiate that my father picked up Delaney's tapes. I'm willing to bet both Delaney's and my father's fingerprints are on the originals. Miss Matthews here, a respected attorney for the City, was with me when we uncovered them a couple days ago. You think we're making this up? You think these are actors? What?"

"If this is authentic, George Spanos will be open to any number of criminal charges," the other attorney said. "If it's a hoax, the station will be crucified."

Sutherland stood, glowering at the two attorneys. "Then what's it to be?"

Getting no response, he turned to the station manager. "Well?" The manager looked back with a questioning shrug. "Okay, fine." Sutherland walked over to the DVD player and ejected the disk, saying as he did, "Kelly, grab those others. We're out of here."

Everyone at the table looked on, astonished, as Kelly scooped up the DVDs from the table, returned them to the shoe box that had housed them, and started for the door behind Sutherland.

"Wait," the station manager shouted. "We'll run it. This is way too big to miss." He looked at the others at the table and said, "End of discussion. It's on me. Since Mr. Sutherland insists on nine o'clock, we push everything back. Andy, you're on, tapes and all. So fasten your seat belts ladies and gentlemen."

\*　　　\*　　　\*

281

On the sidewalk outside the studio, Kelly asked, "You think they'll follow through? Those lawyers were pissing their pants, they were so upset."

"I don't know. But Andy heard me say it would be on the Internet if they didn't. I meant it."

"So where to now? I need a drink."

They walked down Lake Street to Monk's Bar, where they sat in a booth. Over scotches Sutherland told her about his long meeting with Andy Domingo and Matt Fontaine on his boat.

"Why were you so insistent about it going on the air at nine?"

Sutherland didn't want to get into a discussion about his meeting with Tunney, so he hedged. "I wanted it out before the *Sun Times* articles." At least that was partly true.

"Yet you're busy tonight. A date with Red?"

"How'd you know I was busy?"

"When you showed me the text from Domingo, I saw the one from Red, saying she'd pick you up at seven forty-five."

"Sneaky."

"Who's sneaky?" she said. "I thought that was over with her. So what's going on tonight? And don't give me any more bullshit."

"I'll explain it all tomorrow."

"Now. Sandler's dead. You're planning something with Tunney, right?"

"Promise you won't get excited and I'll tell you."

"Just spit it out."

Kelly had that look he'd seen before, the hunched shoulders, the set jaw, the fiery eyes, ready for a fight he was not willing to have. Resigned, he related his meeting with Langer and the meeting planned for that evening. When he finished, she leaned across the table and fixed him with that fire in her eyes.

"See if I understand this. You're getting wired. To talk to a killer. And he'll just admit it all to you?"

"No wire, I'll just record with my cell phone. And *he* called me. Probably to make a deal on the tapes. Once he realizes it's too late, maybe he'll open up about my father. What's he got to lose?"

"Precisely. What's he got to lose if he's already killed a half-dozen people? Langer wouldn't do it, and I wouldn't trust him any more than Tunney. Was this Red's idea?"

"What do you have against her? Christ, she lost her brother. She's after the killer. You would be, too."

"Who knows what Red's after? You know her story, don't you? About her dismissal from the state's attorney's office? Her tennis career?"

"Come on, cattiness isn't like you. She told me about the tennis thing, being kicked off the circuit."

"I met an acquaintance of hers."

"Met, or snooped around for one?"

Kelly scowled and jammed her fists on her hips, ready to take him on. "Trust me, will you? Did you know she was fired for fabricating and suppressing evidence in the state's attorney's office? To get a conviction. They kept it real hushed. Detective Vislowski, who was working with her—and dating her, I might add—got a serious reprimand. Lost a promotion."

"I can't believe this." Sutherland turned in the booth to face the bar. Did it make sense? Suppressing evidence? There was that sometimes-strained relationship between Ronnie and Vislowski, but that didn't prove anything. Sutherland's relationship with her had been just as strained since their brief fling.

"Since then she's worked for three firms and been let go," Kelly continued. "The word in law circles says she doesn't play nice and has a major gambling problem to boot. So you let her talk you into exposing yourself to a murderer. Are you nuts?"

"How else can I resolve this thing?"

"Define resolve. Getting killed? Killing Tunney? What?" She stood up and looked down at Sutherland, her eyes burning and wet, lips trembling. "Why not let the police finish this? The FBI. That's their job."

"You heard Ronnie. They'll never nail him for the murders."

"Red again. At least let the police back you up on this thing."

"They need a warrant. Besides, the police don't care about my questions."

"What's left to find out? You've learned you were wrong about your father. He wasn't a crook, it looks like they invented the whole payoff thing to reestablish his credibility with those crooks. So he wasn't that corrupt hypocrite you despised all these years."

"I wish I could prove that. The tapes pretty much disclose who was responsible for the FBI agent's murder, so that's decided. Now the question is, was my father really acting for the government, or had he decided to disappear with all the money? Branson says the FBI suspected the latter could be the case, which explains why the FBI never released the information about my father's working for them and why they never cleared his name."

"The FBI sees conspiracies in every corner. You don't believe it."

"But I can't refute it."

"And that's why you need a showdown with Tunney?"

Sutherland ran a hand through his hair down to his neck, flinching when he touched cigarette burn there. Too many showdowns lately. "That's just one question. I'm hoping I get a bigger one answered tonight."

"I give up," Kelly said, and she headed for the door.

# Chapter 85

The Corvette eased from the curb in front of Sutherland's building, and he fastened his seat belt. "Have you seen the rest of the tapes? You've had enough time," Ronnie said, shifting into second gear. She wore jeans and a tee shirt, and judging by the bags under her eyes, she hadn't been sleeping well.

"Not all of them. But enough to see a dozen careers about to end."

"What's the plan? When can I see the rest of them?"

"Tomorrow if you want."

"You keep the originals in a safe place? Your apartment was already broken into."

"No one will find them, believe me," Sutherland said.

Downshifting before turning onto the entrance ramp to Lake Shore Drive, Ronnie said, "In your storage unit, I'll bet. In the basement."

"Too obvious," he said. "And the fewer who know, the better."

"You tell your girlfriend?"

"No."

"Then how about this question. What if Tunney offers to buy them from us? You said it was his idea to meet, so that's probably what he's after. Why not sell them? They could be worth millions."

Her increasing fixation on money was getting bothersome, if not worrisome. To what extremes was she prepared to go? "When did all this change from finding the killers and getting Bill the recognition he deserves, to a matter of money or compensation?"

"Why not both? Justice and reparation. They're not mutually exclusive."

"True, but let's not get ahead of ourselves. Play it out tonight and see where we go from there."

Ronnie was quiet as they cruised down the lakeshore, her eyes narrowed and lips tight, as if fighting off a tantrum. Finally she stopped glowering and asked, "You sure the phone will do the job? I have a transmitter with me, if you want. A super-sensitive mic, so you wouldn't have to yell or get that close. It'll pick up a pin dropping."

"I'm cool with the phone," Sutherland said. "I just want to record him admitting he killed my father and Bill. Or say who did. A recording wouldn't be allowed in evidence."

"Maybe not in a court."

He didn't ask what she meant. He could guess. She wouldn't stop until Billy's death was avenged. With due compensation if she had her way, a notion consistent with her intensified interest in money.

"Bait him. Insult him," she said. "Call him a sadist, a fag, a sicko, a crazy man. Just get him to get pissed off and rant, brag, even. I've seen it work."

"I've got a better idea to get him going." Reasoning she'd go ballistic if she knew the tapes might be aired, Sutherland kept it to himself. She'd know soon enough.

A few minutes later she pulled to the curb in front of Tunney's building. Before he got out, Ronnie grabbed his arm and said, "For Billy and your father, we gotta nail him. But remember about justice and reparation not being—"

"I know," Sutherland interrupted as he opened the car door. "I'll call you when I'm done. Meantime, watch the ABC news at nine o'clock."

He turned and started for Tunney's building, but not before seeing Ronnie's eyes widen in shock as she grasped what he meant. As he pushed through the revolving doors, he heard Ronnie's car wheeling around the corner from Michigan Avenue.

# CHAPTER 86

Tunney stared at the television screen and felt a twinge of deep-rooted craving. The set was tuned to the security camera in his building lobby, and Doug Sutherland was approaching the guard's desk. Tunney imagined giving him a large dose of Tunney-inflicted pain, payback for sticking his nose where it didn't belong. A few hours alone with him would satisfy his hunger for a long time.

Knowing that that wasn't going to happen tonight, he tried to suppress his urge by reliving past indulgences of administering pain and death. In a fast-forward flashback, he saw his foster sister drown in a creek, the death of a boy in a game that went too far, a high school basketball teammate that went missing, a college soccer player who presumably committed suicide, a graduate school professor who ostensibly set himself on fire. The sequence of images accelerated, jumping from Canada to Chicago, more than a few ending with a missing person or a body and an unsolved murder.

As Sutherland's face came into focus on the video screen, Tunney felt his mouth go dry, and he had to swallow hard. Swiveling in his chair, he filled a glass with scotch and downed half of it. If only this meeting could end the way he fantasized.

*     *     *

The same security guard that greeted Sutherland on his last visit raised his eyes from the same muscle magazine to watch Sutherland scribble his name and the time, 8:40 PM. In the blank for suite, Sutherland wrote, "Chartered Associates."

"Still hot out," Sutherland said.

The guard turned a page. "The man's expecting you on twenty."

Sutherland walked to the elevators, entered one, and a few moments later stepped out on the twentieth floor. He passed the glass entrance doors to Chartered Associates' private lobby and continued down the corridor to the men's room. After making sure he was alone, he reached into his pocket, took out his iPhone, turned up the recording volume control, and slipped the device into his shirt pocket.

In the mirror, he examined the purple bruise discoloring his deep tan, the bandage still covering the wound on his temple. He forced a smile and placed his index finger on the small scar under his right eye where the boom of his father's sailboat had caught him. He had never seen his father more distressed than those frantic moments when the ten-year-old Douglas Sutherland was retrieved from the lake. Now Doug Sutherland breathed deeply, willing himself to pull this off. He owed it to that man.

He left the men's room and walked to the entrance doors, where Tunney's secretary met him. "You've kept Mr. Tunney waiting. He's in his office," she said with a glare. She scuttled past him into the elevator lobby, and the office door locked itself behind her.

Reginald Tunney, in white shirt and tie, sat behind his antique oak desk, his eyes fixed on a flat-screen television to his right, next to his desktop computer. His suit jacket hung on his chair back, and a near-empty glass rested in a pool of condensation by his left hand. Behind him, over a credenza that matched his desk, hung an oil painting of men, horses, and dogs on a fox hunt. He didn't hear Sutherland approach.

Sutherland studied the broken veins in Tunney's aristocratic nose, the rheumy, gray eyes glued to the flickering screen as if he were in a trance. Watching from the doorway, Sutherland thought how easy it would be to exact the justice the system dispensed so stingily. He only needed a weapon— and an anesthetized conscience. He coughed.

Tunney looked up from the TV screen and in his cultivated baritone said, "Doug, my boy, how'd you get in?"

"Your secretary."

"I thought our security had broken down." Tunney turned the TV off and gestured to one of two chairs in front of his desk. "Touch of the creature? You look like you need one." He revolved his chair and opened the lid of a compartment in the credenza stocked with bottles, glasses, and an ice bucket.

Sutherland sat. "None for me," he said, watching Tunney select a Chivas Regal bottle.

"Highland nectar," Tunney said. He poured, added ice cubes, and swiveled back to face Sutherland. With lips pulled back in a plastic smile, he said, "Cheers."

"Enjoy it. They don't serve that in prisons."

Tunney arched his eyebrows. "My, my. You know something I don't?"

"Only that the past usually catches up on you. Fifteen years or a couple days, doesn't matter. Murder is murder."

"By a couple days, do you mean Gene's unceremonious demise? If so, you and Jules make good suspects," Tunney said. "The two of you were together, and it's well known neither of you particularly liked the fat man."

"It couldn't have been the boy and girl toys you had follow me. They're still in custody. Talking, I imagine."

Tunney sipped from his scotch and smiled. "I doubt it. Facing trespassing and concealed weapons charges won't intimidate them."

"How about a string of connected murders? If that pair you hired helped with your dirty work, I bet they made mistakes. They didn't seem too smart in the tunnel."

Tunney flicked his hand as if shooing a fly. "Suppositions are all rather tedious. Let's cut the shit. You found what you were looking for, didn't you?"

"Three hundred or so recorded meetings. You're a star."

For a second Tunney's poise faltered—he swallowed, and his chin jutted forward. Lifting his glass to his lips, he studied Sutherland over the rim.

After a sip, he said, "That many. The bastard was bad as Nixon. Yet you haven't handed them over. Smart boy. That's why I wanted to talk."

"Let's. Start by telling me what happened on my father's boat the night he died."

Tunney pursed his lips and tipped his head in an almost nod, his yellowish eyes studying his accuser. Finally he said, "Is this where I break down sobbing and confess? Stop that recorder. It insults me."

Sutherland felt a cold shiver. Only Kelly, Ronnie, and Langer knew he was planning to record the meeting. Exasperated, he wanted to reach over the desk and wring the smugness from that face. The man had a few inches and thirty pounds on him, but he was out of shape and on his way to being drunk. Sutherland could take him if he got in the first punch, but then he wouldn't get what he came for.

"You win," Sutherland sighed, pulling out the phone and turning it off, showing Tunney the screen to prove it.

"Don't sell me short like your father did. He was a double-dealing fuck, just like Danny."

"Danny. Our infamous film producer."

"And your ticket to real wealth and power, my boy. You can share in what we've set up. All you have to do is destroy Delaney's opus. Once Spanos is elected, our position will be golden."

"What if I'm not interested?"

Tunney held up his hand, signaling a pause while he turned to replenish his drink. When he faced Sutherland again he said, "Look. You think handing those tapes to the FBI will hurt me? Don't bet on it. There'll be questions, headlines, some red faces, a few resignations or firings, but nobody's going to jail based on fifteen-year-old conversations. The hype will be over before the elections. So what's in it for you?"

"It would prove my father wasn't a crook. That he was working for the FBI all along, that the guilty plea was nothing but a huge put-on, and that he was murdered for tricking you and turning Delaney."

Tunney's mouth fell open, and his eyes narrowed in disbelief as he stared back at Sutherland. After a few seconds he nodded, as if he had just solved an old riddle. He took a swallow of his drink, wiped his mouth, and smiled. "Son of a gun. He was with them all that time? Are you sure?"

"It's in one of the tapes. The FBI confirmed it."

"And for that you want to hand over those tapes? Why? It won't bring your old man back. It's history. No one cares."

"But it will put his murderers in prison. It will keep a corrupt politician from becoming governor."

"Now you're talking nonsense. Delaney's videos won't hurt Spanos or me. You're either bluffing or stupid."

"Your memory of who was there and what was discussed is evidently failing you. Besides, Delaney wasn't the only one recording meetings. Miles Langer did too."

Tunney chuckled. "Miles Langer invented that kind of thing. But Jules destroyed them all. He told me so."

"He kept one."

Tunney shook his head in disgust. "Fucking Jules. He'd only hurt himself if it got out."

"He's not in it. You are, though. Spanos too. Talking about killing Delaney."

"Miles Langer," Tunney said, spitting out the name. "A malicious prick right up to the end. His last chance to say 'fuck you.'" After he tossed back his drink and bringing his glass down with a hard clunk, his total demeanor changed. When his stare returned to Sutherland, he was no longer the reasonable negotiator; he was a menacing and angry adversary. "Where is it now?" he growled.

"Tell me what happened on his boat and I'll let you see it."

"I don't want to see it, you little shit. I want it destroyed, that's what I want. I'm through fucking around. Important people want those tapes gone. I'll have those tapes confiscated before you can say Douglas Fucking Sutherland."

"Want to bet?" Sutherland looked at his watch and realized it was after nine o'clock, the moment of truth. Did the station manager follow through, or did he cave in? "Turn on your TV. Channel 7."

The implication must have registered, because Tunney's face became a mask of shock, disbelief, and fear. "What did you do?"

289

# CHAPTER 87

George Spanos was in his element. Sitting at the head of the dining room table in his Chicago Gold Coast townhouse, a glass of California Shiraz in his hand, glancing down the row of guests paying homage and $10,000 apiece to dine with the next governor of Illinois. His wife, at the far end of the grand table, beamed with pleasure as the CEO of the world's largest fast food chain stood to toast Mrs. Spanos, the hostess. As the gathering raised their glasses, Virginia, George Spanos's seventeen-year-old daughter, barged in from the adjacent sitting room. She seemed out of breath and frazzled, her dark eyes wet with tears.

"Dad, you gotta see this," Virginia said. "It's on TV."

"Ginny," Spanos snapped, "we're in the middle of dinner."

"But you got to," she insisted. "You're on the news."

Spanos looked at his guests, grinning but embarrassed. "I should hope so. That's what campaigns are for."

"No, Daddy," she said as she came closer, cupping her hands to whisper in his ear. "It's about that alderman, the one found buried in that building. Dapper something? You're there with some men talking about killing him. An old video they found."

Spanos felt a combination of vichyssoise, veal saltimbucca, and Shiraz coursing up his esophagus, blocking his speech. It couldn't be. How? A dozen quizzical sets of eyes stared down the table at him as he fought the rising tide from his stomach and the urge to scream. Carefully he set his glass down, swallowing bile and fear and the sense of falling. Finally his wife broke the silence.

"What is it, George?"

The congressman held his hand to his mouth, hiding a belch. Rising, laying his napkin beside the plate, he said, "Excuse me for a moment. I should check this out." He turned and, with his pride rapidly draining, walked out into the sitting room, hoping that his guests would leave before he had to face them again.

# Chapter 88

Tunney grabbed the remote, and after fumbling with it for a few seconds, Andy Domingo appeared on the screen. The piece had apparently already begun because Domingo was saying, "Welcome back to Channel 7's exclusive exposé on the clandestine activities leading up to Alderman Daniel Delaney's murder fifteen years ago. This next clip takes place two weeks after the previous one, where George Spanos, then working for the state's attorney's office, revealed the confidential information to the parties under investigation. We'll see Congressman Spanos disclosing that Alderman Delaney was testifying against the men at the table, including Benjamin Gorman and Eugene Sandler, two coconspirators who have been recently murdered. Also present in the meeting is then-Commissioner Alex Rodriguez of the Chicago Police Department; Miles Langer, who died of natural causes shortly afterward; and Reginald Tunney, a Chicago real estate executive. You will hear the men discussing the murder of Alderman Delaney, whose skeleton was recently uncovered in a downtown building, and hear instructions to George Spanos to further sabotage the prosecution case against the group." The screen changed to black and white as Gene Sandler, fifty pounds lighter and fifteen years younger, rumbled into the room and questioned why they were meeting in Miles Langer's and not Delaney's office.

Tunney stared at the screen in stunned silence. He watched it through to end of the scene without moving, his jaw hanging, a trickle of saliva seeping from the side of his mouth. When the clip was over, as if in a trance, he mechanically turned the TV off with the remote. Then he filled his empty glass to the brim, sloshing scotch over the desk blotter. He gulped down half of the glass, and when he finally looked at Sutherland again, his eyes were yellow pools of hatred.

"You want to know what happened that night?" he said, his face morphing into a malicious leer. "The fat man and I caught him while he was still in the harbor, closing up his boat. He knew that FBI prick was dead, so he thought he could get away. We tore the boat apart but couldn't find Delaney's stuff, so we were about to work on him." Tunney chuckled cruelly. "Too bad he wasn't a better swimmer."

Sutherland had imagined the admission, but not so viciously, not with such malevolent glee. He stared, clenching his jaw, balling his fists, fighting for control while Tunney's admission hung there like the whiskey fumes pervading the room. Then Tunney opened the top drawer and pulled out a dull-gray pistol. He held it loosely in his left hand, pointing at nothing in particular, and then set it down in the middle of the desk halfway between them.

"Go ahead," Tunney said. "You want to. Pick it up and shoot."

It was easily within Sutherland's reach. Should he seize it? His eyes flicked from the gun's dull sheen to Tunney's wide chest. A bullet right in the middle of that scotch-dampened tie? What would it feel like to see the blood seep across his white shirt, to see the surprise in his arrogant face, to see him sputter and die like a deflating balloon?

Tunney watched as if he could read Sutherland's mind. "No? No balls?" He reached into a drawer, pulling out a blue velvet box like the one Langer had. He opened it, revealing Danny's gold-backed tooth propped in its slot. "I sent this to Miles Langer as a warning for what might happen to his son in case he had a deathbed confession. It was Sandler's idea, extracting the tooth before we buried him alive." He'd started slurring his words; his face seemed to be sagging with the effects of the alcohol.

Jules Langer must have returned the tooth earlier today, the same time he had informed Tunney that Sutherland was going to record their conversation. "You must have enjoyed it. You didn't stop with Delaney."

"That pig Scooch? That nosy reporter and his bitch? Part of a long string you'll never know about." Tunney picked up the gun and looked at Sutherland earnestly, as if wanting to explain something profound. "When you merely kill someone, it's over too quickly. Poof. Nothing there but a pile of meat. You want to make it last, make him know you're killing him, that he'll be dead, and make it unbearable while he's knowing it." Tunney slurped a long sip while Sutherland choked back his growing alarm. Langer was right: drunk enough, Tunney was capable of saying anything. Sutherland had to get out of there. The booze, the gun, this man was a ticking bomb.

Sutherland stood up. "I think it's time to leave."

"Wait." Tunney's grip on the gun tensed and he squinted at Sutherland. "I haven't finished yet."

What Sutherland saw when he looked back was Tunney's gun aimed directly at his chest.

"I wanna see what it feels like to pull this trigger on a Sutherland." Tunney leaned forward in the chair, his left hand maintaining a wobbly aim at Sutherland.

There was only eight feet between them. He couldn't miss, even with that unsteady hand. Sutherland's throat constricted, he felt lightheaded, and despite the hot night, he shivered. He stared back, standing paralyzed and waiting.

Tunney's finger slowly tugged on the trigger, and Sutherland sucked in his breath. A maniacal satisfaction spread across Tunney's face as the trigger reached the point of no return and the sharp clack of the hammer, cold metal on metal, signaled an empty chamber.

Several seconds passed. Sutherland exhaled slowly and collapsed into his chair as the tension drained, like air from a balloon. Tunney looked at the gun and said, "Still don't know why I didn't do that to your old man. Only with the fuckin' thing loaded."

"What's the difference? Shooting him or throwing him overboard? You killed him."

"That's where you're wrong. If I'd've done that, he'd have had concrete shoes on. You wanna know? I'll tell you, you little prick." Tunney rummaged through the drawer and retrieved a loaded magazine for the pistol. Fumbling, he pulled back the gun's slide, rammed the magazine in, and released the slide. "Could've shot him any time. There he stood taunting us, saying the tapes would finish us. Gene took a swing at him with the boat hook, but the fucker yanked it away and threw it back at him. Then he just turned around, dove over the side, and started swimming. Middle of the lake. You believe that shit?"

"He wouldn't let you win," Sutherland said, standing again, tensing himself to run or jump or dive for safety. Was the gun Tunney wielded so carelessly the same one that had killed Sandler?

"Lotta good it did. Maybe if I shot you I might win after all." The smile left his face and he grew more serious, his heavy-lidded eyes narrowing as he started to raise his wavering gun hand.

Without thinking, Sutherland lunged across the desk and grabbed Tunney's wrist and bent it back, sending the pistol clattering over the desk and onto the floor. As Tunney lurched backward and swiveled in his chair, Sutherland rolled off the desk onto Tunney's side. He threw all his weight into the first punch—a right, coming from waist level smack into the seated man's face. There was a crack and a grunt as Tunney jerked his hand up to his nose and slid from the chair to his knees, grabbing the desk to stay upright. Sutherland took one step forward and, forgetting his taped finger, hooked a left, recoiling with his own pain when he connected with Tunney's temple. Another right caught the nose again in an explosion of blood. With a final downward right, Tunney fell against the wall, his long legs splayed like a discarded doll's.

Sutherland stepped closer and delivered a kick to the fallen man's ribs, feeling the crunch of bone and cartilage, hearing Tunney's groan a split second later. He wanted to kick again, to strike until the man cried out, "No more." But just before Sutherland launched another kick, the telephone rang, startling him. As if he'd been wrenched from a dream, he suddenly found himself wide-eyed, staring at the simpering heap on the floor.

Sutherland gulped one breath after another, willing his rage to subside. Seeing Tunney's glass, he lifted it and drank, the whiskey dulling the metal taste in his mouth. Tunney groaned and pulled his large frame into a fetal coil. Sutherland watched, wondering how close to Tunney's level his own lust to inflict pain had sunk.

Calmer now, he took one last look at the man who had ended his father's life and walked out of the office, closing the door behind him.

*  *  *

Sutherland reached the ground floor of Tunney's building with sweat streaming down his face and his heart still racing at marathon pace. The guard at the desk looked Sutherland over while his head slowly bobbed to a Spanish ballad on his portable radio.

"You okay, man?"

"Yeah. Just hot up there." Sutherland reached for the pen and noticed the blood spots on his sleeve, smears on his knuckles. The guard noticed them too, and when Sutherland replaced the pen, a red smudge stared up from the register.

"You hurt, amigo?"

"Nothing—an old injury." Sutherland pointed to his bandaged face, turned, and walked away.

# CHAPTER 89

Ronnie was waiting by the curb in her Corvette when Sutherland exited Tunney's building. After he piled in, he stared straight ahead and took a deep breath. From the corner of his eye he sensed she was glaring at him. "You bastard," she hissed. "Why'd you release the tapes? It wasn't your decision to make."

"No choice. I was warned that a judge was issuing an order to confiscate them. They were going to make them disappear. I think the same judge is on one of the videos taking money, so now we can fight it."

Huffing and shaking her head, she put the gear into first and pulled away. "So tell me what happened. You're bloody and reek of booze," she said while accelerating through the gears, reaching third by the time they sped through a yellow light.

"He admitted just about everything, he pulled a gun, and I lost it."

"Is he ...?"

"Something stopped me."

"How about the recording?"

"He knew. Was tipped off." He turned to check her reaction.

"You didn't get it?" she said through clenched teeth, slamming on the brakes behind a car at a red light. "How'd he know?"

"Langer. A setup. I'm not sure what he expected to happen, but he knew that giving me his father's tape would get Tunney's attention." He pulled out his cell phone and called Langer's private number. While he waited, Ronnie peeled off again, muttering to herself. Langer answered, and Sutherland said, "You told Tunney, didn't you?"

"No I didn't. I—"

"Don't bullshit me, Jules. He was drunk and had a gun and could've killed me."

After a moment, in a voice more angry than apologetic, Langer said, "My sister. What else could I do?"

"What you've always wanted to. He's still in his office. Alone and too drunk to see straight."

295

"He'll never do it," Ronnie scoffed in mid-shift, turning onto the Drive.

"If you weren't such an empty suit, you'd free your sister once and for all." Sutherland hung up, trying to imagine Langer entering Tunney's office with a gun, but the image wouldn't gel; Langer wouldn't do it. But then, neither had he.

Ronnie cut around a car on the inside lane. "Tunney admitted everything? Billy too?" she asked.

"And others that he didn't bother to name. He opened up after he saw the Channel 7 piece. The cat's out of the bag and he knows it."

Ronnie braked hard for a slower car, cursing under her breath. She changed lanes and surged off again, winding out second gear a little too long, as if the transmission's whining was her own.

"I would've killed him right there," she said, squeezing the wheel, her knuckles protruding in an angry row.

"I damn near did."

"Damn near doesn't cut it."

She didn't speak in sentences for the rest of the drive to Sutherland's apartment building—the screeching tires, the whining gears, and her mumbled curses said it all.

Upstairs in the kitchen, Sutherland washed the blood from his hands and ran cold water over his broken finger, trying to remember how long the pain lasted the last time. Ronnie sat brooding, elbows resting on the kitchen table.

"Want a drink?" he said. "There's some Chivas in the cabinet."

"You smell like you swam in it."

"Same brand." Sutherland let the water run for several minutes before turning off the tap and starting for the liquor cabinet. Ronnie walked over, touched his arm, and smiled weakly. "I'll make you one. You go shower."

In the bedroom he undressed, throwing his blood-spotted shirt and pants on the floor of his closet. Ronnie walked in with an amber drink on ice. "Here's your scotch. I added some Drambuie for a rusty nail. Sip on that and I'll make you an ice pack for your finger." She turned and left the room.

He took a large gulp from the glass, savoring the sweet combination as it dissolved away the acrid taste from his fight. The warmth spread into his chest and stomach as he finished undressing. In the shower, letting the hot water spill over head and shoulders, he wished it could wash away all the pain and thoughts of Tunney. When he stepped out of the bathroom in his robe, Ronnie arrived and handed him a plastic bag of ice.

"Feel better?"

He sat on the bed and took another drink. "Tired." He placed the ice bag on the bedside table.

"Adrenalin withdrawal. What did he say about the money? He find it on the boat?"

"No." Sutherland flexed his right hand, feeling the damage he'd done, bone against bone. As he yawned, feeling his eyelids grow heavy, he said, "I need a nap."

"All right. I'll wake you in half an hour."

"Sounds like a plan." Sutherland reached to set his glass on the bedside table. He missed, and the glass toppled onto the carpet. He didn't care.

# CHAPTER 90

The first ring of the phone peeled back a thin layer of sleep. The next exposed a slowly seeping ache behind his eyes. The third awakened Sutherland's bladder and the fourth his foul-tasting tongue. Why wouldn't that ringing stop? Through a haze, he peered at his alarm clock—eleven o'clock. Finally the call must have gone to messages.

His entire body seemed to crave something, a deep itch screaming to be scratched or fed. He wanted orange juice, lots of orange juice—and aspirin.

He rolled out of bed and walked naked into the bathroom. Standing at the toilet, he tested his swollen finger and shreds of last night's events returned in wispy images.

The phone rang again. He picked it up and croaked a hello.

"Sutherland? Detective Vislowski. Where've you been?"

"Right here. Why?" Sitting on the bed, he caught his reflection in the bureau mirror. No photographs please.

"Got to talk. About last night and Tunney. You left his place at …" there was a pause as Vislowski apparently consulted something, "Nine thirty? How was he when you left him?"

"Under the weather. Why?"

"What's that mean?"

"Drunk."

"This is serious."

"I am serious. He was on his ass. Smashed." Sometimes English's double meanings were useful.

"Then what?"

"I came home. Ronnie drove me."

"And Tunney was alive, right?"

"Of course. Why? What's going on?"

The phone was silent for a moment. "Tunney's dead. They found him in his office this morning."

Tunney, dead. Sutherland should have felt triumphant. Instead, his stomach knotted, wondering whether his beating killed him after all. He took a breath and asked, "How'd he die?"

"It looks like suicide. Gunshot."

Sutherland exhaled slowly, relieved. Suicide. Perfect. "I'm not surprised. He'd just seen the video of him and Spanos on the television. His world was crashing down. If you search his things, you'll find Delaney's tooth and maybe even more 'parts' of people from other murders. Maybe you'll finally believe Ronnie and me."

Vislowski grunted. "We'll see. I'm going to need a statement from you so don't go anywhere. And another thing: we'll want those tapes. That one you gave the TV channels has been running nonstop. *Sun-Times* has a few stills and a long story."

"What makes you think I've got those tapes?"

"Veronica told me."

"Has Spanos said anything?"

"Incommunicado, but his campaign manager said it's merely a smear, that the tapes are fabrications. That's why the originals are needed. You hear me?"

The interview seemed over. But after a moment, in a conciliatory tone, Vislowski asked, "You haven't seen Veronica, have you? I can't get hold of her at her place."

"You try her hotel?"

"I don't know which one. Sure she isn't with you?"

"Let me check." Sutherland glanced at the rumpled sheets on the bed and a few of Ronnie's red hairs on the pillow. "Nope, not here. Just memories."

There was a crash on the line as Vislowski's phone slammed down.

*    *    *

Sutherland spent the rest of the day suffering from a deep malaise and a dull headache, trying vainly to focus on his business meetings until he gave up and went home. After a nap, he showered, and after watching the six o'clock newscasts airing more of the Delaney and Spanos connection, he sat down to view more of the tapes while nursing whatever it was that had intruded on his clear senses.

# Chapter 91

**THURSDAY, AUGUST 9**

Sutherland trod wearily up the plaza stairs in front of Langer's office building. He hadn't fully recovered from whatever ailed him and couldn't understand how a glass of scotch could have done so much damage. Maybe it was the twenty-four-hour flu. Circling through the revolving door, he met Jules Langer walking toward him from the elevators. Langer had called an hour earlier and asked for this last-minute meeting. He'd sounded anxious, saying it wouldn't wait.

"We aren't going to fight, are we?" Langer said, hanging back a few steps.

"I should wipe you all over this floor, you slimy fuck. You set me up."

Langer held up his hands, maintaining his distance. "I swear. Why would I? Did he admit the murders? What about your father?"

"He dove from the boat to escape being shot. Seven miles from shore it amounts to murder. Just like who knows how many other victims we'll never know about."

"In time it would've been my sister. Tunney's nurses have her so drugged she's incoherent. She'll come out of it, once she's living with me. I'm going to take a sabbatical."

"It's called jail."

"It'll be a while before that happens."

"You can always leave the country."

"Why didn't I think of that?" He gave Sutherland a smile and winked. "I'm on my way to see my sister and fire those Nazi nurses right now. Walk with me, I'm going to Union Station, and then I won't be around."

"Where's you limo?"

Langer shrugged. "I won't be needing it."

As they left the building, an elevated train rattled overhead, the metal-against-metal screech preventing conversation, even thought, until it passed.

Further west they approached the red, white, and blue construction barricades announcing America Tower. Nothing lay behind the barricades but vacant land and hopes. Sutherland asked, "What'll happen to your monument when you take your sabbatical?"

"That's what I wanted to tell you. I've been meeting with Imperial Food Products for their new headquarters. I was way ahead of you on that one. Now you've got a clear field. You owe me."

Good news on the real estate front. Better odds for the McCollum site if Langer was out of the picture.

Crossing the bridge to the west side, Langer looked at his diamond Rolex and said, "I've got a few minutes," and he steered Sutherland to the railing at the edge of the concrete promenade, facing east overlooking the river. Before them, the city's center loomed, a manmade mountain range, its peaks colossal symbols of achievements, egos, and excesses.

They said nothing for several moments, watching the khaki-colored river drift by, hearing horns and brakes and sirens, small sounds in the city's drone. At their feet, a flock of pigeons warbled and fluttered on the esplanade.

Langer laughed. "It just occurred to me how the circle closes. Your father hides the money, then he dies in what looks like suicide. Now Tunney, the guy that killed him, commits suicide and you get the money. You know where it is, don't you?"

Sutherland shrugged. "Actually, I don't."

"It's okay," Langer said with a sigh. "Your secret's safe."

"You're not good with secrets. Telling him about me recording. He had Danny's tooth, so I know you met him."

"Yeah. I convinced him to see you. Told him you had something he'd want, but not what. Figured you'd show him my father's tape and he'd open up."

"How about the keys? You use them later? After I left?"

"What're you talking about?"

"I'm just wondering if it really was suicide, that's all."

"Don't fuck with me, Doug. I hated him and maybe wanted him dead, but that's all." He turned and stomped away toward the entrance to the station.

Sutherland thought, besides a good salesman, Langer was a terrific actor. That or Tunney had guessed about the recorder. And maybe he did commit suicide, just like it looked.

# Chapter 92

**W**hen Sutherland arrived at his office after seeing Langer, his secretary gave him a don't-blame-me shrug and pointed inside. Detective Vislowski sat in Sutherland's chair, leaning back, feet on the desk, talking on the telephone. Seeing Sutherland, the detective removed his black shoes from the rosewood and said into the phone, "Call me back when you've got it. Bye."

"Make yourself at home, Detective," Sutherland said, slumping into the guest chair in front of the desk.

"Impressive project," the detective said, pointing to the wall with the renderings for the McCollum site. "But I hear you've had a few setbacks."

"You follow real estate?"

"Not usually," Vislowski said, fingering his mustache. "But in your case, yes."

"Look, Detective, if you need my statement, fine. But I've got a lot to do today. Did you talk to Ronnie about that night?"

"I didn't talk to her. But one of your doormen said she was there for a while."

"You talked to my doorman?" Sutherland said.

The telephone rang and Vislowski's hand moved toward it.

"You mind? It's still my office," Sutherland said, picking it up. He listened and handed the receiver to the detective. "For you."

"Vislowski." As he listened, Vislowski's scowl brightened into a satisfied grin. "Great. Be there in a half hour. In the lobby."

He smiled smugly at Sutherland. "Care to join me?"

"Where?"

"Your apartment."

"Huh?"

"We've got a search warrant."

"Search? What the fuck's going on?"

"A man died. Under suspicious circumstances. You were in his office, probably had a fight, have at least one motive, and you don't have an alibi."

"Ronnie was with me."

"Not at the time Tunney died. Your doorman saw her leave right before his shift was up. And your fingerprints were on the scotch bottle, the one containing what we think were barbiturates."

"What?" Sutherland ignored Vislowski's grin, searching through blurred memories of Saturday night. No, he never touched Tunney's bottles, never even got close.

"Your prints, clear as day. He's drinking and drugged. Maybe he passes out. Killer stands behind him, puts Tunney's gun into his hand, and blows his brains all over the office."

Sutherland didn't move. His fingerprints on the bottle. Ronnie leaving his apartment.

Vislowski pulled a set of eight-by-ten-inch color photographs from a folder and slid them in front of Sutherland. The first photo showed Tunney's desk with the wall beside it blotched with reddish-brown spots. Tunney was sitting with his torso and arms sprawled on the desk with his head lying on a dark stain on the blotter. Bits of brown and gray speckle were mixed with the blood spattered across the desk. The gun lay in Tunney's upturned left hand, gray metal on gray skin.

Sutherland's mind whirled. Vislowski's description of how the murder might have happened, along with the gruesome photo, painted a picture so vivid it was like Sutherland was returning to the scene in a nightmare.

"When I left, he was drunk and hurt, but he was alive. I signed out. The guard saw me, way before ten."

"You could've come back."

"That doesn't mean I did. What evidence is there he was murdered?"

"Some hair was pulled out. Like maybe it was grabbed to hold his head up when the shot was fired."

Sutherland replayed the picture of Tunney leveling the gun at him and the fear returned, the same paralysis and metal taste he had in those seconds before Tunney pulled the trigger.

The phone rang again. Vislowski picked it up this time. He listened and said, "Kelly Mathews? He's busy."

"Wait." Sutherland jumped up and grabbed the phone from Vislowski. Kelly's name sounded like a lifeline.

"Make it fast," the detective said.

"Kelly."

"Are you all right? And who was that?"

"Detective Vislowski. Here about Tunney's death. You heard?"

"All over the news," she said. "But I've got to see you. Something's odd about that night."

"You're not kidding," he said, watching Vislowski smoothing his mustache. "What do you think's odd?"

"Something happened between Jenny and her friend, so she decided to spend the night with you. She called you at home and on your cell, but no one answered. Finally she called me and I picked her up and we went to your place. We didn't have the keys for the new locks, but the second shift doorman came and we convinced him to let us in. We took a phone call for a Miss Jamison while we were there. It was about a boat with directions to the harbor in Michigan. What's it about, Doug?"

Vislowski coughed and passed his hand across his neck in a cutting motion.

"Not a clue. I'll have to call you later," he said and then replaced the phone.

As Vislowski gathered the photographs, an image flashed into Sutherland's thoughts—flaming hair above Tunney's slouched body. Could it be?

"You know, Detective, if Tunney was murdered, I'm not the only one with a motive."

"Yours are the only fingerprints we've found."

"I don't deny I was there. What about others with motives? Langer—his sister was Tunney's abused wife."

"Maybe."

"Tunney's partners in real estate deals, kinky friends in North Side bars."

"We'll check."

"Ronnie in particular had a motive. Her brother."

"That's enough," he snapped. "We'll sort it out."

"I hit a nerve?" Sutherland watched Vislowski's eyes, saw the initial flash of anger dissolve into an uncertain glaze.

After a moment the detective blinked and said, "Let's go. They've probably started on your place. If it's evidence you want, maybe we can find some."

"Before we go, I want to call my attorney."

"Worried we'll find something?"

"Too late to be worried."

# CHAPTER 93

"**Y**our guys done yet?" Sutherland asked, opening his refrigerator for a beer. Strange, he hadn't seen it that full since Kelly's era—it had actual food in there: sliced turkey, bread, milk, cheese, a few tomatoes, and a head of lettuce. He doubted Ronnie was that considerate, so Kelly must have stopped at the grocery store when she brought Jenny here last night. Pouring the beer he said, "What the hell are they doing back there? Already been at it an hour."

"Wouldn't want to miss anything," Vislowski replied, sitting down at Sutherland's dining room table. He held up a pencil from which hung a ring with two dangling keys. "Recognize these?"

"What do they fit?"

"You tell me."

"This is rich," Sutherland said, shaking his head. "I've got a box full of keys I can't find locks for."

"They found your shirt too. Blood all over."

"Tunney's nose spouted like a geyser. What'd you expect?"

Jocular voices and heavy footsteps preceded two men into the room. The taller one carried a small suitcase in his right hand. "We're outta here, Stan. Finished," he said. "We'll leave a copy of the inventory list."

The other man, balding and eyes too close together, handed Vislowski a sheet of paper. Vislowski studied it, looked up, and said, "Nothing more?"

"The fuck you want? Jesus." They both stared at Sutherland balefully—in one second he was tried, convicted, and hanged.

"Here, take the keys too," Vislowski said, holding out the pencil with the key ring. The balding one let them drop into an envelope, which he put into the taller cop's case.

"Later, Stan," the other said, and both men continued down the corridor to the door.

"Nice guys," Sutherland said.

They heard a mumbled conversation at the door and then a female voice shouted, "Doug?"

Vislowski scowled and said, "Who's that?"

"Sounds like Kelly."

"Get rid of her."

Kelly Matthews appeared around the corner and seeing Vislowski, said, "Ohh."

"Remember Chicago's finest? Detective Vislowski?" Sutherland asked.

"Yeah," she said, frowning. "What's going on?"

"We're done, aren't we, Detective? Finished snooping and sniffing?" He turned to Kelly and said, "They've got this idea Reggie Tunney didn't commit suicide. Came here to search for the smoking gun."

"Search?"

"That's right. What'd your guys find beside keys and my shirt?" Sutherland asked, turning to Vislowski.

The detective sat silently examining the sheet of paper.

"He's not talking," Sutherland said.

"Why not?" she asked.

"He's figuring how to hang it on me so he and Ronnie can ride off into the sunset."

Vislowski looked up with his lower lip distended and eyes narrowed; he resembled a street urchin ready to fight. "Want to know what we found, wise guy? Ought to shut you up."

"Give it your best shot." Sutherland took a sip of his beer.

Vislowski read from the list. "Two keys we have reason to believe will fit the doors to Tunney's parking garage door and office."

"If they're Tunney's, somebody planted them, probably whoever told you that there were such keys," Sutherland said. "Someone who'd like to see me framed."

"A shirt and pants with stains, believed to be blood," Vislowski continued.

"His nose, I told you."

"Brown and gray strands of hair in a pants pocket." Vislowski looked up from the paper and grinned at each of them. He enjoyed this.

"In my pocket?" Sutherland said. How could that be? "Must've been when I hit him." But he knew better. This was getting creepier.

"You hit him?" Kelly asked, the color beginning to drain from her face.

"Well …" Sutherland said. "Tell you later."

"A bottle of capsules—Seconal," Vislowski continued. "Could've been used to drug Tunney."

"What's Seconal?"

"Sleeping drug," Kelly said. "A barbiturate."

"A frigging sleeping drug? Jesus, am I stupid?" Sutherland said, slamming his fists on the table.

"And how 'bout this?" Vislowski said, holding up the list. "A ring box—want to guess what's in it?"

"I know what's in it," Sutherland said, grimacing. "Now you'll accuse me of killing Delaney."

"A tooth. Bet it *is* Danny's."

Kelly inhaled sharply. "What *is* this?"

"Murder," Vislowski said.

"A frame," Sutherland said, tossing down the last of his beer, wiping his mouth with the back of his hand. "She's fooled us both, Detective. She brought me back here after I saw Tunney, drugged me with that Seconal shit, returned to see Tunney, and brought that stuff you found to leave for you to find."

"Sure," Vislowski said, standing. "Just don't go anywhere. After the lab runs their tests on that stuff—hair, blood, et cetera—you'll need your lawyer."

"Wait a minute," Sutherland said. "You're slower than I am. Doesn't this shit strike a chord with you? Déjà vu? You're either the most naïve cop in the world or you're in it with her."

"What'd you say?" Vislowski glowered, clenching his teeth, his jaw muscles protruding like the knuckles on his fists.

"Ronnie disappears with all this evidence left conveniently in my apartment?"

"So?"

"How gullible are you? What happened that forced her to leave the state's attorney's office, the thing that set your brilliant career back a few years?"

Sutherland and Kelly watched the policeman redden and his eyes bulge, as though his shirt collar was choking him.

"I'll tell you the charges," Kelly said. "Red and he were up for fabricating evidence, falsifying reports, and coaching witnesses in the case against one Dennis Karch. Karch went free."

"He was guilty," Vislowski blurted.

"Doesn't matter," Sutherland said. "This is old stuff for Ronnie. Think about it, Detective. Maybe you should search her place too."

Vislowski pushed the table aside, almost knocking Sutherland backward with it. After glaring at Sutherland for a long moment, he stomped out of the room, down the corridor, and out the door, slamming it behind him.

Sutherland picked up his beer glass, saw it was empty, and set it down hard. "Boy, was I stupid. I thought it was Langer."

Kelly started to say something then closed her mouth. Probably going to agree with him, he thought. "I got a couple phone calls to make," he said. "That black widow isn't gonna get the best of me."

307

"You act like this is a game. Didn't you hear that thickheaded cop? He wants you in jail."

"I'll be okay. Just need to clear my head. I've been walking around with a two-day hangover and now I know why. She really did drug me."

Kelly's eyes and mouth opened to some realization. "That's why you were so zonked—you wouldn't wake up. We finally gave up, and I took Jenny to my place to sleep. While we were here a call came in and we overheard it."

"I haven't checked my messages."

"The caller said the boat was in Harbor Springs, Michigan."

"My father's boat. I'll bet Ronnie's searching for the money right now."

"Are you going there?"

"No reason to. Money won't be there. My father left messages saying he was going sailing for a few days. If he said sailing, he meant sailing, as in sailboat, not motoring or cruising. I've got to make some calls."

"That's a straight answer if I ever heard one." She shook her head. "I wish you'd tell me what's going on instead of dancing around my questions. I might be able to help. At least I've got a clear head. When did Red plant that stuff in here?"

"Had to be after she came back from Tunney's. Must have taken my keys to let herself back in. I vaguely remember her waking me up. I thought she was there the whole time." He closed his eyes and saw Ronnie coming to him with a champagne glass in each hand. She was naked, fresh from a shower and from murdering Tunney. Jesus, how she'd played him.

Kelly stiffened. "She came here, after? What she do then? Pop in bed with you?"

"I was in no condition."

Kelly jumped to her feet, her face coloring, eyes blazing. "Did you know that your daughter wanted to spend the night here? You and your little murder-nymph would have been cavorting around in the next room."

"Jesus."

She glanced away, slapped her thigh, and looked back at him, fixing his eyes. "Answer one question, Doug. When was Tunney killed?"

"Vislowski says ten or ten thirty Tuesday night."

"Hmmm." She smirked, narrowing her eyes in an expression both mischievous and spiteful. "See if you can save your ass without me, Mr. Don't-need-no-help-from-no-one." She turned and waltzed out, like she knew Sutherland was watching and wondering.

With the click of the door latch, he felt the panic coming, the butterflies in his gut, the tightening in his chest. He was losing, and that's when it always came, when the prospect of finishing second pushed him to fight harder. But there was a big difference this time. Kelly was right—this wasn't a game.

# CHAPTER 94

Sutherland reviewed the names and phone numbers listed on his iPhone and felt a grain of confidence returning—a sailor with his course laid out on his chart. Doubts still jabbed at him like pesky gremlins, reminding him that Ronnie was far ahead and he needed to rely on too many guesses. He picked up his kitchen phone and punched in the first number on his list.

Jules Langer nearly hung up his cell phone when he heard Sutherland's voice. "I told you," he said, "it's over. Leave me alone."

"Not that easy, Jules. You're an accessory now. To murder."

"Murder?"

"Police suspect murder. If it *was*, your keys were used by the killer."

"But you have the keys—you sent a messenger."

"So that's how it was done," Sutherland said. "Do you remember the messenger company?"

"Just some kid, I think. Why? He said it was for you."

"It wasn't. He leave you anything? A receipt—something?"

"Never even saw him. He just took the keys from the doorman and went. Do you think it was murder?"

"Yes."

Hanging up, Sutherland realized how thorough Ronnie had been. The messenger could've been some freelance guy picked off the street for some easy money. How should he play it now? He wanted to talk to her, but she'd avoid him if she knew he'd caught on. He picked up the phone and, reaching Ronnie's voice mail, left a message. "Ronnie, Doug here. Vislowski is making a case that I killed Tunney. I need your help to clear this up. Call soon. Please."

His next call was to Al Wiley, the harbormaster in Harbor Springs, Michigan. He was a garrulous salt Sutherland knew from *Circe*'s overnights there on his way back from Mackinac each summer. When he reached Wiley he wasn't surprised to learn that *Gabriela II*, renamed *Wet Dream* by her present owner, had been missing from her berth since early that morning. An itinerant deckhand was suspected of motoring off with the twenty-year-old trawler. The Coast Guard had been alerted, but there was no news. Sutherland asked Wiley to contact him if the boat or thief turned up.

Next he tried his apartment building's second-shift doorman, hoping to confirm that Sutherland hadn't left on his shift and that Ronnie came back after the doorman saw her leave. That could explain the keys and other police discoveries, though it wouldn't provide Sutherland a solid alibi since it was possible to sneak in and out of the building unnoticed if you knew how. The doorman wasn't in, but his wife said the police had been looking for him too. She would give him the message to phone.

Hang up, pick up, dial tone, call—this time a boatyard on the Calumet River. "Can I get at her, or is she still buried in the back of the shed?" Sutherland asked when the yard manager came to the phone.

"I'll have to move some other relics to get to her. You goin' fix her up?"

"Just want to check it out. See you tomorrow," Sutherland said and then hung up.

Now he called the phone company and, after escalating it to a supervisor, got an answer to his question: could he get all the phone numbers and times for calls originated from his home phone? No problem.

One last call: Jim Fellows, his attorney. After trying his office again and insisting he speak to him, Sutherland reached Fellows at his vacation home in Wisconsin. He summarized his situation, complete with the keys, Seconal, and tooth found in his apartment. "I told the police you were my attorney."

"Jesus, Doug. You need representation *now.*"

"I called you twice. They didn't tell me you were on vacation."

"You need a criminal lawyer, not me. I'll get that in motion. Call me later and I'll have it worked out. Jesus."

That was reassuring. Sutherland looked down his list and reviewed his arrangements. Now there was nothing to do but wait and try and relax. But as he was about to put his feet up, another thought struck him. On the night Tunney died, Ronnie had asked where he'd stashed the tapes and had suggested selling them for the millions she believed they could bring. A few hours later she had taken his keys while he was sleeping. Had she gone to the storage area and searched for them? She couldn't have found his hiding place, because he'd spent Wednesday afternoon viewing the tapes. Knowing whether or not she'd tried was more than his curiosity could endure, so he took the elevator to the basement and checked his designated storage cage, a four-by-four-foot compartment identified by his apartment number. He'd taken its padlock to secure the empty, unassigned cage where he hid the tapes. A quick look was all it took to see that someone had rummaged through what little the now-unprotected cage contained—just some paint cans, a bike rack for his car, and two empty suitcases. After being stymied, she would have given up, realizing that she couldn't break into each of the remaining hundred or so cages. For Sutherland, though, her attempt was another indication of her deviousness and determination to get her hands on a large amount of cash.

Back in his apartment, gazing out of the window at the sailboats that speckled the lake, he realized how he might forget Ronnie and Vislowski and Branson and all the trouble they represented. A least for a little while.

*     *     *

With the sun setting over the city, Sutherland set *Circe*'s main and jib, cleared the lighthouse on a starboard reach, and settled himself at the helm. Low on the leeward side, warm wind on his face, he sensed the cleansing begin, the events of the last days flaking off him like old skin. And with each wave, each plunge and surge of *Circe*'s hull, he felt new strength flow into him, as if he was drawing power from the surf itself. An hour later, hearing the roar and suck of the rolling waves, watching the foam flash by in the moonlight, he felt the rush of freedom, like the feeling the gulls must have when riding the wind. If only life was always so. Ten miles on the way to Michigan he came about, ready to face what had to be done.

After midnight, with the lighthouse astern and the sails furled, Sutherland sat in *Circe*'s cockpit and contemplated the city, bathing in its illumination. He would stay on his mooring until morning. No one knew he was here, and he always slept well on *Circe*. He would need the rest for tomorrow.

# Chapter 95

At seven the next morning, climbing *Circe*'s companionway, Sutherland was dazzled by a flaming band of sunlight between lake and clouds on the eastern horizon. To the west, buildings reflected the dawn in thousands of burnished-orange windowpanes. He glanced at his watch; things would start happening soon.

He made himself breakfast from dried food and, while sipping his coffee, called his apartment number and entered his access code to retrieve his phone messages.

The first was from the Michigan harbormaster. "Mr. Sutherland, Wiley here. They found that boat—*Wet Dream*. It was beached near Charlevoix. Inside's torn apart and wrecked. Somebody looking for something—drugs, the Coast Guard thinks. Call me if you want."

The next voice he heard was Vislowski's, growling like a bad imitation of Humphrey Bogart. "Detective Vislowski here. I told you to stick around. You got a problem. Better call me fast, buddy." He probably confirmed those keys fit Tunney's offices.

Ronnie Jamison's voice followed. "Doug, I got your message. What's happening? We need to get together fast. Don't let Stanley Vislowski know we're talking. Call me before you do anything." She left a number he recognized as her cell phone.

Eight thirty. His secretary would be in by now. "Where are you?" she said over the phone, unable to hide her worry. "The police called wanting to know. And your attorney called saying it was important, and Ronnie Jamison said she had to see you, that it was urgent. And the FBI called. Doug, are you all right? They said they tried you at home, but you weren't there. That cop was mighty mad."

"That all?" he asked.

"All? Doug, are you all right?"

"I'm fine. I'll call you later."

"But what will I tell them?"

"The truth. You don't know where I am."

He called the number Ronnie had left him. She was in her car and didn't say where she was talking from. She didn't have to. It was a long drive from Charlevoix, Michigan.

# CHAPTER 96

Sutherland sat at an outdoor table in Bounce, a Lincoln Park restaurant, waiting in the warm morning sun. Eleven thirty was early for the lunch crowd, but several of the tables were occupied, and the waiters were finishing with the place settings. The *Chicago Tribune* was spread before him, open to the continuation of the front page headline article:

### FBI TO INVESTIGATE SPANOS'S PAST

Spanos himself hadn't been seen since the first airing of the videotape on Tuesday night. His beleaguered press agent hadn't spoken to or heard from her candidate either but nonetheless insisted that the video was bogus and taken totally out of context. Shouts were already sounding for his resignation from his congressional seat and the gubernatorial race. Sutherland had no doubt that the decision would be hastened by disclosures that the first video was one of many that would implicate the congressman and others in a widespread corruption scheme.

Sutherland watched as Ronnie drove up and parked her Corvette on Clark Street by a bus stop. As she walked toward the restaurant he could sense her fatigue in her listless gait and slumped shoulders. No wonder; she'd had a very busy couple days.

She found him and sat down, her expression the picture of earnest concern. "Doug, I can't believe it. What's happening?" He recognized the bright-green sweater she wore and remembered the seductive grace with which she'd once removed it. Now that evening on Mackinac seemed like a grotesque dream.

"Cut the bullshit," he said. "You know what's happening. Your buddy Vislowski is measuring me for jail stripes."

She picked up her napkin and unfolded it onto her lap, taking more care than the task demanded. "That's just Stanley," she said, "trying to make a suicide into something else. He really can be tiresome, can't he?" She turned her glance away, as if to locate a waiter.

"Tiresome? *Tire*some?" Sutherland said.

"It can't stick, can it?"

"Ronnie, they found your barbiturate that probably drugged Tunney, what they think is his hair, and the keys you left for them to find. I'm hours away from being arrested and it's because of you, so don't … act … innocent." He glared at her, trying to connect with her eyes.

"All right, all right. Don't get upset," she said, glancing momentarily at him. "I can straighten it out with Stanley. I was with you all night."

"But you told him you weren't."

"He's just playing cop games with you. I'm your alibi, so don't worry. I'll talk to him."

"I'd like to hear that conversation. What will you tell him when he asks about your trip to Michigan?"

"Hmm?"

"I could have told you the money wasn't in *Wet Dream* and saved you the trouble."

Her eyes hardened, defensive. Looking at him for a long moment, she must have made a decision. "I intended to share it."

"Share what?"

"Doug, we can work together on this. We both can benefit. You've got a loan due on your McCollum project."

"And you have a pile of gambling debts. Tough to pay them off from a jail cell. If your planted evidence sticks, we'll both be there."

"What do you mean?"

"You've got me nailed good, but if the medical examiner and police rule it murder, you're in it as deep as me."

"Oh please," she said. "That's ridiculous." She saw a young waiter by the door and waved. He arrived, they both ordered Chardonnay, and he retreated, looking grateful to escape the chill around the table.

"Let me give you some facts," Sutherland said. "First, Langer's doorman can ID the messenger who picked up the keys to Tunney's place. Sooner or later we'll find him and prove you sent him, not me."

"As if," she said with a wave of her hand.

"That night you called the guy hired to steal my father's old boat. Knowing I was in a drugged sleep, you gave the thief my home phone number, thinking the message would be waiting on my voice mail when you let yourself back into my place."

She appeared nonplussed for a moment then said, "What good's a message if it's erased?"

"Because when it was being recorded, someone wrote the message down. Someone in my apartment with me at the exact time Tunney was killed."

"Bullshit."

"Kelly and my daughter were there. How else would I know about a phone message from your accomplice in Michigan?"

She said nothing, just studied him from fatigue-ringed eyes.

"You've got no choice if you want to save your own ass," Sutherland said. "The only way the keys and hair and whatever could've got in my apartment was by you—after my alibi left. The doorman didn't see you, so you must've used my keys to the back way."

Ronnie smirked.

"But the doorman saw my daughter and Kelly. They didn't leave until after eleven. After Tunney was dead and the message about the boat came in."

"You can't prove I came back."

"Don't have to. If Vislowski or the grand jury or the DA or whoever insists that Tunney was murdered, I've got an alibi. Do you? I doubt your old flame dislikes me enough to charge you with murder to get at me as an accomplice. So if I were you I'd convince him to lose some of that crap you planted in my place."

Ronnie's cheeks flushed and she said, "Langer. It could have been Langer."

"How would he get into my place? Besides, your fingerprints are bound to be there, his aren't. Not to mention some hair and bodily fluids you left on my sheets."

"Could've happened anytime. Doesn't mean I came back."

"That's for the jury to figure. I've got an alibi and I'll testify against you—bet on it. So unless it's ruled a suicide, we have a stalemate."

Ronnie sipped her water, wiped her lips with her napkin, and opened the menu. She studied it intently as Sutherland watched. Then she closed it and placed it on the tablecloth. She said, "There's no direct evidence. Stanley can't have anything on me."

"You haven't been home yet, have you? I wouldn't be surprised if he got a search warrant for your place too—after I reminded him of your history."

She wrinkled her brow, apparently thinking hard. "There's nothing there."

"Even ex-prosecuting attorneys make mistakes. How will it feel if you're caught in your own frame?"

"You've got it wrong, Doug. I didn't try to frame you. It was to look like suicide, plain and simple."

"No it wasn't. You drugged Tunney then blew his head off, knowing I'd be the prime suspect. My defense? Napping all alone in my apartment. They would've had a field day with me."

"I didn't know they'd search your place."

"Bull. You probably tipped Vislowski to search it."

She stared at something behind Sutherland, her green eyes angry. The waiter came with the wine, set the glasses on the table, and disappeared.

"Well," she said, forcing a smile, lifting her wine glass in a salute. "If you do have an alibi, you're a lucky son of a bitch. Now what?"

"That's up to you." Sutherland sipped his wine. "Judge, jury, executioner. It's still murder." He envisioned her holding the head by the hair, pulling the trigger, watching the spume of blood and brain as the gun went off.

"You expect remorse? It's no big deal," Ronnie said, as if talking about crushing a bug.

Imagining the grisly photographs, the splattered desk, the slouched body, he knew it was true. For an instant in Tunney's office he'd felt a spark of that atavistic instinct and almost acted on it. Whatever stopped him, that fateful phone call or some moral proscription, separated him from the likes of Sandler, Tunney, and Ronnie. He stood up and smiled down on her, feeling, at least in that sense, he had won something. Pulling out two twenty-dollar bills and laying them on the table, he said, "I'll be interested in how Vislowski reacts when he realizes what you've done. Like old times, right? Who was that guy you tried to set up, the scheme that got you fired?"

He watched her face as the words sank in: her eyes hardening, lower lip trembling—a mural of resentment and loathing. "This isn't the end, Doug," she said. "Think you're home free? Keep the money that Billy died for, that he should have lived to enjoy? Uh uh, sweetie. I've got a message for you."

"Forget the money. Consider yourself lucky if you can avoid jail."

"I owe too much to forget the money. Not just gambling markers—I can't even trade anymore, I can't cover my shorts."

"Sounds like a major problem. Tell it to someone who cares."

"Could be yours too. My creditors know about our partnership. They know you have Delaney's original tapes, his cash, and millions in some foreign account."

"What partnership? If they believe all that, they're as deluded as you."

"They know I can't pay them, and their only alternative is what your father hid. I won't be the only one watching you."

Sutherland walked out, feeling her eyes on his back, wishing her words were merely a last cry of defiance, but conceding that they weren't. It wasn't the end.

# Chapter 97

Confronted with Vislowski's surly face, Sutherland's confidence almost evaporated. "Told you not to go anywhere," Vislowski said, pushing through the doorway into Sutherland's apartment. Two steps behind him was Manny López, his partner.

"I slept on my boat. It's not a crime in the law books I've read."

"Don't fuck with me. You're in deep shit. Call your lawyer and tell him to meet us at the precinct."

"We should talk about this, Detective," Sutherland said, backing along the entry corridor.

"You bet we'll talk. Those keys fit Tunney's building and office. And the hair's a match. I'll bet the rest of the tests are even more interesting. You're going to like prison, Sutherland," he said with a wicked grin. "You'll make somebody a pretty wife."

"You're making a mistake."

"Let's go, asshole," Vislowski said, thrusting his chin forward, causing Sutherland to draw back into the apartment. The bully again—the brat on the playground you wanted to smack.

"We'll see who's the asshole," Sutherland said. "You won't get off as easy this time—when they discover Ronnie trumped up evidence again. Does you partner know about that?"

"The evidence is solid," Vislowski said, glancing over his shoulder to see if López had heard. But he was too far away, leaning on the door jamb looking at his fingernails.

"Listen a minute. If we go to the station, it'll be too late—for you *and* her. Like putting toothpaste back in the tube. Hear me out, for your own good."

Vislowski snorted then turned to his partner. "Manny, wait in the car for us while this hump tries to get my sympathy. I can handle him alone."

López waved and shut the door behind him after leaving.

"You got one minute. Sit down." He pointed to the dining room. They walked in and sat facing each other at the table.

"You talk to the second-shift doorman?" Sutherland asked.

"Yeah. He didn't see you leave, but there's a back door you could've used.

He didn't see Veronica come back either. So there goes your story about the stuff we found."

"He didn't tell you about my daughter and Kelly?"

"What about them?"

"If you'd asked, he'd tell you my thirteen-year-old daughter and Kelly Matthews came here at ten thirty and found me sound asleep, drugged by our mutual friend. The phone company, if you bother to check, will list calls made that night. It'll prove my daughter and Kelly were here and show a call made by Ronnie to the man who stole the trawler."

Vislowski pulled a pen and notebook out of his jacket and scribbled a few lines. "What're you talking—what trawler?"

"You'll see. Kelly and my daughter left at eleven with me still asleep. The doorman saw them. Later, Ronnie used my keys to my building's back door to bypass the doorman and bring in the evidence you found."

Vislowski balled his hands into meaty fists and his lower lip hung out like a pugnacious kid's. "You're blowing smoke."

"Have you checked her apartment yet? Find any blood? Or couldn't you be bothered with a search warrant?"

He looked a little embarrassed but said, "Didn't need one. Still got a key. Nothing there."

"How about her hotel? She's been staying in one ever since her brother died. Probably can't pay the bill though. She has serious money problems, the poor dear."

"What hotel?"

"She never said. I'd say it's worth checking."

"I'll find out," Vislowski grumbled.

"What you'll find is that I have an alibi and your choices are simple," Sutherland said. "Either Tunney *did* commit suicide, or someone other than me killed him. And you know who that someone is."

Without warning Vislowski lunged across the table with a right hook. Sutherland pushed against the table, tipping himself backward in the chair, just out of reach of Vislowski's sweeping haymaker. He landed on the floor with a crash and, kicking the chair from under him, sent it skidding across the tile under the table to strike Vislowski at the shins.

Vislowski howled, bending to grab his leg. Sutherland scrambled to his feet, closing his fists, preparing himself, but keeping the table between them. Vislowski merely rubbed his shin and grimaced. "Don't think we're through with this," he said through clenched teeth.

"You should be grateful—she'll owe you big-time."

"You fucking—"

He took a step around the table and Sutherland grabbed another chair, swinging it in front like a lion tamer. Vislowski stopped and put his hand on his gun handle.

"Don't," Sutherland said. "Others know about this. You'd never get away with it."

Vislowski lowered his hand from the gun and his shoulders slumped.

"She's poison, Detective. It's time we both realized it."

# CHAPTER 98

Four hours later in his office, Sutherland closed his file drawers, turned his computer off, and threw the last of his mail into his briefcase. Time to pick up Kelly. The phone rang before he reached the door. It was Jim Fellows, his attorney.

"Thought you'd want this news right away," Fellows said. "For the time being, you don't have to worry about going to jail. The Cook County medical examiner has ruled it a suspicious death, really meaning she hasn't yet decided suicide or murder. The state's attorney wants to take it to the sitting grand jury, and the police can't make up their mind. Your daughter's and Miss Matthews's statements should clear you, but any prosecutor will say they're biased and protecting you."

"So you're not sure?"

"You've been to law school; you know how it works."

"How about publicity? I'm trying to land Imperial Food Products now that the Broadwell deal fell apart. If I'm hung out there as a murder suspect, what chance do you think I'll have?"

"I'm well aware of that, and we've threatened all kinds of hell if your reputation is damaged by some leak."

"Will it stick?"

"So far so good. Your name's been kept out of the public domain."

"How about Ronnie Jamison's? She's the guilty one."

"Are you serious? If you are, we should talk."

"No thanks. I'll live with it. I just got one monkey off my back, I can handle another."

"Speaking of things on your back," Fellows said, "you're going to have an army on you if you don't turn over those tapes. The state's attorney, the FBI, the federal attorney. What are you trying to do?"

"How can they be sure I have more tapes? The paper and the TV station have protected my identity. Besides, they're my property, found in my building."

"They're going to issue a court order any minute."

"By what judge? There's at least three I've identified in those tapes taking bribes. Who can I trust with the originals? I'll keep them and hand in copies. Just like I'm doing for the media."

"All of them? Why?"

"It'll be years before the prosecutors will do anything. If at all, given the statute of limitations. TV, Internet can air them immediately. These corrupt bastards have been hiding for years. They should be outed now."

"They'll stop you. A warrant, an injunction."

"It'll be too late. Easier to ask forgiveness than permission."

# CHAPTER 99

At dinner with Kelly that night in Carlo's, an Italian restaurant in the River North area, Sutherland recounted his meetings with Ronnie and Vislowski and the call from his attorney. "If you and Jenny hadn't come over that night, I'd be in jail right now facing a murder charge."

"Jenny's idea. She had some argument with her friend and called me. The doorman let us in with the new keys, but after noticing Red's shoulder bag on the table, seeing you zonked out in bed, and receiving that phone call meant for Red, I decided we needed to get the hell out of there. I took Jenny to sleep at my place."

"Whatever. I owe you. And thanks for calling Vislowski and giving your statement." He raised his wine glass for a toast.

She touched his glass with hers and said, "I could almost hear his disappointment when I told him. That was only the second or third time you ever asked me for help. Did it hurt?"

"As a matter of fact. But thanks anyway."

"You can pay me back. Interested?"

"What's the payoff?"

"Let bygones be bygones. Bury the hatchet."

Kelly wore a loose silk blouse, opened deeply at the neck, and he had to keep his eyes focused on hers to avoid glancing at the soft curves and shadows where old pleasures lay. He studied those liquid eyes, wide and warm and consuming. "You mean about the landmark thing?"

"What else?"

He thought about how important it had seemed at the time. How heated the fight, how angry her opposition made him. Now it seemed petty. Was it because it was over now, that he'd won and the demolition was a fact? Or was it something else, something to do with him, with what was meaningful and what wasn't?

"Give me time on that one," he said. "I'm still sorting it out. Okay?"

She nodded, and they both drank.

"Then tell me this," Kelly said. "You discovered the truth about your father. His killer's dead. Why the funk?"

"Where do I start? For one thing, I'm not out of the woods. I could still be indicted." He finished the wine in his glass, refilled it, and topped off hers. "Second, if it gets out that I'm a suspect in a murder case, we can kiss off landing Imperial or any other tenant and saving my project. Then there's my ambivalence over Ronnie's getting away with it."

She grimaced. "Ambivalence? She's a murderer."

"She executed a monster who tortured and killed five people we know about, including her brother and, in a way, my father. Some would say she did the world a service and maybe saved a bunch more people from him."

"And framed you for murder."

"There's that too," Sutherland said, frowning. "What's scary is I didn't see it and it damn near worked. I can't turn her in because she's vindictive enough to swear I helped her."

"I'm not surprised she fooled you. Red's smart and attractive. You've got a lot in common. She has a need to win, and fortunately that's where the similarity ends."

"Thanks. The final thing is that my father hasn't been cleared, hasn't been proven innocent of the FBI's suspicions."

"Which brings us to your hang-up on what to do about the money."

"Why do you say that?"

"You ask yourself, should you turn the money in? After all, the cash was skimmed from casinos, then laundered in a sham building sale and destined for the Delaney crowd's secret offshore accounts before your father diverted it for the feds. When the investigation got compromised by George Spanos and the FBI contact was killed, your father changed the plan. So, whose money is it now?"

"You're getting ahead of yourself. What money and where? Cash? Numbered bank account? Which of a dozen countries? What's the number?"

"Now you're being disingenuous."

"I'm not. And my challenge is to convince Ronnie and maybe her gambling buddies that I don't know, or that it's lost somehow, so they'll let me alone. She'll never give up, she's like a junkyard dog. Her bookies, if she does what she threatened, won't be easy to persuade either."

"How will you convince them?"

"I'll let you know when I figure it out. For the moment, I've got other challenges. Tomorrow morning we're seeing Alan Battenfield, the head of Imperial Food Products, about building on the McCollum site. My leasing agent believes we'll be their only real option with Langer's project out of contention. I'll have the only building with enough space within their time frame. Let's just hope that my name doesn't appear in tomorrow's *Tribune* as a murder suspect."

# Chapter 100

The Saturday morning meeting with Battenfield and the relocation committee for Imperial Food Products went as well as Sutherland could have hoped. Battenfield was a big-picture guy and had little patience for details or fluff. He wasn't interested in his headquarters building being a monument, believing it sent a bad message to stockholders, customers, and employees. His attention focused on Sutherland's ability to deliver a practical solution for his consolidation on time and at a reasonable cost. After being satisfied that that was the case, he left the meeting and directed his in-house attorney and real estate director to handle the details.

It took four hours, but in the end, they decided they would use the lease that was almost finished between Sutherland and Broadwell. Frank Mann, Sutherland's leasing agent, and the lawyers on both sides would see to the wording changes while the architect and building engineers would see to the few modifications necessary to accommodate Imperial's requirements.

When the meeting was over, Frank Mann congratulated Sutherland.

"Nothing like having to do the deal twice," Sutherland responded. "You earned your commission this time."

"Talk about timing."

"Let's just get this thing done before something else happens." Like a grand jury indictment for murder.

*     *     *

Sutherland was walking back to his office when his cell rang. It was Ronnie, and she was short and to the point. "Where's your father's other boat? The sailboat."

Sutherland had wondered how long it would take before she got around to exploring that option. Ronnie had admitted she needed money badly. Delaney's cash wasn't found in the McCollum Building or the trawler, why not the original *Gabriela*, the sailboat? Out of desperation she probably hoped that Sutherland's father stuffed the cash into the water tank he'd bought the day he disappeared. She was wrong, of course. Sutherland had sailed *Gabriela* for years, knew ever nook and cranny, and anyway, he remembered seeing the new water tank his father bought in the warehouse when he picked up his father's records.

"She sits in a boatyard rotting away," Sutherland said. "Sad, she was a beauty."

"What boatyard? I haven't time to fuck around."

"You're wasting your time. What if I call the FBI and let them check it out?"

"Doug, please." She was using her seductive voice again. "These guys are serious, they hurt people. You too, if they think you're holding out. I told them half that money's mine, that you owe it to me. Half for your father, half for my brother."

"Half of nothing is still nothing. How much you owe?"

"More than I have."

"You made that bed, you sleep in it," and he hung up. Then he smiled to himself, because her scheming was exactly what his strategy required. Now all he had to do was execute his plan and Ronnie would be off his back for good. She and her creditors could settle their issues among themselves, an ending that Ronnie richly deserved.

*     *     *

Fifteen minutes later, Sutherland had reached Deane Tank, his friend and *Circe*'s navigator for five of his Mac sailing races. He worked for the US Treasury Department in Chicago and was at home when Sutherland called. It was the second time in two days they'd discussed the topic, so little needed to be said.

"Any success?" Sutherland asked.

"It arrived here overnight. Stop by this afternoon or tomorrow. If I'm not home, my wife will be."

"How big is it?"

"Fifty pounds. Too much?"

"Perfect. Thanks, Deane."

"You won't tell me what this is about? A prank, right?"

"There you go again," Sutherland said. "Typical government snoop. Finger in everyone else's business."

"Okay, asshole," Deane joked. "You can buy the beer for the tri-state race."

"Don't I always?"

A few minutes later, Sutherland called another friend, one who worked backstage at the Goodman Theater. Her specialty was stage props, and he arranged to pick up her and her bag of tricks at her workshop the following afternoon.

*     *     *

He had just hung up when the phone rang again. The number on the caller ID was blocked, the voice was unfamiliar, the tone polite and urbane. "Mr. Sutherland?"

"Who's this?"

"A friend of your girlfriend."

"What girlfriend?"

"More than one, eh? Good for you. Mr. Sutherland, I mean Veronica Jamison."

Sutherland's alarms went off. "What's this about?"

"You owe her a large sum of money."

"That's her fantasy. I owe her nothing, there's no money, no debt, and she's not my girlfriend. She's demented."

The caller continued as if he hadn't heard. "Were the articles about your father in the *Tribune* fantasy too? She showed me that alderman's notebook, and her logic is somewhat convincing; there are only so many places the money could be hidden. She owes me a large sum. Since you owe her, in a way, you owe me."

"I see where this is going, Mister … what did you say your name was? I'd like to spell it correctly when I report this extortion to the police."

"She tells me the money is in a boat. Why don't you be reasonable and show us so we can know, one way or other?"

"I make it a rule not to deal with extortionists, and I've got lots of reasons not to trust her. You won't find any money there."

"You've already taken it, then."

"I don't chase after fairy tales. Haven't seen that boat for years. Look for yourself. But if Ronnie Jamison is with you, watch your back." He hung up.

# Chapter 101

The next evening Sutherland was sitting in his dining room with his feet on a chair, bone tired, aching, and dehydrated. On the way home from the far South Side, he'd stopped for some Mexican takeout and a six-pack of Negra Modelo. The enchiladas were gone, and he was nursing his third beer when the phone rang and he picked it up to hear Kelly's voice.

"How did your meeting with the Imperial people go?" she asked.

"Just a few tweaks and we may have a deal, if I can keep the police at bay long enough."

"Congrats."

"Don't jinx me. Now my other challenge: getting Ronnie off my case."

"How's that going?"

"We'll see. I went down to the boatyard this afternoon."

"Your father's sailboat? You said the money wasn't there."

"It isn't. During the time I sailed it, I took it apart and put it together more than once. Knew it wouldn't be on his trawler either. Nevertheless, Ronnie figures since it wasn't in the McCollum or the trawler, it has to be in the sailboat. My father's old purchases at the marine store have her convinced. If it will help me get her off my back, I'll let her go there and find out for herself."

"If you knew the money's not there, why the trip to the yacht yard?"

"Sorry, this phone might be bugged," he said lightly.

"Bull. The police took the microphones out. What gives?"

"I just had to check on something."

Kelly must have been thinking, because there was a long pause. "Tell you what," she said finally. "You running tomorrow?"

"Yeah. I need a good workout."

"I'll join you and treat for breakfast. Meet you at the east zoo entrance, and I'll bring the bagels for after."

"First extortion, now bribery," he said. "Seven too early for you?"

*     *     *

The phone rang just as Manny López was about to leave the precinct after spending a few off-duty hours catching up on paperwork. He was supposed to meet Vislowski for a drink at O'Malley's, the local copper watering hole, to catch a couple innings of the White Sox game. These sessions didn't occur often, especially on a Sunday; Manny's wife wanted him home and didn't approve of some of his drinking buddies, even if they were fellow detectives. Too much time with the other cops and his dinner would be in the refrigerator, ready to microwave. The kids would be in bed, and she would give him the cold shoulder while watching a DVD movie.

The caller was Mel Jackson, an officer López had worked with when he was a patrolman. They'd both made detective the same year, Manny in homicide, Mel in burglary.

"Called you at home, Manny," Jackson said. "Your wife said you were at the station, but I gotta admit, I thought it was bull. You lookin' to get promoted ahead of me?"

"Just cleaning up some crapola reports. What's up?"

"Got something you may be able to use. Pawnbroker on Clark tipped me on Friday. A woman came in with a huge diamond ring, a man's. Had to be worth ten grand or more. Knew from the look of the woman it had to be hot, so even though he could've resold it for ten times what she wanted, he knew we were watching, and he owes me."

"So why call me?"

"I saw that that Sandler guy, the guy whacked in his office, had a pinkie ring stolen."

López, who had been standing, ready to leave, sat down and grabbed a pen. "So, what did he do? We know who she is? Get an address?"

"Slow down. He said she was a Polack, looked like was some kind of maid, a cleaning woman. How could she own such a thing? But he said this was some diamond, made him horny."

"So he didn't take it. What?"

"Like I said, he owes me. He spun her a line, said he didn't have enough cash on hand, said he'd have to get back to her."

"And?"

"Got her name."

"Legit?"

"She's sitting in front of me. Near as I can understand her English, she said she found it on the bus."

"Of course she did. Where does she work?"

329

"Some dump on Ohio. The Bristol Inn."

"Find out what hotel room she, quote, found it in. Then we need someone to ID it as Sandler's. A jeweler maybe."

"How about his initials inside? EPS? His first name was Eugene, wasn't it?"

"And I'm looking at his obit in the paper," López replied immediately. "Middle name Phillip."

# Chapter 102

He was in his running shorts and singlet, locking his apartment door, when his iPhone rang. It was Ronnie, and she sounded frantic. "Doug, can you meet me this morning? I really need to know where your father's sailboat is. They're getting impatient."

"Call me later and I'll give you directions. I'm going for a run, and I'm keeping someone waiting on the path. Back in a couple hours." He hung up, took the elevator down to the lobby and, once on the street, started jogging to the park.

Kelly was stretching her hamstring, her right leg hiked up on the hood of her Audi, when Sutherland arrived. He had jogged through the Lincoln Park Zoo from his apartment, exiting by the eastern entrance into the parking lot. She switched legs and watched as he approached.

"Is that a phone I see?" she shouted. "You planning on calling someone while you're running?"

"It's eight in New York. My attorney's been following Broadwell's situation and where I stand in the bankruptcy line. He said he'd call."

"It'll wait," she said, holding out her hand. "Give it here. I'll put it in the car with your keys."

They ran north along the path paralleling the lagoon, through the tunnel under Fullerton, and past the Diversey Yacht Club. The temperature was already near eighty, and Sutherland was sweating through his tank top and shorts. Just as they reached the entrance to the north parking lot, a white Buick pulled across the path from the street. The car had hardly stopped before Ronnie Jamison jumped out of the passenger side and waved her arms for them to stop.

"What now?" Kelly asked Sutherland as she slowed to a stop twenty feet from the car.

Before Sutherland could answer, the back door opened, and a man swung his legs out and stood. He was medium height and wore shades, a navy-blue suit, a white shirt, a silver-gray tie, and Italian loafers. His steel-gray hair was cut short. He could have been an attorney or investment banker, but Sutherland guessed he was the man Ronnie owed a "large sum," as he had said on the phone.

"Mr. Sutherland," the man said. "And this must be Miss Matthews."

"Let me guess," Sutherland said, remaining a safe twenty feet away. "Mr. Extortion. You here to bust knees?"

"Please. Nothing to worry about. We just want you to take us to that sailboat. We go there, search, and that's it. What could be simpler?"

"You're wasting your time."

"Indulge us. Miss Jamison is counting on this."

"Let's go," Kelly said, loudly enough for the man to hear. "He can't catch us in those loafers."

"True," the man said. "But why not get this over with? No one's interested in hurting you. We're just trying to give Miss Jamison a chance to pay off what she owes."

"Come on, Doug," Ronnie said. "How long can it take?"

Sutherland turned to Kelly and whispered, "You go back to the car. I'll get this over with. Trust me. This will work."

"Are you nuts? You see the guy in the driver's seat? He doesn't have a neck."

Sutherland peered through the front windshield and saw a big man behind the wheel, staring straight ahead. Kelly was correct, his head seemed sit directly on his wide shoulders. "I'll be all right," he said. "Now go."

"What?"

"Go," he hissed, and he walked toward the car. "Okay. What are we waiting for? Where should I sit?"

As the car turned around, Sutherland looked at Kelly, still standing on the path. She was shaking her head, talking to herself. He adjusted the seat belt in the backseat and, realizing how wet he was, said, "Sorry about the sweat."

"No worries. It's a rental," the man said.

"I don't have any keys to the boat. There's a lock on the hatch."

Ronnie turned around and said, "I've got tools."

"I almost forgot. You've got experience trashing boats."

"What's the best route?" the man asked.

"Take Lake Shore Drive to the Dan Ryan."

\*　　\*　　\*

Kelly ran back to her car, cursing and mumbling the whole way. "That stupid, headstrong idiot. What's he thinking? Driving off with a murderer

332

and a loan shark like it was off to the movies. If I ever see him again I'm going to kill him."

She got in her car and was almost out of the parking lot, still fuming, when Sutherland's phone rang. *Probably his New York lawyer*, she thought. She picked it up anyway.

"Hello?"

"Who's this? I'm calling Douglas Sutherland."

She recognized the voice immediately. "This is Kelly Matthews. Is this Detective Vislowski?"

"Right. Where is he? I'm at his building and he's not answering."

"He's with Red, Ronnie. They just left with a couple guys she owes money to. I told him not to go, but—"

"Great," Vislowski said, meaning the opposite. "Where?"

"Some old yard way south on the Calumet River."

"Why a yacht yard?"

"She thinks there's money in a boat there. Sutherland's father's. They practically kidnapped Doug." A slight exaggeration, but who cares?

"You know where? The yard, the boat?"

"Can't remember the name, but I've been there."

"Where are you?"

"In the parking lot by the zoo. I was heading to Doug's to drop off his phone and keys."

"We're there now. When you get here, you can come with us to show us where it is."

"Why? What's the rush?" Kelly asked.

"We have an arrest warrant, and if we don't get there in time, someone could get hurt. Maybe worse."

# Chapter 103

In the rental car heading down Lake Shore Drive, Sutherland took stock of his situation. Ronnie sat in the front seat wearing a white tee shirt and jeans, her red hair tied with a green bandana. The driver, in a black suit and blue shirt, had thick shoulders that slanted up to a roll of solid muscle at the back of his head. Covering his large dome was a bristle of thick, black hair. On Sutherland's right sat the man in a suit fingering his BlackBerry, occasionally touching the screen or scrolling. No one seemed interested in conversation.

"So what do I call you?" Sutherland asked. "Mr. Big?"

The man continued reading from his PDA and said, "Call me Jim."

"How much does she owe you, Jim?"

"A hundred and fifty," he said without looking up.

"Thousand?

"That's right," Ronnie said, turning from the front seat, a sardonic smile on her face. "Happy?"

"Why would that make me happy? Besides, you told me once you could lose or gain fifty thousand in a day."

"Everything's changed. My luck, everything."

"She owes her brokers too," Jim said. "Playing long shots, selling short, maxing out her margin—all risky business. Me, I never bet what I don't have."

"It's a good thing everyone doesn't have that philosophy," Sutherland said. "You'd be out of business." He thought he saw the hint of a smile on Jim's otherwise stony face. "So what happens if the money isn't on the boat? And for the record, I don't think it is."

"We can always sell the tapes," Ronnie said. "The originals. A lot of people would pay big to see them disappear."

"Too late, my dear," Sutherland said. "I didn't trust anyone around here, so I've arranged for a federal judge from out of the area to hold on to them." It wasn't a total lie. He intended to do it but hadn't finished copying them all. The deceit was necessary to prevent Ronnie or Jim from pursuing that option.

"Stupid shit," she scoffed. "They aren't yours to give away."

334

They drove in silence the rest of the way. Lake Shore Drive to the Dan Ryan, exited, and continued to 143rd to Olson's boatyard, where Sutherland's father's sailboat had sat neglected on its cradle for over ten years, ever since it had been hit by lightning and nearly sunk as a result. All of its electrical components had been fried—radar, GPS, and navigation lights.

"Doesn't look like the boatyard business is doing too well," Jim said as he they passed through a gate that was hanging by one hinge. There were knee-high weeds around the vacant watchman's gatehouse, its windows broken and the door missing.

"The old owner died and his kids don't seem to be interested," Sutherland said. "Hoping to sell the land, my guess. Not that it's worth much."

He directed the driver past a row of empty boat cradles. The yard was mostly deserted; most of the boats that were still stored winters there were in the water. They came to a half-dozen sailboats that hadn't been launched, apparently abandoned for the season or forgotten altogether. Halyards slapped and clanged against two of the masts that hadn't been unstepped. At the end of the row they came to the once black, now graying hull of a thirty-foot sailing sloop sitting high on its cradle, its full, five-foot-deep keel a foot off the ground. Its mast lay lengthwise, having fallen from its wooden supports onto the deck, now overhanging each end of the boat, bow and stern, by several feet. Draped over the mast was a tattered tarp that stretched tent-like over the toe rails and down the sides. The years of neglect, elements, and vandalism had torn huge holes in the tarp, and shreds of the loose material fluttered in the light breeze.

"That's her," Sutherland said. "We'll need a ladder. I'll borrow the one over there."

The driver pulled behind the sloop, and everyone got out but him. While Jim and Ronnie walked around to the stern, Sutherland dragged the ladder that was lying under his neighbor's cradle over to his father's boat and leaned it against the transom. The letters on the fading paint were blurry but still readable: *Gabriela*. It had been his father's pride and the source of many happy hours together with his son.

"This is your show," Sutherland said to Ronnie. "For your sake, I hope you're right. Have at it."

# CHAPTER 104

Kelly pulled into the circle in front of Sutherland's condominium building. The patrol car was waiting, its engine running. Detective Vislowski was in the driver's seat, his partner, Manny López, sat shotgun. It had been five minutes since they'd spoken on the phone, and during the entire trip over, Kelly had been debating whether or not to help Vislowski. If he was intending to arrest Sutherland, why should she help?

Vislowski opened his window and motioned for her, shouting, "In the back, Miss Matthews."

She walked over to the blue-and-white and leaned over, looking the detective in the eye. "Before I go anywhere, what's this about?"

"Hop in and we'll tell you on the way. You know where it is, right?"

"It's somewhere near 143rd and the Calumet. I can find it but why should I?"

"This is an official request, Miss Matthews. You're an attorney for the City, right?"

"What's that got to do with it? Is this an arrest? This about Doug?"

"It's for his own good. Get in the back and I'll tell you on the way."

She opened the back door and slid in to the shock of the air conditioning. Still wet from her run, wearing only shorts and a singlet, goose bumps spread like a rash. "Can you turn the air down?"

"Sorry," Manny said as he adjusted the controls.

"Take Lake Shore Drive," she said. "Now what's this about?"

Before she got her answer, Vislowski talked into his radio. "Requesting backup. It's near 143rd and the Calumet. A yacht yard. Can you have a patrol meet us? It'll take us about a half hour. Meet you at the exit."

The voice responded, "What's the call?"

"Arrest warrant. Suspect could be armed." He turned to Kelly and asked, "How many besides Veronica?"

"Two of them," she said. An arrest warrant, and she was helping them. The suspect armed? Doug?

Vislowski was talking into the mic again. "Three others are not suspects but could be trouble. Could be armed. Will call again in fifteen minutes. Out."

When he lowered the mic Kelly didn't waste a second. "Tell me what's happening now, or I may forget where the damn place is."

"Don't be stupid, miss. I'll tell you, just stay out of the way."

*    *    *

Ronnie held up her canvas bag and pointed to the ladder. "I've got the tools. You first."

With a hand on the aluminum ladder, Sutherland said to Jim, "Coming?"

Jim seemed to be considering the grease-soaked ground, the gritty ladder, and the dirt-caked hull. His clean, well-tailored suit didn't have a chance. "I'll have Russ join you," he said, motioning to the driver. "Keep an eye on them." The driver opened his car door and stood, hoisting his heavily muscled torso up onto disproportionately short legs. As he lumbered toward them he gave the impression of an ape in a business suit.

Sutherland climbed the ladder first, followed by Ronnie and Russ. The companionway lock had been torn off and the hatch itself was lying on the cockpit floor. No need for a key. The interior was dark, but Ronnie had thought of that. She produced a bright flashlight from the bag and, from the cockpit, surveyed the cramped area with a sweep of the beam. It was a small cabin, too low for Sutherland to stand upright, and cramped with the three of them. They descended the causeway steps. In the galley were a sink, two cushioned benches doubling as bunks, and a commode behind a bulkhead and faded curtain. Forward was a berth that doubled for sail and anchor stowage. Aft, a narrow bunk partially under the cockpit was separated by a bulkhead from the inboard diesel engine. The air stunk of mildew and diesel fuel, and water covered the cabin sole, apparently from the main hatch, which had caved in from vandalism or when the mast had fallen from its supports.

"Where do you want to start?" Sutherland asked. "There's three freshwater tanks and a waste-holding tank."

"I don't care. We're going to find it if there's nothing left but toothpicks. Start at the front."

"The bow it is," he said, pointing and smiling.

"Here's a crowbar. You first."

The forward cabin was a disaster. Two sail bags were wedged forward into the very prow, the canvas-covered cushion was pooled with brackish water, and the hull liner was peeling off overhead. "Thing's seen better days," Sutherland said, remembering the many nights he'd slept in that space, cozy in its closeness. "There's storage and a tank under the berth," he said, pushing the mattresses aside and lifting the plywood sheet underneath. Inside the locker were two badly stained pillows, a spare anchor, and a coil of anchor line next to the plastic tank. He unscrewed a three-inch-diameter cap and peered in. "Empty," he said. "Let's try the head and main cabin."

"Damn it," Ronnie said, looking over his shoulder, holding the light on the mess. The only sound from Russ, a few steps behind her, was a grunt.

After ten minutes, using hammer, crowbar, and brute strength, Sutherland pulled out the toilet holding tank, which fortunately had been pumped out years ago, saving them from stench. "Your turn," he said, wiping dirty sweat from his forehead. "Try under the port bench."

They crowded into the salon, Russ with his back to the steps leading up to the cockpit. Ronnie handed Sutherland the flashlight and pulled up the port bench, revealing two badly corroded twelve-volt car batteries, one of them split open, and a white plastic box the size of a small suitcase. They all rested in three inches of dark, foul-smelling water.

"Jesus," she cried, shrinking back and holding her nose from the acrid stench. "What happened here?"

"Lightning hit the mast and fried everything down to the batteries," Sutherland said. "That's another of the water tanks."

"Pull it out," she said, getting out of the way.

Sutherland held his breath and hauled out the tank. "Doesn't look good," he said. "The bilge backed up, and it's been sitting in water, diesel fuel, and battery acid. Acid's eaten away at the plastic. But maybe you were right. It was cut open and taped closed again, and the hoses aren't connected." He pointed at the line of wrinkled duct tape forming a square on the tank's top.

"Open it," she said, handing him a knife.

Sutherland could feel her hot breath on his neck while he cut through the tape and peeled back the plastic that formed the makeshift lid. Finished, Ronnie pushed him out of the way and plunged her hand into the open tank.

"Ohhh," she howled. "It can't be."

She was staring at the clump of wet matter clutched in her fist. The mass looked like gray papier-mâché, but there were green flecks here and there and one larger fragment with a clearly decipherable "100" on it. As she squeezed the dripping pulp, a rancid odor emanated, a pungent brew of diesel fuel and battery acid.

"It's rotted away," she screamed. "A fortune turned to shit."

"Let me see," Russ said, bulling his way past Sutherland and grabbing Ronnie's wrist to see what she held. "Is that the cash? What the fuck?"

She didn't seem to hear, merely stared at the broken container of pulp. Then she began to rock forward and back, her jaw muscles contracting, nostrils flaring with the rhythm, eyes hooded and dark. *Bad signals*, Sutherland thought as he started to ease toward the steps leading to the cockpit.

When Ronnie lifted her gaze toward him, she glared like a madwoman—nothing pretty about her now, only a snarling animal, narrowed eyes filled with venom. "You," she said.

He had to calm her, but his throat felt like chalk. "Ronnie, think. The joke's on both of us."

"You think this is funny?" she shrieked. "Billy dead, and this is what I get? No way." Flinging the stinking mush aside, she thrust her hand inside her bag and came out with a pistol. "A joke?" she screamed, trembling with rage, holding the gun with two hands while she drew the hammer back.

Sutherland was as far away as the small salon allowed, but even shaky as she was, she couldn't miss. She raised the gun to aim at his chest, and he jumped to the side at the same time as an explosion echoed around the cabin. On his back on the bunk, he blinked hard and saw where the bullet had slammed into the bulkhead next to him, splintering a gash in the plywood. Incredibly, she'd missed.

Glancing back at Ronnie, he saw her eyes clenched in pain, a dark stain blooming on her shoulder. Her revolver rattled to the floorboards, and behind her, Vislowski peered down from the cockpit, a wisp of smoke seeping from his gun barrel.

"Nobody move," he said. "You're under arrest."

# CHAPTER 105

Half an hour later, Sutherland and Kelly watched the ambulance bounce out of the unpaved boatyard, heaving over bumps and into ruts, carrying the wounded Ronnie away. The red and white van turned right out of the gate and a few seconds later bleated out the first of a fading series of siren blasts. The squads from the local precincts had gone, as had Jim and Russ in their rental car. Sutherland had overheard their statements to Manny López, learning that Jim was really John Lewzyk and Russ was Russell Pietrazak. Both of them lived in Las Vegas. Lewzyk hadn't been in the boat and hadn't seen a thing. Russ merely described what had happened, that Ronnie was aiming at Sutherland and about to pull the trigger when Vislowski, seeing this, shot her. Both guns went off at once. After some argument, Lewzyk and Pietrazak were allowed to leave.

Vislowski was sitting in the squad filling out paperwork and talking on his phone. Having fired his weapon, he had taken himself out of the interview process, leaving it to his partner.

With the flurry of activity after the shooting—controlling Ronnie's bleeding, hauling her out of the cabin into the cockpit, lowering her down the ladder, and treating her for shock—there'd been no opportunity for Sutherland to hear the whole story. What he had learned was that Vislowski had an arrest warrant for murder—not for Sutherland, but for Ronnie Jamison.

As the last of the siren's wail faded off, Sutherland turned to Detective López and asked, "How about a ride? I came with the boys from Vegas."

López glanced at Sutherland and Kelly then looked around and realized all the other police cars were gone. "Sure," he said. "Drop you off at the station. You can get a taxi."

"Have to do better than that," Sutherland said, pulling at his tank top, and pulling out an imaginary empty pocket from his shorts. "Neither of us have a dime on us. And I don't feel like running home."

López scowled then jerked his head toward the squad. "Okay, hop in. Take you back to your lady's car."

For the first minutes of the ride back, no one spoke. Vislowski, in the front passenger seat, was obviously in a dark mood, probably because he knew he had a mountain of red tape ahead and myriad questions to face for firing his weapon and injuring someone. Or was it because he'd had to arrest his old flame instead of Sutherland in the face of the alibi Kelly and Jenny had provided? The only sounds filling the awkward silence were from the police radio, and Sutherland was reluctant to break into the otherwise solemn atmosphere, even to thank the detective for saving his life. He'd been an easy target in that small cabin.

Finally, he could suspend his curiosity no longer. Sitting in the backseat, Sutherland turned to Kelly and whispered, "What did they tell you? Am I off the hook? They charging her with Tunney's murder?"

"Uh uh," she whispered back.

"Then what?"

"Gene Sandler's."

"Vislowski told you that?"

"I wasn't going to direct them to the boat unless they said why they wanted to find you. They said it wasn't for you, it was for her. For Sandler's murder."

"Is that right, Detective?" Sutherland asked, almost shouting over the voice on the two-way radio. "Ronnie killed Sandler?"

Vislowski turned and glowered at them. "I've already said too much. So don't ask."

"Jesus," he said. "She cut off his finger. She only broke mine."

*    *    *

They sat in Sutherland's dining room drinking the colas and eating the hamburgers and fries they'd bought after being dropped off by Detective López. What had started as a run in the park had progressed to an encounter with some loan sharks, a car trip to the far South Side, and a narrow escape from being shot—all on an empty stomach. Sutherland and Kelly tucked into their food like survivors of the Bataan Death March.

When she came up for breath, Kelly asked what must have been on her mind since leaving the boatyard. "You think they bought it?"

"Bought what?" Sutherland mumbled while chewing some french fries.

"About the money. Your dimwitted plan. The one that nearly got you killed."

He washed down his mouthful with a long draft of soda and said, "She must have, otherwise why'd she want to shoot me?"

"What about the loan guys?"

"The big guy saw it and seemed convinced. He'd tell the other one."

"What exactly did they see?"

"A stinking box full of money glop. It was perfect."

"And nearly got you killed."

"I underestimated her. Again. Did you suspect?"

"Something was fishy. Your mysterious trip to the boatyard yesterday. Your agreeability to being hijacked by those well-dressed hoods. Was the money there all along?"

"There never was money there and I knew it. I got a box of shredded currency from the Treasury Department and a couple of trashed batteries, and Gloria Ventura, a prop expert from the Goodman Theater, helped me with the effects. We mixed the confetti with water and acid, and she used some stage tricks to make it look like the tank and tape were old and the money had disintegrated, turned to mush. Then she made the boat look like we'd never been there."

"You didn't think it might backfire?"

"I don't know where the real money went. How else was I going to get them off my back? She'd be waiting, watching me, and those hoods might have gotten rough. I had to make them believe that the money was gone, that it was a dead end."

"Be glad you weren't dead in the end."

# CHAPTER 106

**TUESDAY, AUGUST 14**

When Sutherland arrived at his office the next morning, Eileen was already at her desk talking on the telephone. She held up a finger as he passed and said into the phone, "Hold a second," and handed Sutherland a message slip. "From Kelly Matthews. And Frank Mann called too. Says congratulations and to call him. Does that mean …?"

"Could be. They worked all day and into last night to get the lease hammered out. Wanted it wrapped up before Imperial's board meeting tomorrow."

"So I'll still have a job?" She beamed.

"Me too," he said, passing into his office.

A half hour later Eileen poked her head in and said tentatively, "Miss Matthews on your line?" Her hesitance was a holdover from all the times he'd been avoiding her.

"I'll take it," he said.

"You owe me again, Sutherland," Kelly said as soon as he picked up.

"What this time?"

"Our hacker. There's a geek that works on the City's website. I had to go to court for him six months ago when he was discovered messing with some girl's Facebook. I think he can do it."

"When can he come?"

"How about now?"

*    *    *

Thirty minutes later Kelly entered, looking more like a high-priced attorney than one of the City's legal staff—conservative, blue linen suit jacket and slacks, silk blouse, and a designer scarf. Behind her was a tall, scrawny, acne-faced redhead with a receded chin and a large, hawk-shaped nose. He wore sneakers, jeans, and a tee shirt and carried a small gym bag.

"This is Jeremy Hopkins," Kelly said.

The young man's handshake was firm, but he never met Sutherland's eyes. "Hi," was all he said.

"I made some notes that might help," Sutherland said, handing him a notebook page covered with words and numbers related to his father. "Wife's name, street names, phone numbers, cars, colleges, like that."

"Okay," Jeremy said, taking the paper but hardly looking at it. "Where's it at? It's an old one?"

"At least fifteen years." Sutherland gestured for them to follow and led them to the cubicle with the desktop. When they arrived, Jeremy sat down and powered up the CPU and monitor. While he waited for the prompt, he took a floppy disk from his gym bag and slipped it into the slot.

"How long do these things take?" Sutherland asked. "You want a coffee, something?"

"Won't take long."

Kelly and Sutherland looked over Jeremy's shoulder while the password prompt popped up and disappeared, the computer growled, the hacker typed, waited, typed, waited, and after a few minutes, a menu for all of Bernard Sutherland's files opened up.

"Just like that," Sutherland said. "So much for security."

Jeremy returned to city hall, leaving Sutherland and Kelly to browse through the files. There were folders for correspondence, model text for leases and partnership agreements, cash flow pro formas, and management reports—everything one would expect a landlord and former attorney to store on his computer. His personal finances were there as well, all of his bank accounts and his stock and bond portfolio.

"Judging by these assets," Kelly said, sitting next to Sutherland as he scrolled through folders, "he was a wealthy man at the time of his death. Did you know that?"

"Not as much as you think. His trawler was financed, and he had mortgages on the McCollum Building and his house. He left me two hundred and fifty thousand in a trust," Sutherland said. "I only touched it once and paid it back out of guilt for using what could be considered tainted money."

"But it wasn't," Kelly said.

"Tell that to the FBI. The bastards kept quiet all these years, letting everyone think he was dirty. That's going to change."

He scrolled through a few more menu items until he stopped at one entitled "Offshore." Opening it revealed a spreadsheet, each line containing a foreign bank name, routing number, account number, account name, phone number, and owner's real name.

"Holy shit," he said.

"Whoa. The mother lode," Kelly said. "Look at those names. There's fifty or so, each with their own secret bank data. Panama, Grand Cayman, Costa Rica, Bermuda, Switzerland. The IRS will have a field day. I see judges, police officials, aldermen, lawyers, a county controller, and all of our old friends: Delaney, Sandler, Tunney, Langer, Gorman, and look, even Spanos."

"But look at that," Sutherland said, pointing to the last name on the spreadsheet. "Oxfam at the Banco de San José. Isn't that the organization that helps victims of earthquakes and tsunamis? Why deposit dirty money in an account for an international charity?"

"I can't believe those crooks were interested in solving world hunger," Kelly said.

"Another mystery," Sutherland added. "I'm going to print this and make some calls."

# CHAPTER 107

## WEDNESDAY, AUGUST 15

FBI agent Mark Branson greeted Sutherland in the lobby of the FBI's Chicago building the following morning. He'd called the night before after learning of the shooting and of Ronnie Jamison's arrest. The meeting was supposed to be informal, just wanting to "tie up some loose ends, fill in some missing pieces." At first, remembering the threats and allegations the agent had made, Sutherland hadn't felt inclined to meet. Why should he? There had been no official FBI investigation. Branson's interest was personal, part-time, and possibly unauthorized. Furthermore, the FBI and the federal prosecutors had treated his father shabbily. He had been working for them at great risk, yet by all public historical accounts, he was a disbarred attorney and felon associated with a corrupt cabal.

Sutherland planned to change that using the media, but perhaps meeting with Branson could get the official process rolling. So he consented to the meeting after Branson agreed to squeeze out more information on the charges and evidence against Ronnie. Vislowski and López had refused to shed any more light on the arrest, and there had not yet been any announcement to the news media. How was it that he never suspected her of killing Sandler, yet that's the way it appeared?

After a perfunctory shaking of hands in the lobby of the FBI building, Branson suggested they get a coffee at the café around the corner.

"Just like last time," Sutherland said. "Meet at the FBI offices to make it look official and then split."

"Busted," Branson said, smiling. It was the first time Sutherland had seen anything but a stone-hard or angry face on the man. "But there will be a real investigation now. The tapes you found started it, after sitting dormant for fifteen years."

They left the building and turned the corner, dodging a group of tourists on an architecture tour. "You going to be part of the new investigation?" Sutherland asked, holding the door to the café.

They sat next to one another at the counter. "We're talking about it," Branson said. "Just the initial stages, for continuity. Anyway, the thing I wanted most was justice for John Durham's murder, a good friend and boss, and for George Spanos to be exposed for the slime bag he is. I always had a bad feeling about him."

"According to this morning's paper, he's dropped out of the governor's race and resigned from the House."

"Only the beginning. He's up for serious federal charges. Toast. That's one of the reasons I wanted to see you. To thank you."

*Surprise, surprise. After weeks of harassment, threats, and accusations, the G-man thanks me.* Sutherland couldn't think of a response. He felt anything he'd done was purely out of self-preservation. Sure, there had also been an undercurrent of curiosity over his father's part in the drama, wanting to know what kind of man he really was. But solving cold FBI cases had never been his goal. Fortunately a waitress preempted any comment when she asked for his order. "What'll it be, hon?"

"Coffee and a toasted bagel," he said. Branson opted for iced tea.

"Which brings me to your request," Branson said. "The evidence is still being assembled, so it took a while for me to get the straight scoop from the prosecuting team. Seems that Ronnie Jamison had been using a room in a cheap hotel after her brother was killed."

"Right," Sutherland said. "She tried to pick up the notebook story where Bill Jamison left off and was understandably worried that she'd be next. She never told me where she was staying."

"Paid cash, under an assumed name, meaning the police never could search it for evidence after Tunney died. They looked in your and her apartments, but not her hotel. So there was no way to confirm your claims that she framed you."

"That's what I told Vislowski. But she was arrested for Sandler, not Tunney."

"It was Sandler's pinkie ring that caught her. It turned up at a pawnshop."

"Jesus. I knew she owed money, but that was beyond stupid."

"Wasn't her. A hotel maid lifted it from her room and tried to pawn it. Shop owner turned her in, and they found Jamison's room and the pruning sheers she used to cut off Sandler's finger. They may get her on Tunney's murder as well, because there was other evidence found that could rule out suicide."

"No wonder Vislowski was so angry. Given their history, he should have suspected, especially after what I told him about framing me. Probably will crater his career. But the main thing that strikes me is this: what made her as bad as the monsters she killed?"

"A question I ask all the time. When you find an answer, call me," Branson said, squeezing lemon into the iced tea the waitress had set before him. "Couple other things. The police took a good look at that crap you cooked up on your boat. It *was* currency, once, but it didn't happen the way you wanted Miss Jamison to believe."

"I had to make it look good, even drew it out, acting like I was clueless. She and her loan shark buddies had to be sold. My way of getting rid of them."

"What about the real cash?"

"That's just it. I don't know. Never did. But how could I convince them? Or you, for that matter?"

"It's probably still somewhere in Chicago. I know that if it shows up, you'll turn it in." He winked. "Now let's talk about the videotapes. You gave some copies to the media, but the originals will be needed if there's to be indictments. The judge who was about to issue the court order for them resigned after seeing himself on one of the tapes on TV. But the federal prosecutor will come after them. Make it easy on yourself and give them up." He sucked up a mouthful of iced tea through the straw and then pushed the glass away.

"They can have them—along with some other information I found on my father's hard drive. The identity of about fifty secret offshore bank accounts."

"Now you're being smart. Bank accounts? With names? Beautiful."

"Under one condition."

Branson frowned. "Don't be difficult."

"I want my father completely exonerated. Not pardoned, but totally declared innocent of any crimes, his disbarment reversed, everything. I want his reputation cleared. Officially. The FBI, the City, the state. And finally, I want an apology."

"You can't be serious."

"Look at this," Sutherland said, unfolding the printed sheet of account numbers and placing it in front of Branson.

Branson scanned the sheet and whistled. "Fantastic. Why'd you black out the account numbers?"

"You'll get it all when I get what I want. I made some phone calls. It took a while, but I managed to get in touch with an official for Oxfam, the last name on the sheet. It turns out that from about fifteen years ago until the day my father died, they were getting periodic gifts, sent anonymously by wire to that account. On the day my father died, they received a gift of five million dollars. You can check for yourself. That's why I want an apology."

Branson sighed then stood up, holding out his hand to shake. "I'll see what I can do. With the cash still missing, there may be some doubters, so it may take a while."

"It's been fifteen years. I can wait a little."

# EPILOGUE

Weeks later, TV chatter and sensational headlines once again made Illinois corruption national news. George Spanos's ignominious departure from the political scene was only the beginning. Every day, with each new disclosure, there was another firing, resignation, or retirement. The term "no comment" seemed to echo around the state every time a microphone was thrust into the face of the latest casualty. Danny Delaney's murder, the recent serial killings, and the group's web of corruption had become part of the popular culture.

Ronnie Jamison's arrest and indictment for the murder of two of the cabal's leaders was chum for local call-in shows and national TV pundits. Wasn't killing Sandler and Tunney, the murderers of her brother, an FBI agent, and half a dozen others, justifiable homicide? She did what the impotent police and the FBI couldn't do. But while vigilante types came down on her side, staunch law defenders argued vociferously against her actions. The debate wouldn't end soon, and the trial, when it took place, promised to be a circus.

No mention was made of Ronnie Jamison's character. By media accounts, she was a respected attorney-turned-day-trader who got caught up in her brother's blockbuster exposé on corruption. The fact that she had tried to frame Sutherland hadn't been disclosed, but it was sure to come out when he testified. The prosecution team had already met with him and were shocked to learn the extent of her cunning and deceit. Adding to the murder charges, she'd framed him, stolen and trashed a boat, attempted to steal and sell the Delaney tapes, and fingered Sutherland as a co-debtor to loan sharks. Defense money was flowing in from vigilante factions, but when the defense team eventually deposed Sutherland, it wouldn't like what he had to say.

His father's name and photograph had made the front page after the FBI's news release outlining his indispensable involvement in exposing Delaney's criminal web. The Bureau tried to justify their previous reticence by claiming they were protecting other agents and ongoing investigations.

A week later, the governor announced a complete exoneration with a description of the sham bribery conviction and the reason for it. It seemed that it was the only way Mr. Sutherland could gain the full trust of Danny Delaney and his coconspirators.

The media only mentioned in passing Bernard Sutherland's son, along with the McCollum Building. It seemed the hiding place of the tapes or their discoverer didn't seem to matter. That was fine with Doug. He had a development company to run and an office tower to build, and even though the signing of Imperial Food Products had enabled him to secure his financing, he didn't need any more notoriety. Seeing his name in the same paragraph with Delaney and his ilk made him nervous. People make connections whether they realize it or not.

*　　*　　*

At seven thirty on a Friday morning, Sutherland was sitting in his office preparing for another long day when his phone rang. Eileen was down the hall making copies, and when Sutherland answered, Kelly crooned, "Good mornin', sunshine. Starting early again?"

"I'll be with my contractor's team all day. Want to finish it early so I can get in a game of squash before the dinner." His lenders were sponsoring a celebration for him and his brokerage team that night.

"What time you picking me up?" she asked.

"Seven. That why you called?"

"More important than that. You read the paper this morning? The *Trib*?"

"Not yet. Why?"

"Read the letters to the editor. You'll love it. See ya at seven."

Eileen had put all the daily papers in an empty cubicle for anyone in the office to read. There was a week's worth at any time, and Sutherland found that day's *Wall Street Journal*, *Tribune*, and *Daily News* stacked next to a scattered pile of old issues. Standing, Sutherland scanned the first letter in the *Tribune* letters, a citizen complaining about the election debate format. He quickly went to the next one and after the first sentence had to take a seat while he read.

> I was pleased to read of the governor's and the FBI's clearing of Bernard Sutherland's name after fifteen years of duplicity. Based on what we now understand, their apology was a long-overdue and feeble act of vindication. For reasons I will explain, I never believed the lies spread about the man. Whether it was poor journalism or government misinformation to cover up a botched corruption investigation, we may never know. The result is the same: the tarnishing of a good and generous man's reputation.

We now learn that his guilty plea for attempted bribery was an FBI-conceived ruse to convince a corrupt circle that Mr. Sutherland was as crooked as they and could therefore be trusted. After his death, neither the FBI, the city, nor state authorities attempted to set the record straight. Worse, the FBI went on to imply that Mr. Sutherland absconded with millions in illegal funds. Since we've learned that this was untrue, that this money was donated to a respected international charity, the FBI was pressured into admitting its mistake. What isn't known, and the reason I always believed in his innocence, was because on the day he died he came to see me.

Fifteen years ago I was the newly assigned head of the Chicago Salvation Army. A man came to see me and gave me a suitcase telling me that it contained ill-begotten cash that should be used to do good. He'd seized it from crooks, and since no real victim could be identified, the public should benefit from it. When my staff and I counted it, we were astonished to find more than two hundred thousand dollars.

The man never gave his name, but several days later I saw his photo in the paper and recognized him: Bernard Sutherland, who had gone missing from his boat on Lake Michigan. Whether it was an accident or suicide was never fully resolved, but the press delighted in stressing his criminal record, his close association with the notorious alderman Delaney, and the suggestion that he might have planned to disappear with a large amount of money. The truth is finally out and puts a lie to all the disparagement. Now the shame is not Bernard Sutherland's, but the FBI's.

Major Dennis R. O'Donnell, retired.

"Finally," Sutherland said, putting down the paper. Shuffling through the pile of old newspapers, he found the issue covering the governor's exoneration of Sutherland's father on the front page. The item included a twenty-year-old photo of a handsome man shaking hands with the then-mayor. Sutherland gazed at the photo, his eyes brimming. "I'm sorry, Dad," he croaked, choking back sobs. "I never should have doubted."

THE END